DARKNESS AND THE GRAVE

JOHN TOLLIVER

SEVERED PRESS

HOBART TASMANIA

DARKNESS AND THE GRAVE

WWW.SEVEREDPRESS.COM

ISBN: 978-1-925711-09-7

CHAPTER ONE

Katie Barnes
Day 0

"Good afternoon Buffalo!" the pant-suited anchor said cheerily into the camera. *"Our top headline at this noon hour is that two massive hurricanes are currently bearing down on the United States! Hurricane Teresa is threatening the Gulf Coast and projected to make landfall near Bay Saint Louis, Mississippi tomorrow evening! Let's turn to Meteorologist Bill Breilly for the latest on Hurricane Teresa. Bill, what can you tell us about Teresa?"*

The camera cut to the rotund weatherman. *"Well, the National Weather Service indicates that Hurricane Teresa is going to make landfall as a Category Four hurricane. Mandatory evacuations have been underway for a few days now in and around Bay Saint Louis, Mississippi. It is estimated that Teresa will cause storm surges of around fifteen feet where it makes landfall and will cause heavy flooding inland from rain. If you have loved ones in Southern Mississippi or Alabama or Louisiana, now is the time to urge them to evacuate if they haven't already."*

"Now Bill, what about Hurricane Victor?" the anchor called from off screen.

"Well Tanna, we aren't going to get it quite as bad as folks downstate will," Bill gestured at a map of Upstate New York. *"We expect Victor to drop torrential rains on New York City in addition to all the wind and the storm surge. It's expected to weaken to a Category One hurricane before it makes landfall. It will weaken further as it makes its way inland, but we can still expect heavy rain here in Buffalo, possibly up to a foot, and tropical storm force winds for the next couple of days starting late tonight. Please be careful out there folks! We are talking about a potential of quite a bit of rain over a period of a few days. Don't drive through flooded streets, stay away from downed power lines and make sure you have ample food and water. The rain should clear out before Halloween on Saturday, but be aware everything will still be very wet. Be careful out there folks."*

"Now, we go to correspondent Brent Fulker in Boston, at the home of District Attorney Linda Ferber. Brent, what do we know about the explosion at the District Attorney's house?"

Katie turned the television off and walked up to the bathroom to dry her hair. She had come downstairs after her shower to watch the news. She needed to go up to the University at Buffalo's North Campus in

Amherst in the evening to work on a research paper that was due by the end of the semester. She was going to write on the significance of photography as a communication medium for her Art History class. Since she was a photographer, she was delighted that her teacher had allowed her to choose that topic.

She frowned at the mirror when she removed the towel from her hair. Her wavy blonde hair would need to be straightened. She heated the straightener up and waited. At last she used it to straighten her shoulder-length hair.

She arrived at the library around 6:00pm, after dinner. Her fiancé Joel dropped her off and then left to go watch Game Seven of the World Series. It was getting dark as she walked up to the library, but by this time clouds obscured the setting sun. It would soon begin to rain. She paused in the plaza and stared up at the large blocky brick building. She found it quite imposing.

When she entered, she noticed that most of the students who were normally there studying had gone back to their dorms to wait out the storm. She noticed a tall, lanky man ogling her as she walked past the circulation desk. She recognized him as a lacrosse player.

"Hey Sweet Cheeks!" he called out.

Katie glared at him and he quickly looked away. She walked to the back of the room and climbed a set of stairs to the mezzanine level. She laid her bag on a table and pulled her white laptop out. Once the laptop had booted to its home screen, she walked over to the Art section to grab some books. When she returned, she sat a heavy stack of hardcover books down next to her computer, plugged her headphones in and started listening to Broken Bells. Then she started reading, making photocopies and taking notes. Gradually her mind wandered.

She had been mesmerized by the clarinet opening for *The High Road* ever since her uncle in Toronto had introduced her to it. He had introduced her to many good bands. Her thoughts drifted to recent events. Joel had returned from a trip to Italy with his parents a week before. He had surprised her with tickets to Game Four of the World Series in Washington D.C. She had been so excited!

She supposed that her older brother Robby was to blame for her intense love of baseball, but really Major League Baseball had been quite unusual over the summer and fall. In the National League the San Francisco Giants, the Chicago Cubs, the Washington Senators and the Saint Louis Cardinals had all made it to the Division Series of playoffs. Over in the American League the New York Yankees, the Oakland Athletics, the Seattle Mariners and the Kansas City Royals had all made it to the Division Series.

The Cubs beat the Giants in five games and Washington beat Saint Louis in five games to advance to the National League Championship Series. In that series, Washington beat Chicago in five games to advance to the World Series for the first time ever! Over in the American League, Seattle beat Oakland in five games and the Royals beat the Yankees in five games to advance to the American League Championship Series. That series had been decided by a single run in Game Seven when Seattle Mariners Third Baseman Mikel Roznov hit a walk-off home run in the Thirteenth Inning to send the Mariners to their first ever World Series.

The Senators had won the first three games of the Series and were one win away from their first ever World Series trophy. Katie had grown up in Baltimore, so she had rooted for the Senators in the Orioles' terrible years. She was really hoping that Washington would win Game Four. Plus, both teams were going to be starting their best pitchers. Washington was going to be sending Chaz Macon to the mound. The right-hander was in his second year of pitching at the Major League level and had pitched freakishly well through the entire season. He finished with a 30-4 record and a ridiculous 1.12 earned run average. He was practically guaranteed the Cy Young Award!

Seattle was sending Chris Nuñez to the mound. Nuñez, who was nicknamed the Cuban Missile Crisis for his blindingly fast four-seam fastball was Seattle's last hope. He had finished the regular season with a 33-5 record and a respectable 3.43 earned run average. If anyone was going to get Seattle past Game Four, it would have to be Nuñez.

Katie and Joel had arrived in D.C. early in the afternoon the day before the game. As they sat relaxing at the Jefferson Hotel, Joel smiled at her.

"What are you smiling at?" she asked.

"You," he said. "Want to go eat dinner somewhere fancy tonight?"

"Sure," she had replied.

"Ever been to the Presidential Steakhouse?"

"I haven't, where's it at?"

"Down by the Tidal Basin. They have really good food. Steak and potatoes, that kind of stuff."

"Sure, let's go."

They had gotten ready and then taken a taxi down to the Tidal Basin right before sundown. She had worn a simple turquoise dress with large white polka dots. He wore a light blue button up shirt with a plaid bowtie and black suspenders and a pair of gray dress pants. As they walked into the restaurant she looked back toward the Basin and saw the cherry blossom trees painted resplendent shades of gold by the sunset's golden light. She turned toward the restaurant and looked up the Ionian columns surrounding the building. She thought they made it look quite presidential.

They were seated near a window facing south at a small table. She watched the sky fade from a rich magenta to a deep purple and then to indigo as the city lights outside lit up. The inside of the restaurant was quiet; a violinist and cellist sat in the corner playing Beethoven. The air smelled strongly of grilled beef and potatoes. She ate an eight-ounce sirloin steak with a baked potato. Joel had a large side of prime rib with mashed potatoes.

"Joel, this has been great!" she exclaimed as she placed her handkerchief on the plate; she had barely been able to eat half of the steak. "Should I share a photo of dessert with the internets?"

"No, I want you to enjoy dessert with your mouth Kate, not some dumb piece of technology."

A server brought out dessert. Joel said he had arranged for something special. Katie's curiosity had been piqued, but he had told her not to look at the cake until he said she could. Her anticipation grew. Finally, he told her to look down.

She gasped, covering her mouth with both of her hands.

A silver ring with a single marquis-cut diamond was mounted on a sugar rose in the middle of the cake. Joel was on one knee; he had slid from his seat without her even noticing!

"Kathryn Marie Barnes," he said as he grabbed her left hand and pulled it toward him. "Will you marry me?" He slid the ring onto her finger.

She had been overwhelmed. Of course she said yes!

The next day she and Joel went to a pep rally before the baseball game and then headed to Senators Park. At 7:15pm Chaz Macon threw the first pitch and the game was on. Both pitchers maintained a shutout through eight innings, with Nuñez actually maintaining a perfect game. Trouble brewed though.

In the top of the 9th inning, Macon walked the first batter, Kelly Shopach and then gave up a bloop single to Nuñez. Then he hit their leadoff hitter, Jake Greenwood with a pitch, leaving the bases loaded. The Senators management immediately made a pitching change, putting their star closer, Donovan Granger in.

Granger had led the Major League in closes for the previous three seasons. It seemed like the game would remain scoreless for the time being. Sure enough, he struck out the next two batters. The crowd went nuts, wild with anticipation. Seattle's Third Baseman Mikel Roznov stepped up to bat. Granger had Mikel Roznov down to a 1-2 count when he pitched a fastball high in the strike zone. Roznov connected and the ball arced upward. At first it looked like it would be caught. The Senators outfielder leapt at the ball to catch it, and it sailed over his glove by about four feet to give the Mariners a 4-0 lead as Roznov had just hit his first career grand slam.

The stunned crowd grew quiet momentarily. They began cheering again when Granger struck out the next batter for the third out. They grew silent again when Nuñez struck out three batters in a row in the bottom of the 9th inning to win the game for Seattle, thus staving off elimination, and completing a perfect game.

Nuñez's perfect game was only the second perfect game in postseason history and marked the first time more than one no-hitter had been pitched in postseason play. Katie had been amazed!

A clap of thunder interrupted her thoughts. She looked up and saw one other student packing his things up. She watched as he walked out into the lightly falling rain. She felt a yawn coming on. She stood up and stretched. It was just after 9:30pm. By now Joel would be at their favorite sports bar, The Bouncing Buffalo to watch the baseball game.

She looked back down at the table at the literary descriptions of daguerreotypes and Kodachrome and Leica. She sat back down and got back to work as she listened to music.

She was lost in the work of photography and Indie music when suddenly her phone vibrated. She glanced down at the LCD screen as the lyrics echoed in her ears. "We'll become silhouettes when our bodies finally go," she mumbled. She realized it was after midnight now. She looked around the library and saw that it was empty. She also saw that it was now pouring down rain outside. She closed her eyes and listened to the rain pelt the exterior of the building. Even here, in the depths of the library, she could hear the roar of the storm.

Katie looked down at her phone again and saw that she had a text message from Campus Services! *What could they want at this hour?* she thought. She shook her head; it was probably just something about the storm. Maybe classes for the next day had been canceled. She unlocked her phone and opened the text message.

"Quarantine initiated. All students to remain indoors where they are. If ill, please contact Campus Health Services ASAP," she read the text message aloud. Quarantine? What was going on? She called Joel.

"Kate, where are you?" He sounded worried. He usually only called her Kate when he was nervous.

"I'm at the library at the North Campus. What's going on? I just got a text message from Campus Services."

"I did too. The bar sent everyone home about an hour ago. They were saying on the news a little while ago that a statewide quarantine with curfew has been initiated. They said anyone caught outside would be arrested. The National Guard and police are enforcing it apparently."

"So what, am I just supposed to ride out the hurricane in the library?" she asked.

"Are you there by yourself?"

"I think so."

"I guess you are. I'm sorry Katie. I'm stuck at a friend's house near the main campus. I'd come get you, but they sounded pretty serious about arresting people."

"Why are we under quarantine?"

"They said Owasa Disease was to blame. I don't really understand because I didn't think Owasa Disease was contagious."

"Isn't that what Austin's grandma ha?"

"Yeah."

"Wow, I hope she's okay."

"Yeah, I spoke to Austin earlier today. He said his grandma passed away yesterday."

Katie gasped. "I'm sorry to hear that."

"Yeah, I gave him our condolences."

Austin was Joel's roommate and best friend. He had gone home a week earlier to be with his parents in Pittsburgh after his grandma had gotten sick.

"Are you going to be okay?" Joel asked.

"Yeah, I guess so. I have music to keep me company."

"Okay, well look, keep in touch with me. If you need me to, I'll come get you."

"I will, I love you Joel Ryan!"

"I love you too. You know, you're missing the game. It's getting wild. Macon just gave up a bunch of runs. Wait, what?" He sounded startled.

"What? What's wrong?" she asked.

"Washington put their closing pitcher on the mound a few minutes ago and he just collapsed on the mound."

"Donovan Granger collapsed?" she gasped.

Suddenly the power in the library went out.

"Great, the power just went out," Katie said. "What happened? Granger just collapsed on the mound? Is he okay?"

"I don't know. Do you need me to come get you?"

"I'm okay. I'm not afraid of the dark you know."

"Yeah. Oh my, they're performing CPR on Granger!"

"Oh no!"

"They just said he's dead! How on Earth did that happen? Wait, they're saying he was sick before the game. Someone is suggesting Owasa Disease."

Something clattered among the bookshelves, somewhere behind Katie. It sounded as though someone had just knocked a bunch of books off a shelf.

"Joel, I'm going to call you back," Katie whispered. "I just heard some noise and I'm going to go check it out."

"What? Kate, I'm going to come get you!"

"No Joel," she whispered. "It's probably just a mouse or something."

"Kate, call me back when you know what it is. I want you to be safe."

"I will. I love you Joel."

"I love you too. Be careful. And call me back!"

"I will! Bye," she whispered as she hung up the phone.

More books crashed to the floor behind her as they were knocked off the shelves. Katie turned around and strained to see what was making the noise in the darkness. She opened the flashlight app on her phone and looked down the aisle the noise had come from. The dim white beam faintly illuminated the aisle. Books were scattered on the floor about fifteen feet from her and she noticed a brownish red liquid on the floor. She walked toward it and realized it was blood.

"Hello? Is anyone there?" she asked nervously. It was possible, she reasoned, an animal had gotten in through a vent on the roof and was maybe injured. Maybe it was an injured possum. She jumped when more books thumped on the floor a few aisles over. "Hello?" she called out. "Is anyone there? If someone's there, please respond!" She noticed a hint of panic entering her voice.

A gurgling noise that sounded like a strangled growl came from a few aisles over.

She cautiously walked back to the table and moved laterally toward where the sound had come from. She shined her light down the aisle and saw someone at the end of the aisle shuffling around the corner. A line of blood trailed behind the person.

"Hey! Are you okay?" she yelled.

The person stopped and staggered backward. They paused when Katie was in their line of sight. Another growl, this one more ominous. Katie couldn't tell in the dim light who they were.

"Hey, are you okay? You look like you're hurt," she said, her voice quaking with fear. Something inside told her this situation was wrong.

The person made a motion like they were sniffing the air. Suddenly a flash of lightning illuminated the whole library. For a brief instant Katie locked eyes with the person, or rather what was left of the person. In that brief instant, she saw the figure fully revealed.

His clothes were torn and blood-stained. He was shoeless and his feet were covered with dozens of small cuts. He had large lacerations all over his arms. His mouth was open in an expression that looked like hunger. And his eyes, oh those bloodshot eyes! His eyes were dead and lifeless yet full of rage and hunger. This person was no longer a man but a ravenous monster.

Katie screamed as the man began to stagger toward her. She stood frozen in fear until he was only a few feet away. She retreated toward her laptop as he continued his approach.

"Stop!" she warned him.

He growled and reached for her.

Instinctively, Katie grabbed her laptop and swung it hard into the creature's face. He stumbled backwards and let out an inhuman shriek as the shattered screen of the laptop clinked to the floor. She threw what was left of her laptop at him and ran down the stairs toward the library's entrance.

Another flash of lightning revealed dozens more of the creatures in the plaza approaching the library. She turned and ran through the hallway toward the Charles B. Sears Law Library. It seemed like such a long run but she finally reached the library, closed the door and crouched behind a short bookshelf nearby. Her panting was the only thing she could hear besides the rain. The rainfall had intensified outside; sheets of rain pounded the building.

Then she heard it, another low gurgling noise. It was coming from the other side of the bookshelf Katie was hiding behind! She heard a retching noise and a splash on the carpet. She had to put her hand over her mouth to stifle a gag as a wretched odor filled the room. Suddenly her phone rang and she screamed, startled. It was Joel! She heard the creature on the other side of the bookshelf growl and she knew she had been revealed.

"Joel!" she whispered intensely. "You have to come save me! Help me!"

"Kate, what's going on?" he asked.

"I don't know! There are people who aren't people anymore trying to get me! One of them is a few feet away from me!"

"Whoa, slow down Kate, you're not making much sense. Who is trying to get you?"

"Joel! People who aren't people! I don't know, maybe they have Owasa Disease!"

"I'll come get you right away! Where are you?"

"I'm in the Sears Law Library!"

"I'll be there as fast as I can!"

There was pounding on the door behind Katie. That was when she became aware there was something else in the room with her beside the vomiting creature. There were several something elses in the room with her. Growls sounded all over the room.

Katie looked around frantically at the shadows. The room was dimly lit by emergency lights, but she couldn't see anyone else in the room with her. She did see an elevator on the far side of the room though. Maybe there was a stairwell nearby! She could climb the stairs and hopefully find a way out through one of the upper levels of the building.

She stood in a crouching position and began to creep toward the elevator quietly. Suddenly she heard a growl behind her. She turned and saw a dozen of the infected people emerging from the shadows behind her. They were reaching for her. She screamed and ran.

When she reached the elevator, she saw there were no stairs nearby. She turned around and saw that she was surrounded by bloodthirsty creatures that were slowly moving in.

Suddenly the lights came back on! She turned and started feverishly hitting the call button for the elevator. The creatures were approaching.

They were twenty feet away.

"Come on!" she yelled.

They were fifteen feet away.

"Come on!" she screamed, tapping the call button frantically and pounding on the elevator door with a clenched fist.

They were ten feet away.

She pounded on the elevator door with both hands.

They were five feet away. They were reaching for her. They were clawing at her.

Finally, the elevator door opened and Katie fell into the elevator with a cry. The door closed right behind her. She reached up and hit the button for the second floor and took a deep breath as the elevator began to ascend the shaft.

The elevator dinged and the doors opened exposing the second floor. The power went out again as she stepped out on to the balcony above the library below. She looked down and saw the monsters clawing at the elevator door below. Mercifully, she seemed to be alone up where she was. She turned and ran out of the library across the skywalk to Park Hall. She pulled her phone out and called Joel.

"Joel! Go right on Augspurger Road when you get here! I'll meet you in the lot in front of Park Hall! Where are you now?"

"I'm just a couple of minutes away. Are you okay Kate?"

"Yes, I am for now. Hurry!"

She ran down an emergency stairwell and threw open a door leading out to the parking lot. It was pouring down rain. She took off sprinting toward the street. She saw more infected people staggering around the parking lot. She ran past them toward the road. She saw Joel's car turning on to Augspurger Road as she ran across a muddy median. She waved her arms to flag him down.

He drove past and spun the car around. Then he drove up and stopped. Katie opened the door and jumped in.

"Are you okay Kate?" he asked.

"Yes! I'm okay."

He leaned over and kissed her.

She saw more infected people staggering toward the car.

"Go Joel! We have to get away from them!" she yelled.

He floored it and they sped away.

"What was wrong with those people?" he asked.

"I don't know Joel. I just know they chased me around! I think they wanted to kill me!" She started to cry. She felt the tears flow down her cheeks.

"It's okay Katie. It's okay. You're okay now, you're safe with me," he tried to comfort her.

"But what's going to happen? What if this is happening everywhere?"

"We have each other Katie."

As they turned on to Bailey Avenue from Grover Cleveland Highway, Katie saw a police roadblock ahead. A police officer in a raincoat waved at them to stop so they stopped. The cop motioned for them to exit the car.

"Are you sick?" he yelled over the roaring downpour.

"No!" Joel yelled back.

"Why are you out?" the cop asked.

"He had to come pick me up from my school's library! I was in danger there! I was being chased!" Katie yelled as she shivered in the rain.

"Who were you being chased by ma'am?"

"I don't know!"

"Alright, stand there with your hands up, the both of you," the cop said. He walked over with another police officer and they both patted Joel and Katie down before handcuffing them.

"I'm sorry, but we're going to have to take you downtown," the other cop said. "We will send someone to check out the library. However, you violated curfew and the law is clear. Where is the library?"

"UB's North Campus!" Joel yelled. "Why are you arresting us?"

"Son, you violated an Executive Order from the President of the United States!"

The cop led Joel and Katie toward a police car. Katie started crying again; she had never been arrested before! She began to panic. They were going to die now! She was certain of it. Everything began to grow dark all around her.

CHAPTER TWO

Randy Eccleston
Day 0

"I hear that whoever wins tonight's game is going to be at fault for causing hell to freeze over!" a balding man sitting at the bar yelled as he lifted his beer stein.

Randy laughed. "Who are you rooting for Casey?"

He shrugged. "I don't know, I've never really been into baseball."

Randy laughed again and punched him in the arm. "Whatever man, I know you're pulling for Washington."

"No, I think that's you who is pulling for Washington."

He and Casey had been friends since high school. They had met in marching band. Randy had played saxophone, Casey had played the percussion instruments. Casey had been a Goth then and had kept his black hair long since becoming an adult.

"Hey, looks like Adam, Jill and Missy are coming back," Casey said, pointing.

Randy turned and saw his best friend Adam walking up with his girlfriend Jillian. "Washington's closing pitcher just gave up the tying run!" he yelled over the clamor of the tavern.

Randy shrugged. "So?"

"So? The guy is like the best closing pitcher since Bruce Sutter! Donovan Granger is a frighteningly good pitcher, so this is a bit uncharacteristic of him."

"Who wants some longnecks?" Missy, Casey's girlfriend, asked as she walked up with a bucket of beer.

"I'll take one," Randy replied.

"Me too," Casey said.

"Hey, what just happened?" Adam asked, pointing at the nearest television.

Randy looked up and saw that the game had been replaced by a screen with vertical colored bars.

"I'll bet that storm on the East Coast is affecting the signal!" Casey suggested.

"How? The game is in Seattle and we are in Saint Louis!" Adam replied.

"So what?" Randy said. "You know all that network stuff is distributed these days. If a squirrel chews up a power line in Boston, then Houston loses its internet signal."

"Hey wait!" someone in the bar yelled as a news desk appeared on the screen manned by a sports commentator. The bar became very quiet.

"Folks, I'm sorry to say this to you," the commentator said grimly, "but it appears that Donovan Granger collapsed on the mound and has died."

Several people gasped.

"We have received reports that he was complaining of flu-like symptoms before tonight's game and well, those reports appear to be substantiated. If you're just tuning in, Donovan Granger, star closing pitcher for the Washington Senators has collapsed on the pitching mound and has died."

Suddenly, a television that had been displaying an MMA match switched to a screen with vertical colored bars.

"Man! I had money on that fight!" someone yelled.

"Who were you pulling for?" the bartender asked.

"I bet on the Comeback Kid!"

"Well, you guys want to head back to my place?" Casey asked.

"I guess. We can commiserate there. At least the beer will be cheaper," Adam said.

They all stood and exited the bar. They were in a hipster neighborhood just west of downtown Saint Louis. It was warm and breezy as they walked into the night.

"You excited about going back to work?" Jillian asked Randy.

"What, to the blood bank?" he asked.

"Yeah."

He shrugged. "I guess. It's pretty boring working the midnight shift."

She laughed. "I'll bet vampires come in all the time to cash their checks."

"Huh?"

"You work in a blood bank."

"Oh!" Randy laughed as they descended a set of stairs toward a commuter train platform.

He, Adam and Jillian were in Saint Louis visiting Casey and Missy. They had moved to Saint Louis after college so that Casey could play guitar in a band. They lived in a little town called Shiloh to the east of Saint Louis, in Illinois. As the group reached the platform to wait for a train, Randy thought about Chicago. He decided he was looking forward to returning home. He hadn't seen his brother Todd in a few months.

"Attention passengers, the next east bound train is approaching and will arrive at the platform in thirty seconds," a monotone voice boomed from loudspeakers over the platform. *"Please remain behind the yellow line until the train has come to a complete stop. Thank you for riding Metrolink!"*

Randy heard a train whistle and looked down the tracks. The single headlight of a train approached. The white and red commuter train slowed to a stop as it reached the platform. Randy and his friends stepped in and realized they were the only ones on the train.

"Huh, I guess a lot of folks are glued to a TV," Adam said quietly as the train slowly accelerated away from the station.

Randy sat down and watched the city race by through the window. Suddenly the train was in a tunnel. Adam sat down next to him. He shook his head.

"You okay man?" Randy asked.

"You know, I should be. I'm not even a Washington Senators fan! But I mean, a great pitcher just died in the Ninth Inning of Game Seven of the World Series! I guess this is a World Series that probably won't ever be decided."

"Hey, are we slowing down?" Missy asked suddenly.

Randy looked out the window and noticed the stone walls of the tunnel moving by ever slower. The train suddenly stopped.

"What the, what's going on?" he asked.

"We stopped," Casey said. He walked to the front of the train car and then returned. "This train must be automated. There's no operator."

"Hmm," Jillian said. "I wonder what happened. Was there some kind of power outage?"

"Who knows?" Adam asked.

They sat there for about twenty minutes. Suddenly a loudspeaker in the ceiling of the train car crackled. *"Attention passengers, quarantine has been enacted. Please remain where you are. Attention passengers, quarantine has been enacted. Please remain where you are."*

"Quarantine?" Randy asked. "What?"

"Hey, do you guys have cell service?" Missy asked.

He pulled his iPhone out and frowned. "No."

No one else had service either.

"Now what?" Adam asked.

Casey walked toward the front of the train car and fumbled at a small lever above the door. The door popped open.

"What are you doing?" Jillian asked.

Casey laughed. "I'm going to see what's going on. Besides, aren't you guys hot in here? I figured we could use a draft."

"Casey Newburgh! Get back here!" Missy yelled.

"Relax Melissa Sanders," he said sardonically. "I'll be right back. Look, the riverfront is just ahead. I'll go see what's going on. I think there's a station up there. I'll be back." He hopped out of the train car.

Missy growled. "He's so stubborn!"

"Indeed he is," Adam said.

The lights on the train flickered.

"Maybe we should follow him," Jillian said.

"No, let's stay put until he gets back," Randy replied as he stood and walked to the open doorway.

Suddenly he heard footsteps in the tunnel. He turned toward the others and put his finger over his mouth.

"Hey guys, I'm uh, I'm being arrested," Casey said suddenly from outside the train car.

Randy turned and gasped. A police officer in riot gear had a machine gun pointed at the small of Casey's back. He mumbled something into a radio mounted on his vest and jabbed Casey with the point of the rifle.

"Keep marching son," he said curtly. "And the rest of you, stay in that train car. Do not leave it!"

"Wait Officer!" Missy yelled, running to the open door. "Where are you taking my boyfriend?"

"Missy, just get back in the train!" Casey yelled.

"Shut up!" the cop yelled as he hit Casey in the back with the butt of his rifle.

"Casey!" Missy screamed as he fell to the ground.

The cop spun around and pointed his rifle at the friends in the train. "Get back into the train. Now!" he barked as Casey slowly stood back up.

Randy pulled Missy back as the open door closed automatically. Suddenly the train car began moving in reverse. They rolled past Casey and the police officer. Missy was crying.

"Where are we going?" Adam asked.

"Back to the last station I guess, why?" Randy asked.

"We left the main line about five seconds ago."

"What?" Randy looked back down the tunnel. Sure enough, they appeared to have branched off from the main tunnel. "Where are we going?"

The train car slowly rolled to a stop in a darkened train station. Suddenly the interior of the train car was illuminated by spotlights from the platform.

"Everyone inside the train! When we open the doors, slowly step out on to the platform with your hands in the air!" someone yelled.

The doors slid open and Randy stepped out of the train car with his hands up. The lights were blinding. He heard the others follow.

"Cuff them and take them to the quarantine ward!" someone else yelled.

Suddenly Randy was being handcuffed and pulled away from the platform. He was led into a brightly lit hallway with white tiled floors and white walls. He saw that another cop was the one pulling him.

"Where are you taking me Officer?" he asked as he blinked.

"To a holding cell son. You were out violating quarantine."

"But Officer, how? We got on that train before quarantine was announced!" he protested.

"Doesn't matter. We caught you and your friends out on the tracks after quarantine was announced. We're going to detain you until we receive further instructions on what to do."

"Can't I call a lawyer sir?"

"No."

"Am I under arrest?"

"Yes."

"You didn't read me my rights. Don't I have the right to an attorney and a right to see a judge?"

"Son, habeas corpus was suspended a half hour ago by the President of the United States. We were ordered to arrest anybody who violates curfew," the cop replied as he led Randy onto an elevator. "We're doing this for your own safety."

"Where are my friends being taken?"

"They'll be processed and then brought to the same cell you'll be in," he replied as he pushed the button for the eighth floor.

Two hours later they were all finally reunited; all of them except for Casey that is. They were held in a large jail cell with a bare concrete floor. Metal benches with crude epithets scrawled on them lined three of the walls. The fourth wall was just a large wall of metal bars.

"This is great!" Jillian said, throwing her hands up. "They took my phone!"

"Yeah, they took mine too," Randy said as he sat down on the bench. "I wonder what's going to happen to Casey?"

"Me too," Missy said solemnly. "They wouldn't tell me where they were taking him."

"How is this legal?" Randy asked.

"Man, I guess the government can just suspend civil liberties," Adam sighed.

"What's all this quarantine business about, anyway?" Randy asked.

"Who knows?" Adam replied. "Maybe there's an epidemic of bird flu or something."

Two cops stood near the cell in the hallway talking. Randy motioned for the others to be quiet as he strained to hear the conversation.

"I understand the Air Force is going to destroy all of the bridges between Missouri and Illinois to stop the rioters," one cop said.

"How many of those rioters are infected, do you think?" the other cop said.

"Who knows? I just know they have the guys downstairs wearing riot gear and face masks. The directive from DHS said not to come in direct contact with anyone's bodily fluids in their bulletin. That Owasa stuff is nasty."

"Yeah, I heard it makes most people act like zombies."

"I heard it makes them die like they have Ebola."

"Whatever it does, I don't want to catch it."

"You don't live in Illinois, do you?"

"No, I live out west of here. So I wouldn't be affected by the bridge situation anyway."

Suddenly a radio crackled. One of the cops mumbled something. "I'd better get downstairs Sandoval. There are protesters gathered outside the building."

"Be careful Tyrone."

"Thanks man, you too."

Randy heard a metal door slam.

He looked at the others. They needed to escape soon if they wished to make it out of Saint Louis.

"What were they talking about? What's Owasa?" Missy whispered.

"I don't know," Randy replied quietly. "Sounds like some kind of disease."

"You all talking about Owasa Disease?" the cop asked as he walked up to the cell.

Randy nodded. "What is it?"

"A nasty virus son. You don't want to catch it."

"What does it do?" Jillian asked.

"It causes terrible pain, vomiting, diarrhea, fever. Then it drives you mad and you become violent. It causes you to bleed from your eyes and your mouth and your nose and your ears. By the time it kills you, you will have likely wished for death many times."

"That sounds awful," Randy said.

He nodded grimly. "Yeah. And now we've got all those rioters out there, who knows how many of them are infected?"

"How does one get infected?"

"All it takes is exposure to an infected person's bodily fluids. Then you're probably going to die."

"Yikes."

He nodded. "I'll be over there if you all need anything."

"Sir, we live in Illinois. How are we supposed to get back over there if the military destroys all the bridges?" Adam asked.

The cop shrugged. "I don't know." He turned and walked away.

"Guys!" Missy whispered. "I have an idea. Just work with me here."

Randy nodded. "What is it?"

"I'll pretend to be infected. When the cop comes over here, you all need to pretend that you're at risk of being infected by me. When he opens the cell, tackle him and we'll lock him in here."

"How will we get out of here?" Adam asked quietly.

"We'll have to improvise," Randy said.

Missy coughed. "Guys, I don't feel so good," she said as she sat down on the floor.

"Officer!" Jillian yelled. "One of our friends doesn't feel good!"

"Just relax!" he yelled. "She's probably okay."

"Officer! I think she's going to be sick!"

Suddenly Missy vomited.

The cop sighed and walked over. "What seems to be the problem?"

"I don't know!" Missy screamed, in tears. "I feel terrible!"

"Have you been drinking tonight Miss?"

She shook her head. Suddenly she fell over and began to convulse.

The cop quickly unlocked the cell door and entered. "Stay back all of you!"

Randy locked his fists together and struck the cop in the back of his head as he knelt over Missy. He fell over with a cry as Adam grabbed his gun. Missy jumped up.

"You! You were faking! Get back here!" the cop yelled as he spun around on his hands and knees.

"If you move I'll shoot you," Adam said quietly.

"What do you want?" the cop asked.

"Our freedom."

"I'll take these," Randy said as he snatched the cell keys from the cop.

"Don't worry, we're not going to hurt you," Adam said as he and Randy backed out of the cell. Jillian and Missy stood in the hall.

Randy closed the cell door and locked it as the cop stood up.

"You're not going to want to go out there!" he yelled. "The rioters are worse than this!"

"We'll have to take our chances," Randy said.

"Here!" Jillian yelled.

Randy turned and saw that she had several nightsticks in her hand. He walked over and took one. So did Missy.

He saw a map on the wall and studied it. "Looks like this door leads to a hallway that leads to a stairwell. We might be able to escape through there."

They exited the detainment area and walked down an eerily quiet hallway toward a door marked "Exit."

"Do you think that cop was right?" Adam asked.

"About what?" Randy replied.

"The rioters. What if we get exposed to whatever they have?"

He shrugged. "Just don't get anyone's blood on you and you should be fine." He pushed a steel door open and they walked out into a stairwell. "I guess we're not going to get our phones back, huh?"

"No, I guess not," Missy replied. "I wonder how Casey is."

"Hopefully he escaped and can meet us at his house. I guess we should shoot for heading there," Randy said as they descended the stairs.

Ten minutes later they reached an exit. Randy opened the door and they walked out onto a loading dock. He could hear protesters nearby, on the other side of the building he assumed.

"Where to now?" he asked.

"You guys are lucky Casey liked to visit Saint Louis!" Missy said, laughing. "This way, down the alley! We should be able to get to Spruce!"

They all took off following her. The alley was dark and there were puddles everywhere. They ran past a sleeping homeless man. As they came around the corner they almost ran into the back of a large crowd of protesters gathered in the police station's parking lot.

"Give us back our loved ones!" a long-haired man yelled from the back of the crowd. He waved a large sign over his head.

Missy pointed to the parking lot across the street. Randy and the others followed her across Spruce into a parking lot adjacent to a large hotel.

Randy heard a scream from above and he looked up just in time to see a woman falling from an upper floor of the hotel. She hit the ground with a sickening thud, her limbs splayed. Three men leaned out of the window she had leapt from, stretching their arms toward the ground. Something looked off about their gaze.

"What just happened?" Jillian asked.

"She got pushed by those guys!" Randy yelled. "Run!"

They ran below a raised section of highway away from the scene. They were all breathless by the time they neared Busch Stadium.

"Guys! You made it out!"

Randy looked up as his friend stepped out of the shadows. "Casey!"

Missy ran to her boyfriend and tearfully embraced him. "I thought I'd never see you again!"

He laughed. "Here I am! And look! I got this cool gun!" He brandished a machine gun.

"Where did you get that?" Adam asked.

"That cop that was holding me at gunpoint. I knocked him out and took his gun. How did you guys escape?"

"We tricked a cop at the police station," Randy replied. He walked up to Casey and hugged him. "I'm glad you're okay."

"Me too. Me too man."

"We've got to get out of here," Randy said. "The military is going to destroy all of the bridges to Illinois soon."

Casey nodded. "Let's go! Follow me!" He took off running.

The group followed him through crowded streets full of rioting protesters. Cars all around were ablaze. They ran past looters throwing bricks through shop windows. Randy noticed they ran past several people who appeared to be vomiting blood.

"This way!" Casey yelled as he turned right on to a street choked with cars.

The group wove around cars stopped in the road; most were abandoned. They ran under an overpass and up the approach to the Eads Bridge.

Suddenly Randy saw why the cars were stopped as he and his friends froze. Several military trucks had blocked the road in a makeshift roadblock. Armed soldiers stood at attention in front of the trucks as a mass of protesters waited restlessly.

"What now?" Missy asked breathlessly.

"I don't know," Casey said.

A soldier suddenly yelled something and began shooting at the protesters. The other soldiers joined him in shooting as the armed men fell back behind the trucks. The protesters surged forward, toward the trucks.

"What? Something's not right here," Casey said. "Come on! We'll run down the sidewalks!"

Randy and the others hopped a railing and took off down the sidewalk, parallel to the surging mass of protesters. Many of them looked ill.

"Hey! Get back behind the roadblock!" a soldier yelled, pointing his gun at Randy.

"Don't shoot!" he yelled.

"You infected?"

"No sir!"

"Then run for your lives!"

Randy ran as fast as he could, the others alongside him. The sounds of the crowd began to fade behind him. He glanced south and saw the city lights reflecting off the river far below. He heard jet engines in the distance.

"Run guys!" he yelled.

As they neared the east bank of the river, an airplane rushed overhead. Suddenly another bridge just upriver was enveloped in a fireball and began to collapse as a missile struck it. The Eads Bridge then shook violently and Randy was thrown off his feet. He looked back as a fireball erupted from the deck perhaps five hundred feet behind him. He stood back up and helped Jillian and Adam up. Then they resumed running.

When they reached the eastern terminus of the bridge the road divided. Casey pointed down. Randy looked and saw a train station below.

"We can hide there until things die down," Casey suggested.

Randy nodded. "Come on guys." He looked back toward the city. "We can wait down there for a bit and catch our breath. Who knows what's next!"

CHAPTER THREE

Andy Gibson
Day 0

The radio crackled as clouds drifted across the southern horizon.

"Bald Point Thirty-One-Thirty-One, this is Ops Houston, do you copy?" a friendly female voice asked.

"Ops Houston, this is Bee Pee Thirty-One-Thirty-One, I read you loud and clear. Go ahead," Andy replied, pressing the button on the microphone.

"Good afternoon Andy!"

"Hi Betty."

"So I just wanted to confirm that we will be evacuating y'all from your platform this evening. The first helicopter will arrive at Eighteen-Hundred hours, you copy?"

"Roger that Ops. Y'all are cutting it close, aren't you?" he asked.

He heard laughter. *"I'm sorry, you know we run things on a shoestring budget,"* she replied apologetically.

"It's fine. We'll be watching for the helis this evening. Anything else?" he asked.

"No sir," she replied.

"Alright, this is Bee Pee Thirty-One-Thirty-One, out."

Andy sat the microphone on the desk and looked out over the rolling sea, wondering if there would be a platform to return to. News had broken a few days before that Hurricane Teddy was going to pass directly over BP3131, necessitating an evacuation.

As the crew waited for the helicopters, Offshore Installation Manager Carl Becker came up to the Communication Room and sat down next to Andy.

"Gibson, I think you've got some great mettle!" he said, patting Andy's back.

"Thanks sir," he replied.

"Now, we've had this talk before. I want you to call me Carl."

"Sorry Carl," Andy replied.

Becker laughed. "No problem at all! You ready to get off here?"

He nodded. "Maintenance has been working all day on mothballing the platform and Production and Well Services have been working together to taper off production. I think Sappins said at Thirteen-Hundred Hours that extraction had been shut down and that most of the oil and gas onboard had been pumped ashore."

"That's good, yeah, I saw that he had reported success. You live close to shore?"

Andy nodded. "Yeah, in Bay Saint Louis, Mississippi, you?"

"Sort of, I live up in Monroe, Louisiana near my grandbabies. You've got a little boy, right?"

"Yeah, Isaiah Alexander Gibson," Andy said, smiling. "He just had his first birthday back in August."

The older man smiled. "You have any pictures?"

20

"Have any pictures?" Andy laughed. "Of course I do!" He pulled his phone out and opened up the picture gallery. He showed Becker a photo of the little, chubby brown-haired boy with a toothy grin who was his son.

The older man smiled. "He's cute. He looks just like you."

"Thanks."

"You're welcome."

"So what's going on with your prostate cancer? Is it still in remission?" Andy asked. Carl had told them he had cancer a while back.

He laughed. "Well, you know it's the craziest thing. I got that treatment from my doctor back in July and when I had my checkup a few weeks ago, they said I was completely cancer free, they couldn't find any sign of cancer in my body!"

"That's insane!"

"Yeah. My wife called me yesterday and told me I needed to make an appointment with my doctor when I get home though. The treatment was recalled a couple of weeks ago. Apparently it causes serious adverse effects in some people."

"That's no good," Andy said. "I hope you'll be okay."

"Well, it did cure my cancer, so I guess if it winds up blinding me or something I can just retire early."

"Yeah, that's true," Andy said as he watched the waves on the sea intensify.

Later, Andy walked down to wait for the helicopters in the galley. Some crew sat around playing cards, the Well Services team was discussing procedures to bring BP3131 back online after the storm and others occupied themselves with reading. Andy split his attention between looking at pictures of his wife and son on his phone and reading old issues of Wired Magazine.

At 6:05pm they were all still waiting when Third Mate Dale Speith entered the room. "Hey, Gibson! We need you up in the Comm Room," he said, motioning at Andy.

Andy stood and followed him out of the galley and up to the Communication Room. Carl, Carlos, Mitch, and Mike Speer, the Well Services supervisor stood around Sterling. Sterling was sitting at the desk with the radio unit and he had a scowl on his face.

"We've been trying for twenty minutes to reach someone," Sterling said, glancing down at his watch. "They're now ten minutes late! I can't get a chopper, I can't get Operations, I can't even get HQ!" He threw his arms up.

"We need to be off this platform by Twenty-Hundred Hours or we'll have to ride out the hurricane," Mitch said darkly.

"Anyone ever rode out a hurricane on a platform?" Dale asked.

No affirmative response came.

"Ops Houston, Ops Houston, this is Bald Point Thirty-One-Thirty-One, do you copy?" Sterling said, microphone in hand. "Ops Houston, Ops Houston, this is Bald Point Thirty-One-Thirty-One, do you copy?"

He turned a dial on the transmitter and muttered something under his breath.

"HQ Nola, HQ Nola, this is Bald Point Thirty-One-Thirty-One, do you copy? HQ Nola, HQ Nola, this is Bald Point Thirty-One-Thirty-One, do you copy?"

The only sound that came from the radio was a faint hiss punctuated occasionally by a soft crackle. The team murmured as tension grew.

"Okay, Andy, I need you to do me a favor," Carl said.

"Yes sir?" he asked.

"We need to make secondary preparations in the event those helicopters don't come. I want you to grab another crew member and verify that everything out on the open decks is secured. Likewise, I want you to double check that oil and gas production are shut down."

"Yes sir," Andy said. Then he turned and descended the stairs to the galley.

"Hey, what's going on?" Milo Jennings asked. He was one of the cooks. Andy's best friend Royce had introduced Andy to Milo during his first week on the platform. Royce had insisted Milo knew the secret for barbequing perfect ribs.

Milo did know the secret, actually. His biological father lived in Memphis and had once worked at a restaurant called Rendezvous. He had taught Milo how to barbeque as a high school graduation present.

Milo lived on an old plantation with his mother and stepfather just outside Mobile, Alabama. His great-great-grandfather had been a former slave who remained on his plantation after the Civil War, working as a servant for his former master. Milo's grandfather managed to save up a sizable amount of money and buy the plantation in 1981.

"We're still waiting on the helicopters," Andy said. "Hey Royce! Take a walk with me."

The short muscular man laid his cards down on the table and followed Andy out of the galley. They walked through a bulkhead to the stairwell and descended to the main deck.

"What's up?" Royce asked as they walked.

"Becker wanted us to make sure everything is secured out on the open decks," Andy replied as he opened the door.

"What's going on with the helicopters?" Royce asked as they walked out onto the main deck. A warm wind blew steadily from the south as the sea roared below.

Andy shrugged. "They've been trying to get in touch with Ops for almost a half hour. They haven't gotten a response, so no one knows. Maybe the helicopters are on their way."

"What if they don't come?" Royce's concern was apparent.

"Then I guess we'll ride out the storm," Andy said as he glanced up at the derrick towering over the deck.

The derrick towered high over the deck, reaching more than two hundred feet toward the sky. It was flanked by two red cranes. In front, the safety flare apparatus reached out over the Gulf. Behind the derrick, the accommodation module stood five stories high. The control room was on the first deck, the galley was on the second, the communications room on the third, and the helipad on the roof. The rest of the module was filled with crew quarters. Theoretically the platform could accommodate up to one hundred and twenty crew but it rarely had that many due to CPG's staffing policies.

Bald Point 3131 was a spar platform; meaning the machinery and accommodation decks were built atop a large metal cylinder that had a diameter of about eighty feet and a height of about six hundred feet. The bottom of the cylinder was filled with heavy ballast and the whole thing was anchored to the seafloor with twelve mooring lines.

Each cabin had its own bathroom and TV. There was a library onboard and a gym. The rooms weren't luxurious, but they weren't exactly spartan either.

Below the main deck all of the equipment dedicated to keeping the oil pumping up from the depths of the crust normally whirred almost constantly. It was strange to hear nothing but silence from two whole decks, but the situation demanded such extreme measures.

Everything appeared to be secured. Tools were strapped to the deck, so there was nothing loose.

Andy walked over to the driller's shack and verified that production had stopped. Then he walked back out on the open deck to Royce.

"You think we'll be okay if we ride the storm out here?" his friend asked.

Andy shrugged. "I think so. I mean we're on a spar platform. So I think we'll be okay."

"Yeah, I guess I just don't like the thought of this thing sinking."

"We do have lifeboats."

"Yeah, but do you really think we'll have time to get to them if the ballast tanks fail? Besides that, I don't think those lifeboats are designed to float in a hurricane."

Andy laughed. "You make a good point. The lifeboats won't be much good if we're at the bottom of the sea."

"That's not funny! I don't like the thought of ending up almost half a mile below the surface!"

"There *are* worse ways to die you know. At least we'd just end up being crab food."

"That's morbid."

"And unlikely! The mooring lines will probably hold! Besides, these types of platforms are weighted so that they won't bob up and down in heavy seas. If I recall correctly, this platform was hit by Hurricane Ike and it came through just fine. Just don't come out here for a smoke!"

Royce laughed. "You think anyone smuggled cigs out here?"

"Better not have!" Andy exclaimed as he watched the sun dip below the horizon. The western sky was painted in brilliant hues of orange, red and purple. The sea below roiled furiously as clouds moved in from the south.

"You think Shelly and Isaiah are okay?" Royce asked.

He nodded. "Yeah, Shel probably has the house's windows boarded up and is probably at her parents' house up in Hattiesburg. I guess I should call her, you know, let her know I might have to ride out the storm here."

Royce laughed. "You haven't told her yet?"

"How would I have? We still don't know whether the helicopters are coming or not."

"Fair enough."

Andy pulled out his phone and tapped the phone tile on the screen. He dialed Shelly's number.

The phone rang several times.

"Hello?" he heard her warm voice.

"Shel? It's Andy, did you and Isaiah make it to your parents'?" he asked.

"Andy!" she exclaimed joyfully. "We did, Isaiah slept most of the way. You getting ready to get on a helicopter?"

"Well, about that. We can't get a hold of Operations or Headquarters. We're not sure what's going on, but the helicopters haven't come yet. They're late."

"Oh no!" she said worriedly. "What are you guys going to do?"

"Well, worst case scenario, I guess we are going to have to ride out the storm out here."

"Oh no! Andy, is there some other way for you to get home?"

"Well, maybe if they had tried to evacuate us sooner, I'd have a better plan B. I guess I'd better look for a new job when I get home."

"Eddie said the Forest Service is hiring firefighters up in Idaho," she said.

"Oh yeah? I guess I could use a change of scenery. Tell your brother I'll look into it."

"I will. When am I going to hear from you?" she asked.

"I'll call you again when we know for sure whether we have to stay here or not. I love you!"

"I love you too Andy. Wait, hey buddy, you want to say 'hi' to daddy?" Andy heard her ask. "Hang on honey, I'm going to put it on speakerphone for Isaiah. Hang on," he heard her fumbling around on her phone. "Okay, still there Andy?"

"Yeah, I'm still here," he replied.

"Ha! Is that daddy? Is that daddy on the phone?" he heard her say in baby talk.

He heard a childish laugh and Andy felt himself involuntarily smiling. "Hey buddy!" he said happily. "How are you doing?"

"Da? Da!" he heard the reply.

He also heard noise on the call.

"No no," he heard Shelly say. "We don't hit the phone."

"I love you Isaiah!" Andy said.

"Oh!" she squealed. "You should have seen him! He just got the biggest smile ever! He misses his daddy!"

"I know," he said. "His daddy misses him."

Andy heard more scratching noises. "Okay, it's off speakerphone," she said.

"You wish you had a Windows Phone, don't you?" he teased.

She laughed. "I know *you* wish I did."

"Shelly, I love you!" he said.

"I love you too! Be careful!" she said.

"I will be. Tell your parents I said hi."

"Okay," she said. "You're going to call me back once you know what's going on?"

"Yes."

"Okay, I love you Richard Andrew Gibson."

"I love you too! Kiss Isaiah for me."

"I will. Say 'bye bye daddy!'"

"Bye buddy!"

The call disconnected. Andy looked out on the rolling sea as the last vestiges of twilight faded into darkness.

"I guess we should get back inside!" Royce yelled over the wind and sea.

"Wait! Let's go make sure the lifeboats are ready! You know, just in case! I'll check this side! You check that side!"

Andy walked over to a stairwell and descended to the lifeboat area. He looked at each of the two lifeboats. The large bright-orange pods looked more like streamlined coffins than lifeboats. He opened the back door of one of the boats and climbed inside. He tested the electricity to make sure the boat powered up and down without any issues. Then he climbed out and repeated the test in the other lifeboat.

When he was finished he climbed out of the second boat and examined the rails both lifeboats sat on. Each boat faced slightly downward, secured on a set of rails. In the event of launch, the brake would be released and the boat would plummet nose-first eighty feet into the Gulf. The boats were constructed using buoyant materials, so even if the back door was left open, the boat would still resurface within ten seconds.

Andy found himself hoping the boats would never need to be used. He turned and walked back up to the main deck. Royce was waiting.

"How'd your boats look?" Andy asked.

"They looked fine man, yours?"

"They looked good."

"Good, let's get inside. I think it's going to start raining soon."

"Oh? You're a meteorologist now?" Andy joked.

Royce laughed. "You know it man."

Andy turned and followed him inside and they climbed the stairs up to the galley. The crew looked restless.

"Wait here," Andy told Royce. "I'm going up to the Comm Room to see if there's any update."

"Okay," his friend said.

He turned and walked back to the stairwell and went upstairs to the Communication Room. The officers were still trying to contact CPG.

"Any luck?" he asked.

"No," Carlos replied tersely. "We've tried HQ multiple times and Ops. We've all tried calling the executive staff with our cell phones. Nothing! It's like we've been cut off!"

"We still looking at Twenty-Hundred hours as the deadline?" Andy asked.

"Yes," Becker said. "If we haven't contacted anyone by then, we will advise everyone to head back to their cabins and batten down the hatches."

At 8:00pm Carlos went down to the Galley to break the news to the crew: they would ride out the hurricane on the platform. Andy climbed the stairs to the helideck and pulled his phone out.

It was windy outside and clouds obscured the stars. It would probably begin raining soon. He looked at his phone and dialed Shelly's phone number.

The phone rang several times.

"Hello?" he heard her ask. Her voice sounded staticky.

"Shelly? It's Andy."

"So, what's going on? Am I going to see you tonight?" she asked expectantly.

"No, I'm afraid not. We're going to have to wait out the storm here."

"That's ridiculous!" she protested.

"I know. I'm not happy about it either."

"When will I hear from you again?" she asked.

"I don't know," he replied. "It all depends on when Petrocom gets service restored after the storm, if we can get off the platform soon after the storm and if cell phone service is still up for y'all."

"I don't like that."

"I don't either, but we'll have to make do. Is Isaiah asleep?"

"Yeah, I put him down about a half hour ago."

"Did he go down easily?"

"He fussed a little bit, but I think he was pretty tired from all the packing and driving today."

"Okay, well, I'd better go. I love you!" he said.

"Hello? Andy? Are you there?" he heard her ask. "Hello?"

"Shel, I'm here, I'm here!" he exclaimed.

"Hello, Andy? Andy?" she asked. "And-" The call dropped.

Andy looked down at his phone's display. He had no service. Petrocom must have proactively deactivated their network.

He growled. *Well, at least I got to talk to Shelly and Isaiah earlier and she knows what's going to happen,* he thought to himself. He walked back downstairs to the galley. The crew seemed angry.

"So we're stuck on this rig?" Chef Lester Keel asked angrily. "That's ridiculous!"

"We know you are all very angry because of this news. We are too. We plan to file formal complaints with Bee See when we get back ashore," Becker said.

The frustrated murmuring continued.

"Look, time is of the essence here. Go back to your cabins. It's probably going to start raining soon," Sterling said. "And please, once it starts raining do not go outside on the main deck for any reason except a call to evacuate to the lifeboats. This is a major storm that's going to pass over us with wind speeds of up to one-hundred-and-fifty-six miles per hour. Based on the last weather report we got from NOAA, it looks like the eye is going to pass about thirty miles east of here. Be careful guys."

The guys all stood up and slowly exited the galley. Royce and Milo nodded at Andy as they walked past.

"Hey," Andy said, grabbing Royce's arm. "If you and Milo want to kick it in my cabin, I'll be up there in a little while."

He nodded. "Sounds good man."

Andy walked up to the Communication Room. Sterling was sitting at the radio still trying to contact Operations.

"Ops Houston, Ops Houston, this is Sterling Williams, Chief Safety Officer aboard Bald Point Thirty-One-Thirty-One, do you read me?" He sounded frustrated.

He sat the microphone down on the desk and looked up at Andy. He shrugged.

"Bee See's going to have a field day with them, leaving ninety-two people on an offshore installation in the middle of a hurricane!" He threw up his arms.

"I agree sir," Andy replied. "Have you tried contacting the Coast Guard?"

He nodded. "Nothing there either!"

Andy frowned. What was going on?

"It's just ridiculous! You're telling me they couldn't charter any helicopters? They could have just sent a support boat a couple of days ago and we'd be fine!" Sterling waved his arms some more.

"Do you think this platform will hold?" Andy asked.

"Well, the spar design's supposed to be pretty sturdy. I reckon the spar itself will be fine. The derrick, however, might get blown over. It's a good thing we shut down production."

"Yeah, I could see things getting pretty messy if we left the oil and gas going."

"At least if there was an explosion, I guess, the rain, wind and sea would kill the flames pretty quickly," he laughed darkly.

Suddenly the fax machine beeped. Sterling spun around and grabbed the printout. He read it carefully and grimaced.

"What is it?" Andy asked.

Sterling looked up at him, lowering the paper. "Teddy's been upgraded to a Category Five storm. Maximum sustained wind speeds of one-hundred-and-seventy-four miles per hour. We'd better hang on. If we get through this okay, I'm going to kill whoever's responsible for leaving us out here."

"Yeah," Andy replied. "This is bad."

Around midnight it began to rain outside. The winds gradually picked up and began to shake the platform.

Andy played poker with Royce and Milo into the early hours of the morning. Around midnight, Engineer Blake Meyers joined them. They talked about family back home and what they expected to find when they finally got home.

"My house is up on stilts, but that won't do it any good if Bay Saint Louis takes a direct hit," Andy said. "The guy we bought it from told us that he had to rebuild it after Hurricane Katrina hit. He said that when he was finally able to return home, all that was left was a plate from his wife's china collection and a single stilt bent at an angle."

Everyone whistled.

"That's why you live inland away from the shore," Blake said.

"If a Category Five storm hits your house, it's going to blow your house down, whether it's made of straw, sticks or stone," Milo said. "I trust that my Momma and stepdad will be alright."

"Well, my family all lives in North Carolina," Royce said. "So I don't think I'll be seeing anything from the hurricane except higher homeowner's insurance premiums."

Everyone laughed as the sea thrashed outside.

"Hey Andy, did you read the latest issue of Wired?" Blake asked.

Andy nodded as he looked down at his cards. "I did."

"You read the cover story?"

"About the guy in Macau who got assassinated by Mossad?"

"Yeah. That's crazy isn't it?"

Andy shrugged. "I guess. I mean, what was his name? Xintao? He's not the first guy to be iced by a state agency. I'm surprised the DEA wasn't going after him, with all the drug trafficking he was involved with."

"Maybe they'll make a movie about it one day."

Andy nodded. "That'd make for some good cinema, I'd imagine."

The crew wound up riding out the storm for five whole days. Andy spent his time reading magazines, playing poker, watching movies, and sleeping. Miraculously, the rig didn't sink and didn't take serious damage. The storm just passed right over them.

Finally, on November 3rd, at dawn, Andy awoke to see sunlight outside. He walked up to the main deck and saw scaffolders at work up on the derrick.

"Hey Andy, looks like we were pretty lucky!" Senior Driller Nathan Howell said.

"Yeah, it does. What are they doing up on the derrick?"

"Inspecting it. They found a few places where bolts had been stripped away. So they're inspecting and repairing as they go," he said.

Andy nodded. "Thanks. How'd you fare riding out the storm?"

He laughed. "Watched movies. Lots of movies."

"Sounds like a nice break."

"It was!" He laughed again.

Andy walked up to the Communications Room and saw Sterling sitting at the radio.

"I still can't get anyone. It looks like the storm tracked west toward Texas, so it's possible HQ and Operations are pretty badly damaged. I guess we can give them a few days. But here's the thing," he leaned over the desk toward Andy. "I tried reaching the Coast Guard this morning too. Nothing."

"Hmm," Andy stroked his chin. "You think the damage is that bad?"

He shrugged. "From Destin to Houston?"

"I don't know," Andy replied. "Could our radio equipment be damaged?"

Sterling shook his head. "No, I had maintenance check that out a little while ago. Fyodor confirmed everything was working alright."

"That's strange."

"Yeah. And to make matters worse, we've got a number of crew missing."

"Who?" Andy asked.

"Let's see," he replied, glancing down at a list. "Hal is missing, so are Tinson, Grubb, Towson, McRoberts, Lucas Fisher and Frank Diaz. Moses is missing. We searched the platform and can't find them. With the missing floor hands, Peter Rivas, one of the other floor hands reported that they all went outside two nights ago to smoke. Why that wasn't reported until now is beyond me! Needless to say, Mister Rivas won't have a job when we finally get a hold of HQ! He may even face criminal charges."

"Are we going to mount a rescue operation?" Andy asked.

"With what? We're on a platform that's, thankfully, still anchored to the seabed! We have no way to mount a rescue operation! If they were all knocked overboard, their bodies may be halfway to Louisiana by now!"

"True," Andy said.

"And in addition to *all* of that, Becker has the flu!" He threw his arms up.

"Geez."

"Yeah. I guess we'll keep trying to reach shore, and in the meantime work on getting everything here back up and running. Carlos is acting OIM while Becker is sick."

"Thanks, I'll have my team do a drill this evening."

"Thanks Andrew."

"You're welcome sir."

Later, Andy pulled his phone out to try to call Shelly. He grimaced when he saw that no service was available.

"Petrocom must have gotten hit pretty hard," he mumbled.

He walked around his room thinking. If Teddy had caused a lot of damage back home, it was likely Shel's phone wouldn't be working. He decided to try calling her parents from the satellite phone in the galley.

Andy left his room and walked downstairs to the galley. It was fairly quiet in the large cafeteria. He walked over to the satellite phone kiosk and dialed Shelly's parents' phone number.

"We're sorry but the network you are attempting to reach appears to be experiencing technical difficulties. Please try your call again later. Goodbye!" the automated message said.

He tried calling her cell. Same error message.

He placed the handset back in its cradle and frowned. He had hoped to reach Shelly and Isaiah; he was somewhat anxious about their wellbeing.

When a hurricane had struck the Gulf Coast a few years earlier, Andy had been on a platform off the coast of Southeast Brazil in the Lula Field. He recalled that he hadn't been able to get a hold of Shelly for a week after the storm, but he finally did.

"Patience," he said softly. "I need patience."

CHAPTER FOUR

Jim Gibson
Day 1

"You coward!" he yelled as a grenade exploded next to him. "Even the noob tube is better than that!"

"Say that to my shotgun," Jim said into the headset, laughing.

Colors danced across the television as Jim shot the heavily armored character in the face with a sawed-off shotgun. Jim's opponent yelled so loud he could hear him over the headset.

"Hey Vik! Calm down buddy!" Jeff yelled at Jim's roommate, laughing. "I can hear you over my headset! It's after midnight on a weeknight man! Some people probably have class tomorrow!"

"I can hear you too Vik. Besides, you know," Jim paused as Vik killed his character. "You're likely to get a spawn kill."

Vikram laughed as the match drew to a close.

Thunder suddenly shook the whole building. The remnants of Hurricane Vicky were moving in, threatening to deluge the area with rain. News reports had said New York City was going to be hit with the most powerful hurricane it had ever experienced. Of course, that meant folks in Buffalo would get whatever was left after the storm moved ashore. Jim imagined his mom and stepdad were glad to be on the other side of the country for the deciding game of the World Series.

He stood up to stretch, gazing out the window of his dorm. It was raining hard outside. The south campus of the University at Buffalo stretched to the south of the dorm and in the distance, partially obscured by curtains of rain, the VA Hospital stood tall, a luminous sentinel in the night.

Jim sat back down to resume the carnage. While the new match loaded he glanced down at his phone; it had been vibrating all night long. According to Cortana he had 20 missed calls and 124 text messages!

He thumbed through the list of missed calls. His mom had tried calling him a dozen times, his dad had tried a few, his sister had a few and his brother Phil had a few. What was going on? He started to dial the number for voicemail when there was a loud knocking on the door to the dorm.

Jeff and Vik turned to see what had made the noise. Jim stood and walked over to the door. It was late, who would be knocking at his door at 1:00am on a school night? He peered out the peephole.

There was no one there. Suddenly, a tall man wearing white face paint staggered up to the door. He had bloody clothes on and looked like he was dressed up as a zombie.

"Come on man!" Jim yelled. "Halloween's not until Saturday!"

The man growled in response.

"Real convincing man! You know Sigma Phi is having a zombie party on Saturday! You should go! Your growl is pretty convincing!" Jim yelled, laughing.

Then Jim heard screams come from down the hall and the pale man turned and shuffled toward the source.

Jim opened the door and poked his head out. He saw a woman down the hall who had multiple people dressed as zombies on top of her. Fake blood was everywhere.

"That's not funny guys! Come on, some people have class tomorrow!" he yelled.

Someone exited a dorm room closer to the group with a baseball bat in hand and bashed one of the costumed guys in the head. The man fell down with a growl.

"Hey! Why'd you do that?" Jim yelled, stepping into the hallway.

"Dude! There's a quarantine!" the guy with the bat yelled back. "Agh!"

Another costumed man had bitten him in the ankle. The man with the bat fell over and began convulsing and foaming at the mouth as blood poured from his ankle.

"What the...?" Jim asked, startled.

He suddenly felt hands grab him from behind and pull him back into his dorm. It was Jeff!

"Dude, did you see the text message from Campus Services?" he asked, handing Jim his phone.

"No, what is it?" he asked.

"Just read it."

Jim opened the text message from Campus Services.

"Quarantine initiated. All students to remain indoors where they are. If ill, please contact Campus Health Services ASAP."

"What's that all about?" he asked aloud.

"I don't know," Vik replied, pushing the couch in front of the door. "But I suspect it has something to do with the altercation down the hall."

"Altercation? I think someone died!" Jim replied incredulously.

"Eaten by zombies?" Jeff asked skeptically.

He shrugged. "I don't know. The guy with the bat totally got bitten in the ankle by one of the guys dressed like a zombie. Dude with a bat started foaming at the mouth then."

"You don't think Sigma Phi is pulling a Halloween prank, do you?" Vik asked.

Jim shrugged again. "I don't know. Maybe they're pulling the prank to make light of Campus Services' instructions."

Jeff turned the Xbox off and turned it to the news.

"And as Vicky moves into the Buffalo Metro, it has been downgraded to a tropical storm," the mustachioed news anchor said. *"Now folks, remember, the quarantine means you should stay in your home until notified it's okay to leave. If you or anyone you're with is displaying symptoms of Owasa Disease, the authorities want you to hang a red sheet or towel in your window. If you don't have a red sheet or towel, a red shirt or jacket will suffice. A medical professional will be by to assist you as soon as possible. We now return you to your regularly scheduled programming."*

Jeff turned the TV off. "Sounds pretty serious."

Jim nodded. "Yeah, it does."

He sat down on the couch and looked at his phone. He had text messages from his mom and his brother imploring him to call them. He tried dialing out. No luck, he couldn't place an outgoing call. He tried texting them. No luck. He tried his voicemail. Miraculously, it connected.

"Hey loser!" his brother Phil said in the first message, left at 10:30pm, *"You watching the news? Call me back."*

"Jim," he heard his mother yell over the roar of the crowd in the next voicemail message, *"The pitcher for the Washington Senators just died on the field! Wait, what's that Steve? Oh my! Oh my!"* She screamed. *"James, we are going back to the hotel. Please call me when you get this. I love you!"*

"Hey! It's your dad! You been watching the game? Washington's pitcher just died on the mound! Anyway, call me." His dad had left the third message.

"Hmm," Jim said.

"Your mom at the game?" Jeff asked.

He nodded. "Yeah, I never understood why Steve was a Mariners fan."

"Me neither," Jeff replied, sitting down. "Then again, your dad works for the Detroit Tigers. Maybe she married Steve to spite your dad."

Jim laughed. "Maybe. Man, Steve was such a..." he paused, shaking his head. "Never mind. I guess we might as well play more Hail of Bullets."

"You don't want to watch a zombie movie?" Vik asked, surprised.

"You know what? Yeah, let's watch Night of the Living Dead," Jim said. "Hey Jeff, where's Connor?"

He shrugged. "I guess he's out with Giselle."

"Huh," Jim replied, as he placed the DVD in the disc tray.

"Aren't you a bit freaked out about this?" Jeff asked.

Jim looked down at his phone. He held it up to his face. "Hey Cortana, what's going on?"

His phone made a dinging noise and then he heard, "Quarantine has been enacted. No other information available."

He repeated his question.

"I'm sorry, I do not seem to have an Internet connection. Please try again later," his phone said.

He looked at Jeff. "I guess we'll have to wait to see what's going on anyway."

Jeff shook his head. "Fine, let's watch the movie. Maybe you'll have cell service again later. I don't have cell service either."

"It's probably just the storm," Vik said.

"Okay, we'll watch the movie," Jim said.

He thought about his mom as the protagonists of the movie sought shelter in the farmhouse. He had grown up in a nice townhouse in the Upper East Side in New York City. His older brother Andy, older sister Vicki, older brother Phil and he had enjoyed a pretty comfortable childhood as his mom had inherited a bunch of money from her grandparents shortly after Phil was born.

His parents divorced when he was three and then his mother had married Steve Rojas. Steve was a managing partner at Rojas, Platt and Gaul Managing Partners. Jim never did like him. He had been rude to Jim and always seemed to prefer Tyler, Jim's younger half-brother.

Jim's dad took a position as a radio broadcaster for the Detroit Tigers and moved to the Motor City soon after the divorce. Jim flew out to visit him one weekend a month during the school year and one month per summer when he was a kid.

Jim's brother Phil was three years older than he was. After he graduated from high school and received his Bachelor's degree in Mathematics from the City College of New York four years later, he came to Buffalo to get his Master's Degree from the University at Buffalo. Jim followed him out to Buffalo to work on his undergraduate studies after he had finished high school.

Vicki was his older sister. She had moved to Chicago with her husband Todd in the year Phil had graduated from high school. She was a nurse in the Windy City. Andy was the oldest. He had moved away after high school and only returned every couple of years to visit on Christmas. He worked on offshore oil platforms and lived in Alabama with his wife and son.

Jim sat there on the other couch wondering how everyone was doing as the zombies surrounded the farmhouse in the movie. Gradually, the growling noises in the hallway outside the dorm quieted down.

At 3:20am, he was awakened as his phone vibrated. He had a text message; it was from Campus Services.

"Students, please remain where you are. Police and National Guard will be by as the rain lets up to release you. Please call us if someone in your dorm is ill."

He looked around. Jeff and Vik were both asleep on the floor. The movie had returned to the menu screen. Jim fell back asleep.

A pounding on the door woke him up. It was still dark outside and raining. He stood and walked over to the barricaded door. He peered out the peephole. Connor and Giselle stood there, soaking wet.

"Hey! Jim! If you're in there, please let me and Giselle in! There are zombies out here! *Zombies!*" he called out. He knocked again.

"Hang on," Jim said as he moved the couch that was barricading the door. He then opened the door. "You guys okay?"

"Yes!" Connor said tersely as he and Giselle walked in.

Jim closed the door and locked it. "Where have you guys been?"

"Walking here in the rain," Giselle said as her jacket dripped rainwater into a puddle on the tile floor.

"I see that. So you guys saw real zombies?" Jim laughed. "Sigma Phi was pulling a prank last night, everyone on this floor was dressed up like zombies. They even simulated a guy getting turned into a zombie and a woman getting eaten. Man, their pranks get crazier every year. Oh, and how did you guys get here? You know there's a quarantine in place, right?"

"Jim, I don't think those were actors last night. There's totally a dead lady at the end of the hall. She got eviscerated," Connor replied, grimacing. "And yes, there *is* a quarantine in place! But when zombies broke into Giselle's house, we ran, and came here. I expected to see more police, but..." he shrugged, "I didn't."

"You guys walked here all the way from Tonawanda?" Vik asked.

"Yep," Connor replied.

Jim whistled. "And you guys didn't get eaten by zombies?"

He didn't smile. "No. Did you hear me man? There's a woman's corpse in the hallway!"

Jim's smile faded. "You did say that, didn't you? I thought you were kidding."

"He wasn't," Giselle said. "Go see for yourself."

Jim moved the couch again and walked out into the hallway. He looked down toward where the action had been the night before and saw a woman lying in what appeared to be a pool of blood.

He walked toward her and gasped as he reached her. Her abdomen had been torn open and she had been disemboweled. Jim felt dizzy and nauseous.

He turned away from the co-ed's corpse, leaned over and threw up on the floor. As his stomach heaved, suddenly the lights went out. His vomit made a wet sound as it splashed on the floor in the dark.

He coughed and stood back up as the retching stopped. He wiped his mouth with his shirt and heard a scratching noise on a nearby door. He heard more growls come from other dorm rooms.

"Guys?" he called out. His voice echoed in the hallway.

"You okay? It sounded like you just hurled!" Jeff yelled.

"Yeah, I did hurl. There's definitely a dead woman down here."

"Uh, what happened to the lights?" Jeff asked.

"Power must have gone out. It's raining pretty hard out there."

Jim started walking back in the direction of his dorm room, feeling along the wall. He passed doors that were pulsating as furious scratching sounds issued forth. Finally, he made it back to his dorm room.

"It should be daylight out soon," Vik said.

"Good, my phone's almost dead," Giselle said in response.

"Yeah, my iPhone got soaked on the way here," Connor said. "Lousy phone."

Jim re-entered his dorm.

"Well guys, me and Giselle are pretty tired," Connor said, stretching. "All that walking in the rain can make one quite sleepy. I think we're going to walk next door to my dorm and change into some dry clothes and sleep."

"Okay, be careful," Jeff said.

"We will," Connor said. "We've got some furniture I could rip apart to kill zombies, if the need arises."

Jeff grimaced. "You mean my table?"

Connor shrugged, grinning. "Possibly. That's okay, Ikea has more of them I'm sure. Goodnight all!"

Jim pushed the couch against the door after they had left. "I'm pretty beat too."

Vik nodded, "Yeah. I guess we might as well sleep some more."

"Yeah, is it okay if I stay here?" Jeff asked. "I'd rather not sleep next to the lovebirds."

"Sure," Jim said.

Jim awoke around noon. He stood up, stretched and looked outside. It was still pouring down rain. The streets were nearly empty, except for a stopped police car blocking the road. Its lights were flashing and the driver side door was open. There was no cop in sight though. He turned and walked back to the couch in the front room. Jeff was laying on the floor snoring. The power must have come back on at some point during the morning, as the clock on the stove was flashing.

He tried calling his mom again. His phone still wouldn't connect to the network. He turned the TV on and saw that a video outlining the conditions of the quarantine was looping. He sighed. What was going on?

Jim tried to remember what he had heard about Owasa Disease, but kept drawing blanks. As a film student, he hadn't really been following that part of the news lately.

He got up and walked into the kitchen. What did he want to eat? He opened the cupboard and scanned the shelves. Ramen sounded good.

He pulled a couple of packets out and set them on the counter. He pounded his fists on each packet a few times and heard the distinctive crunch as bricks of noodles were broken up. He then opened a cabinet and pulled a saucepan out.

He filled it with water and put it on the stove. After he turned the burner on he pulled some chicken out of the fridge. He had grilled some chicken a few nights before in the Quad and had some left over.

He then cut up some broccoli and carrots from the fridge and waited for the water to boil. When it did, he emptied the packets of noodles into it and added the chopped vegetables and chicken. Then he waited.

He heard footsteps behind him.

"What are you making?" Jeff asked sleepily.

"Ramen with chicken and vegetables. If you want some I can add more noodles," Jim replied.

"Sure man."

He added a couple more packs of noodles. When it was finished cooking, he poured some of the water out. Jim spooned some of the steaming noodles into a bowl and walked back into the living room. As he sat on the couch, Vik walked out of his bedroom.

"What did you cook Jim? It smells good."

"Ramen with chicken and vegetables. There might be some left after Jeff finishes making his bowl, if you want some?"

"Sure, that sounds good!"

Vikram Patel had come to America with his family from India when he was two. He had grown up in Houston and had come to UB to study Mechanical Engineering. He had been Jim's roommate since their second year of college.

Jeff, on the other hand, had been Jim's friend since they had been six. He had lived a block further down East 73rd from where Jim's mom lived. His dad had been a senior analyst at some investment firm where he ran some department that dealt with buying Treasury bonds. He and Jim went to school together until their sophomore year of high school.

That fall, Jeff's dad's investment bank collapsed and he lost his job. Jeff's parents were forced to sell their townhouse, which, in retrospect, miraculously sold very quickly. They moved to Queens and then Jeff and Jim only got to hang out occasionally until college.

Around 2:00 pm, Connor and Giselle knocked on the door and Jim let them in. They all watched some more zombie movies and talked about what they would do when the quarantine was over. Surely the authorities were clearing areas of zombies, right?

CHAPTER FIVE

Katie Barnes
Day 0

"Let's get going," the police officer said as he climbed into the squad car. "Hey, why are you crying?"

Katie was practically hysterical. "Please don't take us downtown! Please! Just take us home, please officer! I'm so sorry we broke curfew! Please just take us home! Please! Please!" she cried.

Joel placed a comforting hand on her back. "Officer, I understand you have protocol to follow, but please take us home. That's where we will be safest. I can assure you neither we nor anyone in our household is infected. We can happily abide by the rules of quarantine there," he said calmly.

The officer sighed. "Where is home?"

"One Hundred Allenhurst Road, we can prove that's where we belong," Joel replied.

"Keep quiet about this son. I am clearly violating the law," the cop said quietly as he reached up and switched his dashboard camera off. "However, I also think I'm doing the right thing."

The squad car pulled to a stop in front of Katie's house a few minutes later. As the cop let Katie and Joel out, he said, "Be careful. Barricade yourselves inside. We don't know fully what's happening, as the military won't share much information with us, but we know people from the CDC have been called in. Don't let anyone in your house, you understand?"

Katie nodded.

"Thank you, officer," Joel said.

They turned and walked up to the porch as the police officer drove away. When they reached the covered porch, Katie turned and hugged Joel tightly.

"Katie, I don't know what's happening but I will protect you. No matter what," Joel said solemnly. They stood out there for a long time embracing as the wind sprayed them with rainy mist. Finally, the front door creaked open. Katie opened her eyes and saw her roommates' friend Megan standing there.

"Kathryn Barnes!" she exclaimed and ran out to turn Katie and Joel's embrace into a group hug. Soon Katie's roommates Rachel and Michelle and another friend named Amber joined in.

"Can we go inside? It's kind of unpleasant out here," Katie said.

She walked up to her bedroom to change into dry clothes once they were inside. She grimaced when she saw her reflection in the mirror; mascara and blush were running down her face and made her look like a horror movie actress. As she changed out of her drenched clothing she removed her phone from her pocket. She was surprised to see it was still dry. She tried to call her Aunt Catherine, but was unable to get her phone to dial out.

"I guess everyone is trying to make phone calls right now," she mumbled. She sat down at her desk and turned her desktop PC on. She remembered that her shattered laptop was still in the library up in Amherst. She shook her head as she logged in to Skype. She tried video-calling her aunt.

A grainy face popped up on screen. "Katie? Is that you?"

"Yes Aunt Catherine."

"Oh, the image quality is horrid!"

"It is. Are you okay?"

"Yes, I'm at my hotel right now. They've asked us to stay put as quarantine has been enacted. So right now we are just biding our time." Katie thought she saw a nervous smile flash on her aunt's face. Catherine had been invited to an art conference in Paris. "At least I can see the Eiffel Tower from my hotel room."

"Good. It's comforting to see you're okay."

"Is everything okay Katie?"

"No. We're under quarantine too. And some psychopaths tried to kill me at the library tonight! I'm okay now, the police said they'd go investigate, but still."

Catherine's face darkened. "What happened?"

"I don't know. I was in the library doing some research for a paper and suddenly I was being chased by several crazy people who I think were infected with Owasa Disease. I ran and got away, but it was still terrifying."

"I'd say! Are you okay?"

Katie nodded. "Yeah, I think so. I have Joel, I have my roommates here at home and several of their friends are here too. I think we'll be okay. We've got enough water to last a while and we have a bunch of canned goods in the basement."

"Katie, please be careful. I don't know why such stringent quarantine measures have been enacted, but they make me feel unsettled, like something terrible is happening."

"You be careful too Aunt Catherine."

"I'm sure this will all blow over in a few days. But just know I love you Katie. I've loved you like a daughter ever since you came to live with us. You know Martin loved you like a daughter too."

"I know Aunt Catherine. I love you too! Be optimistic though, like you said, this will all blow over soon. At any rate, we are getting the remnants of a hurricane here, so we are stuck inside anyway."

The image quality degraded significantly and the audio became staticky. "-- -- love --," was all Katie heard Catherine say before the call disconnected.

"Aunt Catherine?" Katie asked. She tried calling her aunt back but the connection timed out. "I guess the internet is down now," she muttered angrily. She thought about the last conversation they had. When Katie had returned from D.C., she had gone up to her room and Skyped Catherine.

"Hey Katie! How are you?" Catherine had asked.

Katie had quietly lifted her left hand as a grin spread across her face.

"Oh my! Kathryn Marie! That's marvelous! What a big diamond! Tell me all about it!"

Katie had recounted the trip to D.C. to her aunt.

"Oh Katie, I'm so happy for you and Joel! Keep me updated! You know, it's been thirty years since I got married, but I know a thing or two about wedding planning," Catherine had said.

"Of course Aunt Catherine, I'll keep you in the loop! When do you get back from Paris?"

"November Twenty-Seventh. I leave tomorrow."

"Wow! They have a lot planned for you, don't they?"

"Yeah. At least it's in Paris and not somewhere in the tundra." Catherine had laughed.

"We wrap up finals here in the first week of December. I'm going to try to talk Joel into coming home with me for at least part of Christmas Break. I know he's never been to Toronto."

"That sounds great Katie. Let me know what he says. Don't forget to tell him I make the best Christmas snicker doodles!"

The rest of the conversation had already faded from Katie's memory. Catherine was Katie's mother's sister. After Katie's mother died, Catherine and her husband Martin had taken Katie in and practically raised her. They were the reason Katie had developed a faint Canadian accent.

She had gone to live with them in Toronto when she was fifteen. It had been really tough at first, but she bonded with her aunt over a shared interest in art. Catherine worked at the Art Gallery of Ontario and did work as a photographer on the side. Martin was a marketing executive for Rogers Communications. He had become a father figure to Katie. He would take her on camping trips to the Ontario wilderness in the summer and take her to go Christmas shopping in Montréal and Vancouver. Katie missed him. He had suffered a heart attack and died right after Katie's second semester at the University at Buffalo had started. It had been rough, but Martin had taught her how to be strong, so she had weathered the loss.

Nevertheless, Katie missed their weekly phone calls, so she talked Catherine into weekly video calls. As she sat there reflecting on her relationship with her aunt, she recalled a text message she had received from Joel right after they had returned from D.C. She pulled her phone back out and looked at the message.

"Austin is heading back home to Pittsburgh tonight. His folks called. His grandma has Owasa Disease."

Owasa Disease. In just a matter of weeks, a virus that had been intended to cure cancer had begun infecting people. Katie recalled the night her household had learned of Owasa Disease. She had just gotten home from school and everyone had been glued to the TV. The Federal Government had just announced a recall of a cancer treatment called the Noble Treatment. It had been developed from an exotic African virus known as N'zo Bat Lyssavirus (NBL). NBL was a genetic relative of rabies. An American scientist had isolated the virus from a cave in Côte d'Ivoire and it was quickly recognized as a leading candidate for a type of cancer treatment known as oncolytic virotherapy, a treatment that involved using viruses to attack cancer cells. It had been genetically manipulated to become a virus that could destroy all forms of cancer and it was deemed a modern day miracle.

Early on, Katie believed it was what her family should have had when she was younger. Her younger brother had died from brain cancer when she was eight. He had only been four years old! Then her mother died a few years later from bone cancer. Cancer had shattered her family.

In spite of being hailed as the greatest medical accomplishment in history, NBL mutated somewhere along the way and began to cause rabies-like illness in those who had received it. It killed everyone who developed the illness that was eventually dubbed Owasa Disease after a researcher in Africa who had first isolated the N'zo Bat Lyssavirus.

Katie thought about her father. She hadn't talked to him in years, not since he had sent her to Canada to live with her mother's sister. She shook her head; those thoughts would have to wait. She went downstairs to join everyone. They were watching the television intently as tropical storm force winds howled outside, lashing rain against the side of the house. She took note of who was in her living room. Joel sat alone on a love seat. Her roommates Rachel and Michelle sat on the couch alongside Megan. Rachel's friend Amber sat on the floor next to her boyfriend Anthony.

"Hey, so what happened in the World Series? Did the Sens end up winning?" she asked.

"No, Donovan Granger died on the mound and then they pulled the broadcast, so we have no idea what happened. Something really bad must have happened because ESPN simply quit giving updates about five minutes after they pulled it," Michelle replied.

"Oh," Katie said.

"I saw on Twitter that supposedly Granger came back to life as a flesh eating monster and attacked his catcher and they had to shoot him," Anthony said darkly.

"Shut up Anthony, how could you say something like that?" Amber glared at him.

"Sorry Amb, I shouldn't have said that," he replied.

"Well guys, I guess we are stuck here for a while. Who wants to play poker?" Rachel asked.

Gradually everyone grew tired. Joel and Anthony barricaded the front and back doors with some furniture and drew the shades on the windows. Anthony volunteered to keep watch and the others all went upstairs to sleep.

Katie woke up around ten the next morning and saw that everyone else was still asleep. Anthony had dozed off at some point. He was asleep at the top of the stairs snoring softly. It was still pouring down rain outside and windy. She had assumed, based on the previous night's events that she would have a fitful night of nightmares and tossing and turning. She had slept quite soundly, however.

She showered and then went downstairs to see what the latest updates were. She turned the television on and discovered it was just looping a recording giving quarantine instructions. Every channel was like that, with each station having recorded its own message. She scratched her head.

"Well, I guess I'll watch it rain," she muttered to herself. She walked over to the window, sat down on the couch and turned around to watch the rain fall. It was coming down in thick sheets outside. The streets were empty.

"Hey early bird," Joel said, walking down the stairs.

"Hey."

"Did you put any coffee on yet?"

"Not yet, I needed a hot shower more."

She heard Joel rummaging around in the kitchen. "Where do you guys keep the coffee filters?"

"In the cabinet above the stove," she replied distractedly. A tree in the neighbor's yard across the street started to lean precariously over the neighbor's car. "Hope they have good insurance," she murmured quietly.

Joel sat down next to her a moment later. "Katie, in the craziness last night, I never found out what happened exactly. I'm sorry I didn't try to listen better."

"It's okay," she replied. "I'm in a better frame of mind to describe it now."

"So what happened in the library?"

"I heard a noise, like someone had knocked some books off a shelf right after the power went out. I couldn't tell what was causing it because I had been in the library by myself. I saw blood on the floor, and heard more crashing. I saw someone stumbling around among the bookshelves, but I couldn't make out who they were. I called to them but got no answer, except a creepy gurgling noise. A flash of lightning lit them up, and I saw that whoever this guy was, he was seriously ill, injured, and looked like he was dead. Those eyes. Those cold, lifeless eyes..." Katie trailed off and shuddered.

"Did he attack you?"

"Yeah, he came after me and chased me. So I hit him in the face with my laptop and ran. I started to run outside and saw there were more people outside just like him. Some appeared to be grievously injured. So I ran to the Law Library and hid in there. I thought I was alone until you called and then I guess they were alerted to my presence because suddenly there were a lot in the room with me."

"I'm sorry," he said, putting his arm around her.

"It's okay, you couldn't have known. So I ran, and miraculously an elevator was working, and I got away and ran to you."

He hugged her tightly. "I'm glad you're okay. You know, after seeing them chasing after us last night, I believe you. What do you think was wrong with them?"

"I don't know, maybe they were infected with Owasa Disease."

"They sound more like zombies."

"Yeah, they do. I don't know though, maybe they can be cured. I would hate to be called a zombie if I were just horribly ill."

"Yeah, I guess zombie might be kind of demeaning."

Katie heard footsteps coming down the stairs.

"Hey guys," Amber greeted them. "Is that coffee I smell?"

"Yup," replied Joel. "The best part of waking up."

"Ha, yeah," she replied.

Joel hugged Katie again. "Look, no matter what happens, we are in this together."

"Thanks Joel, that really means a lot."

Everyone else woke up a little after noon. The night seemed to have taken its toll on everyone, as all were exhausted.

At 1:00pm the power went out.

"Ugh, really?" Michelle complained.

"Well, don't forget we are in the midst of a tropical storm!" Anthony replied.

"He does have a point you know Michelle," Megan said.

"Yes! I know! I'm just upset that now I have to shower in the dark. At least we have a gas stove, so we can still cook."

"I'll go down into the basement and take stock of how much food and water we actually have," Katie offered.

"Why don't I go with you?" Anthony said.

"Sure," Katie replied as she grabbed a flashlight and went into the basement. Fortunately, it didn't appear to be leaking much.

"Man Katie, your basement is really creepy," he said.

"Yeah, tell me about it," she said as she approached the shelves of canned goods.

The house had been built in the early 1920s. The basement had a low ceiling and row after row of metal shelves stocked with mason jars when Katie, Michelle and Rachel had moved in. They had removed the mason jars and replaced them with canned goods and bottled water in the meantime.

No one, however, could figure out why there was a toilet in the middle of the basement, connected to a water supply, without any walls around it. They just laughed about it usually.

In the midst of counting cans, Katie realized she didn't know where Anthony had gone. "Anthony?" she asked, walking to the end of the shelf. She turned the corner.

"Boo!" he yelled, jumping at her.

"Ah!" she screamed and dropped the flashlight. "You jerk!" She punched him hard in his arm.

"Hey, I just wanted to see how you reacted to the zombies last night!" he said, laughing.

"That's not funny," Katie said angrily. "Go upstairs. I can count our food and water alone."

He walked back upstairs, chuckling to himself.

"What a jerk," she said out loud. She picked up the flashlight and went back to work.

They had 25 gallons of drinking water, enough food to last a week and 3 additional flashlights. As she turned to go back upstairs, Katie saw something else sitting in the corner. "That could prove useful," she said, walking toward the bat.

She had discovered the old wooden bat in the attic when they had moved into the house. She grabbed it and walked back upstairs.

"Ready to play baseball?" Joel asked when he saw her.

She laughed. "Maybe. I figured this might make defending myself a bit easier."

"Hey Katie, we are going to play a few rounds of Hold 'Em, you want in?" Megan asked.

"Not for now, I might join in later," Katie replied as she walked over to the living room window and sat down. She laid the bat on the floor against the wall. The storm howled outside.

Katie recalled when Hurricane Isabel hit Baltimore. It was a few months before her mom died. She was still in pretty good spirits then and Katie had watched the storm come through with her. Luckily their house was in a higher area of Baltimore, so they escaped most of the flooding. The basement did not, however, and Katie remembered her father and older brother Robby working hard to save valuables from the basement. She remembered her mother found the whole thing quite amusing.

Katie had played outside after the storm while neighbors cleaned up their yards. The air had been thick with the aroma of sawdust and pine resin and abuzz with the sound of hundreds of chainsaws revving and cutting nearly simultaneously.

Her reverie was interrupted when she saw a military Hummer driving down the street. A Buffalo Police truck followed it. The street appeared to be flooded with about half a foot of storm water.

"I guess they're out making sure no one is violating the quarantine," Joel said as he sat down next to her.

"Yeah, I'm sure that people are really considering skipping out in the middle of a hurricane," she replied sardonically.

"Tropical storm," Joel corrected her. "It got downgraded right before you called me from the school."

"Oh."

Throughout the day Joel tried unsuccessfully to reach his family and Austin. He couldn't get through on his cell phone and the Internet was still out.

"I hope they're okay," he said.

"I'm sure they are," Katie said, hugging him.

They joined in the poker game around 4:00pm and transitioned to playing poker by candlelight as it got dark outside. The storm gradually calmed outside.

Around 11:00pm everyone went to bed. Joel volunteered to keep watch while they slept.

The next morning Katie was startled by Joel leaning over her, breathing heavily.

"What's going on?" she asked, sitting up.

"Nothing," he laughed. "Another mostly uneventful night. The neighbor's tree did fall over on his car though, around three. Katie, I don't know how you can sleep so heavily!" He laughed again. "It woke everyone else up because it set his car alarm off!"

She shrugged. "I've always been a good sleeper."

"You'd sleep through your own eulogy!"

"Yeah? I'll be dead when my eulogy is read, so I hope to sleep through it," she replied.

"Good point."

She stood and looked outside. It was still raining lightly, but the wind had died down. Branches and leaves were down all up and down the street. The neighbor's BMW lay flattened and mangled beneath the remains of a two-hundred-year old oak.

At 9:00am the power came back on. The cable and Internet were still out, so they spent the rest of the morning watching zombie movies. It only seemed appropriate.

While they ate lunch, after the second movie, they heard a man's voice being amplified outside. They all ran to the window and saw a National Guard Humvee approaching.

"Attention citizens of Buffalo. The quarantine restrictions have been expanded. Please continue to remain inside and await further instruction. We advise you to barricade your doors, if possible, and have a secure room in your house to retreat to, if necessary. If anyone in your household is ill with signs of Owasa Disease, please hang a red towel, red sheet or red shirt in a window facing the street and isolate them in an interior room. Medical personnel will come as soon as possible to treat the ill. Please continue to await additional information," the Humvee broadcasted the message on a loop from a loudspeaker as it drove by slowly.

"What a great introduction to Twenty-Eight Days Later!" Rachel said excitedly as she walked to the television. It was her favorite zombie movie.

At 4:00pm, the power went out again. They resumed playing board games and poker.

At 6:00pm, they heard a woman's scream from outside. They watched in horror as they saw a woman in the middle of the street being attacked by a group of people who appeared infected. As the infected set upon the woman, Katie noticed a large group of them shuffling up the street.

"Guys, upstairs, now!" Joel hissed quietly.

Everyone ran upstairs. Katie ran to the foot of the stairs and watched from just outside the field of view of the front porch. An infected man approached the door and scratched at it, sniffing the air. Katie saw his eyes and saw the same look in them she had seen in the library, the same cold deadness mixed with intense fury and hunger. After a few tense seconds, he turned and stumbled off the porch.

The wave of infected individuals passed through fairly quickly and after about a half hour, the street was quiet again. The poor woman who had been attacked lay in the middle of the street in a pool of blood, clearly dead.

That evening everyone was still processing what had happened in the street.

"What was wrong with those people?" Megan asked, still horrified.

"They were obviously sick," Rachel replied.

"But sick people don't suddenly become violent!" Megan protested.

"They do sometimes," Amber replied. "When I was ten my cousin got bitten by a rabid dog. For some idiotic reason he didn't tell anyone. So when he developed symptoms of rabies, they took him to the hospital. He had to be restrained!"

"No dear, people don't usually become violent when they contract rabies," Rachel replied. "They do sometimes need to be restrained though."

"I think you are all missing the point here. What kind of illness makes someone become homicidal?" Anthony asked.

"Wait! What's going on out there?" Megan asked in horror, pointing out the window.

Katie turned and saw the dead woman sit upright and slowly rise to her feet. Then she shuffled away.

Michelle ran upstairs to the bathroom. Retching sounds echoed down the hall.

"How did that just happen?" Anthony asked in horror. "How did she just return to life?"

"She didn't!" Amber said, annoyed. "She returned to 'life,'" she said, making exaggerated quotation marks with her fingers.

"Yeah, but how?" Anthony repeated.

"Maybe she wasn't really dead?" Katie guessed.

"Yeah, but Rachel said there was no way someone could have survived that!" Anthony exclaimed. "That lady had been eviscerated!"

"Well, that's true," Rachel said. "But I guess maybe it is possible."

"But how could she be in any condition to just get up and walk away?" Joel asked.

"I don't know. Sorry, we haven't gone over *surviving grievous wounds* in any of my classes!" Rachel replied, becoming frustrated.

"I'm going to go check on Michelle," Katie said, standing up and making her way upstairs. She walked to the bathroom door and knocked. "You okay Michelle?"

"Yeah," she replied as the toilet flushed. She opened the door. "I guess I was just a bit overwhelmed by what just happened."

"Yeah, it was pretty horrifying," Katie replied.

"What do you think's going to happen?" she asked. "I mean I haven't been able to get a hold of my family at all. I tried everything!" She started to cry. "Are they all going to end up like that?"

Katie hugged her. "Let's go sit down in your bedroom."

They walked to Michelle's room and sat down. They were quiet for a long time. Finally, Katie spoke up. "I'm sure your family is okay."

"You really think so?"

"Yeah, I mean they all live out in the middle of nowhere in Wyoming, right?"

Michelle nodded.

"See? If they aren't near a city they have nothing to worry about."

"Thanks Katie."

Everyone fell asleep around midnight. Anthony kept watch on the stairs with the baseball bat. Everyone realized they needed to be extra vigilant given the circumstances.

Later on, Katie was jolted awake. What time was it? She felt around for her phone. It was dead. It was still dark out. She saw Joel's watch. The glowing hands indicated it was 3:05 am.

What had awakened her? She looked around and was just starting to fall back asleep when she heard it again: a thump from downstairs. It sounded like it had come from the front door.

She heard glass break. She bolted upright and looked around. No one else moved. Several people were snoring softly. She quietly stood up and tiptoed out of the bedroom and down the hall to check on Anthony. As she reached the stairs, she saw Anthony slumped over, leaning against the wall about halfway down. He was snoring. He had fallen asleep! She quietly ran down to him and shook him. He stirred.

"Anthony! Wake up! Be quiet, I think someone is trying to break in!" she whispered tersely.

"Huh?" he replied in a daze.

"Anthony! There is someone in the house!" Katie whispered again.

He sat up and looked around. "There is?" he whispered back.

"Yes!"

He stood and quietly made his way down the stairs with the bat. Katie followed him. There, in the front of the living room, they saw the source of the noise; the woman they had watched die in the street earlier was climbing through the front window, sniffing at the air. She seemed unaware the broken glass in the window frame was slicing her hands open.

"Are you okay Miss?" Anthony asked quizzically as he shone his flashlight on her.

The woman looked up at Anthony and hissed, baring her teeth.

"Anthony! Why did you do that?" Katie whispered angrily.

"Katie! I had to see if she was okay!" he replied defensively.

"Anthony! She's dead! We watched her get disemboweled out in the street earlier!" Katie's voice had taken on a hint of panic.

The woman finished climbing through the window and began to advance toward Anthony and Katie.

"Miss, you look like you're hurt!" Anthony said. "Let us help you."

The woman growled in response as she staggered toward Anthony and Katie.

"The bat Anthony! The bat! Hit her with the bat!" Katie yelled.

He froze, unsure of what to do.

"Anthony! Hit her with the bat!"

He remained frozen. The woman was getting closer to their position at the bottom of the stairs. Katie heard stirring upstairs.

"Anthony! Hit her with the bat!" she screamed.

The woman was just an arm's length away. Her intestines dangled from her open stomach. She growled again.

Katie wrenched the bat out of Anthony's hands and swung it into the side of the woman's head. It made a sickening crack as the woman stumbled to the side into the wall. Picture frames clattered to the floor and broke.

"Kathy! What are you doing?" Anthony yelled hysterically.

The woman growled and started to approach again. Katie swung the bat at her head again. And again. And again. And again. Every swing of the bat produced another sickening cracking sound. At last, the woman fell to the floor and Katie delivered a final blow with the bat. The woman didn't move anymore. Katie dropped the bat and it clanged to the floor.

"Kate! What happened?" Joel asked from behind.

Anthony was sobbing hysterically behind her.

"I killed her Joel," Katie said mutely. "I killed her."

A light swept over the living room. Blood and fragments of bone and brain were everywhere: on the walls, on the floor, on the ceiling, on the bat, on Katie's hands and face, on Anthony. Katie looked down and saw that she had crushed the woman's head; nothing was left recognizable. Katie suddenly felt nauseous.

"Katie! Was that the same lady from the street earlier?" Rachel asked.

Katie spun around and saw everyone standing at the foot of the stairs. Michelle and Amber had gone white. Rachel looked like she was going to vomit. Joel's face was tight with worry. Suddenly the room began to spin around Katie and she felt dizzy. Then everything went black.

The next thing she knew she felt hot and flushed. She opened her eyes and stared up at the ceiling. It was dark in the living room. Someone had turned the lights back off.

"What happened?" she asked.

"You killed an infected woman and then fainted," Joel said as he cradled her head in his lap.

Katie slowly sat up and looked around at the bloody carnage. She saw that everyone else must have gone back upstairs, everyone except Joel and Anthony.

"Anthony! I don't know what you thought you were doing, but you did multiple stupid things tonight that could have gotten us all killed!" she yelled angrily at the pathetic man who sat glumly on the loveseat. His white shirt had splotches of blood all over it. He looked shell-shocked.

"Katie, calm down," he replied remorsefully. "Go upstairs and go back to sleep and I'll finish the night down here."

"No. You go upstairs and get some sleep. You're a coward. I will stay downstairs and keep watch and protect us. I'll do a better job than you. I won't fall asleep. I won't chicken out when there is a bloodthirsty monster staggering toward me. You coward. Go upstairs and go to sleep. I couldn't sleep now even if I wanted to," she replied coldly.

"I'm sorry!"

"No you're not. Now go upstairs!" she glowered at him.

He stood and skulked upstairs, his head down.

"The girls and I decided we would clean up in the morning," Joel said quietly. "Katie, you saved Anthony's life tonight and our lives as well! I knew I picked a great fiancée!" He kissed her.

"Joel! I'm covered with nastiness!" she protested.

"And I love you despite the nastiness!"

"Gee, thanks."

"No problem. I'll keep watch with you."

"No, I'll be okay. I'm wide-awake now. Angry too."

"You sure?"

"I'm positive Joel. Go back to bed."

"Okay," he said reluctantly. He stood and walked back upstairs.

Katie walked over to the stairs and sat down, picking up the now bloody baseball bat. She mulled over what had happened. She was seething with anger toward Anthony. That idiot could've gotten them all killed!

She reflected on her family. Everyone else had family they were worried about. All Katie had was her aunt. She hoped Catherine would be okay, but she knew her aunt was a smart woman, and Katie expected her to be fine. Aside from her, however, Katie was alone.

Her mother had died when Katie was eleven. Her little brother died when she was eight. Her older brother Robby had died when she was in high school. Then her father had cracked and shipped her off to Canada to live with an aunt and uncle she barely knew. While that had turned out well, Katie still nursed a strong grudge against her father for essentially abandoning her.

He had been away with work a lot when she was little, but she had some good memories from then. He loved his job but hated how it took him away from his family. When Katie's little brother died her father became distant. He would come home from work but wouldn't be as present as he could have been.

Then when her mom died, her father just started ignoring her and Robby. He would come home from his trips and just retreat to his office, engrossed in more work. It just got worse when Robby went off to college.

Robby. Her big brother. Katie sighed out loud as she thought of him. She had so much fun with him growing up. She had looked up to him in so many ways. The summer before he went off to college was just great! It was probably the best summer she had ever had.

And then Robby died. And it was more than her dad could bear, so he sent her to live with her aunt and uncle. She was a broken girl who needed healing and love from her daddy, and she never received it. Instead Katie had to find healing in the winter winds sweeping off Lake Ontario and in the forlorn paintings of Tom Thomson and in the quiet stillness of Algonquin Provincial Park. She hadn't spoken with her father in more than five years. She had wanted him out of her life in much the same way he wanted her out of his.

She didn't want anything to do with him.

CHAPTER SIX

Randy Eccleston
Day 1

Gunfire erupted across the river as the friends sat down on benches on one side of the rail station beneath the bridge's roadway. The station's power was out. Casey held Missy and Adam and Jillian sat quietly beside Randy as he tried to figure out what had happened. What was Owasa Disease? He remembered hearing about MERS and Ebola and SARS, but never Owasa Disease. Why was a virus causing such a violent response by the authorities?

"We should try to get to my house when everything dies down a bit," Casey said quietly.

Randy nodded as the others murmured in agreement.

"What happened over there?" Adam asked. "I mean, the military just destroyed bridges into Saint Louis!"

"I don't know," Randy replied. "That virus the cop was talking about must be a pretty nasty bug."

"I'd say!" Jillian exclaimed.

"Why do you think those soldiers started shooting at people?" Missy asked.

"They probably panicked," Casey said.

"But why? They weren't just shooting at a few people, they opened up!"

"You didn't hear what the one soldier asked Randy?" Adam asked. "He asked if Randy was infected. When Randy said no, the guy screamed at us to run!"

"Hey wait!" Randy said urgently, putting his index finger to his lips. "Listen!"

Screams erupted from a nearby casino. Gunfire rang out from the parking lot.

The others looked at him in alarm.

"We'd better be ready for whatever might come our way," he said nervously.

Suddenly he heard a train whistle. He looked up and saw a Metro train approaching from the east at a high rate of speed.

"They've got to stop!" Adam exclaimed. "The bridge is out!"

The train careened past the train station, its wheels screeching on the track. It then flew over the edge of the tracks and plunged into the river with a horrifying crash.

Jillian screamed.

"What the…what just happened?" Casey asked.

"That train just flew off the tracks," Randy said quietly. Missy and Jillian were both crying.

"We've got to get to my house!" Casey whispered urgently.

"No, not yet. Don't you hear the gunfire?" Randy asked. "How far are we from your house? Twenty miles? It's dark, we don't know what's going on down there, and at least up here we're somewhat out of the way."

"Randy, all we have is this one machine gun with its single clip. Besides, we don't know if the military is going to bomb anything else!"

"No Casey, Adam has a pistol he lifted from a cop," Randy said.

"It's only got six bullets in it. We do have night sticks at least," Adam replied.

"Okay, but still," Casey said.

"How did you get that gun, anyway?" Adam asked.

"I knocked the cop that arrested me out and took it from him!" Casey replied defensively.

"Look!" Missy said, pointing at the casino.

Randy turned and saw people fleeing from the entrance of the building as several dozen people staggered out.

"What's wrong with those people?" Adam asked.

"They look sick," Jillian replied.

Randy watched in horror as one of the staggering individuals tackled a person and began clawing at them.

"What is he doing to her?" Jillian asked.

"He's attacking her," Casey replied quietly.

"Look alive guys, there's a stairwell right over there and one across the tracks. We'll need to keep our eyes peeled," Randy said.

"What if one of those people comes up here?" Missy asked.

"I'll shoot him," Casey said, patting the gun.

"What? Why? Those people are sick!" Jillian protested.

"Yeah, and they appear to be feasting on innocent bystanders down there. Unless we want to be on the menu, I'm shooting any of them that come up here."

They watched the terrible scene unfold for a while. Suddenly a cry came from the nearest stairwell. Casey jumped off the bench and crept over to the corner near the stairwell. He peeked around the edge and motioned for Randy to join him.

Randy tiptoed over and peered around the railing. A security guard lay in the darkness weeping. Randy could just make out a shadowy figure standing over him.

"Please no! Please no!" the man yelled as the shadowy figure leaned over him and growled.

Randy leaned back against the wall as the man screamed in agony. After a few moments, he became silent.

"That man is eating him," Casey whispered.

Randy nodded, growing nauseous.

"Seriously, he just ripped that guard's intestines out."

Randy shook his head, horrified.

Casey leaned back against the concrete pillar. He sighed quietly and gripped the gun tightly.

"This is bad," Randy murmured.

He nodded. "If one of those people comes up here, I'll unload on him."

Randy nodded and glanced at his watch. It was 1:30am. Screams and periodic gunfire rang out down in the parking lot of the casino. Gradually the parking lot fell quiet. Missy and Jillian sobbed quietly behind Randy and Casey as wet splashing sounds echoed up from the stairs. Eventually, that too fell silent.

Randy looked up at the crescent moon as it dimly illuminated the night sky. He must have nodded off at some point because suddenly sirens started going off all around. The sound startled him awake.

"Quarantine has been enacted. Take cover immediately," a voice rang out all around. Then sirens resonated for thirty seconds and the message repeated.

Randy looked at his watch. It was 2:43am. The others were looking around quietly.

"The sick person is gone," Casey whispered over the clamor of the sirens. "He stumbled away about a half hour ago."

Randy nodded.

Gunfire erupted across the river in the city.

"This is bad," he mumbled quietly.

Casey nodded. "Yeah, it is."

At 3:00am, the message quit repeating and was replaced with a constant shrill siren.

Adam, Jillian and Missy huddled together on the bench as Casey and Randy sat near the stairwell.

"You get any sleep?" Casey asked.

"I nodded off for a little bit earlier."

He nodded.

"Why don't you get some shuteye?" Randy suggested.

He shook his head. "You think I could sleep in this?"

Randy chuckled. "Good point."

"What do you think we should do?" he asked.

Randy shrugged. "I don't know. You have family in California, don't you?"

He shook his head. "My mom died four years ago and who knows where my dad is? I haven't seen that deadbeat since I was little. I've got nothing in California. What about you?"

"I've got an older brother in Chicago, about a mile from my house."

He nodded. "Yeah, what's his name?"

"Todd. He's got a wife named Vicki and they have two little girls."

He nodded. "My vote is to head back to Chicago, see if your brother is still alive," he said. "Besides, I'm sure Adam and Jillian want to head back to Chicago too."

"We'll see," Randy said.

"See what?" Adam asked.

"Casey and I were discussing our next steps."

"We're heading back to Chicago, right?" Adam asked.

"Is that where you and Jillian want to go?" Randy asked.

He nodded. "We were talking about it over there. Jill wants to go back, you know, see if we still have a home."

Randy nodded. "What about Missy? What about your house Casey?"

Missy shook her head. "There's nothing for us there. We were going to be evicted within a few days anyway. You know Casey lost his job a few months ago."

"What about supplies? Is there any food at your house Casey?" Adam asked. He nodded. "A bit."

"So at dawn let's head to Casey's," Randy said, "and then let's head to Chicago."

"Let's leave now," Jillian suggested.

He shook his head. "It's dark. We don't know what we will encounter between here and Casey's, but it will be easier to see in daylight. Besides, with all the gunfire around us, I'd be concerned that someone would mistake us for one of those sick people in the dark."

The others nodded.

"At dawn we'll follow the train tracks to Shiloh, to Casey's house."

Everyone huddled in the dark for the last few hours of nighttime as gunfire continued across the river in Saint Louis.

At dawn, they rose and began making their way down the railroad tracks toward Casey's house in Shiloh. As they made their way down the inclined tracks the emergency sirens all around fell silent.

"What do you think happened last night?" Adam asked Randy as they walked.

Randy shook his head. "Something bad. That cop was talking about a nasty virus. I guess that's what happened. Look!" He pointed west toward Saint Louis. Several of the office towers were ablaze, sending columns of thick black smoke skyward.

"What kind of virus causes people to become homicidal?"

Randy shrugged. "I don't know. I mean rabies can cause violence."

They passed through a deserted plaza in front of several municipal buildings a short time later. Several stray dogs ran through the plaza, sniffing at the wind. It was eerily quiet.

"Where is everyone?" Adam asked.

Randy raised his arm and everyone froze.

"It's really quiet," Casey said.

He nodded. "Something's not right. Where are the police? Where's the National Guard? Casey, be ready with that gun. Guys, if you see any weapons you could use to defend yourselves, grab them."

The others murmured in agreement.

They continued on through the plaza and followed the railroad tracks past several blocks of buildings in various stages of decay. Some of the buildings had trees growing through the windows.

"Behold East Saint Louis!" Casey said, chuckling nervously.

"This place looks like it has seen better days," Randy said quietly.

They entered a residential neighborhood as they continued on.

"Look!" Jillian whispered. "There are red sheets in the windows of every house!"

"Abandoned police cars too," Missy said.

"Be alert guys," Randy said.

They came around a bend in the tracks and Randy saw a raised section up ahead that appeared to rise over a highway. He ran ahead and climbed the sloping track until he was perhaps fifty feet above the highway. He looked down and gasped.

The interstate was choked with abandoned cars around which hundreds of people shuffled aimlessly. Many of the individuals below were covered in blood. All of them possessed an ominous gait that suggested something terrible.

The others caught up to Randy, panting.

"Hey! You ran off on us - whoa!" Casey gasped, looking down at the throng of people.

"They look infected," Missy said.

Casey raised his gun.

"Wait!" Randy whispered urgently. "You don't have enough bullets to kill all of them! Besides, we don't know if they're homicidal like the others were!"

"You ever seen Dawn of the Dead?" Casey asked, raising an eyebrow.

He nodded. "This is real life though, this isn't fiction! We don't know what those people have, but they surely aren't zombies! We don't even know if what they have can be treated!"

Casey chuckled. "So you think the apparent collapse of society in the immediate area is happening independently of this?"

Randy shook his head. "No, but an epidemic of a debilitating and deadly disease could quickly cause a breakdown of normal societal structures, without a zombie virus. I mean, I think Hollywood has all but debunked the idea of the zombie."

Casey shook his head again. "I disagree."

"Look," Randy said, putting his hand on his friend's shoulder. "I agree with you that we should keep our distance from them. Regardless of what they have, I don't want to catch it."

"Me neither," Adam said. "Come on, let's keep moving. You'll both have time to argue later. Let's get going before those people notice us."

They continued on and descended to the other side of the interstate. They passed a desolate train station and more houses with red sheets and towels hanging in the windows. Some houses seemed to have scratching noises coming from the doors.

They walked all day, past abandoned cars, under overpasses, through thick woods and past desolate buildings that had long ago been vacated. Finally, around 4:00pm, Casey cleared his throat.

"We need to climb down to the road down there and follow it north for about a mile," he said, pointing up ahead.

They climbed down to the road and followed him north. Randy realized he hadn't seen any signs of life since they had crossed the interstate that morning. Even the birds were quiet.

As the sun began to near the horizon, he and the others followed Casey and Missy into a subdivision up to a house at the end of a cul-de-sac. This house was the only house in the neighborhood without red sheets in the windows. The sun slowly sank below the trees at the opposite edge of a field behind Casey's house.

They entered the quiet house and all heaved a collective sigh of relief once Adam closed the door.

"We made it," Jillian said, laughing.

Randy nodded. "Hey Casey, turn the lights on."

"I would, but the power seems to be out," he muttered.

"Great! I guess we'll be sleeping in the dark!" Jillian sighed.

"Hey, help me eat the food in the fridge. It's going to go bad," Missy said.

She opened the refrigerator and in the fading light, Randy saw a cheesecake, leftover steak, leftover chicken salad and a bag of lettuce.

"Let us feast!" he cried dramatically.

CHAPTER SEVEN

Andy Gibson
Day 7

The next day, Andy ate lunch with Royce and the other guys on his team: Alex Giles, Matt Carlton, Nick Flaugher, Eric McClintock, Justin Ragan, Kevin Sampson and Jeremy Edwards.

"What a storm, eh boys?" Eric asked as he took a bite of a chicken sandwich.

Suddenly there was a loud bang outside and alarms began sounding.

"Go to your stations and get your gear! Jeremy, assess the situation and come report to us!" Andy yelled as they all leapt out of their seats.

Andy ran to the Fire Team staging area. He hurriedly opened his locker, donned his overalls and his fireproof outerwear and then his helmet and boots.

"We're going to go down there expecting a blowout!" he yelled to his team. "Even though we know that isn't possible, we are going to go expecting the worst. Matt, I want you, Eric and Nick to prepare hoses from Side A. Royce, I want myself, you and Kevin to prepare hoses from Side B. Jeremy and Justin will evacuate any injured to the Infirmary. Let's do this!"

Jeremy ran into the room panting.

"Report?" Andy asked.

"The north storage tank on the main deck is on fire. The production techs were supervising a welder while he was welding a line closed and it appears there were hydrocarbons in the line."

"We've got to get out there! B Team, with me!" Andy shouted.

They ran down the stairs and out of the accommodation module. Andy paused when he reached the main deck. The ten-thousand-gallon storage tank was veiled in thick black smoke. The deck in front of it was awash in orange flames. A man lay still near the flames, face down.

"Come on!" Andy yelled. They ran to the Side B hose kit and quickly assembled it. Kevin turned the activation valve and they moved toward the flames.

From this angle Andy could see that the flames were only ten feet from the storage tank. If the tank caught fire, it could explode and possibly destroy the entire platform.

With his free hand, he grabbed the radio on his lapel. "A Team, wait for us to douse the flames with PKP, when we have knocked the flames down, foam the whole area including the tank! We must keep it cool!" he barked.

"Roger that!" he heard Matt reply.

Andy grabbed the lever on the nozzle, switched it to the left hose and glanced over his shoulder. "Ready!" he yelled. He pulled the lever back and a stream of violet powder erupted from the pointed nozzle toward the flames. The burning pipe was quickly enveloped in a low purple cloud and the fire was extinguished.

At the same time an ivory stream of foam arced over Justin and Jeremy, who were tending to the unconscious man, and quickly coated the pipe and the storage tank.

Andy released the lever and his team laid the hose on the deck. He then ran over to Justin and Jeremy.

"What's the status of the victim?" he yelled.

"Sir, he's dead," Justin replied as Jeremy continued CPR.

Andy stopped when he reached them. It was intensely hot. Andy looked down at the badly burned dead man. His coveralls were charred. He was bloody and his face was scorched beyond recognition.

"Do we know who that was?" Andy asked.

Justin shook his head. "Not with certainty."

He turned and looked around as the foam bubbled on the hot deck. "Any other victims?"

"Not that I can tell sir," Jeremy said as he ceased resuscitation efforts.

"I've got two victims over here!" Matt yelled from over behind the pipe.

Andy turned and ran to him. Another man, who was clearly dead, lay face down on the deck, the back of his head caved in. Another man lay nearby, severely burned but conscious.

"Raul? Raul Simpson?" Andy asked.

"Andrew, hello," the burned man rasped back.

"What happened?"

"Mike and Elliot," he replied, coughing.

"Mike Speer?"

"Yeah."

"Alright guys, we need to get a medic up here. We're going to need to get Raul to the Infirmary," Andy said.

"Here, I grabbed a backboard!" Andy heard a voice behind him. He turned and saw Oscar Mendez, one of the Production Techs, standing behind him holding a bright yellow backboard.

"Alright, let's get him on it!" Andy barked. "Be gentle!"

Oscar laid the backboard on the deck and they carefully moved Raul onto it. Andy looked down at the burned man.

"Hang in there Raul, you'll pull through!" he said. He looked up at Matt and Alex. "Guys, get him to the Infirmary."

"Yes sir!" Matt said, as he and Alex lifted the backboard and carried Raul away.

Andy turned and surveyed the scene. A thick layer of fire-suppressing foam coated the deck and oil storage tank. Steam rose from the foam and in places the violet hue of Purple K was visible beneath the foam. Royce and his team shut off the spray of foam. Royce walked over.

"What happened?" Royce asked.

"I don't know," Andy replied. "Let's interview witnesses and see what's going on."

"What happened?" someone else asked from behind.

Andy turned and saw Kenny Shafer, lead of Fire Team B.

"Hey Kenny," he said. "There was an explosion and fire up here. We've got the fire under control, and we have the injured man evacuated to the Infirmary. Two were killed."

"Whoa," his counterpart replied. "We train for this stuff but man, that's awful. How'd it happen?"

"We'll have to interview some witnesses and review surveillance footage," Andy said.

The next day Raul Simpson died. The crew held a funeral service for the three men killed in the accident as well as the eight men presumed dead in the storm.

On the November 6th Andy wrote the official report of what had happened for BSEE:

At 12:16 on Wednesday November 4, an accident occurred on the North side of the Main Deck of Platform 3131 - Bald Point owned by Cypress Petroleum Group. The platform had recently taken a direct hit from a Category 5 hurricane, Hurricane Teddy. The maintenance crews were repairing damage caused by the storm.

At 12:00, Production Technician Raul Simpson took Welder Elliot Harvey to a 15" diameter oil pipe that ran across a portion of the main deck near an oil storage tank. The tank contained approximately 10,000 gallons of crude oil. The pipe had been punctured by a fragment of airborne debris during the hurricane and needed to be patched.

As Mr. Harvey prepared his equipment to repair the pipe, Well Services Supervisor Mike Speer came over to talk to Raul. It is not clear what they were talking about.

At 12:10 Mr. Harvey opened the valve on his acetylene tank and lit his cutting torch. He began cutting around the puncture site in the steel pipe. The perforation in the pipe was noted as approximately 3" in diameter and irregularly shaped. The perforating agent was never located but was presumed to be a structural bolt that was stripped from the derrick during the storm by the wind.

Mr. Harvey proceeded to remove a panel of pipe measuring approximately 4" x 4" as Mr. Simpson and Mr. Speer observed. At 12:15, approximately 30 seconds before the explosion, Mr. Harvey switched to his welding torch and moved the patch over the weld site. He activated the torch and began welding it in place.

At 12:16 an explosion occurred which killed Mr. Harvey and Mr. Speer almost instantly. They both received 2nd and 3rd degree burns over 75% of their bodies in addition to receiving physical trauma from the blast wave. Mr. Simpson was thrown backwards by the blast about 15 feet and received 2nd and 3rd degree burns over 60% of his body.

The explosion ignited oil remaining in the pipe and ignited the exterior of the storage tank. Fire Team A was mobilized and successfully extinguished the fire using a twin agent spray of Purple-K and AFFF foam at 12:22.

Mr. Harvey and Mr. Speer were deceased when located by the fire team. Mr. Simpson was grievously wounded but still conscious when found. He was evacuated to the Infirmary where he died the next day.

The primary cause of the incident has been determined to be ignition of hydrocarbon residue by molten metal. As Mr. Harvey was welding the patch in place, hot liquefied steel poured into the pipe where it came in contact with oil and gas that had pooled in a bend and ignited the pool of hydrocarbons. The flame flashed upward through the pipe until it emerged through the opening where the patch was being applied. It engulfed Mr. Harvey and the heat caused his tank of acetylene to deflagrate due to thermal failure of the small tank's valve.

The failure by either Mr. Harvey or Mr. Simpson to examine the interior of the pipe to verify the absence of flammable substances is mystifying. They clearly violated a well-established safety practice and it is not known if this was deliberate or accidental.

The safety valve that was in place to prevent backflow of oil within the pipe held up and thus prevented an even worse catastrophe. The prompt response of the fire safety team almost certainly saved lives.

Andy placed the report in the filing cabinet near his desk and shook his head.

"Such a waste," he murmured.

On the morning of November 14th, a pounding on the door of Andy's room awakened him. He rose from bed and opened the door. Royce was standing in the hallway; his face was pale.

"Becker's dead," he said.

"What?" Andy asked. "You're kidding!"

"I'm not man. Doctor Kulik went to check on him this morning and he was dead. I heard he had bled out all over his room," he whispered the last part.

"What?"

"I know! That doesn't sound like the flu to me."

"He's really dead?" Andy asked.

"Yes!"

Suddenly the loudspeaker in the hallway crackled.

"All able-bodied crew report to the galley for a briefing on OIM Carl Becker," the voice crackled through the speaker.

Andy dressed quickly and followed Royce down to the galley. By the time they arrived, it was packed. Carlos, Mitch, Dale, Sterling and Merle stood in the front of the room, grim expressions on their faces.

After a few minutes, Carlos stepped forward and motioned for silence. He cleared his throat. "As you all may have heard, OIM Carl Becker was ill with flu-like symptoms for more than a week. This morning at Six-Hundred hours, Doctor Dan Kulik went to his room to check on him. When he entered the room, he found Mr. Becker had passed away at some point in the night."

The room filled with audible murmurs as the crew expressed their shock.

"Now, I know we are all confused by this tragic turn of events. We will be having a memorial service for Carl this evening, as soon as the medical staff has determined the cause of death. If you have been in contact with Carl since he became ill, we ask that you would go to the Infirmary following this meeting as you may have been exposed to his illness. Finally, as per company policy and maritime standards, I am now the acting OIM. That would naturally make Mitch the new OTL and Dale the new Second Officer, but we will need to await confirmation from Operations before we can issue the promotions," he said. "If you have any questions, feel free to come see me."

The murmurs faded to stunned silence. Some crewmembers visibly wept; others sat completely still. Nevertheless, everyone on board the Bald Point platform was shaken by this turn of events.

Royce and Andy walked upstairs to the Officers' Quarters to see if Doctor Kulik was still attending to Becker. As they walked down the hallway Andy heard a woman's horrified scream come from the direction of Becker's room.

He looked at Royce and they sprinted down the hall toward the commotion. When they arrived on the scene Andy saw Doctor Claire Maclin standing near the door with her hands on the sides of her head. She shrieked again. In front of her, Carl Becker was attacking Doctor Kulik.

"What's going on here?" Andy asked as Royce stood beside him in disbelief.

"He- he attacked Dan when Dan was taking his measurements! I- we thought he was dead!" she screamed.

"Dan! Carl! Stop!" Andy yelled, shoving past her into the large room. Blood pooled on the carpet. He realized Dan was bleeding profusely from his wrist. Andy ran to Carl and wrapped his arms around the older man's torso. He jerked backwards and heaved Becker off of Doctor Kulik.

The old man growled at Andy and batted his hands at him. He felt ice cold and his skin possessed the pallor of a dead man. He growled again and struggled.

"Carl! Carl! Stop! What are you doing?" Andy pleaded as the OIM tried to turn around to face him.

"Doctor Kulik!" Doctor Maclin yelled. "Are you okay?"

Doctor Kulik coughed. "He bit me! The OIM bit me!"

Carl bleated loudly and started to kick his legs. He didn't seem to be breathing. Andy felt something wet and cold slide over his forearm.

"Andy! Let go of him and run!" Andy heard Royce yell over the commotion.

"Why? He's a danger to Doctor Kulik! Get them out of here!" he yelled back.

"Andy! His intestines are dangling over your arm!" Royce yelled.

With a grunt Andy lifted the old man and turned him so that he was facing away from the door. Carl bleated again and growled, arms flailing about over his head.

"The doctors are out! Come on man!" Royce yelled.

Andy threw Carl against the wall, face first, and jumped backwards. The man spun around and hissed at him. He saw that Becker's abdomen had been sliced open and his viscera were spilling out. The old man reached for him and staggered forward.

Andy ran backwards and jerked the door shut as he exited the room. Doctor Kulik clutched his arm as Doctor Maclin cried.

"What just happened in there?" Royce asked.

"I don't know!" Andy exclaimed.

"Becker, he's- he's- this shouldn't be possible," Kulik gasped.

"Why?" Andy asked.

"He's dead."

"Uh Doctor Kulik? Dead men don't move and bite folks," Royce said.

The door shook and Andy heard Becker growl behind it. He heard clawing at the door.

"How sturdy is this door?" Andy asked.

"Pretty sturdy actually," he heard a voice from behind. Andy turned his head and saw Tyrell Cook and Robbie McBride, both of whom were security guards.

"Tyrell! Robbie! Thank heavens you guys showed up!" Royce exclaimed.

"You want to tell me why you are all standing outside our deceased OIM's room?" Tyrell asked. "What's going on? Why is your arm bloody Andrew? What happened to Kulik?"

Becker scratched at the door from inside again.

"And *who* is in the OIM's quarters?"

"Becker! Carl Becker is!" Claire shouted.

"Step aside," Tyrell instructed.

"Officer Cook, Carl bit me. He's going to bite you too if you open that door!" Doctor Kulik yelled.

"Step aside Andrew. I don't want to have to make you step aside," Tyrell repeated.

"Okay," Andy said. He stepped aside as Tyrell and Robbie readied their batons.

Robbie turned the knob and pushed. The door wouldn't open.

"Something's leaning against the door!" he exclaimed, pushing against it.

Becker growled and suddenly the door flew open. Robbie almost fell into Becker's bloody arms.

The security man gasped as Becker lunged at him. He instinctively swung his baton upward into the pallid man's chin. With a sickening crack, the nightstick made contact with Carl's jaw and he staggered backwards away from the door into the bed.

"Sir! I'm so sorry!" Robbie yelled as Tyrell gasped.

"He's alive?" the Security Chief cried out.

"Look at him!" Royce yelled. "Whatever he is he needs to be barricaded in his room!"

Robbie nodded quickly as Becker sat up and growled at them. He had pieces of bloody skin stuck between his teeth. His eyes were bloodshot and possessed a lifeless gaze.

"Close the door!" Andy yelled as Becker labored to stand up.

"Close the door!" Doctors Maclin and Kulik yelled.

"Close the door Robbie!" Tyrell yelled as Becker lurched toward the open doorway.

Robbie snapped out of his trance and yanked the door shut. The door thumped as Carl walked into the door. The dead man let out a frustrated shriek.

"What- what was wrong with Carl?" Tyrell demanded.

"I don't know sir," Robbie replied. "He- he- I had to hit him!"

"I know that Robbie. He was far more aggressive than the grievous wounds he had would warrant," Tyrell said.

"I checked! I checked his vitals!" Kulik yelled. "He definitely did *not* have a pulse and he definitely was *not* breathing! Please remember, *I* am a doctor!"

"Dan," Andy said. "There's no way! How would a dead man attack you and try to attack us?"

"How would a living man be able to attack us while his intestines are hanging out?" Royce asked.

"Did Captain Becker ever seem like he had a problem with drug abuse?" Tyrell asked.

"What?" Andy asked. "That's preposterous!"

"You know, this does sound like what them bath salts do," Robbie said suddenly. "I mean folks have become monstrously violent while under their influence and have even wounded themselves while on them. One guy I read about even took a knife and cut his own face off. Doctor Kulik, did you or Doctor Maclin cut his belly open?"

"No," Kulik replied.

"Then how did that happen? And really, it sounded like I broke his jaw when I hit him. Shouldn't that have knocked him down and put him in intense agony?" Robbie asked.

"That's a good point Robbie," Tyrell said. "Here's the deal. We need to file an incident report. But, we also need to monitor him. I can lock that door, and it should hold against him. However, we want to wait for him to come down from whatever he took."

"If he's alive you realize he may succumb to his injuries if we leave him alone, right?" Claire asked.

"Claire, that's a risk we'll have to take I think," Kulik said. He shook his head. "He's dead. I think he already succumbed to whatever he had."

"Alright, Robbie, you stay here. No one gets into that room unless it's me, you or a doctor. We will check on him in an hour. Doctor Kulik, please go to the Infirmary. That bite on your forearm looks nasty!" Tyrell said. "And you two," he pointed at Andy and Royce, "don't tell *anyone* about this until we know what's going on, got it?"

Andy nodded. Royce did too.

"Alright, now get out of here. And take a shower Gibson! Get that bloody mess off your arm!"

Around midnight, the Maintenance Supervisor Scott Maniczewski ran into the galley where Milo and Andy were sitting eating dinner. His face was flushed.

"Somebody! Come quick! Doctor Kulik killed Doctor Maclin!" he yelled.

Andy jumped up and several of the crew followed him to the Infirmary where Doctor Maclin lay face down in a pool of blood. Doctor Kulik crouched in the corner eating something from his hands.

"Doctor Maclin!" Andy yelled. "Doctor Kulik!"

Kulik looked up at him and growled, baring bloody teeth. His white shirt was blood-soaked. He appeared to have numerous scratches on his pale face. His face was the same shade of greenish white that Becker's had been. He growled again and resumed eating the bloody mass clutched in his hands.

Scott pushed past Andy and bent over Claire.

"Claire?" he asked. He put his hand on her shoulder and shook her. She didn't move. He turned her onto her side and immediately turned away, vomiting.

"Kulik!" Andy heard Tyrell yell. He too shoved past Andy and looked down at Claire. "What happened?" he yelled.

"Her face," Scott said weakly. "It's...gone."

"Dan! Stand up with your hands in the air!" Tyrell yelled, pulling his Taser out and aiming it at the bloody man.

Kulik tilted his head and growled.

"Drop what's in your hands!" Tyrell yelled.

Kulik shrank into the corner, muttering something as he went.

"This is your last warning! Stand up with your hands in the air or I will fire!" Tyrell yelled.

Kulik growled.

Tyrell adjusted his aim and fired. The cartridge activated and two electrodes embedded themselves in the mad doctor's cheek. He didn't flinch as the barbs pierced his skin. As the current began to arc over the wires to him, he jerked and dropped the crimson mass he had been clutching. He stood up and staggered forward two steps before falling face down on the floor twitching.

Andy heard gasps and turned to see a number of the crew gathered behind him watching the horrifying spectacle. He turned back around and saw Tyrell approaching Kulik. He gasped as the bloody man forced himself up into a sitting position. He growled at Tyrell again.

"Dan! What happened?" Tyrell asked.

Kulik stood up and lunged at Tyrell. The security guard leapt backward out of his reach.

"Dan! If you don't stop, I will be forced to escalate my use of force! Do you understand?"

Someone vomited behind Andy.

The doctor staggered toward Tyrell. Tyrell removed his pistol from its holster. He leveled it at Kulik.

"Dan! Stop now or I will shoot with deadly force! Stop!" Tyrell yelled.

Kulik growled and lunged at Tyrell again.

Bang!

The doctor fell at the security guard's feet. At last he was still.

"What is going on here?" someone yelled. Andy turned and saw Sterling and Doctor Shah standing in the doorway of the Infirmary.

"Claire! Dan!" Shah cried out, running into the room.

"Doctor Kulik attacked Doctor Maclin," Scott said from a sitting position near Claire. "He ripped her face off and ate it."

"What?" Sterling asked in disbelief.

"Yeah, Tyrell shot him to death because he was trying to attack him," Andy said.

"Alright, everyone but Scott, Andy, Doctor Shah and Tyrell back to your rooms now!" Sterling yelled angrily.

The crowd dispersed quickly. Sterling sighed loudly.

"*What* is going on? Can somebody please explain it to me?" he demanded.

"Doctor Kulik attacked and killed Doctor Maclin," Tyrell said. "And then when I happened on to the scene he attacked me. I had to use lethal force to stop him."

Sterling looked at Andy. "Really?" he asked.

Andy nodded.

"Why would Doctor Kulik become violent?" he demanded.

Tyrell shrugged. "He was attacked by Becker earlier and bitten."

"Wait, did you just say he was attacked by OIM Carl Becker, who is dead?" Sterling asked.

Tyrell nodded.

"Why didn't anybody tell me about this? You aren't making any sense. Why would Carl attack Dan? And for that matter, how could he? He's dead!" Sterling exclaimed.

"See for yourself sir," Andy said.

Sterling looked at Scott who was crying now. "Scott, Scott! Pull yourself together! I need you to help Doctor Shah get this room cleaned up! If you need to grab some lease hands to help, do it. Follow Doctor Shah's orders."

Scott nodded.

"Tyrell, take me to Becker's room. I demand to know what's going on!" Sterling said.

CHAPTER EIGHT

Randy Eccleston
Day 2

Around midnight Randy was awakened by a scratching noise at the front door. He sat up in the darkened living room and looked around. What was that?

He slowly stood up as the scratching continued. He crept over to the front door and peered out the peephole. In the dim moonlight he could just barely make out the shape of a woman standing on the front porch. She was clawing at the front door and growling softly. Suddenly she staggered backwards and bent over. He heard retching and splashing sounds; she was vomiting.

He stepped back from the door and felt a hand on his shoulder.

He spun around, night stick raised, and saw Adam.

His friend threw his hands up. "Hey, sorry!" he whispered. "What's that noise out there?"

"An infected woman," Randy whispered. "She's throwing up right now."

"What should we do?"

He shrugged. "I guess I could run out there and subdue her, but I don't know how many others there are, and I'm not sure she's homicidal. She looked curious and tired."

"Maybe she'll go away?" Adam asked.

"I hope so."

"How contagious do you think that disease is?"

Randy shrugged. "I hope it's not airborne. I mean, with all of the blood and stuff, if it is contagious I'd imagine it is bloodborne."

Adam nodded. "You work in a blood bank, I guess you'd be knowledgeable about that kind of stuff."

He shrugged. "I guess. I don't know. Just don't come in direct contact with any of their body fluids. Besides, we should keep our distance anyway."

"Hey, the scratching finally stopped."

Randy turned and looked out the peephole and saw the woman shuffling away. He nodded at Adam.

"I guess one of us should stay up to keep watch," his friend said.

He nodded. "I'll do it."

"You sure?"

"Yeah, I'll do it."

"Alright, good night Randy."

"Good night Adam."

It began to rain around 2:30am. As Randy sat on the couch staring out the window at the yard, he began to think about his brother Todd. He wondered how he was.

Todd was three years older. He and Randy had been pretty close in their childhood. He had gone off to Rutgers University after high school and had obtained a business degree. With that, he managed to start up a successful microbrewery in Chicago where he later settled down and married a woman named Vicki.

Randy, on the other hand, had gone to Northwestern University near their parents' home. With that thought, Randy wondered about his parents and whether they were okay. He thought about their house in Lake Forest, north of Chicago. So many memories.

He shook his head. He didn't know if he would ever see his parents or his brother ever again. He sighed. Though he didn't know, he would try to find them.

CHAPTER NINE

Adam Doss
Day 2

"Hey Adam, wake up sleepyhead!" Jillian laughed playfully.

Adam opened his eyes and sat up. They were in a bedroom at Casey's house. He looked at the walls that had been illuminated by the morning sunlight. Numerous posters for different metal bands hung all over the room. He chuckled at some of the band names.

"God Fodder," he said, laughing.

"You think that's a good one?" Jillian asked, laughing. "How about Sewageface?"

He laughed. "That is a good one but I think Skeletonwitch is better. How long you been up?"

"I don't know, maybe a half hour," she replied, smiling.

He and Jillian had been dating for six years. They had begun dating in college at Northwestern University. Her red hair shone dazzlingly in the morning sun.

"What, do I have something on my face?" she asked.

"No, I just think you're pretty is all," he replied kissing her.

"Alright love birds, we're going to get going in a little while," Casey said as he walked by the bedroom.

"Okay Casey," Adam said, standing up and stretching.

"You sleep well?" he asked.

"Yeah, for the most part. Around three o'clock I got woke up because there was an infected lady scratching at the front door."

"What? What happened?" Casey asked nervously.

"Nothing. She scratched at the door for a little while and then stumbled away. Randy said he'd keep watch for the rest of the night."

"Okay, I'll go check on him," he replied. "I think we have some cereal if you guys are hungry?"

Adam nodded and turned to Jillian. "You hungry?"

She nodded.

"Let's go get breakfast."

He walked downstairs and heard Casey and Randy laughing from the living room. He walked in and saw Randy sleepily rubbing his eyes. "How did it go?" he asked.

Randy laughed. "I must have nodded off at some point."

He nodded. "We'll have to all be careful about that," he said.

"Yeah, if those are indeed zombies, falling asleep could get us all killed!" Casey said, laughing as he punched Randy in the arm.

"I'm telling you, Hollywood has all but debunked the zombie myth!" Randy said, laughing as he returned the punch.

Casey feigned pain. "That hurt man."

"What hurt?" Adam asked.

"He shot down my theory!"

Adam laughed. "Casey, for all of our sakes I hope those aren't zombies. I hope Randy's right."

"We'll find out," Casey said. "And I agree. I hope I'm wrong."

The group set out after breakfast and as they walked out of Casey's subdivision, Adam heard yelling down the road.

"Hey look! There's a lot of people down there!" Missy said.

He looked and saw police cars down near a college.

"You hear that?" Casey asked.

He nodded. The drone of a helicopter could be heard to the north, near all of the clamor.

"We probably shouldn't go that way," Randy said. "We don't know if those people are infected or not."

"Yeah, besides, we're all violating the quarantine rules," Adam said. "The police would arrest us or worse."

"How do we want to try to get to Chicago?" Casey asked.

"Well, the police are probably going to be out enforcing the quarantine and there are probably infected people on the roads too, so we should stay off the roads," Randy said. "We could retrace our steps on the railroad tracks we walked down yesterday and follow a line north. That way we'll stay off the roads but still be able to head north without walking through fields or anything."

"Agreed. Let's go, before the crowd heads our way," Jillian said nervously.

They walked back to the tracks and walked for hours. By noon the sun was high overhead, scorching them as they walked north on railroad tracks running parallel to Illinois Route 3. They had spent the morning retracing their steps along the Metro Link line and had followed a diverging set of railroad tracks north. They crossed a creek and Adam saw an oil refinery up ahead. Oil storage tanks sat off to the right of the tracks. He and the others had seen a few infected people as they had walked and had passed abandoned police roadblocks.

"Hey, did you guys hear that?" Missy asked.

"Hear what?" Casey replied.

"I don't know. It sounded like a scream off in the distance."

"I didn't hear it," Casey said.

"Either way, let's pick up the pace guys, I'd like to get away from populated areas as soon as possible," Randy said.

"Agreed," Adam said. "When are we going to stop for lunch?"

"I think I see a park up ahead. We'll stop there," Randy said.

They walked further ahead and stopped at the park off to the left of the tracks. To the right of the tracks a fallow field stretched toward oil storage tanks perhaps a quarter of a mile away. To the left, behind the park, lay a neighborhood of houses that all had red sheets hanging in their windows.

"What's with all the red sheets?" Jillian asked.

"I think they have something to do with the quarantine," Randy replied.

Casey handed them all peanut butter sandwiches they had made that morning and they chowed down.

"Hey look," Adam said, pointing. "That house's window is broken. See? That red sheet is flapping in the wind."

"Hey yeah, you're right," Randy said. "Be alert guys."

Suddenly Missy screamed.

Adam spun around and saw an infected man stumbling toward them. His eyes were bloodshot and his skin was gray. His face was stained brown with dried blood. His clothes were torn and he had large chunks of glass protruding from his forearm.

Without thinking Adam pulled out the pistol he had pilfered from the cop less than 48 hours before and aimed it at the man.

"Adam!" Jillian screamed. "What are you doing?"

"Stop where you are!" he yelled at the sick man.

The man growled at him and stumbled forward.

"I'm serious! Stop right there!"

"Adam! Put the gun down!" Randy yelled.

Adam placed his index finger on the trigger. The cool metal tab felt firm under his fingertip.

"Adam! Stop!" Jillian yelled as the infected man came within six feet of the table where they were all gathered.

"This is my final warning! Stop!" Adam yelled.

The man stretched his arms toward Missy.

Adam squeezed the trigger and the gun recoiled backwards with a loud bang. The man fell backwards as a red spray erupted from the back of his head.

Jillian screamed as Randy ran to the now dead man.

Adam dropped the gun and sat down on the table, stunned that he had just killed another man. Everything started spinning around him

"Adam!" Casey yelled. "Adam!"

Everything went black.

He had a headache when he came to. Jillian was kneeling by his side.

"What happened?" he asked.

"You killed an infected man," she replied quietly.

It all came back to him.

"I shouldn't have done it. I'm sorry Jill."

She shook her head. "He was coming toward us. You made the best decision you knew to make."

He sat up and looked around. The others were sitting at the picnic table with somber expressions on their face.

Randy stood and walked toward him.

"Hey," Adam said.

He nodded. "Don't feel too bad. I don't think he would have survived much longer anyway. I followed the trail of blood he had back to the house with the broken window. He looked like he had lost a lot of blood and, honestly, given what I know about the human body, I'm really not sure how he possessed the strength to stumble toward us."

Adam shuddered, remembering the ghastly expression on the man's face.

"You okay?" Randy asked.

He shook his head. "I killed a man."

Randy patted him on the shoulder. "I think you did what needed to be done. Remember the other night on that train platform? That infected guy eviscerated another man in the stairwell. For all we know, that guy you shot could have ended up doing that to one of us. Plus, he was probably contagious."

Adam shrugged. "What about the legal ramifications? I just killed a man!"

"I don't know, but it looks like civilization has completely collapsed. I mean, where have the police been? Where has the military been? When we left the train station, there seemed to be no one left. Why haven't we seen anyone walking north? The only people we've seen have been infected."

Adam nodded.

"Guys, I hate to say this but we need to get going," Casey said, clearing his throat. "We've got a really long way to go yet and we don't know how many more infected people there are nearby."

Adam stood up slowly. "Yeah, we should get going." He looked and saw that the dead man had been covered with a sheet.

"You sure?" Jillian asked him. She looked worried.

He nodded, eager to put this episode behind him.

The group continued on, walking north. They passed several tanker cars stopped on the tracks. Gunshots rang out in the distance.

"Look alive guys, things could get serious real quick," Casey said as they continued on.

As they came around the end of the line of tanker cars, Adam looked toward the residential neighborhood they were passing and saw dozens of infected people walking down the street, going in the opposite direction. He nodded at the others and they hurriedly continued north, away from the crowd of blood-vomiting people.

"This is bad," Jillian said quietly as they walked down the tracks.

Adam nodded quietly and put his arm around her.

"Tell me this will be okay Adam, please," she implored him.

He nodded again. "Yeah, it will be okay."

"You don't sound confident."

"I'm not confident," he replied. "I think civilization might be collapsing."

"You know, following the Black Death in Europe, people thought it was the end of the world," she countered. "But humanity survived."

"Yeah, humanity did survive," he quipped back. "But society collapsed. That epidemic killed so many people that feudalism couldn't sustain itself. Historians estimated at one time that the plague killed a third of Europe's population in the Fourteenth Century. Just think, if this epidemic just kills a third of the Earth's population, think about how that would dramatically reshape civilization, probably in a negative way."

She frowned. "You're such a pessimist."

He chuckled. "I'm an accountant. I'm trained to see the world in terms of unlikely profit and probable loss."

She laughed and punched him in the arm. "That might be so, but you're still a human being!"

He chuckled and replied in a monotone voice, "No, I am not. Your boyfriend Adam Doss has been replaced by a calculator strongly resembling him."

She laughed again.

"Hey guys, what's going on over there?" Missy asked suddenly.

He looked up at her and saw her pointing toward a tank farm to the right that appeared to be several hundred yards away. He saw some people standing on top of one tank. Suddenly a huge fireball erupted from one of the tanks and a second later the ground shook with a loud boom.

"Oh my! Those people are on fire!" Jillian yelled, pointing.

Several dozen burning figures ran across the field away from the inferno for a few seconds before they fell to the ground and remained motionless.

Adam gasped.

Several more tanks exploded, sending enormous columns of black smoke skyward.

"Let's quicken our pace guys," Randy said.

"But what about those people?" Missy asked.

"Nothing can be done for them Missy," Casey said gently.

The group continued on, eager to distance themselves from the oil refinery.

Military helicopters flew over them toward the refinery as they walked on.

They walked for what seemed like hours through alternating patches of forest and field. After a while they approached a rail bridge that appeared to go over a major road. Adam heard weeping. He jogged ahead of the others and stopped when he reached the rail bridge.

Stretching away from the bridge in both directions along the road, hundreds of people were converging on a spot just ahead, past the northern terminus of the bridge. They were all walking slowly. Most had backpacks or were carrying bags.

"Look! There must be a train station up ahead!" Randy exclaimed.

Adam, Randy, Casey, Jillian and Missy walked across the bridge and saw that the throng of people had indeed converged on the railroad tracks and were continuing north on them.

"Where to now man?" Casey asked Randy.

He shrugged. "This is still probably safer than the streets."

"What if someone's infected?" Jillian asked.

Randy shrugged again. "I guess we'll have to run and put some distance between ourselves and them. Let's just try to walk faster than the crowd and get past them quickly."

The group walked on ahead and came alongside the crowd. The throng stretched ahead as far as the eye could see. All of the people looked tired, hungry and scared. There were a lot of families with little children. Adam grimaced when he realized that.

He thought about his own family. His dad's family had immigrated to the United States when his dad was a teenager to escape the totalitarian regime of East Germany. He would regale Adam with stories of their dramatic escape when he was a kid. His family settled in Valparaiso, Indiana where Grandpa got a job teaching mathematics at a community college. Dad had two siblings; an older brother named William and a younger sister named Deborah. Of course Aunt Debbie and Uncle William had kids too. So Adam had quite the extended family growing up.

He frowned as he reflected on the good times he had with them. Would he ever see any of them again? He was startled out of his thoughts by shouting up ahead.

"I told you to grab my gun!" a tall man yelled as he raged at another, shorter man beside him.

"I'm sorry Newton!" the accused man replied, throwing his hands up.

Newton grabbed the man by the collar of his shirt and dragged him out of the throng. Adam and the others passed them as Newton began beating the smaller man in a clearing on the side of the tracks.

They continued on around a bend in the tracks that changed their direction from northwest to what Adam judged to be roughly north-northeast.

"Where are you all from?" a woman asked him as he walked by her.

"Chicago, originally," he replied as he slowed down.

"Oh my! That's a long way from here. You trying to get home?"

He nodded.

"I'm from Saint Louis," she said.

"Where are you going?" he asked.

"The National Guard told us to go northwest to a safe zone they set up just north of Jerseyville. They promised us freedom and safety if we could make it there."

"Wow. Good luck."

"Good luck to you too! Be careful out there, don't get bitten by any of them zombies."

He nodded. "You too."

They soon came to a split in the tracks; one track continued north-northeast and the other split off going northwest. The throng all followed the split to the northwest, while Adam and the others went in the other direction. They were alone on the tracks once again. Eventually they emerged from the trees into a large field the tracks cut across.

Randy cleared his throat. "See guys? I told you we'd be fine."

Adam laughed. "Yeah, did you hear where those people are all going?"

He shook his head.

"The National Guard apparently told them there was a safe camp set up in some town north of here called Jerseyville."

He frowned. "We must have passed a thousand people."

Adam nodded. "I'm not sure I buy it, but whatever."

He shrugged.

They walked for several more hours and passed through a desolate little town called Brighton. It appeared to have been evacuated as the streets were empty and quiet.

"This place gives me the creeps," Missy said.

"Me too," Jillian said.

Adam put his hand on the grip of the pistol instinctively. He had tucked it into his waistband after they had left the park earlier that afternoon.

"Just keep walking guys," Randy said quietly. "Be alert too. It will be getting dark soon. I want us to get out of the town before we settle down for the evening."

Gradually houses gave way to what appeared to be miles of barren fields stretching toward the eastern horizon. They walked on.

"Well, this place looks as good as any," Casey said as the sun began to near the western horizon.

"There's no shelter," Missy said plaintively. "You think we should just sleep on an open field?"

"It's that or break into someone's house," he replied. "I'd rather not break into a house and meet the business end of a shotgun being held by a frightened homeowner or worse, run into a family of infected people."

"Casey has a point," Randy said. "We can take turns sleeping. Plus, it's still warm out. So we won't have to worry about getting too cold tonight."

"I stuffed a couple of sleeping bags into my backpack, in case anyone is interested. No one has fleas or head lice, right?" Casey asked.

That made everyone laugh.

"That settles it," Randy said. "We'll sleep out here."

CHAPTER TEN

Jim Gibson
Day 1

"Hey! I have an idea!" Vik's excited statement woke Jim the next day.

"Yeah?" Jim asked sleepily, opening his eyes and squinting them in the morning light.

"Yeah! You know, I have a toolbox full of hand tools. If the people up here are really zombies, we need to figure out how to defend ourselves against them, right?"

"I guess," Jim replied while rubbing his eyes. "If they're anything like they are in the zombie movies, it will take a blow to the head to kill them."

"Are you listening to yourself?" Giselle asked incredulously. "What if those people are just sick?"

"Giselle, we saw people try to kill them on our walk here! Remember the guy we passed who shot one of them dozens of times in the chest?" Connor replied.

"Connor, that doesn't mean anything. You know drug addicts can sometimes withstand horrific trauma."

"Okay, so why don't we find out?" Jim asked.

Vik ran to his room and Jim heard the clanking of metal on metal. His roommate returned holding a claw hammer in one hand and a small pry bar in the other hand. "Which one do you want Jim?"

Jim sat up. "I guess I'll take the pry bar. Now everyone get out. I'd like to get dressed!"

Everyone left the suddenly crowded bedroom. Jim closed the door and got dressed. He pulled on a pair of blue jeans from the floor then he put on a Yankees shirt and pulled a blue UB hoodie over it. He finished by putting his black Onitsuka Tigers on and walked out to the living room with the pry bar in his hand.

Vik stood in the living room wearing a pea coat and a ski mask.

Jim laughed. "I don't think the mask is going to do much to protect you from getting bitten."

His roommate narrowed his eyes to a slit. "Some face protection is better than none."

"True. You ready to do this?"

"Yes. The noises out there faded earlier, they might have congregated at the other end of the hall."

"Okay, let's do this!"

Jeff pulled the couch away from the door and Jim opened the door. He was hit immediately by the stench of rotting flesh.

"Get the air freshener!" Vik yelled, pulling his hoodie up over his mouth and nose.

Jim ran out into the hallway and saw a zombie-like person about ten feet away.

"Hey!" he yelled at the ghastly man.

The man turned around. Jim recognized him from a writing class. His eyes were bloodshot. His nose looked broken. His clothes were torn and he had several bite marks on his arms. He narrowed his eyes and growled. Then he started staggering toward Jim.

Jim raised the pry bar in anticipation. When the ghoul came within range Jim struck him in the chest hard with the flat side of the pry bar. The man staggered back about five feet, seemingly uninjured. Jim struck him again and while he staggered back again, he showed no signs of pain or injury.

"Okay, let's escalate this," Jim muttered. The man stepped toward him again and Jim swung the flat side of the pry bar up into the man's chin. He fell backwards as the cold steel produced a sickening cracking noise in his face. Jim deduced he had just broken the man's jaw.

The man stared up at him for a moment and then climbed back to his feet. He seemed unaware of any pain or injury. He staggered toward Jim, hands outreached. Jim looked down at the pry bar. It was black with the prongs painted a bright yellow. There was now a little blood on the tip.

"Try puncturing his chest!" Vik yelled from the open door behind Jim.

"Why aren't you out here?" Jim asked, noticing a group of around a dozen more individuals like this man slowly shuffling down the hall toward him.

"I figured I'd let you be the guinea pig!" Vik said, laughing. "I figured I'd jump in if you needed my help."

"Thanks," Jim said, swinging the pointed end of the pry bar into the man's chest, to the right of his sternum. Reddish black blood splashed out of the horrific chest wound Jim had just created. The man staggered backwards, but appeared to not feel any pain. Jim wrenched the pry bar out with some difficulty. Blood splattered on the floor as he stepped back.

"I guess you have to try the head next!" Jeff yelled.

"And the peanut gallery speaks again!" Jim yelled swinging the pointed end of the pry bar down into the man's skull. He let out a grunt as his skull made a horrible splitting sound and he fell to the floor motionless.

"I guess they are zombies," Jim said, disturbed by what he had just done.

Vik jumped out into the hallway and ran ahead of Jim, planting the claw end of the hammer into the forehead of the first advancing zombie. It collapsed to the floor.

Jim moved forward over the now dead zombie and stepped ahead of Vik, swinging the pry bar down into the skull of the next zombie, a history major he had taken on a date once.

They worked their way down the hall until they reached the spot where the dead co-ed had been. She was gone. Both men were panting when they reached the end of the hall. Jim turned and saw that he and Vik had killed more than a dozen zombies. He looked and saw that all of the doors in the hallway had been opened.

"How do you think those doors got opened?" Jim asked, between breaths.

"I don't know," Vik replied. "Wait, do you see that sticking out of the elevator?" He pointed down the hall.

A camouflaged leg was sticking out of the partly open elevator doors.

They walked down the hall, stepping over dead zombies. Jim peered into the elevator. The light inside flickered. A dead soldier lay on the floor; he had apparently killed himself. He had several bite marks on his leg.

"Whoa," Vik said.

"Yeah," Jim stepped back, looking up and down the hall. After a moment he walked back to his dorm. Jeff and the others were waiting.

"So, I guess we need to determine what we are going to do," Jim said.

"What do you mean?" Jeff asked.

"Well, we have more than a dozen dead bodies out there. It's going to get to smelling pretty awful up in here before too long."

"It looks like the rain is letting up," Connor said. "Maybe the police will show up soon."

"There's a dead soldier in the elevator. I'm not sure rescue is coming. I mean, how long has it been since we heard from anyone outside of this building?" Jim asked.

Vik walked back to the dorm holding the soldier's pistol. "I thought this might be useful. Any of you guys have experience with a gun?"

"I do," Connor said. "My dad's a cop."

"Cool," Vik said, handing the pistol to Connor. "Be careful with this."

"Yeah, I know," Connor replied.

"Okay, here's what we can do," Jim said, clearing his throat. "I don't know about you guys, but I am worried about my family. I have dozens of missed calls from every member of my immediate family from the night all of this started. We are going to wait for the rain to taper off and give it a day. If there is no sign of rescue I'm going to leave this place. My brother lives to the south of here, at the old New York Central Terminal Tower. He may be okay, he may not be. I don't know, but I must find out."

"I'll go with you Jim," Jeff said.

"Me too," Vik said.

"I guess we will too," Connor said, looking at Giselle. She nodded.

"I don't know what awaits us out there, but it must be bad. It's not even raining that hard and we haven't heard anything from Campus Services or the police or the National Guard or the news. I mean, they've been looping that same video on the quarantine rules since at least yesterday with no interruption," Jim said.

"Dude, we're your friends. You're like a brother to me. We have to stick with you," Jeff said. "You know, in those zombie movies, things usually get bad when the main characters go off on their own."

He has a good point, Jim thought.

Later on, the afternoon of the 30th, it quit raining. The streets were still quiet though. On Halloween Jim and his friends only saw a few zombies shuffling down the street. They spent the evening packing. The power also went out that day. On the morning of November 1st, everyone awoke at dawn. The power was still out and by now Jim was the only one whose cell phone still had juice.

He packed a couple of changes of shirts, socks and underwear in his backpack. He also packed a metal water bottle along with a pocketknife, a compass and a vintage Dist-o-Map, all of which had been given to him by his Grandpa Fred when he graduated from high school.

The Dist-o-Map was probably the coolest thing Fred had given Jim. It had 6 pages with maps corresponding to each region of the United States with a 7th page that showed the whole country. Each major city had a little hole punched in the page next to it. At the top of each page was a dial one could turn, each major city was marked on the dial. The way it worked was, one would spin the dial until the name of the city they were starting in was lined up with an arrow marked at the top of the page. Then, the mileage to each major city was shown in the little window next to the cities. Jim thought it was an ingenious idea. Plus, it seemed more reliable than GPS.

He led the way out of the dorm into the hallway where the smell of decay was nearly overwhelming. Some of the dead zombies were bloated. The group carefully stepped around the corpses as they walked to the stairwell. It was warm in the hallway.

Jim walked to the metal door blocking the stairwell. He peered through the reinforced glass window and saw a couple of zombies staggering around in the stairwell. He looked back at the others, taking stock. He had his pry bar, Vikram had a hammer, Jeff had a baseball bat, Connor had the soldier's pistol and Giselle was unarmed.

"Alright, there are zombies out there. Here's what we'll do. I will go first, followed by Jeff. Next will come Giselle and Connor and Vik will bring up the rear," Jim said. "Okay?"

Everyone nodded and took their places.

"Let's go!" Jim said, opening the door and walking into the stairwell. He planted the pry bar in the skull of the closest zombie to him while Jeff bashed the head of another with his bat.

They walked down the stairs from the sixth floor. Thankfully, they only encountered a few more zombies along the way. When they exited into the lobby of Clement Hall, Jim was startled to find it zombie free. The group walked through the darkened lobby and exited to the driveway.

The sun was still hugging the eastern horizon, behind the golf course that was across Bailey Avenue. They started walking.

"It's kind of warm for this time of year," Giselle said.

"Yeah, it is," Jim replied. "Hey, Connor didn't tell us much about you. What were you studying?"

"International finance," she replied. "You guys?"

"Film," Jim replied.

"Film," Jeff said.

"Mechanical engineering," replied Vik.

"Oh, that's cool! I always tease Connor for being a chemical engineering student! You know, I call him a nerd and stuff. I hope this isn't offensive, but I see that he keeps good company."

Everyone laughed.

"No offense taken Giselle. So, where are you from originally?" Jim replied.

"Miami, you?"

"I'm from New York City."

"Me too," Jeff said.

"I'm from India, actually," Vik said.

"Wow, that's cool," she said. "Any of you guys have girlfriends?"

"They always kid with me that my girlfriend must live in a textbook because I am so studious," Vik said, laughing.

"Ha, no, I don't really have time for one," Jeff said dismissively.

"What about you Jim?" she asked.

"Well, I'm currently single," he replied. "There was this one girl who was in one of my classes that I asked out a couple of weeks ago, but she just got engaged, so yeah."

"Huh, that sucks," she said.

"Yeah."

"Plus he just got out of a relationship with a crazy lady!" Jeff said, laughing.

"Yeah, Alyssa was pretty crazy," Jim said sheepishly.

"Alyssa Horn?" she asked.

"Yeah, you know her?"

"Know her? She had the dorm room next to mine freshman year. Talk about a drama queen!'

"Yeah," Jim said awkwardly, rubbing the back of his neck. "She was an endless source of drama."

"Remember how she told her friends you tried to poison her?" Vik asked. "That was terrible."

"Yeah, it was. She backed down when I threatened to sue her. I mean, she acted like she was the only one who got food poisoning from that Greek restaurant up in Amherst," Jim said angrily.

"Zorba's?" Giselle asked.

"Yeah."

They walked past the VA hospital. Zombies stumbled around in the plaza in front of the building.

"Look alive guys," Jim said as several zombies turned and started advancing toward the group.

Vik raised his hammer, let out a war cry and ran at a zombie. He struck its head and it crumpled to the ground.

The others quickly dispatched the zombies with disturbing efficiency. They continued on in silence.

As the group crossed under Kensington Avenue, Jim saw people ahead exiting their homes, looking around.

"Excuse me!" a short Hispanic lady asked as she approached Jim and his friends. "Do you have water? I am very thirsty."

"I'm sorry miss," Jim replied, looking at the others. "We don't have any."

She looked disappointed. "Okay, thank you anyway," she said as she walked away.

Jim looked at Connor as they walked further on. "Don't pull the gun out unless we are in a position where we need to use it, okay?"

He nodded.

The people exiting their homes looked disheveled and hungry. Jim wondered how long the power had been out down here. He shook his head, wondering why the police and National Guard had failed so miserably. What happened?

Jim heard gunfire and screaming behind him. He spun around to see zombies attacking people who had left their homes about a hundred yards back. They were attacking men who fell weakly as the women and children behind them screamed and turned to run.

Jim and his friends didn't have water to offer these people, they didn't have food and they didn't have shelter. They did have crude implements with which to save the people from the snapping jaws of death though.

With that thought in mind Jim raised his pry bar and yelled, "We have to go back there and save them! Let's crush some zombie skulls!"

Jim heard Vik, Jeff, Connor and even Giselle let out aggressive cries. He ran forward through a wave of screaming women holding crying babies and planted the angled prong of his pry bar in the forehead of the first zombie he came to. It collapsed with a grunt.

Jim heard the others engage in similarly visceral combat. Vik's hammer found its targets with precision. Jeff's bat crushed zombie heads with devastating speed. And as Jim heard gunshots ring out, he learned Connor was a dead eye with a gun.

The group killed at least four-dozen zombies in just a few minutes, striking down the hellish monsters before they could devour the widows and orphans. By the time Jim killed the last zombie, the women and children stood in stunned silence behind his friends. Dead and dying victims of zombie attacks lay on the pavement all around Jim, the wounded moaning in agony.

"What do we do with the people that got bitten?" Jeff asked.

"I don't know. It looks like five of them are still alive," Jim replied, turning. He looked at the survivors he and his friends had saved. "Are any of you doctors or nurses?"

A few raised their hands.

"Okay, there are wounded men and women behind me. They need your help," Jim said.

He noticed Giselle hugging a woman who was weeping softly.

"Can you handle this?" he asked the volunteers.

They all nodded.

"Alright, this is your neighborhood. Remember, the zombies came unexpectedly, but now you can prepare. Barricade yourselves in your homes."

"And then what?" a woman with messy hair asked. "We've barricaded ourselves in our homes for the last three days!"

"Ma'am, I don't know if you realize this or not, but we just saved your lives!" Vik said.

She put her hands on her hips. "Go back to India! Why are you even in this country?"

"Ma'am, my parents brought me here when I was a little boy so that I may have a better life than they had in Mumbai. Do I assume correctly that your ancestors came here for the same reasons?"

She narrowed her eyes. "We don't need your help! In fact, if you all were just passing through, then get going!"

Jim cleared his throat. "We will be going now. My friend is right though; if we hadn't come back you'd be some zombie's happy meal. But, we will be going now. Have a good day!" he turned and nodded at his friends.

They continued on, pushing past the surly woman. As Jim and his friends passed her, she glared at each of them and when they had all passed her, she spat on the ground.

They walked on for a while.

"Some people are so ungrateful!" Vik said later, as they passed a payday loan building.

"Yeah, ignorant too," Jeff said.

"They probably won't be the last ones we'll meet," Jim said.

Sometime later Giselle approached him. "So Jim, you said your brother lives just to the south of here. What about the rest of your immediate family?"

He shrugged. "My mom and stepdad live in Manhattan, over in the Upper East Side, but they were in Seattle for Game Seven of the World Series when the quarantine was declared, so I have no idea if they're okay or not. I have an older sister who lives in Chicago with her husband; they have two little kids. I have another older brother who lives in Alabama with his wife; they have a little boy I think. And then my dad lives in Detroit. He works for the Detroit Tigers."

"Wow. How long have your folks been divorced?" she asked. "Wait, that's probably too personal."

"No, it's okay. They got divorced when I was three. I was the youngest, so I think it hurt my brothers and sister more. My mom discovered that my dad had several mistresses, and that was the last straw. He took a job with the Tigers and moved to Detroit shortly after the divorce was final. I had to visit frequently, so I saw my dad as I was growing up, which was nice. Steve, the guy my mom married a couple of years later was a tool. He never really paid any attention to me. They had a kid of their own, Tyler, about a year after they got married, and of course he showered Tyler with all sorts of attention.

"Andy, my oldest brother, moved as far away as he could as soon as he could. Vicki, my sister, moved away as soon as she could. Phil, my other brother, did as well. And then, of course, I skipped out and moved here."

"That sucks," she replied.

He shrugged. "Nothing that can be done about it now except avoid making the same mistakes my mom and dad made."

"You seem like you turned out alright."

He laughed. "Only because of people like my grandparents and Jeff's parents."

"All those years I thought you just liked my mom's cooking!" Jeff said, laughing.

"I did! My mom could barely boil water!" Jim shot back.

By the time they reached Broadway, the sun was starting to descend toward the western horizon. They turned right on Broadway and continued southeast. Most people in this area of town were still heeding the quarantine, but a lot of houses had red sheets or red towels hanging in the windows.

"You suppose those houses have zombies in them?" Vik asked nervously.

Jim nodded. "Probably."

Every now and then they would hear an explosion in the distance followed by gunfire.

Soon Jim saw the tower Phil lived in to the left, in the distance. They passed under a railroad bridge and turned on to Memorial Drive. The sun hung near the horizon to the southwest when they reached the New York Central Terminal complex.

The whole facility had once been a bustling train station but had been abandoned and left to the elements sometime before Jim was born. Around the time he graduated from high school though, a real-estate firm began renovating the whole complex and had converted the tower into apartments and the terminal into a shopping area. The last time Jim had been there, a few weeks before, it had looked cool. It had a nice vintage feel to it.

As they walked up the road toward the complex though, Jim's heart sank. It didn't seem likely that Phil was still alive. Dozens of zombies shuffled about in the plaza in front of the terminal. Broken windows ringed the tower, and dead bodies lay on the ground at the tower's base. Jim couldn't see Phil's twelfth floor apartment from his vantage point but he realized it was likely Phil was now a zombie.

"Alright guys," Jim said grimly. "My brother may or may not be alive in there. Right now, it doesn't look good. If you want to continue without me, go ahead. I realize this might be where we scatter as you all have family too. But, whether you go in with me or not, I have to go see for myself if my brother Phil is still alive."

"Dude, we stand behind you. Connor and Giselle may have never met Phil but me and Vik have. We will go in with you," Jeff said.

Jim raised his pry bar and ran to the zombies. He heard the others running behind him. In the crimson twilight, he swung his pry bar down into the forehead of the first zombie he encountered. He and his friends hacked their way through the group of zombies until they reached the entrance to the terminal. Jim pulled the door open and was relieved to see in the quickly fading daylight that the vast hall was empty.

Everyone walked in and Vik closed the door behind them. Their footsteps echoed in the cavernous chamber.

"Man, this place is creepy in the dark," Jeff said.

"Yeah," Jim murmured. He realized they had left the dorms without a flashlight. There was still some light in the terminal, but it would probably be completely dark within the tower.

He pulled his phone out and turned it on. The battery stood at 11%. He activated the flashlight on it and motioned toward the tower's entrance.

"This way," he said as he walked to the door. He pushed it open and stepped into the dark void.

It was quiet in the lobby. Jim led the others to the stairwell and entered it. He started climbing as the others followed him.

He walked up one floor, up to the mezzanine.

Then two floors.

Then three.

They climbed higher still.

"How old is your brother?" Connor asked.

"Twenty-Four," Jim replied breathlessly.

"Cool."

As they ascended, Jim became aware of a scratching noise. It grew louder as they climbed higher. He realized they weren't alone in the tower.

CHAPTER ELEVEN

Adam Doss
Day 3

Adam sighed as the little campfire crackled and began to die. He grabbed a medium sized log and laid it on the pile and watched it gradually catch fire. He had walked with Randy back to a farm house they had passed a mile earlier as the others set up a small camp. Randy had spied a stack of firewood next to a gray shed behind the farm house when they had been walking north and he had suggested they pilfer some wood to build a fire.

Adam and Randy had each grabbed as much wood as they could carry and had walked back. Then they built a campfire and Adam had agreed to take first watch with Casey while the others slept in a half circle around the fire.

"So what were you doing before all of this?" Casey asked as the fire made a popping noise.

"I was an accountant for a law firm called Dodson and Walsh in Chicago," Adam replied.

Casey whistled.

"It wasn't as interesting as you'd think," he said. "What did you do?"

"Well, I was working as a sound engineer at a recording studio over in Saint Louis until about four months ago," Casey replied, staring into the fire.

"Then what did you do?"

"Well, I got canned because I was late one time too many."

"Oh."

"Yeah, it sucked. Missy had to pick up more hours at Wal-Mart but it still wasn't enough. We were just a couple of days away from the sheriff showing up to foreclose on the house."

"That's rough man."

He nodded. "Yeah, it is rough. Was rough, anyway."

"You're from Chicago originally, right?"

"Yeah, you?"

"No, I'm from Northern Indiana originally. I moved to Chicago after college. Why'd you move to Saint Louis?" Adam asked.

"I wish I could say it was because of the sound engineer job, but I moved after my parents divorced a few years ago. It was a really acrimonious divorce and I just couldn't stand being near either of my parents. They were just so self-absorbed and bent on extracting as many assets as they could from each other."

"That sucks."

"Yeah, it did. Whatever, they can rot for all I care. My mom was a jerk and my dad was a complete idiot. I'm glad I moved to Saint Louis. I wouldn't have met Missy otherwise."

"How long have you guys been together?"

"Just a little over two years. How long have you and Jillian been together?"

"Since college."

"That's a long time."

Adam nodded.

"Yeah, Missy had this ex named Matt that was stalking her when I started dating her. I beat him up one night outside a bar and he left her alone after that."

"Yeah, some people just need to have some sense knocked into them I guess."

Casey chuckled. "Do they ever."

"So that cop in Saint Louis, the one who arrested you, you knocked him out?"

Casey stared at him for a moment. "I shot him."

Adam's jaw dropped.

"He was going to shoot me, so I kicked the gun out of his hand, grabbed it and shot him."

"You killed a cop?"

"What was I supposed to do? He was going to kill me! Besides, you shot a guy today too," Casey said defensively.

He nodded. "No, I understand, I guess. I guess I was just taken aback, that's all."

"I get it. I'm not going to apologize though. That cop was going to kill me. You've seen all the shootings over the years; cops shooting unarmed people."

"I believe you."

"Don't tell Randy."

"What? Why not?"

"I don't know. I just have a feeling he wouldn't take it as well as you just did. I'll tell him when the time is right."

"Okay," Adam said. "I won't tell him."

"Thanks."

He nodded.

"Hey, I'll be back," Casey said, standing up.

"Okay, be careful."

He chuckled. "Well, you know, when nature calls."

Adam nodded, laughing.

He walked away, into the darkness.

Adam stared into the fire and reflected on the last forty-eight hours. They had fled from Saint Louis the night before and were now heading north. The military had demolished all of the bridges out of Saint Louis. Quarantine had been declared and it appeared that the police and military had largely abandoned their posts.

Casey had killed a man, and Adam had killed a man. He thought back to that horrifying moment when he had pulled the trigger and watched as the man's brain sprayed out behind his head in a red mist. Adam had consciously decided to pull the trigger because he thought the man was a clear danger. He was just a few feet away from Missy and looked like he was going to bite her. Adam thought he made the right choice.

What about Casey? Had he made the right choice? Adam realized he had no way of knowing if what he had said was true. Maybe the cop had panicked and decided to kill him. Adam just didn't know. He realized he didn't really know Casey all that well. Casey had been Randy's friend since high school and they had played in a metal band together back then. Adam hadn't met Randy until college.

He shrugged. "Judge not," he mumbled quietly.

He looked down at his watch. It was 2:07am. Had he and Casey really been out here talking for six hours?

His thoughts were interrupted by footsteps behind him. He was about to turn and welcome Casey back when he felt something cold and hard against the back of his head. He heard a click.

"Don't move," a gravelly voice quietly instructed.

He thought about reaching for his pistol when he heard more footsteps.

"Do as you're told and we won't kill you," the gravelly voice said.

"What do you want?" Adam asked quietly. Jill, Randy and Missy were all soundly asleep. Where was Casey?

"We're going to take your women, your guns and your supplies. Try to do anything squirrelly, and we'll rape your women in front of you and then kill you and your male friends. Now, stand up," the voice said as someone grabbed Adam by his arm and jerked him into a standing position. He felt the pistol get pulled from his waistband.

"Hmm, this is a police gun. Did you kill a cop to get this?"

Adam shook his head. "No."

"That's funny. I killed one to get mine."

"All right folks, it is time to get up!" another man yelled. Adam heard a gunshot and flinched.

The others all woke up suddenly.

"What's going on?" Randy asked.

"I was just telling your friend here that we are going to take your women, your weapons and your supplies," the gravel-voiced man said.

"You can't do this," Randy said.

"Yes we can son."

Suddenly three gunshots rang out in front of Adam in rapid succession.

He heard several thuds behind him as Jillian and Missy screamed.

He turned and saw three men dressed in leather jackets and blue jeans lying dead on the ground, bullet holes in their heads. He spun back around and saw Casey emerge from the shadows holding the machine gun. The barrel was smoking.

"Casey!" Missy yelled as she ran to his arms.

"You just saved our lives!" Adam exclaimed.

Casey shrugged. "I've seen trash like that before. They think they can just take whatever they want. Well, they can't."

Adam realized he was shaking.

Randy walked over and hugged Casey too.

"Thanks Casey," Adam said.

"No problem man. We're in this together."

He nodded. Whatever had actually happened with the cop in Saint Louis, Adam realized it didn't matter now. Casey had just saved their lives.

"You okay?" Jill asked as she walked up to Adam.

"Yeah, you?"

"Yeah."

They spent the rest of the night talking and at first light they plundered the would-be robbers. Each man had been armed with a Forty-Caliber Beretta semi-automatic pistol. Additionally, they had stored some meager rations and ammunition in one backpack. Adam and the others took it all and set out at dawn, walking back to the railroad tracks and continuing their journey northeast.

"You must be tired Adam," Jill said as they climbed up on the ridge the tracks ran along.

He shook his head. "Actually, I feel okay."

She laughed. "I know I'm tired!"

He put his arm around her as they walked.

"Sorry I suggested sleeping out in the open field," Randy said.

"It's fine man," Adam said.

"No really, I could have gotten us all killed."

"Really Randy, it's fine. How could you have known we would get ambushed?"

"Yeah," Missy said. "Besides, we're going to all make mistakes. Thankfully Casey had his gun ready. What were you doing anyways Casey?"

Casey laughed. "I walked away to pee."

They all laughed.

They passed through a small town called Shipman about an hour later and continued on. At noon, they stopped to eat lunch in the parking lot of an abandoned feed store to the side of the railroad tracks.

"We haven't seen anyone since last night. What do you guys think is going on?" Jill asked.

Adam shrugged. "Maybe everyone is heading toward that camp the National Guard set up."

"No, I'll bet most people have become zombies," Casey replied as he ate a handful of peanuts.

"Whatever is going on, we'd better be cautious," Randy said. "Tonight, we need to find an abandoned store or office to sleep in. We're lucky we didn't see any of those infected people last night."

Adam nodded. "Yeah, that would probably be a good idea."

"What do you think we'll find in Chicago?" Missy asked.

"Who knows?" Adam asked.

"You know, there's been a road running alongside the tracks most of the way up here and I haven't noticed any cars driving along it. I saw a few abandoned police vehicles yesterday while we were walking, and some roadblocks that had been abandoned, but no cars," Casey said.

"I noticed that too," Adam said.

"When do you think the other shoe is going to drop?" Casey asked.

"What do you mean?" Randy replied.

"I mean, when do you think we're going to see the other end of this? I mean, all we've really seen so far is abandoned towns. Where are all the people?"

"I don't know Casey, I don't know."

After lunch, they continued north along the railroad tracks into a little town called Carlinville. They passed several abandoned neighborhoods. The eerie stillness that had pervaded nearly every town they had passed through continued.

The only sound they could hear was the sound of the wind blowing leaves through the empty streets.

"Hey look!" Randy exclaimed. He ran forward.

"Wait up!" Adam yelled as he took off after his friend.

He stopped about fifty yards ahead and Adam stopped alongside him and gasped. There, piled in a lot next to an Amtrak train station were dozens of naked corpses. The smell of decay was overpowering.

"Oh my," Casey said as he caught up.

Adam heard Jill vomit behind him.

"What happened?" Randy asked. "There must be at least forty corpses here." He walked toward the pile and stopped about two feet from them.

"Be careful man," Adam said.

"They look like they were sick. They all have gunshot wounds to the head too," he said. He turned and walked back to the others.

"Is this the other shoe?" Missy asked warily.

"I don't know. Who put those bodies here? And why were they all shot?" Casey asked.

"Who shot them?" Adam asked.

"I don't know if I want to find out," Casey said darkly.

"Come on, let's keep moving," Randy said. "Casey's right."

Jill walked up to Adam as they continued on. "That was horrible."

He nodded. "I'm worried those aren't the last bodies we are going to see."

The sky grew cloudy as they walked. Soon a light rain began to fall.

Jill walked closer to Adam and he put his arm around her. "It'll be okay Jill," he said.

She nodded.

"Hey guys! We've got a problem!" Randy yelled as they crossed a street.

Adam looked west down the street and saw hundreds of sick people walking toward them. Most had dried blood on their shirts and many of them looked like they were dead.

One of them growled and reached toward the survivors. The crowd was maybe a hundred feet away.

"Run guys!" Casey yelled.

Everyone took off running as the sick people moved onto the tracks behind them.

They ran through the rest of the town and followed the tracks into a large field outside the town. Adam turned and saw the horde of sick people fade behind them.

Everyone stopped to catch their breaths after they had gone a little further.

"That was close!" Randy panted.

"Those people looked like they were dead!" Missy exclaimed.

"They might have been!" Casey gasped.

"Now come on," Adam protested. "Dead people don't walk!"

"They do if they're zombified!"

Adam shook his head. "No, you and Randy had this conversation yesterday. Zombies are fictional! They don't exist!"

"Guys, calm down," Jill said. "Whether or not they were zombies, they were definitely sick. I think a continued strategy of avoiding them is wise."

Adam nodded. "Sorry Casey, I...I don't know."

"It's fine man, it's been a stressful week," he replied, patting him on the back.

"There's a town up ahead," Randy said. "Let's find a place there to settle in for the evening and rest. I know we're all probably exhausted from last night and today."

They continued on into a tiny little town. The stillness pervaded this little hamlet too.

Adam followed Randy up to an abandoned feed store and was surprised to find the front door unlocked. Both men entered and looked around. The store was indeed empty.

"Hey, we could stay here?" Adam suggested. "We could all sleep in the back room and take turns keeping watch."

Randy nodded. "That sounds like a good idea."

They walked outside to the others.

"This is where we're staying tonight," Adam said. "We'll take turns on watch. Who wants first watch?"

Randy nodded at him. "I'll take it."

They walked back into the store. Adam looked down at his watch. It was 5:00pm.

"The back room is small," Jill said, "but it should work."

Adam yawned. "I think I'm going to go take a nap."

She laughed. "You must be exhausted Adam!"

He nodded, laughing. "I am."

"Get some rest man," Randy said.

"I will. Holler if you see trouble."

"I will," he said.

Adam walked back to the back room with Jill and the two sat down in the dark.

"Adam, I love you," she said quietly.

"I love you too Jill. I know this is all scary." He put his arm around her.

"It's just so crazy. A week ago, we were at the airport getting ready to fly to Saint Louis. And now? I don't know if there is a home to return to in Chicago. And what about my family? What if they're not okay?"

He sighed. "I know. I just, I don't know."

"After we get to Chicago can we go to Cleveland?"

He nodded. "Of course. We'll go through Valpo to make sure my family's okay and then head to Cleveland. Maybe we can at least get a car in Chicago."

"Yeah, that was awesome of Randy's brother to drive us all to the airport so we didn't have to pay for parking."

He nodded and yawned. "I think I'm going to lay down and get some sleep."

"Okay," she said. "Goodnight Adam. I love you."

"I love you too," he said. "You can stay in here if you want."

"I might go out and talk to the others while you sleep. I'm sure they're going to try to figure something out for dinner. I'll try to save you some food."

"Thanks Jill. Goodnight."

He laid down in the dark room and quickly sank into a dream-filled slumber..

"Look at the view!" Randy yelled.

"Wait up man!" Adam yelled back, panting heavily as he followed his best friend up the mountain. He gasped when he reached the top. The Pacific Ocean stretched out for what seemed like an eternity ahead of the two men. Cabo San Lucas lay to the southwest.

"Thanks for suggesting this," Randy said as he sat down on a tree stump.

Adam nodded. "Dude, sometimes you just have to get away from everything. How many credit hours did you take last semester?"

"Twenty."

"You're crazy!"

"You took what, eighteen?" Randy asked.

He laughed. "I guess I did."

"So the pot just called the kettle black, huh?"

He laughed again.

"What did Jillian think about you coming to Mexico for a month to backpack?"

He shrugged. "She was cool with it."

"You guys have been together for what, three months?"

He nodded. "I like her a lot."

"I can tell."

"She took me to meet her folks a few weeks before you and I came to Mexico."

"Oh yeah?"

"Yeah, they're pretty cool. Her dad Roger's a pretty skilled woodworker. He builds furniture and stuff."

"Sounds pretty cool."

"Yeah, man. I don't know. I know it's pretty early, but I think she might be the one."

Randy laughed. "Yeah, it is a little early."

"Hey, wake up. Wake up Adam."

He opened his eyes and saw Jill leaning over him.

"What time is it?" he asked.

"Eight AM," she replied. "On Monday."

"Monday? As in the Second of November?"

She nodded.

"I slept for two days?"

"A day and a half, really."

He sat up.

"You seemed exhausted. Casey was too."

He laughed. "Are we just going to stay here?"

She laughed and punched his arm gently. "No, we're going to head out in a little bit. Do you want some fish?"

"Fish?"

"Yeah, Randy caught some fish in a creek this morning."

"Sure."

She walked out of the back room and Adam laid back down to stretch. He couldn't believe he had slept so long. When she returned he sat back up and took the paper plate she held out. Sure enough, there was a cooked fish on it.

"This is delicious!" he exclaimed as he took a bite of the fish.

She laughed. "Yeah, it did all turn out pretty good."

After he finished eating he stood up and walked out to the sales floor of the feed shop. Everyone was gathered around the counter poring over a map.

"Hey guys!" he called out.

"Hey sleepyhead! Welcome back!" Casey laughed.

"Hey yourself," he said. "How long did you get to sleep?"

Casey chuckled.

"He just got up a few hours ago," Missy said.

"I see you got your beauty sleep too then."

Casey laughed again.

"Where are we headed today?" Adam asked.

"According to this map we are about twenty-five miles south of Springfield. I'm thinking we should try to make it to Chatham, a town just south of Springfield, by nightfall," Randy said.

"Agreed," Casey said. "We can cover that distance in one day."

"It's kind of chilly in here," Adam said.

"Yeah, I mean, I guess the weather is catching up to us," Randy said. "Jillian found some jackets in the closet of an abandoned house for all of us. I hope you guys are all soccer fans."

Adam laughed when Jill handed him a red track jacket. "Viva la futbol!" he exclaimed as he put it on. It had an Italian flag on the back of it.

"You look good in it," she said.

"Thanks Jill, you don't look too bad yourself. You look pretty cute."

CHAPTER TWELVE

Katie Barnes
Day 3

Katie was awakened around eleven by the banging of hammers. She sat up and looked around. A quiet conversation was being held downstairs. She stood and looked out the window as she stretched. The sun was out and the pool of blood on the street appeared to have been mostly washed away by the last bit of rain. Shredded leaves and branches were everywhere. She turned and walked out of the bedroom. She went downstairs and saw the others hard at work cleaning up the wreckage from the night before.

The woman's corpse was gone and most of the blood had been cleaned up. The house smelled strongly of the pungent aroma of bleach. The broken glass had all been swept up and Katie saw what the hammering had been coming from; the men were outside boarding up the windows.

"Hey girl!" Michelle greeted her as she reached the base of the stairs.

"Hey. How can I help?" Katie replied.

"You've already helped us. We saw you last night. You saved all of our lives," Rachel said. "Thank you."

Katie shrugged. "I just did what needed to be done. What happened to the body?"

"Buried in the backyard. Joel and Anthony did it. Anthony seems pretty sorry about last night," Amber replied.

"Well, it's going to take some time before I'm okay with him. His actions could have gotten us all killed. Thank heavens that I heard the window getting bashed in! If I hadn't woken up and gone downstairs, he would have been a sleeping meal for that lady and we all would've too!" Katie exclaimed.

"I know, just remember, he is human and he made a mistake," Amber said.

"Yeah, but mistakes can be fatal. He's lucky his didn't wind up being fatal," Katie replied. Then she stepped out to the front porch. "Ignoring the quarantine are we?" she asked Joel.

"Just doing what we can to make sure last night doesn't repeat itself," Anthony replied.

Katie ignored him. "So Joel, what's the plan?"

"Well, we are going to finish boarding up all the windows on the ground floor and then discuss our next steps," he replied.

"Okay," she said and looked down the street. Trees had been blown over on cars and tree limbs were everywhere in yards. It appeared everyone else in the neighborhood was still barricaded inside his or her home.

Joel and Anthony finished boarding up the windows shortly after noon. Everyone then sat down as a group over lunch to discuss what was next.

"Has anyone been able to reach their families?" Rachel asked.

"I spoke to my aunt the night the quarantine started on Skype. She was in Paris and was okay, aside from being confined to her hotel," Katie replied.

"I talked to my mom the night it happened too, I was talking to her on the phone when the quarantine was announced," Anthony said.

"Where is your mom?" Rachel asked.

"She and my sister live in Racine, Wisconsin."

"My dad said he was fine. I texted him the night the quarantine was enacted," Amber said.

"Anyone else?" Rachel asked.

The silence answered the question for her.

"Okay, my dad lives in Pennsylvania," Rachel said.

"Mine are in D.C. and Chicago," said Joel.

"Wyoming," Michelle added.

"Tampa," said Megan.

"Don't despair guys, the National Guard will probably be returning today or tomorrow," Rachel said, moving on.

"I don't think they will be Rachel," Michelle said.

"Why not?"

"Where were they when all hell broke loose on our street yesterday? If that was happening here, it was almost surely happening elsewhere. Where were they?"

"Maybe they were overwhelmed," Rachel said defensively.

"If they were overwhelmed, I don't think they'll be in a position to help us," Katie added. "It might be a long while before we get help. I mean, who knows if our power being out is simply a consequence of the storm or if it's something worse?"

"She's got a good point," Megan said. "But really, I'm pretty scared at this point. I don't know if my family is okay, I do know that this is likely the worst disaster to ever befall mankind!"

"Hey guys, listen!" Joel said urgently. The group grew quiet. "Do you hear that?"

"Hear what?" Amber asked.

"Exactly. Shouldn't we hear birds and other wildlife?"

Everyone got up and walked out on the front porch. The neighborhood was still. They couldn't hear any birds, or any vehicles.

"Shouldn't we at least hear military vehicles driving around?" Joel asked.

"Happy Halloween!" Katie said sardonically.

That night, Katie, Joel and Rachel went out to the backyard. Joel pulled a ladder out of the shed and set it up against the house. Rachel climbed up first, and then Katie followed. Finally, Joel climbed up last.

"The stars are pretty. You can really see a lot without the city lights," Rachel said.

"Yeah, look toward downtown," Katie replied.

Downtown Buffalo lay several miles to the south. Between here and there, it appeared several buildings were on fire. Downtown itself was shrouded in darkness. All around the horizon was devoid of any city lights. Darkness held them tightly in its autumnal embrace.

The next day it became clear the curfew imposed by the quarantine order was being disregarded. Furthermore, it became increasingly clear the National Guard wasn't coming back.

Neighbors started exiting their homes a little after 9:00pm. Then a huge group of people came walking up the street. They looked disheveled, dirty and thirsty.

One woman wearing a red flannel shirt walked into Katie's yard. She looked hungry and had two small kids in tow. Katie and Rachel watched from upstairs as the others peered around them.

"We shouldn't let anyone who comes to the door in," Katie said quietly. "They could be sick or they could be looking to steal from us or hurt us."

"Katie's right," Rachel said. "If they have Owasa Disease, they might not be showing symptoms yet."

The lady knocked on the front door. "Hello?" she called out. "Is anyone home?" She knocked a few more times and continued on to the next house with her two children in tow.

"Mommy," a young voice called out. "I'm thirsty."

"Me too mommy!" another child said.

"I know babies, I know," the woman said as they walked away.

"Get off my property!" the neighbor from across the street yelled at a couple of people in his yard. He was peering out a window on the second floor of his house.

"We just need some water man!" a skinny man cried out. "South Buffalo ain't had no running water for two days!"

"I don't care about South Buffalo! Now what did I say? I said get off my property! This is your last warning!"

"Sir, please!"

The man in the window pointed a rifle at the supplicant on his lawn. One of the people in the yard ran out of the yard, but the beggar remained.

Bang!

The beggar collapsed, and people on the street screamed in terror, fleeing away from the neighbor's house. The neighbor disappeared into the shadows of his home.

"Alright guys, it looks like tensions are high out there," Joel said. "Don't let anyone in from outside."

"Not even them?" Michelle asked sarcastically, pointing at a group of four bearded men who kept pointing at different houses and talking amongst themselves.

"Seeing as how they look pretty shady, I'm going to say no," Joel replied, chuckling.

Anthony came up to Katie later. "Katie, I'm really sorry about the other night. I failed you and everyone else pretty terribly."

She looked him in the eye. "I realize that. Still, you endangered us all. I don't know if I'm ready to forgive you yet."

"Fair enough. Hey, did I call you Kathy the other night?" he asked.

She tilted her head. "Yeah, I think you did."

"I'm sorry about that too," he said as he walked away.

"Joel, I'm going out to the backyard for some fresh air," Katie said and walked downstairs.

She inhaled a breath of fresh air as she walked out to the backyard. A sycamore stood tall in the corner of the yard, reaching skyward; somehow the centenarian titan had weathered the fury of the storm. The sun's rays felt invitingly warm upon her skin.

"Katie, I love the way the sunlight makes your hair look divine," Joel said as he walked out on the deck.

"How does it look now?" she asked as she twirled around.

"Resplendent."

"I love you Joel," she said warmly.

"I love you too."

He walked out into the yard and hugged her. They stood there for what seemed like a long time as the sun warmed them. The peaceful moment was snapped by the sound of another gunshot from the street. Anthony ran out on the porch.

"You guys had better come see this."

Katie and Joel walked back inside and went upstairs. They reached the window just in time to behold a group of several dozen infected people attacking some of the beggars on the street. People were screaming and running around in a panic. Several people were shooting at the infected people.

Katie watched in horror as one Infected was shot six times in the chest and simply kept staggering forward. The shooter ran out of ammunition, threw his pistol at the Infected and ran in the opposite direction.

The neighbor across the street fired at several Infected from his window perch, hitting them in the heads. They fell and didn't get back up.

"Head trauma is what kills them," Katie said quietly.

Most of the group sat down on the floor, unwilling to continue watching the carnage. Megan began to weep softly. Katie continued watching with Joel. Eventually the screams died down, the gunfire became sporadic and distant, and the infected people shuffled down the street to the next block.

"So what happens to those people?" Amber asked later. "The ones who were begging for water? Do we just abandon them to those monsters?"

"I hate to be the one who says this," Joel said, "but what other choice do we have? We don't even have enough food to last the seven of us another week!"

"So we just let them get eaten? We just let them get turned into monsters?"

"I'm afraid so Amber, I mean, what do we do? If we let those people shelter with us they could have Owasa Disease themselves, they could have ill motives. They could just be a greater drain on our resources. It's a terrible situation, but I don't think we really have a choice."

She shook her head.

That night Joel kept watch. Rachel and Katie both stayed up for a while talking to him. They all went back up on the roof briefly around nine and looked toward downtown Buffalo. Several of the distant skyscrapers were ablaze and the whole sky had an eerie orange glow.

When they went back inside, Joel pointed out some people who were walking door-to-door trying doorknobs. "Looters," he said quietly.

The looters approached the neighbor across the street's house. He fired one shot, hitting one in the chest. The surviving looters fired back at him, hitting him. He fell out of his window with a strangled cry.

Joel hugged Katie tightly. "Go get some sleep ladies. This night will probably have more horrors you don't need to see."

Everyone was awakened around midnight by unearthly shrieks coming from outside. Megan wept quietly in the corner. She had her fingers in her ears.

Joel whispered, "The people killed earlier are coming back as Infected."

"Okay, we need to get out of here," Katie said.

"Agreed. My dad has a cabin down in the Alleghenies we can hide out at," Rachel said.

"I'll stay here in Buffalo," Anthony said.

"Me too," Amber said.

"I will also," Megan said as she wiped her eyes, trying to regain her composure.

"Okay. So it will be me, Katie, Rachel and Michelle. You guys sure about that?" Joel asked.

"Yeah, we can make our way back to Amber's house. She has a bunch of food and supplies and she only lives a few blocks from here," Anthony replied.

"Alright, we'll set out early in the morning," Joel said.

"We can take my car," Rachel volunteered.

The next morning, they rose before dawn to pack and say goodbye to one another. As the sun was coming up Katie stood at the top of the stairs stretching as Joel finished zipping his duffle bag up. "So what do you think would have happened if Granger hadn't died in Game Seven?" she asked.

"I think the Senators would have come back and won it," Joel said as he walked out to the hallway with his brown duffel bag. "Let's go load our stuff up. Where are your bags?"

"On the porch," Katie replied as she made her way downstairs and walked out to the front porch. It was warm and humid outside and the neighborhood was mercifully quiet. The street had several pools of congealed blood that had collected near the curb. She heard a cough behind her. She turned and saw Amber walking through the door.

"Katie, I just wanted to clear the air. I know this might be the last time we see each other," she said.

"Yeah," Katie replied.

"I'm sorry for the occasionally snide way I've acted toward you."

"It's alright Amber, really," Katie said.

Katie realized that Amber had been crying. Makeup was streaked on her cheeks. "I don't know if I want to go with Anthony."

Katie looked at her. "Then don't."

Amber sighed. "I wish it were that easy."

"Why isn't it?"

"Because I love Anthony."

"Yeah, but you saw how he almost got us killed a few nights ago!"

Amber shrugged. "I know, but I think he means well."

Katie frowned. "Yeah, but the road to Hell is paved with good intentions. Sweetie, meaning well doesn't translate into surviving long in this."

Amber shrugged again and looked down at her feet. "Yeah, I know. But we do have a lot of food at my place and we can just hunker down there and wait for help."

"Amber, I don't think help is coming."

"Yeah, but if it doesn't we can always move on when we run out of supplies."

"I don't know Amber, what about Megan? What does Megan think?"

She sighed. "I don't know. She's just so shaken up by everything, I guess she's a little shell shocked."

"Are you sure you don't want to come with us?"

"What would Megan do?"

"She could come with us too. There's safety in numbers."

"No, I...I think we'll be fine."

Joel walked up from the yard. "Hey ladies," he said. "Want to help me start loading our vehicles up?"

"I need to go finish packing, actually," Amber said. "It was nice talking Katie," she said as she walked back into the house.

Katie grabbed her two duffle bags and walked down the steps of the porch. Joel followed behind her.

"Sorry if I interrupted your pow wow," he chuckled.

She shook her head. "I just don't understand why she and Megan are going to follow Anthony."

He laughed. "I think it's the other way around. I think Megan and Anthony are following her."

"Whatever, I just don't understand why they're okay with him being in their group."

He shrugged. "Anthony's not that bad."

Katie glared at him. "Joel, he almost got us killed a few nights ago!"

He threw his hands up after he laid a bag in Rachel's SUV. "I know! I know! But people do make mistakes Katie."

"Yeah, and besides, he just gives me the creeps."

"Is it the thin moustache he possesses?"

She glared again.

"Oh, you're mad because he called you Kathy. I get it. I do, but you know, Kathy does have a nice ring to it."

She laughed and punched him in the arm. "Joel Ryan, you can always make me laugh!"

"Let's go back in and get more bags. I think Michelle is done packing," he said.

After they finished loading up the cars, they gathered in the front yard and stood in a circle.

"Guys, I'm going to miss you," Anthony said.

"We'll miss you too Anthony," Joel said, hugging him. "Be careful out there."

Megan sniffled. "I'm going to miss all of you girls!"

"We'll miss you too Megan!" Michelle replied.

At that, they tearfully bade each other farewell, boarded their vehicles and drove away. Katie wondered if she would ever see Megan or Amber again. She, Joel, Rachel and Michelle headed south to the freeway; Joel drove. They passed by burned out military vehicles and piles of bodies. It didn't take a degree in rocket science to see the quarantine had failed.

As they slowly turned onto the freeway, Katie realized their plan needed some modifications. The freeway was jammed with abandoned cars; their hulking SUV simply wouldn't fit.

"Wait, I saw a moped dealership not too far back!" Michelle exclaimed.

"It's worth taking a look, I suppose," Joel said, pulling out. "I think I know which one you're talking about."

They turned around and drove for a few miles until they came to the dealership. Unsurprisingly, the place had been abandoned. Amazingly, however, it looked as though a full stock of brand new mopeds were available.

Joel walked up to the dealership and found the door locked. He looked around, grabbed a stone from the garden and threw it through the glass door. The glass shattered, but as the power was out, no audible alarm sounded.

The four survivors went in and grabbed four mopeds. The keys were in the office as were some helmets. All of the mopeds were fully fueled, but Joel grabbed extra fuel to carry on each one. Then they loaded up what supplies they could from the Toyota and set out. Joel led in front, on a black moped, Katie was next on a turquoise moped, Rachel was next on a pink moped and Michelle was last on a green moped. They returned to the freeway and drove onto it. The cars were close together but there was enough room in between to fit the bikes.

They had driven a few hundred yards when Michelle screamed. Katie skidded to a stop and saw the cars they had been passing contained Infected in them. Most had their windows rolled up, so it was just bloodied hands banging on glass. Some had their windows down though, allowing greedy claws to reach for passersby.

"Are you okay?" Katie asked.

"Yeah, just a little shaken. How far are we from the next exit?" she asked.

"I think about half a mile," Joel replied.

"Could we maybe just get off the freeway there and take the back roads to Rachel's cabin?" she implored.

"Yeah, I guess we should. It would be safer," Joel said thoughtfully.

So they sped to the next exit, weaving carefully between the rows of cars and the rows of bloodied hands grasping toward them. At last they came to the exit and left the highway. Katie noticed they had exited in a burned out section of town.

Joel led the way south out of the city. Katie saw tired looking people, hungry looking people, angry looking people and people who were knelt down on the ground weeping as they drove south. They passed roving bands of gangs armed with crowbars and they passed bands of Infected who would briefly chase and then give up.

Katie sighed. So many stories. Who were those people? Who had the Infected been? Sick people who had been promised a cure but given snake oil? Unfortunate people whose families had received the Noble treatment who then were infected following the imposition of quarantine?

Gradually city transitioned to suburb that gradually became rural farmland. Katie was astonished by how few signs of civilization there were. The only signs of civil authority she had seen were burned out police cars and soldiers who had been infected. The rapid breakdown of society was both surprising and disturbing. What had happened?

Around noon the group stopped at a rest area just south of Buffalo to eat lunch. Joel took the bat and walked around, checking the buildings to make sure they were alone. Katie heard a brief struggle and Joel emerged from the main building with a grim look on his face and a bloodier bat.

"There was one in the bathroom. They were stuck in a stall. I put them out of their misery," he said.

Everyone washed their hands with hand sanitizer and sat down to eat lunch; cheese and crackers.

"So Joel, where are you from originally?" Michelle asked.

"Well, when I was born we lived in Chicago. We moved to Washington D.C. when I was eight," he replied, chewing on a piece of cheese. "Katie still occasionally teases me for liking the Cubs."

Katie laughed.

"Any brothers? Sisters?"

"Yeah, I have two brothers. I'm the middle child. My older brother is five years older than I am. He is a missionary in Southeast Asia, or he was," his face darkened. "I think he was in Thailand, Bangkok maybe. It might have been Bangladesh. My younger brother is a year younger than me. He's studying criminal justice at the University of Tennessee."

"Wow," Michelle said. "Your parents did a good job."

"Thanks."

Before the group got back on the road, Joel peeked in a car parked at the rest area. He opened the door. "Look what I found!" he yelled as he pulled a crowbar out.

"Awesome! I can see how that would be useful!" Katie yelled excitedly.

"Well, let's get going," he said, strapping the crowbar to his back.

They continued on. They drove until it started getting dark. Joel motioned toward a gas station on the side of the road. They pulled into the parking lot.

"How much further is the cabin?" he asked Rachel.

"It's still a few hours away at this pace," she replied.

He furrowed his brow. "I guess we'll need to stop for the night soon. I don't like this place, but we might not find another more suitable place before it gets dark. At least we can sleep in the cooler and rotate watch."

Joel and Katie searched the building for Infected, but it was empty. They pushed the bikes into the mechanic's garage and went back to the cooler.

They did rock-paper-scissors to see who would stay up first and second and so on. Katie won, so she chose to go first. Rachel would go second. Michelle would go third. Finally, Joel would go last. They would each take a shift two hours long.

"Goodnight Katie Bee," Joel said.

"Goodnight Joel, I love you."

"I love you too."

"Goodnight Katie," Michelle said.

"Goodnight Katie," Rachel said, adding, "I'll see you in a few hours."

"Goodnight guys," Katie said, sitting down in a chair near the freezer's entrance, bat in hand. From her vantage point she could see the front of the store and see outside. The front of the store faced west.

Once the sun dipped below the horizon, useful light faded quickly. The sky faded from orange to blue to black. The stars gradually appeared.

Katie listened carefully and was relieved to hear crickets chirping. She could also hear coyotes call to one another in the distance. She hoped the night would be uneventful.

Sure enough, her shift passed without incident. She woke Rachel up at 10:00pm.

"Get some sleep Katie," Rachel said as Katie handed her the bat.

"I will. Holler if you need help," Katie said. Then she walked into the freezer and lay down next to Joel. She covered up with her jacket and sank into dreams quickly.

She looked at her dad. This was a dream she had frequently. They stood in the airport's terminal.

"I'm sorry honey, but your aunt will do a better job than I could have," he said mournfully.

"Dad, I don't understand. Why are you sending me away?" she asked, puzzled and hurt.

"I can't handle the pressure now. I'm afraid that if you stay with me, you will die next."

"Come on dad, let me stay!"

"I can't, I'm sorry. Your aunt and uncle will be waiting for you in Toronto. Be looking for their sign. You'd better hurry, I think they just made the final call for your flight."

Katie looked at him as her vision grew blurry through tears. He was really abandoning his fifteen-year-old daughter.

"I'm sorry," he said as he hugged her tightly. "Know that I love you and I will come to visit when I can."

She nodded, trying not to cry, trying not to make a scene. She stepped back from him, wondering why he wasn't crying.

"Goodbye Katie," he said quietly.

She nodded and turned and walked through the terminal to her gate and crossed the gangway to the airplane. She was grateful she had a window seat.

Katie had no idea what to expect in Toronto. She had no idea what living with her aunt and uncle would be like; she had only seen them a few times. She had no idea if she'd ever talk to her friends in Baltimore again and she had no idea how well she'd make new friends in Canada. She didn't even know how long this flight would last!

She settled into her seat and put some ear buds in. She pushed play on her Zune, hid her ear buds' cable and music player and closed her eyes as the music started.

She faintly heard the plane's engines rev up and felt the plane begin accelerating forward.

"When I was younger, I just wanted to be like you."

The plane tilted upward and left the ground.

"You were my hero, my inspiration, my daddy."

The D.C. Metro area faded below into lines and grids of amber lights arrayed on the former tidewater marshes and was then eventually obscured from view by gathering clouds. Katie looked around the airplane's cabin. There were all kinds of people seated, presumably on their way to Canada.

"In my mind's eye, you never left but that doesn't change how you left that day."

She was nodding off.

"Tell me where you are now, did you fly to the moon? Did you fall in a volcano, lost in the jungle? I know you're never coming back, I know I'm left all alone."

"Tell me where you are now," she quietly mumbled before drifting into oblivion.

CHAPTER THIRTEEN

Adam Doss
Day 5

They reached the outskirts of Chatham, Illinois just before noon. They had seen smoke rising from the horizon from about ten miles out and as they approached, Adam saw why; several buildings were ablaze all over town.

"Be alert guys," Casey said as they followed the railroad tracks into a business park.

"Whoa," Missy said as they walked by four charred corpses on the side of the tracks.

"Let's try to get through town quickly," Adam said.

It took about an hour to walk through the deserted town.

"Hey, look. We must be crossing Lake Springfield," Randy said.

Sure enough they were surrounded on both sides by a lake. They continued on.

"Oh man!" Casey yelled.

"What?" Adam asked.

"Look! The bridge is out!" he yelled.

Sure enough, as they neared a short bridge over the lake, Adam saw that it had collapsed. "Now what?" he asked.

"I guess we need to retrace our steps," Randy said. "We'll have to get off the tracks and find another bridge over the lake or go around it even."

They turned around and walked back toward the town.

"What do you guys think about trying to find a car?" Jill asked as it began to rain.

"We might have a hard time getting from here to Chicago if the roads are blocked," Randy said.

"So we can get a big pickup truck or something and go off road to go around blockages," she retorted.

"So we should steal a car?" he asked.

"It's going to take us a long time to walk to Chicago, Randy. It's getting colder. And we don't even know who or what we will encounter between here and there. At least if we're in a car, we can quickly escape a threat. I mean, we've almost been robbed, we've been chased by infected people, we've seen piles of bloody corpses! I mean, this has just been something out of a nightmare!"

Adam cleared his throat. "Jill's right Randy, we should at least try to find a car."

Randy stared at him for a moment.

"They're right, Randy," Casey said.

He sighed. "Okay, let's try to find something."

Twenty minutes passed as they doubled back to a road that ran under the railroad tracks. They climbed down from the rail bridge and walked east on the road. They soon came to an apartment complex to the left.

"Let's look in here," Randy said. "Anyone know how to hotwire?"

"I do," Missy said.

"Okay, let's start looking."

As they entered the parking lot, Adam saw a vehicle that would be perfect. "Look at that truck!" he exclaimed.

A bright blue Chevrolet Silverado with an extended cab was parked about twenty yards to the left. They ran to it and Randy laughed when he peered in the window.

"We won't need to hotwire it after all," he said. "They left the keys on the seat!"

He opened the driver's side door and unlocked the other doors. Everyone climbed in. Casey climbed in the front seat with Randy and Adam sat in the back seat with Jill and Missy.

Suddenly Adam heard an angry yell. He turned and saw a rather large man walking toward the truck from a nearby apartment. He had a crowbar.

"Come back here! I'm going to skin all five of you!" he screamed.

"Randy, we need to go," Adam said quietly.

"I know Adam! I'm trying to figure out which Chevy key is this truck's!"

"Hey Earl! Hey Tad! Get out here! Some fools are trying to jack our ride!" the man yelled.

Two more men dressed in leather jackets walked out of the apartment. One had a shotgun.

"Randy, we really need to go!" Adam said more urgently.

At last the truck roared to life. Randy shifted the truck into gear as the man with the crowbar came within six feet of it. The truck jumped backward out of the parking spot and Randy turned it around quickly. Then they sped off, leaving the trio of angry men behind.

"That was close!" Jill exclaimed.

"Yeah, it was," Randy said, laughing nervously.

A few minutes later they pulled on to Interstate 55 and headed north.

"The roads are remarkably clear," Adam said, peering out the window at the empty highway.

"They are," Randy said. "This is a marked difference from Saint Louis."

"Hey look," Casey said, pointing ahead. "Are those military vehicles?"

They passed a trio of burned out Humvees that were stopped on the shoulder of the highway.

"Yeah, I think they were," Missy said.

They drove past some infected people shuffling along the highway as they crossed Lake Springfield.

"I guess eventually all those people will die," Jill said morosely.

"If they're not already dead," Casey said.

"Whatever."

Adam closed his eyes for a moment.

"Hey Adam," Randy said. "Wake up."

Adam opened his eyes and looked around. Jill and Missy were asleep. It had quit raining. They were approaching a roadblock on the highway. It appeared to be abandoned. He hadn't even realized he had fallen asleep. "Where are we?" he asked.

"Just south of downtown Bloomington," Randy replied. "This is the second roadblock we've passed in the last three miles."

The truck stopped.

"We'll have to get off at the last exit we passed and try to go around the roadblock" Randy said as he turned the truck around.

"We've passed a lot more military vehicles as we've driven north," Casey said. "They've all been wrecked."

"Hmm," Adam said as they drove off the interstate. They turned north on to South Main Street and drove on past several burned out cars. Soon they passed several large piles of charred corpses.

"What's with all the burned out vehicles and bodies?" Casey asked.

"I don't know," Randy said. "I'd like to not find out."

Jill stirred and sat up.

"Where are we?" she asked as she leaned against Adam and rested her head on his shoulder.

"Bloomington," he replied.

"Indiana?"

"Illinois," Randy said.

"Oh. Why aren't we on the highway anymore?"

"Roadblock," Adam said. "We had to get off to go around."

"Oh."

They drove past a parking garage and several tall buildings. Suddenly Adam heard a loud pop and then a grinding noise from the back of the truck.

"Man, I think we have a flat tire," Randy said as he slowed the truck to a stop in front of a small park.

Adam got out and saw that the rear driver's side tire was flat.

"What did you drive over?" he asked Randy.

He shrugged. "I don't know."

Adam stooped to peer under the truck. "Well, it looks like there's a full-sized spare on the undercarriage," he said. "Here, look under the back seat and see if the tools are there to remove the spare and jack the truck up. Ladies, you're going to have to get out."

Casey pulled out a jack and a tire iron and handed them to him.

He grabbed the tire iron, crawled under the truck and began loosening the spare. "One of these bolts is rusted on real good. Hold on guys," he said.

No reply came. He just assumed the guys hadn't heard him and kept working.

A few minutes later one of the bolts finally popped loose with a loud squeal.

"Finally!" he exclaimed. "I'm making progress. Guys? Hey guys?"

He looked and saw Randy's, Casey's, Jill's and Missy's feet. They were standing together. He also noticed two pairs of boots standing about five feet away.

He crawled out from under the truck and looked up at the hot barrel of a flamethrower being held by a soldier in an olive hazmat suit.

"Get up slowly," another soldier in a hazmat suit instructed him.

He stood up slowly and noticed that both soldiers were wielding flamethrowers.

"Who are you?" he asked.

"We are members of the Wolf Pack," the first soldier replied. "You are trespassing on land currently held by the Wolf Pack and are thus under arrest. You will come with us."

"What if we don't want to?" he replied. "We're trying to get to Chicago."

"And you're also violating quarantine," the other soldier replied.

"Son, do as you're told or my partner and I will barbeque you and your friends," the first soldier said with a sinister laugh. "You will now walk north to the next intersection."

Adam joined the others and they began to walk north away from the truck. He heard a whooshing sound behind him and turned to see the truck was now ablaze. The other soldier was standing about thirty feet from it, spraying bursts of fire at it.

Adam winced as he watched the Silverado burn up; all of their weapons and supplies were inside. He turned back around and continued on.

Suddenly two gunshots rang out. He spun around and saw both soldiers fall to the ground, dead.

"What the...?" he asked.

He heard a whistle back near the intersection they were being marched to. He looked up and saw two men standing there. One of them waved at him and the others to come forward.

Adam and the others ran to them.

"Hey! I'm Jamie Daniels and this is Juan Vega! We are glad to have rescued you!" the taller man introduced himself.

"I'm Randy Eccleston, that's Adam Doss, that's Casey Newburgh, that's Missy Sanders and that's Jillian Wilson," Randy said.

"We just rescued you from some rogue soldiers," Juan said.

"That's the good news," Jamie said.

"What's the bad news?" Randy asked.

"This city is full of about five hundred of them, they all have flamethrowers and the city is also full of zombies."

CHAPTER FOURTEEN

Randy Eccleston
Day 5

Randy and the others followed their rescuers through alleys and backyards, leaping over fences and walking around cars as they moved away from downtown Bloomington.

"Where are you all from?" Jamie asked as he shot at a trio of infected men.

"We're all from Chicago originally but we are coming from Saint Louis," Randy replied.

Jamie stopped and looked at him. "So where are you headed?"

"Chicago."

He chortled and they kept going.

"What's so funny?" Randy asked.

"You," he replied. "You realize that in less than a week, civilization has completely collapsed, right?"

"Yeah, we saw the military blow up bridges in Saint Louis."

"Okay, and you've seen all of the zombies wandering around right?"

"Why are you calling them zombies?"

Jamie shook his head. "Because that virus, whatever it is they catch, it kills them and then brings them back from the dead as zombies."

"You've seen them die?"

"I watched my aunt succumb about a week ago. She was vomiting blood and had an awful fever right before she died. Then she died. I watched her stop breathing. She had been dead for about five hours when I heard a groan come from her bedroom. I walked back there and saw my aunt sitting up on the bed! I just about had a heart attack! She chased me around the house trying to bite me. Finally, I crushed her head with a dumbbell and she stopped."

Casey whistled. "See Randy? I told you they were zombies."

Randy glared at his friend and then looked back at Jamie. "I'm sorry to hear that man."

He shrugged. "Thanks. It's tough. I was living down in southern Illinois, near Carbondale but my family is all from up here originally. So when things went down, I drove up and made it as far as my aunt's house here in Bloomington. Then, after she died, I saw all the soldiers come in. They torched my aunt's house and I barely escaped. I ran into Juan and he invited me to stay with him while we tried to figure out a way to escape from the perimeter the soldiers have set up."

"Hey, hold up," Juan said.

Everyone froze alongside a garage. Juan motioned for them to lean against the side of the garage.

A Humvee carrying soldiers in hazmat suits drove by.

Juan nodded a few seconds later and they continued on.

"So Juan, you live here in Bloomington?" Adam asked.

He shook his head. "No, I actually live in Normal, just north of Bloomington. My house is just down the road from Illinois State University."

Juan was a short, chubby Hispanic man, a sharp contrast with Jamie's tall, pale, thin figure. Randy wondered about both men. Could he trust them? Had he and his friends leapt from the proverbial frying pan into the fire?

They followed Juan and Jamie to a large Victorian-style house at the corner of North Linden Street and East Poplar Street. The address was 2015 East Poplar.

"Is this your place Juan?" Jillian asked.

He nodded as they walked up the steps onto the covered front porch.

"It's beautiful!" she exclaimed.

"Thanks ma'am," he replied. "I bought it about ten years ago and I've lived in it ever since. That's the great thing about these college towns; lots of large, older houses. Come in guys, come in."

Randy and the others followed him into a spacious living room. He and Jamie sat down at opposite ends of a couch. Randy sat down with Adam and Jillian on another couch and Casey and Missy each sat down in recliners.

"This is nice," Casey said.

"Thank you," Juan replied. "I'm afraid we will need to introduce ourselves again. I seem to have forgotten all of your names. I'm sorry."

"It's okay," Randy replied. "I'll start. I'm Randy Eccleston."

Adam cleared his throat. "My name is Adam Doss."

"I'm Jillian Wilson, but most people call me Jill," Jillian said.

"I'm Casey Newburgh," Casey said.

"I'm Missy Sanders," Missy said.

"I am Jamie Daniels," Jamie said.

"I am Juan Francisco Vega," Juan said.

"So let's get down to brass tacks," Jamie said. "You all stumbled into a warzone."

"I noticed," Randy said.

"As I said earlier, there are roughly five hundred rogue soldiers patrolling this area. They set up a perimeter all around Bloomington and Normal. The west side of the perimeter follows I-Seventy-Four. The northern side follows I-Fifty-Five, and the south and east sides follow Veterans Parkway. As best we can tell, the soldiers' strategy is wait and torch. They are moving systematically through both cities torching every zombie they find, arresting and summarily executing every uninfected person they find, and torching any buildings they find that are inhabited by either zombies or uninfected people."

"Where did they come from?" Adam asked.

"The day after quarantine was declared, they seized the airport on the east side of town and they set up a perimeter around the cities. It would seem that almost everyone living in Bloomington-Normal became a zombie," Juan said.

"How did you get here Jamie?" Randy asked.

"I made it in before they closed the perimeter on the southwest side of Bloomington."

"Who are they?"

"The best we can tell, they are soldiers from the Army who went rogue following the imposition of quarantine. They act like they're following orders from afar, but who would be commanding them to torch innocent civilians with flamethrowers?" Jamie replied. "It doesn't make any sense."

"When were you guys planning on escaping?" Missy asked.

"Well, that's the thing. Their perimeter is pretty solid. We have been exploring night and day and haven't found a vulnerability yet," Juan said.

"Where have you looked?" Jillian asked.

"Southeast and south. From directly east of here all the way around to Southwest Bloomington," Jamie said.

"So there are still unexplored areas of the perimeter?" Randy asked.

He nodded.

"You know, that's a large perimeter for five hundred people to patrol. There's got to be a hole somewhere."

"Maybe so. I hope so," he said, laughing. "This has been terrible. Just terrible."

Randy nodded.

They sat there for a while in silence. Randy looked down at his watch. It was 5:30pm.

"Hey!" Jamie whispered. "Do you hear that?"

Randy tilted his head and heard the sound of diesel engines. The sound was growing louder.

"Get down on the floor!" Juan whispered urgently.

Everyone slid off the couches and laid on the floor.

"That's the Wolf Pack. They're on their evening patrol. They'll come through again in six hours," Jamie whispered.

"They'll kill anyone they see," Juan added.

Randy nodded.

Several vehicles slowly rumbled past the house. He heard shouting down the street and the squealing sound of brakes.

"No! Please!" a man yelled.

Then Randy heard the most terrible sound he had ever heard before, a sound like the sound a gas stove makes as a burner lights, but instead of the sound lasting for just a split second, it lasted for what seemed like an eternity. Then, in the midst of the whooshing, he heard a man and a woman screaming almost inhumanly. After a few seconds, their howls fell silent. Then after a few more seconds the terrible swooshing fell silent too. There were footsteps. Several engines spun up and then the rumble of diesel engines faded into the evening.

Everyone laid there for a long time in silence. Finally, Jamie spoke up.

"It's safe to sit up now."

Randy stood up and walked to the window. Just down the street lay two bodies, still ablaze. He shuddered.

"That's terrible," Adam said quietly as he walked up alongside Randy.

Randy nodded quietly.

Juan cleared his throat. "They did that to my partner and his family three nights ago, before I ran into Jamie. I was over at their place, checking on them. You know, we were all confused by the quarantine. Why was a cancer drug causing contagious illness? I knew my business partner's mother had received the treatment just a few weeks earlier, so I had gone over to his place to see how he was doing."

Randy nodded.

"Well, Ray said his mom had called a few days before and said she had been okay. He had a covered porch. We were sitting on it; me, his wife and their little boy. We were talking about the soldiers that had reportedly seized control of the city. They had imposed martial law.

"Suddenly, an APC pulled up in front of the house and four soldiers wearing olive green CBRN suits got out. They were wearing large tanks on their backs and holding flamethrowers," he shuddered as he said that.

"You see, I knew what a flamethrower looked like. My family immigrated to the United States when I was five, back in Eighty-Four. I was born in Ciudad Manté in Tamaulipas, Mexico. We fled drug violence. One of my earliest memories is watching DEA agents torch fields of marijuana from my bedroom window. I knew what a flamethrower looked like.

"So the four soldiers walked slowly upto the front porch as the APC waited. Ray asked them what they wanted and they stopped about fifteen feet from his stoop and stood in silence. He got up and walked out to them, asking if they needed help. Without saying anything, they sprayed him with a flamethrower for two seconds," he paused. "And I watched my best friend and business partner burn to death," his voice cracked.

"And I yelled to his wife and son to run. I stood up and we ran into their house. But where I ran out the backdoor, I didn't realize until it was too late that they had run upstairs. I stopped on the back porch and screamed for them. But then I saw a soldier walking quickly toward me, the nozzle of his weapon pointed at me. There was no time, I had to flee. I ran. I ran for what seemed like a long time. I kept expecting to suddenly be ablaze.

"When I finally stopped, I turned around and saw smoke rising into the sky in the direction his house was in. They killed my best friend and killed his wife and little boy. I walked by there yesterday, me and Jamie did, and I saw their bodies laid out in the front yard in front of the charred ruins of the house." He shook his head wistfully. "Those soldiers don't care about our safety or wellbeing. They are simply following some secret directive. They are nothing more than thuggish murderers and arsonists."

Randy nodded. "That's terrible."

"It is."

Adam hugged Juan.

"Thank you Adam," he said. "Thank you Randy."

Randy nodded. "You're welcome Juan."

They walked back into the living room and sat down on the couches. In the fading light, Randy saw everyone else was eating from what appeared to be MREs.

"Where did you guys get those?" he asked.

"Same place we got guns and flash bang grenades," Jamie said. "We stole them from a parked supply truck near the southeast corner of the perimeter."

Randy nodded. "Do you have any more?"

He laughed. "We've got plenty. Pick your poison, we have spaghetti and meatballs or beef stroganoff."

"I guess I'll take the stroganoff."

"Very well, I'll be right back," he said before disappearing into another room. A moment later he returned and handed Randy a small squarish cardboard box.

"Thanks."

"No problem."

Randy pulled a tab off the side of the box and pulled the flap back. He then pulled out a plastic tray containing a brown bag of stroganoff, a small bag of potato chips, a plastic fork, and a little bottle of Tabasco sauce. He picked up the bag of stroganoff and studied it. There was a small disc on one end of the bag with instructions to squeeze it and then place the bag in the tray. He squeezed the button and immediately felt the bag grow warm. He set it down in the tray and waited. A few minutes later, he tore the bag open and poured the hot noodles into the tray. Honestly, it smelled delicious.

"Thanks," he said, as he took a bite of hot creamy noodles.

"No problem Randy," Jamie said.

"You are all welcome to stay with us until we figure out how to escape," Juan said as it grew dark outside. "I hope that has been obvious."

"Thanks," Randy said. "Why are you guys doing this?"

"Because, we have to band together man," Jamie said. "If we scatter, we will either be eaten by zombies or be killed by crazy people."

He nodded.

"So tomorrow Juan and I are going to get up just before dawn and set out to explore the perimeter, see if we can find a weak spot. If you guys are willing to accompany us, we can actually split into two groups and probe different areas. We can get the perimeter assessed more quickly that way," Jamie said.

Randy nodded. "How do we want to split the groups?"

"Well, why don't you send two or three of your folks with Juan and I'll accompany the others?"

"Casey, do you and Missy feel comfortable going with Juan tomorrow?"

Casey nodded. "Yeah."

"Yeah," Missy said.

"Okay then. Me, Adam and Jillian will go with you Jamie."

"Great, we'll set out in the morning," Juan said. "You are all welcome to sleep anywhere on the second floor of this house. I am going to go to bed."

"Goodnight Juan," Jamie said.

"Goodnight, it was nice meeting you all," Juan said as he stood and walked to the stairs.

"I am going to retire for the night too," Missy said, standing up.

"Me too," Casey said. "Goodnight guys."

"Goodnight!" Randy said.

He sat there silently for a while with Adam, Jillian and Jamie. At length, Jillian spoke up.

"So Jamie, how old are you?" she asked.

"I just turned thirty-three about a month ago," he replied.

"Happy belated birthday," Randy said.

"Thanks," he said. "What about you guys?"

"I'm twenty-six, Jillian is twenty-four and Randy is twenty-five" Adam said.

Jamie nodded.

"Do you have any other family, like kids?" Jillian asked.

He sighed. "I have one daughter. She'd be sixteen now. I haven't seen her in ten years."

"That's crazy! What happened?" she asked. "Wait, if it's too personal, I understand."

"No, no, it's fine. I went to prison when she was three and her mother stopped bringing her to visit me a few years later. Then her mother divorced me and they moved far away. I got out of prison a few years ago, but I haven't been able to find them."

"Why'd you go to prison?" Adam asked.

"I helped some friends rob a gas station in Kentucky about thirteen years ago. I drove the getaway car and knocked an employee out who was standing outside talking on his cell phone. Of course, the take was pitifully small, but we used it to fuel our heroin habits. We got arrested a few weeks later. I was charged the same as the others, with armed robbery, assault and I was also charged with miscellaneous drug charges. The prosecutor sought a sentence of forty to fifty years in a state prison against me. Ultimately, I accepted a plea bargain where I testified against my two accomplices and was only convicted of the assault and drug charges; the robbery charge was dropped in return for my cooperation. I was sentenced to fifteen years at the Kentucky State Penitentiary. They let me out after ten years on parole."

Randy whistled. "That's crazy."

He shook his head and for a moment Randy was worried he had taken offense. "No, it's just the fruit of one bad decision after another. You know, I could blame it on my upbringing. My dad scooted when I was four, my mom married some scumbag named Dwayne. Dwayne used my mom, my siblings and myself as a punching bag, he dragged us back and forth across Appalachia looking for work. We lived paycheck to paycheck throughout my childhood relying on government aid; we wound up getting evicted from more trailers than I could count. There were times my little sister literally had no diapers or formula for days, there were times me and my brother went days without food, I mean, I could keep going on. But the reality is that while I had a lot going against me, I embraced my identity as Hoosier trailer trash.

"I made bad decision after bad decision. I married my girlfriend when I was seventeen and dropped out of high school that year when I knocked her up. I began smoking pot when I was fifteen and that escalated to prescription drug abuse and heroin use by the time my daughter was born. I was unable to hold down a job and resorted to theft to pay for my drug habit. I'd disappear for days into a drug-induced haze and emerge hungry for more. I led my wife into the same habit and one day I came down from a high and realized my daughter had run out of diapers the day before. I had become what I hated." He sighed.

"So, when I made the decision that night to help my drug buddies rob a gas station, it was one more terrible decision in a long line of terrible decisions. I'm surprised I got off so easy, really; that was the seventh time in four years that I had been arrested. Taking that plea deal was probably the best decision I had made upto that point.

"Tamara, my wife, came to visit me every now and then but it was hard. I was held in Western Kentucky, all the way across the state from where she and Maddy lived. The first time she came to visit me, she looked like she was near death. She said that the State had told her to go to rehab or they'd take Maddy away from her, and she wasn't sure what to do. I talked her into rehab and didn't see her again for almost a year. But then she came to visit and brought our daughter. She looked a lot better and Maddy looked good too. She told me she had gotten off drugs and that things were looking up. She visited a few more times and then quit coming and then she filed for divorce a few years later."

"Wow," Jillian said.

"Are you still using? Drugs, that is?" Adam asked.

He shook his head. "No. I relapsed earlier this year after my mom died, but I was just finishing up rehab when all this went down, so I've been clean now for about four months."

Randy nodded.

"It's a daily battle, but I guess this a good situation to be in. It's not like there are any dealers left to buy from."

"Good point," Adam said.

"So where are you going to go from here?" Randy asked.

"I don't know," he replied. "I guess I hadn't really thought that far ahead."

"I see."

"I mean, I guess I just had this vague plan to come here to see if my aunt was still alive, and then she died. I ran into Juan and saved him from some soldiers and we have been together since, but that was really just a couple of days ago."

"Okay."

"What does Juan have planned?" Jillian asked.

"I guess he just wants to get out of Bloomington-Normal. I don't know where he wants to go after that."

"You guys could come with us?" Randy suggested.

Jamie looked at him for a moment before replying. "To Chicago?"

"Yes."

"To Chicago," he repeated. "Hmm, it sounds like there are probably an awful lot of zombies there. Why are you guys going to Chicago?"

"It's home," Randy said. "Plus, for me anyway, I have an older brother who lives there and parents. I'd like to see if they're okay."

He nodded. "I get it."

"Yeah."

"Well, I guess that's better than wandering around aimlessly," he said. "I'm in."

CHAPTER FIFTEEN

Katie Barnes
Day 6

She felt someone shaking her gently. Katie opened her eyes and looked up at Joel.

"Hey sleepy head, let's get going. The sun just came up. Rachel said we can probably make it to the cabin by noon if we leave now." He was smiling.

She rubbed her eyes. "Quiet night?"

"Yeah. Michelle woke me up a half hour early because she heard something outside. When I went to go look, I saw our intruder was a raccoon. It ran off when it saw me," he chuckled.

Katie laughed and yawned. "Yeah, let's get going." She walked outside and saw that Michelle was refueling the mopeds. "How's she doing that?" she asked Joel.

"The pumps still have some emergency power I guess," Joel replied, shrugging.

"Hey guys, I found some packaged pastries in the gas station. They should still be good," Rachel said, handing them all cheese Danishes.

Katie wolfed hers down. It tasted good.

They set out on the road again, with Rachel in the lead this time and Joel in the rear. The countryside gradually became hillier and more forested. Katie noticed a sign welcoming them to Pennsylvania and the Allegheny National Forest as they drove past.

After winding down multiple rural roads for what seemed like hours to Katie, they finally arrived at the cabin around noon. It was in the middle of a clearing, surrounded by tall beeches reaching toward the clouds. The cabin itself was somewhat modest, looking like it had a few bedrooms. A stone chimney jutted up on the side of the building. The front porch was covered and there appeared to be a scarecrow propped up in the swing.

As they all pulled to a stop, Rachel's face twisted in horror. "Daddy?" she asked, her voice trembling. She leapt off her moped and ran toward the scarecrow. "Daddy!" she screamed.

Katie and the others ran up behind her. The figure Katie had mistaken for a scarecrow was Rachel's father. He was wearing a pair of denim bib overalls and appeared to have been dead for more than a week. Rachel hugged his corpse, weeping loudly. Michelle walked up, hugged her and looked at Rachel's dad, tilting her head.

"Huh, I thought I just saw his eyes open a bit," Michelle said, leaning over him. She put her hand on his shoulder. Unexpectedly, he turned his head quickly and bit her hand, his jaw clamped on her flesh. She began to scream loudly as Rachel jumped backward with a shriek.

Joel stepped in and swung the crowbar down into Rachel's dad's head. The corpse released Michelle's hand and slumped over.

"Michelle! Are you okay?" Katie ran to her. Michelle's right hand was streaming blood from where he had bitten her, in the webbing between her thumb and index finger.

Michelle nodded, crying. She clutched her hand.

"Let's get you inside and wash it out!" Rachel exclaimed.

"Wait Rachel, we need to make sure there aren't any other Infected in the cabin!" Joel exclaimed.

"Okay, so you guys clear the cabin while I treat Michelle's hand," Rachel said urgently.

Katie and Joel ran inside and searched the rooms.

"The house is clear Rachel!" Katie yelled.

Michelle was rushed into the house and Rachel helped her wash her hand out and put a bandage on. A couple of hours later, everyone finally felt like they could relax. They would have to make sure Michelle's hand stayed clean, but it seemed likely she would be okay.

Joel built a fire in the fireplace as the sun set outside. Katie locked the doors and drew the shutters on the windows. Rachel sat down in front of the fire and was quiet for a really long time. Finally, she spoke.

"Daddy was a good man. He worked hard at a steel mill for many years and he had just retired a year ago," she paused to wipe some tears from her face. "He and Momma loved one another dearly."

"I'm sorry Rachel," Katie said, hugging her.

"It's okay. I mean, I guess people die. We've seen more people die in the last few days than I've ever seen die. I don't want us to ever reach the point where death is meaningless to us, but I guess we need to get used to it. It's probably going to be a while before things get better out there."

Joel approached. "I found a large bottle of Cabernet in the wine rack. You ladies want to share it?"

They drank from the bottle, passing it around.

"I know I've told you about Junior and my mother," Katie said later. "But I haven't told you much about Robby. I just said he died when I was fifteen and then I was sent to Canada to live with my aunt. I've never told you how he died.

"I remember we went to a baseball game in Kansas City. The Royals crushed the Orioles that day, but it was the most fun I had ever had. Robby had moved south to D.C. for school a few months earlier and I was really missing having him around. My dad was just easier to deal with when Robby was there. So it was a great surprise to wake up one day and see Robby eating breakfast in our kitchen, talking to our dad. I skipped school that day and we drove to Kansas City from Baltimore for the game the next day.

"After the game, we drove back and listened to one of our favorite bands, Death Cab for Cutie. They hadn't released an album for a few years so we just listened to a couple of older ones and we just listened to them over and over and over again, the whole way back from KC," she laughed.

"He went back to school the following Monday and got busy with classes. He had always been a bit of a geek and he just poured himself into his studies. The last time I saw him was when he came home from school the second weekend in November. He was stressing out about some research paper he had due at the end of the semester, and I remember him telling my dad he wanted to change his major to molecular biology. He gave me his favorite Orioles hat before he left to go back to school. He said he had gotten a new one a few weeks before and wanted me to have his old hat.

"I called him on the Fourteenth because I had just had a fight with our dad. Dad had just been freaking out on me because I was failing a class, I think it was algebra. I was really upset. And Robby just comforted me and calmed me down and told me he loved me. I remember he made some corny joke about the Orioles and said he'd be back Friday and would take me down to D.C. to see the sights.

"I remember I told him I had already been to D.C., a lot of times! And he just laughed and said that we would plan a beach trip for the following spring then. I told him I loved him and said goodbye. I was so ready for Friday," Katie said, sighing. She took another drink from the bottle of wine savoring the warm feeling in her throat.

"And then on Thursday night the phone rang. The landline rang. I remember thinking it odd because no one ever called that line. I figured it was a telemarketer or someone calling from the county jail. For some reason our phone number was really similar to the county jail's, so we would occasionally get collect calls from people trying to get free legal advice. Robby would actually accept the calls when we were younger and just give those guys crazy legal advice. We thought it was hilarious until our parents got the phone bill. They didn't think it was so funny."

The others laughed at that revelation.

Katie continued. "Anyway, the phone was ringing. My dad had just sat down for dinner and I had been in the bathroom washing my hands and I was closest to the phone, as it was in the den, so I answered it. It was one of Robby's friends from school, his name was Subhash. He asked for my dad. He sounded upset. So I got my dad, and I remember the conversation like it happened yesterday:

117

"'Hello? Yes, this is. What? Oh God, what? Is he okay? Oh no! Where are they taking him?'"

"I remember he hung up and looked at me."

"'Your brother has been in an accident. We must go to him.'"

Katie sighed. "So we drove to the hospital. I remember I was freaking out the whole time, and my dad just wasn't saying anything! We finally reached the hospital just north of the District, and when we went in, Subhash and Robby's girlfriend Emily were sitting in the waiting room. Subhash looked really nervous and Emily's mascara was streaked down her face; she had been crying. The doctor came out to talk to my dad and he had a grim look on his face and my dad just calmly nodded while the doctor expressed his condolences. I found out what had happened.

"Robby had been on his way to get some dinner for he and Emily when another car coming the other way had crossed the center line and hit Robby's car head on. The driver of the other car was killed instantly; he was ejected from his car. Robby wasn't. He had been trapped in the wreckage and had called Subhash, asking him to call us. I remember Subhash was just so sad. We all were.

"Robby's aorta had been torn and while he seemed fine when the paramedics arrived, by the time they got him to the hospital he had bled to death," Katie felt tears begin rolling down her cheeks. "The doctor said we could go back and see him and I remember how peaceful he looked. He didn't look like he had been in a terrible accident; he just looked like he was asleep.

"The funeral was on a cloudy day the next week. The ceremony was nice and afterward my dad told me he couldn't handle raising me and he put me on a plane with some of my belongings and sent me to Toronto to live with my aunt and uncle."

Everyone was quiet for a few minutes.

Finally, Michelle spoke. "That's heavy. Rachel, I'm so sorry for your loss."

"Thanks Michelle. And Katie, thank you for sharing that," Rachel said.

"Guys, I'm pretty tired. I think I'm going to turn in early," Michelle said.

"Goodnight."

Rachel, Joel and Katie stayed up fairly late talking about each other's upbringings and finishing off the bottle of wine. Gradually the fire in the fireplace reduced itself to glowing coals as the embers faded from white to orange to a deep crimson.

When Katie awoke the next morning, she couldn't find Joel. Where was he? She dressed and stepped out into the chilly morning. The sun had just risen above the horizon and its light filtered through the morning fog and the trees.

She saw Joel standing over a patch of freshly dug dirt holding a shovel about a hundred feet from the cabin.

"What are you doing early bird?" she called out to him.

He turned and walked back toward her. "I just buried Rachel's father. I felt it was appropriate to give his body some dignity."

Katie hugged him. He was sweaty from the work. "You're a good man Joel Ryan."

"Thanks," he replied, patting her back.

They turned and went back inside and ate breakfast. Around 9:00am, Rachel got up. A half hour later, Katie heard noise in Michelle's room.

"Guys, I don't feel so good," she cried out. "I feel hot!"

Rachel and Katie went to check on her. Katie put the back of her hand against Michelle's forehead.

"You're burning up!" Katie exclaimed.

Rachel carefully unwrapped Michelle's hand. It looked red and puffy around the bite. Rachel frowned. "It looks like the bite's infected," she said. "Hang on, I'm going to go grab a thermometer from the bathroom." She left the room and came back a few moments later with an infrared thermometer. She swiped it across Michelle's forehead and waited for it to beep. When it did she furrowed her brow. "One-Hundred-Point-One degrees. You definitely have a fever. Based on that and your hand, I'd say you have an infection. If we could get a hold of some amoxicillin or Cipro, that might help."

"Hey, we passed a pharmacy in the last town we drove through," Joel said. "It was in a strip mall. I'll go check and see if they have any antibiotics. You guys stay here."

"Joel, you can't go alone!" Katie exclaimed, grabbing his arm.

"Katie, I have to go alone. You have to stay here. We can't leave Rachel and Michelle alone. Besides, I have a crowbar," he forced a nervous smile.

"Well, be careful! I'm going to have a hard time forgiving you if you don't come back!"

"I will be. I love you," he leaned over and kissed her before he left.

After he left, Rachel cleaned out the bite wound on Michelle's hand. Katie went into the living room because she didn't want to watch. She heard Michelle crying out in pain.

A few minutes later Rachel came out and sat down across from Katie. "She's going to try to rest. I told her I'll be checking her temp every couple of hours." She shuddered. "I feel terrible that she got bitten. Her hand is pretty bad. The inflammation has it puffed up to almost twice its normal size and the area around the bite is as red as a cherry," she frowned. "I hope Joel gets back quickly with antibiotics. Otherwise I don't think we'll be able to save her hand."

"What? You think we might have to amputate her hand?"

"In the absence of a medical facility to provide intravenous antibiotics, yes. Otherwise she could go into septic shock. I mean who knows what kind of bacteria were living in my dad's mouth? The mouth of a living human being is one of the filthiest places, as far as microbes go. I'd imagine the mouth of a dead human is worse."

Katie and Rachel sat there quietly for a long time. The sounds of the forest were all they could hear. It was actually comforting. Right before sundown, Katie heard the sound of a moped approaching.

"Joel!" she got up and ran outside. Sure enough, Joel was driving up.

"Hey! I got some antibiotics!" he shouted triumphantly as he pulled to a stop. He and Katie walked in and he handed them to Rachel. Rachel then disappeared into Michelle's bedroom.

"What took so long?" Katie asked.

"Well, let's just say the strip mall wasn't empty. I had to kill about a dozen Infected. Then I had to get into the pharmacy. Then I had to find the antibiotics. Then I had to high tail it out of there," he sighed. "Busy day!"

"Well, I'm glad you're okay," Katie said as she hugged him and kissed him on the cheek.

Rachel came outside. "I gave her some antibiotics. Her fever hasn't gone up since this afternoon. We'll see how she does and go from there."

On the morning of November 4th, Michelle's fever had dropped and the swelling in her hand had gone down significantly. In the afternoon, however, the fever returned and shot up to 102°. She also developed chills and back pain.

On the 5th, she had little bright red circles all over her arms and legs and her back pain worsened significantly. Rachel warned Katie and Joel to stay out of Michelle's room, as it was likely she had some kind of virus. By the end of the day, Michelle's fever had hit 106°.

On the 6th, she began to bleed from her gums and nose and complained of constant back pain. The next day she began vomiting blood and became delirious.

On the 9th, Rachel exited Michelle's room around noon. "Michelle just died," she said quietly.

Katie got up and ran to her, to hug her.

She rebuffed Katie. "Don't hug me. I have some of her blood on me. We don't know what she had so we don't know how contagious it is. It's probably blood-borne though. Let me go take a hot shower and then we can hug." She was trying to be stoic.

As Rachel walked to the bathroom, Katie sat down, stunned by the news.

"My roommate just died," she said, looking at Joel.

He came over and put his arm around her. They sat there quietly for a while, while Katie wept. Rachel came out of the bathroom a few minutes later and came over. Katie stood up and hugged her. Both women were crying now. Joel stood there quietly.

Suddenly a growl came from Michelle's bedroom.

"Michelle?" Rachel asked, confused.

Katie heard the groaning of bedsprings and heard footsteps on the floor. Michelle, or rather what was left of Michelle, shuffled into the doorway. Her face was white and mottled with dried blood. She had a pained expression frozen on her face. And she had the same eyes as the other Infected, the same mélange of cold death and hot fury. She growled when she saw Rachel and staggered toward her, arms outstretched.

"No, it isn't Michelle anymore," Joel said, grabbing his crowbar. "Stand back, and please don't watch."

Katie pulled Rachel back and covered her eyes. She began to resist, so Katie whispered in her ear, "How do you want to remember her? I want to remember her as the goofy roommate who sometimes put DVDs in the DVD player upside down, who mistook peanut butter for mayo and ate a BLT with a thick helping of PB. I don't want to remember her as this."

Rachel relaxed. Katie closed her eyes and heard the whoosh of the swinging crowbar and heard a sound like the claw end of a hammer meeting a honeydew. Katie heard a thump on the floor.

"It's done," Joel said grimly. The crowbar clanked as it hit the floor. "Katie, can you help me carry her body outside?"

Katie turned and nodded.

Rachel said, "I'll clean up her room."

Katie grabbed Michelle's ankles and Joel grabbed her wrists and they carried her outside; she was surprisingly light. They set her down in the grass about twenty feet from the porch and Joel went to retrieve the shovel. When he got back he began digging a grave for her.

The afternoon sun was at 45° above the horizon when Joel finished digging. The hole appeared to be about five feet deep. He and Katie gently lowered Michelle into the grave and Joel covered her body with dirt, filling in the hole.

Rachel came out as they were finishing. "The cabin is clean."

"Okay," Katie replied walking to her. She hugged Rachel. "We'll get through this."

Rachel nodded. "I know." She rubbed her eyes. "It just hurts so much!"

"I know," Katie said as they walked back into the cabin.

Joel stoked a fire in the fireplace as it got dark outside and they all reminisced about Michelle.

"Do you remember the first day of class when we found out she was going to be our roommate?" Katie asked.

"I do! I remember we thought she was just a hilarious ginger!" Rachel laughed. "She did and said the funniest things! Remember the time she got us temporarily banned from UB Stadium?"

"I do! Remember when she talked us into going to Niagara Falls on the hottest day of the year? Remember how she kept saying Canadian guys were hot?"

Rachel laughed, nodding. "I remember she kept saying American Falls was a rip-off compared to Horseshoe Falls."

They laughed until they were crying. Joel sat beside Katie, quiet the whole time. She looked at him. "Are you okay Joel?"

"Yeah, just processing what happened today."

She hugged him.

The next morning, Joel and Katie got up at sunrise and took a walk down to the Allegheny Reservoir. Rachel had told them about the reservoir and had said it was about a quarter of a mile east of the cabin. Sure enough, they reached the edge of an escarpment that sloped down to a small rocky beach. They ambled down to the rocky beach and sat on a large rock together. It was a little chilly out.

"This is beautiful," Katie said.

"It is," Joel replied.

They sat there quietly for a little while, watching birds fly south over the reservoir.

"I guess anyone who gets bitten by someone who's infected is likely to become infected themselves," Joel said thoughtfully as a large grey heron swooped down to land in water about thirty feet away. It landed with a splash.

"Yeah, I guess so. I guess that's how it spreads."

"Yeah, it would seem to corroborate what Rachel suggested about it being a blood-borne disease. Plus, it looks like the disease part of it, before you die, is pretty awful. If I get it, please kill me before it gets bad."

Katie didn't know what to say, so she quietly nodded.

"We need to see how much food is in the cabin. We also need to see if there is a rifle in it. If there is, we could go hunting over the winter to find food. If there isn't, we need to consider moving on."

"Yeah, I guess so," she said, watching as the heron stabbed its bill into the water, spearing a small fish.

After a while they walked back to the cabin. It smelled like pizza when they walked in.

"Hey guys, I made some pizza," Rachel said cheerily.

"It smells delicious!" Joel exclaimed.

Pepperonis and peppers and sausage and tomatoes covered the cheesy surface. It sat upon a circular black stone, which must have been a pizza stone. A case of beer from the fridge sat on the counter.

"You guys are just in time. I just took it out of the oven," she said, slicing into it with a pizza cutter.

Katie and Joel sat down and ate the pizza, which turned out to be delicious.

"Rachel, this is really good!" Katie said, mouth full of hot gooey cheese.

"Thanks!" She blushed a little.

"Rachel, we need to talk about our future plans," Joel said, before he took a sip of beer.

"Okay, can't we just stay here?" she replied.

"Well, how did you cook the pizza?" he asked.

"I used the gas oven."

"Propane?"

"Yeah, oh..."

"Is the heat in here propane too?"

"Yeah."

"And the electricity?"

"It runs on a generator."

"How will we get food? Eventually we are going to eat through what we have here," he said.

"Well, my dad kept a rifle in the master bedroom. We could hunt. I think that's what I was planning on. We could make it work. We have a fireplace too."

"Rachel, spring won't come for five months. You know winters up here get really cold. And snowy," Katie chimed in.

"The fireplace will do a decent job of warming the main room, but it will take a lot of firewood to keep the main room reliably warm. Now, we still have maybe three or four weeks of bearably warm weather before it gets cold. If we stay here until the first snow, which by my estimate is an optimistic guess at how long our food and propane will last, we will be stuck trying to get mopeds out of rural Pennsylvania on unplowed, unsalted roads in the dead of winter. We won't have food. We won't be able to get medicine if we need it. I am fairly confident that if we stay here, we will die, whether it's in this cabin or in the woods. We need to leave as soon as we can," Joel said passionately.

"Where are we going to go?" Rachel asked, throwing her hands up in the air.

"Let's make our way south, toward warmer areas of the country. Look, we can pass through Pittsburgh and see if we can find Austin. He lives just north of the city in Summer Hill," he said, raising his eyebrows.

Rachel furrowed her brow thoughtfully. "Hmm."

"Rachel, I agree with Joel. It's a bad idea to stay here for the winter. This was a good place to hide out for a couple of weeks, but we need to get going soon," Katie said.

Rachel nodded.

"Tonight, let's have a feast and then tomorrow morning, let's head out. We should be able to make it to Pittsburgh by day break," Joel suggested.

"Sounds like a plan," Rachel said.

Rachel thawed some ground beef and Katie went to work cutting up vegetables for salad and sauce. Rachel began boiling a pot of water and started sautéing the beef. Katie prepared the salad and heated up some bread in the oven. A little later, Rachel stirred in the vegetables and spaghetti sauce with the browned beef. Then she started cooking some angel hair noodles.

Joel walked over to them. "That smells amazing ladies!"

"Thanks, it will be ready in a few minutes," Rachel said.

When it was done, they sat down to eat together. As they broke bread, Katie realized she was grateful for two friends she could rely on. She wondered if Joel and she would be able to marry in this new frightening world. She wondered if Austin was still alive. She wondered what they would find in Pittsburgh. And quite unexpectedly she found herself wondering if her father was still alive.

The man didn't deserve to be. Yet Katie found a long dormant yearning rising within her. She wanted to see him again. Maybe it was time to finally forgive him.

She quickly dismissed such thoughts from her head. They had a busy day ahead tomorrow. After dinner she would pack their stuff. She had no idea what to expect, but realized she could face anything as long as Joel was with her.

CHAPTER SIXTEEN

Jim Gibson
Day 4

Jim passed the eighth floor and heard scratching behind the fire door.

As he reached the landing for the ninth floor the crescendo of feverish clawing peaked.

"This is creepy," Giselle said, panting.

"Thank you Captain Obvious!" Connor said sarcastically.

"Come on guys," Jeff said. "I know things are tense, but we have to keep going and pray those doors hold up."

Jim continued on. The tenth floor had no scratching behind the fire door. The eleventh was similarly quiet. The clawing faded below as he and his friends rose. He became aware of another sound above, but this wasn't the sound of feverish hands scratching at doors.

He stopped. "Hey, do you guys hear that?"

"Yeah, what is that?" Vik asked.

Connor laughed. "I guess someone's alive up there."

The pulsating sound became more discernible as Jim ascended the stairs to the twelfth floor; it was the bassy thump-thump of a well-endowed sound system.

"I like big butts and I cannot lie!"

The lyrics became decipherable as Jim reached the landing below the twelfth floor. He saw light filtering through the narrow gap below the fire door.

His friends all laughed as they realized they were improbably hearing the jams of Sir Mix-a-Lot. Jim was tired by this point and he knew his friends were likely exhausted too, having walked up twenty-eight flights of stairs.

He walked up to the fire door and put his ear up to it, straining to pick out something besides old school rap. He heard laughter and clinking dishes. He thought he detected a familiar voice but couldn't determine to whom it belonged.

He looked at the others and shrugged. "I guess I'll knock and see who's home." Jim turned and pounded on the steel door with his fist.

The music continued unabated.

He pounded some more, harder this time.

Still no response.

He pounded and yelled, "Hey!" as loud as he could.

Finally, the music quieted down and footsteps approached the door.

"Who's out there?" a familiar voice asked.

"Antoine? Antoine, is that you?"

"Maybe, who's asking?"

"This is Jim, Phil's brother. Please tell me Phil is still alive!"

"Jim Gibson?"

"Yes!" he yelled.

"You infected?"

"Infected with what?"

"Owasa Disease man!"

"Oh, the zombie virus? No!"

"How do I know that?"

"I feel fine!"

"That's not how it's measured man! Have you been bitten or scratched by a zombie?"

"No."

"Gotten any of their blood in your mouth, eyes or open wounds?"

"No!"

"Who's with you?"

"Jeff, Vik, Connor and Giselle."

"Who are Connor and Giselle?" he asked suspiciously.

"Connor is Jeff's roommate and Giselle is Connor's girlfriend. Now come on, is Phil alive?" Jim asked anxiously, growing tired of the interrogation.

"Are any of them infected?"

"No! Is Phil alive?"

The inquisitor grew quiet for a moment. Jim became anxious. Had Phil died? Had he become a zombie?

Suddenly Jim heard the tumblers turn as the door was unlocked. The door opened and he gasped. His brother Phil stood there, grinning. Antoine stood behind him.

"You're alive!" Jim exclaimed, embracing his brother.

"You're alive as well," Phil said, hugging him.

"Come in guys," Antoine said, motioning to the rest of the group. He closed the door once they were all inside and locked it.

"Come on in," Phil said as he walked down the hallway.

"What is all of this?" Jim asked.

"All of what? We had to secure the entire floor because," he knocked on an apartment door as he walked by, "these doors aren't exactly secure. Somehow we managed to be the only ones on the floor who weren't living with people who became zombies. We killed all of the zombies and decided to just leave the apartments all open."

"How do you guys have power? And where are all the dead zombies?"

"You've got a lot of questions little brother!" He laughed. "We moved all of the dead zombies to the floor below us and sealed them in a couple of vacant apartments. It was a gruesome job, but it had to be done."

"And the electricity?" Jeff asked.

"Well, you guys remember how they put solar panels on the roof of the terminal a couple of years ago? It was as simple as getting into the electrical room up on the top floor of this building and flipping some switches. We had to cut the power going back into the grid, as that was drawing away useful electricity and we had to cut the power going to the other floors and the rest of the terminal complex. That part was as simple as flipping the switches on some breakers. Now, we have electricity! And, the battery system down in the attic of the terminal will provide extra power for cloudy days in the winter."

"Wow," Jim replied. "That's impressive."

"I thought so myself," he replied.

"What about the elevators?"

"We switched those off. We thought it made the building less secure."

Antoine laughed. Antoine Hughes was Phil's roommate and best friend.

"Oh hey Jim!" a familiar voice said up ahead. Jim looked up and saw Sherry Walker saunter out of his brother's apartment.

"Sherry?" he asked, puzzled. Sherry had been Phil's on-again, off-again girlfriend and had most recently been his ex-girlfriend.

"Yup, in the flesh!" she said, laughing.

Jim looked at Phil. He smiled and shrugged.

They entered Phil's apartment and he motioned for them to sit on the couches. Jim sat down and stretched out.

"So, you guys walked from UB?" he asked.

"Yeah," Vikram said.

"Hmm, how many zombies did you encounter?"

"We encountered them in waves. There was a small wave at the VA, a large wave between there and Broadway, and a few stragglers between Broadway and here," Jim replied. "Of course, there were also quite a few in the plaza down there."

Phil nodded grimly. "Well, it's been a few days since any of us has heard from civil authorities. I don't want to rule out the possibility of rescue, but it seems pretty slim."

"Yeah, the government basically confined everyone to their homes without any further instruction. We encountered people who had been without food and clean water for days," Giselle said.

"Yeah, but from what I observed police were only around to arrest curfew breakers that first night. After that, they were incognito," Antoine said.

"So you guys are just holed up here?" Jim asked.

"Well, we have electricity still, and could for the foreseeable future. We still have food, although even with all of the apartments up here, we will run out eventually. And water, well, we have some miscellaneous means of obtaining it I guess," Phil replied.

"What do you mean, miscellaneous?" Jim asked.

"Well, most of the apartments up here have large supplies of bottled water. I'd imagine most of the other floors are in a similar state. Once those are gone, I guess we'll have to rely on rainwater and snowfall. We'll set up a rainwater catchment system on the roof of the terminal soon, between the solar panels."

"And what about us? How long are we welcome to stay here?" Jim asked.

"Jim, you're my brother. You and your friends are welcome to join our group and stay as long as you want or need to. You guys can all take an apartment and sleep in there. You're also welcome to join the three of us in our training regimen."

"Training regimen?" Jeff asked.

"Yeah. We watch zombie movies in the morning to analyze good anti-zombie strategies, we exercise in the afternoons, and we read in the evening."

"That sounds hardcore," Connor said flatly.

"It might be, but you never know. Right now this is a safe area, but it might get swarmed by zombies or something. Plus, we will eventually need to go find food out there. We might as well be in the best shape possible."

Later that night, after everyone else had gone to bed, Jim stayed up playing chess with Phil.

"So, you thought you might never see me again?" Phil asked.

"I feared that, yes," Jim replied as one of his pawns took one of Phil's knights.

"I feared that for you as well. I'm glad you're okay."

"Have you heard from mom?"

Phil shook his head. "I missed her call, and by the time I tried calling her back, the phones were all down. I did talk to dad and Vicki though."

"Oh?"

"Yeah, I was talking to dad when the fiasco in Seattle happened last week."

"Oh yeah, what happened?"

"Washington's closing pitcher collapsed on the mound after giving up the tying run to Seattle. He actually died on the mound. They pulled the broadcast right after he died, but Twitter was filled with reports that he came back to life and attacked his teammates."

"Wow."

"Yeah, dad was pretty shocked too. I actually heard him express concern for mom when he told me about the game. You know, her and what's his face were there with Tyler. Dad actually said he hoped they all were okay. And that was about the time the quarantine started. It was nationwide apparently."

"Wow, what did dad have to say about it?"

"He said it kind of reminded him of Nine-Eleven, just like the way people seemed to be panicking. He thought the government was overreacting and this would all blow over within a day or two."

They both laughed. "Dad was always optimistic at odd times," Jim said.

"Yeah. I haven't heard from him since then."

"Yeah," Jim nodded grimly. "But we're both still alive, so that means he might be too."

"Yeah, I don't want to rule that out. Dad's a tough guy."

"So what about Vicki?"

"I talked to her earlier that same day. She had just gotten home from a shift in the ER where all she dealt with were folks who had Owasa Disease. She said it was the most horrifying illness she had ever seen. She told me people were coming in with it who had never received the Noble Treatment. She said that she and Todd were going to probably hole up in their house if it got bad."

"Noble? What's that" Jim asked quizzically.

"Yeah! The Noble Virus. It was a virus some researcher in Baltimore created as a cure for cancer. Man, did you just not pay attention to the news last week or the week before?"

Jim shook his head.

"Late night gaming, I understand," Phil said, laughing. "Anyway, people who received this treatment had their cancer cured. The guy who created it won a Nobel Prize or something like that. Well, after a few months being cancer free they'd come down with this horrible disease where they had symptoms like rabies and then started bleeding from their eyes and mouth and stuff. Then they would die. They'd always die."

"That's awful."

"Yeah, and often there would be reports of strange noises coming from caskets at these folks' funerals. So the hospitals all adopted policies of immediate cremation. As it turns out, guess where all the zombies came from?"

"Wait, all the zombies we've encountered are people who recovered from cancer?"

"Well, not all of them. Check!"

Jim looked down at the chessboard. Phil had his king in check. He moved a pawn to block. "So how did other people get this disease?"

"Well, it looks like it spreads in a way similar to rabies. It spreads via contact with bodily fluids. So people who received the treatment got sick and died and then came back as zombies and bit the people they were living with, or bit neighbors, etcetera etcetera."

"So what happens if you get bitten?"

Phil shuddered. "You get Owasa Disease. Except, it usually moves a lot faster. Owasa Disease normally takes a few days to kill. If you contract it via a bite or contact with bodily fluids, it kills in anywhere from a couple of days down to a few minutes. Then the person comes back as a bloodthirsty zombie."

"How did you find that out?"

"This floor had about a dozen tenants last week. They all turned into zombies. We watched a few of them die after being bitten. Jim, it was terrible."

"So what you're saying is that I shouldn't get bitten?"

"Yes. If you get bitten, even though you're my brother, I will kill you. And I hope you would do the same for me. Even without the zombie part, it just looks like an awful way to die."

Jim nodded. "On our way here, we helped some people. They had wandered out of their homes and were attacked by zombies. We killed all the zombies, but some of the people were bitten by them. They've all turned into zombies by now, haven't they?"

Phil nodded. "If they haven't yet, they will."

Jim looked down. He had made a horrible mistake that would likely result in more people dying.

"You told the survivors to take care of the wounded, didn't you?"

He nodded.

"Don't beat yourself up Jim. I mean, you didn't know. There's no way you could have known."

"Phil, this is playing out a lot like the zombie movies do. I mean you guys are watching through zombie movies to develop strategies, aren't you?"

"Jim, if I had come to you last week and said that zombies were going to be here now, would you have believed me?"

He shook his head.

"Exactly. We've been put in a situation no one has any experience with. You were leading your friends, right?"

"I guess."

"The leader has to make decisions with the information he has available. He doesn't have the luxury of seeing all things at once. So he has two choices when it comes to situations he's never encountered: do nothing or make a decision and stick to it. You did the best thing you knew to do. Would you act differently now? Of course you would. But, you have to realize those people will probably get eaten by zombies either way. The chances, in the long run anyway, aren't much better for us."

"Checkmate," Jim said.

"What? How did you...? Argh!" He laughed.

"Thanks Phil, that helped."

"What did? The advice? Me letting you beat me?"

Jim laughed. "Both I suppose."

"Well, I'm glad I could be of service!" he said sarcastically.

Jim stood up and walked over to the window in the kitchen. It faced northwest, and to the left Jim could see downtown Buffalo in the distance. It was ablaze. Office towers burned in the night.

"The city's on fire, isn't it?" Phil asked, walking up behind him.

"Just downtown."

"For now. Just wait. People are rioting all over the city. At least that's how it appeared this morning, judging by all the columns of smoke."

"Man, how do you think mom and Steve are?"

"I hope mom's okay. She and I haven't seen eye to eye on much lately, but she's still our mother. Steve, honestly I couldn't care less about him."

"Yeah. He was a jerk. Have you talked to Andy lately?"

Phil shook his head. "No, I haven't talked to him since shortly after Isaiah's first birthday. He sounded like he was doing well then, but now? Who knows?"

Jim shrugged. "He's probably out on an oil platform anyway."

"Yeah. Hey, I meant to ask you if you'd heard about the DA in Boston getting assassinated?"

"I heard a bit, what happened again?"

"Someone, they think it was the mob, planted a bomb in her refrigerator. When she came home from a meeting, she opened the fridge to get something and boom!"

"That's crazy."

"I know. And, here's the crazier part; you know Steve's firm was getting investigated by her office, right?"

"What? Why?"

"I don't know little brother. Her office thought they were committing securities fraud or something probably."

"Wouldn't surprise me. Steve was a scumbag."

"Even so, he might be the only family we have left."

Jim punched his brother. "That's not funny."

"Sorry."

"It's fine."

"Anyway, little brother, I am going to bed. Sleep wherever you want, all of the apartments on this floor are unlocked."

"Thanks. Hey, I meant to ask. What's up with you and Sherry?"

Phil laughed. "Well, we aren't exactly dating and we aren't not dating. I guess you could say it's complicated."

Jim laughed. "Okay then. Goodnight."

"Goodnight Jim."

They spent the whole month of November training vigorously. Six days a week the schedule looked like this: in the morning, everyone watched zombie movies and practiced on zombies who were occupying the fifteenth floor. After lunch, they spent a couple of hours working out and then after dinner they read. One of the apartments on the twelfth floor had an incredible library within it.

The twelfth floor apartments were all two-bedroom apartments with an open floor plan. A bathroom and two bedrooms ringed the living room/kitchen. The first night there, Jim slept on Phil's couch but moved into an apartment down the hall that looked over the terminal concourse. He saw the shiny solar panels reflecting sunlight most days.

The apartment he moved into appeared to have belonged to an old man who had worked for an airline, apparently as a pilot. The walls were decorated with metal signs bearing old airline logos, and aviation memorabilia lay on shelves throughout the apartment.

There was a watch with a steel band on the nightstand next to the bed Jim slept in. It was an analog wristwatch with a TWA logo in the center of the face. The face had three dials set in it; a dial that rotated to display a moonlit starry sky and a sunlit sky alternately, and two smaller dials that displayed date and day of the week. The logo on the reverse side of the watch identified it as a Breitling. The right side of the watch had a dial to adjust time, a dial to adjust date and a fat dial whose function Jim couldn't figure out. The watch appeared to be custom made. He took the watch for himself as the owner was now deceased.

Phil also made everyone pack "bug out" bags; in the event they had to leave the building quickly, they would have all of the gear they needed to survive outside. Jim's bag had all of the items he had packed before leaving the dorm as well as a winter coat attached to it with gloves, a scarf and a hat. It also had a four-pound bag of trail mix and several pocket notebooks. He secured all of the additional items from closets in abandoned apartments throughout the building.

The wristwatch was probably the most prized possession he found. He found a manual for it in the nightstand and learned the fat knob whose purpose had been inscrutable was actually an emergency beacon that could be activated by twisting and pulling.

The group slowly cleansed the tower of zombies and explored the rest of the complex. Phil and Antoine searched endlessly for the room containing the batteries attached to the photovoltaic panels on the roof but were unable to find it. Nevertheless, they figured everyone would be fine as the batteries should have an inverter attached to prevent overcharging.

For all the bad blood Phil and Sherry once had, they got along very well, to Jim's surprise, almost like they were attempting to get back to a point where they could date again. That said, the redheaded Sherry turned out to be a pleasant woman to be around. Jeff, Vik and Jim occupied their free time by playing video games and reminiscing about childhood.

On the afternoon of Thursday, December 3rd, it was cold and snowy outside. From Jim's vantage point fourteen stories above the street, he saw zombies shuffling about stiffly in the cold. Antoine had gone downstairs with Connor and

Giselle a few hours earlier to search for the battery room. The sun broke through the cloud cover at dusk and painted the sky an angry shade of red.

Antoine and the others were still downstairs when Jim, Phil, Sherry, Vik and Jeff had dinner. Sherry cooked some chicken breasts stuffed with provolone with rice and vegetables, all pilfered from the freezers in the twelfth floor apartments. The food smelled delicious. As they ate, they mused about recent events.

"You know what really caused the zombie outbreak?" Phil asked facetiously.

"What?" Vik asked.

"The possibility of the Seattle Mariners winning the World Series!"

Everyone laughed at that thought. They had all been baseball fans before. Phil and Jim were Yankees fans, Jeff was a Mets fan and Vik was a Rangers fan.

"Do you guys smell that?" Vik asked some time later.

"Smell what? A delicious dinner?" Jim asked.

"No, I smell something, like something is burning."

Jim sniffed the air. He smelled it too, the faint odor of smoke.

"Sherry, you turned the stove and oven off, right?" Phil asked.

She nodded.

Jeff got up and walked out of the apartment, in search of the source of smoke.

"Guys! You might want to come see this!" he yelled from his apartment.

They all ran to his apartment and looked out the window. Bright orange flames leapt skyward from the roof of the concourse, illuminating the night sky in a garish color. Suddenly the power went out, plunging the floor into darkness.

"Guys, grab your bug out bags and let's head downstairs!" Phil yelled.

"What about the others' bags?" Jim asked.

"Grab them! Hopefully they'll make it out too!"

They hurriedly grabbed their bags and made their way to the fire door. Jim had his backpack on with his coat tied around it and held his pry bar in one hand and a flashlight in the other hand.

Phil opened the door and they started down the stairs. As they descended, the air became thick with smoke.

"Pull your shirts over your faces guys! And duck down, we don't want to suffocate!" Vikram yelled.

They continued their descent but paused around the fifth floor. Jim heard pained screams coming from below accompanied by hurried footsteps. He and the others ran down to investigate and almost ran into Connor as he carried Giselle upstairs.

She was moaning in agony and in the dim light appeared to be badly burned. Connor was covered with soot.

"Guys! There's a fire!" Connor said breathlessly.

"Where's Antoine?" Phil asked.

"He's dead!"

"Come on! We've got to get out of here! We have your bags!" Jim said urgently.

They continued down the stairs as Giselle moaned in pain. When they reached the mezzanine level, Phil and Jim ran over to the windowed door that looked out upon the interior of the terminal.

The massive hall was ablaze. Flaming timbers fell from the ceiling and Jim saw one of the ceiling vaults collapse.

"Come on, let's go this way!" Phil said, running down the stairs. Everyone followed him out the side door of the tower. Jim gasped when they made it outside; there were hundreds of zombies in the courtyard.

The others immediately surrounded Connor and Giselle in a circle and began fighting off the insatiable undead. The cold night air was filled with the smell of smoke and decay and the sounds of war cries and the zombies' roars. The group hacked their way through the horde until a ring of corpses lay all around. Then Jim and Vik helped Connor and Giselle over the dead zombies and everyone made their way across the plaza as flames burst out of windows in the tower behind them. They stopped in a small grove of trees a few hundred feet from the tower and Connor laid Giselle down in the snow. Her moans had become quiet by now.

"Come on Giselle, hang in there," he said quietly, holding her hand.

Jeff shone his flashlight on her and Jim gasped as he beheld the severity of her injuries. Her shirt had melted into her skin and the flesh on her arms was charred.

"What happened Connor?" Jeff asked.

"We found the battery room. It had zombies in it. When we got in, Antoine swung his knife at one and pushed the zombie into an electrical cable. His knife's blade nicked the wire and he electrocuted himself. At the same time, the zombie burst into flames and we had just enough time to escape the room before the whole attic area ignited. A burning timber fell on Giselle. I went back to rescue her and I lifted the beam off her," he paused, showing his hands. The skin was red and blistered. "She's going to die, isn't she?"

"I don't know man," Jeff said.

"She is. None of us are doctors. None of us have the degree of medical knowledge necessary to treat her. It's snowing, it's cold and we don't have a sterile environment for her. I'm no pre-med student but even I know this looks bad," he said glumly.

Giselle moved her legs a little.

"Even if she lives through the night, we have no way to fix her wounds. Her shirt melted into her skin. I mean, that will get infected. So even if she survives through the night, she's going to die of infection," he said.

The tower was ablaze now, flames shooting forth from every window.

"Guys, we need to get somewhere that's easily defendable," Phil said urgently. "We just killed several dozen zombies, but more will come. We also need to get Giselle out of the cold."

"Let's try over there!" Vik said, pointing to the neighborhood that sat across a field from the terminal complex.

"I guess that's as good as we can do for now," Phil said quietly. "Let's go!"

Connor scooped Giselle up into his arms. She whimpered.

"I know babe, I know. We'll get you to shelter soon," he said.

"Why Connor? Why? My arms are on fire!" she cried out.

Jim and the others ran across the field in a circle around Connor and Giselle. Phil led the way, Vik and Sherry had each side and Jeff and Jim ran behind everyone. Jim looked around, trying to see if zombies were near. They were, of course.

The snowy field was slippery beneath Jim's feet, but somehow he avoided slipping. He and the others finally reached a small one and a half story house.

Phil tried the door and found that it was unlocked. The smell of death emanated from the darkened portal.

"Alright, me and Vik are going to go inside to make sure there are no zombies. Jim, you, Jeff and Sherry will stay out here with Connor and Giselle. Okay?" Phil said.

"Yeah," Jim said.

They ran in. Jim saw several zombies moving across the field toward the house in the light cast by the blazing tower.

"I'm sorry Connor, I'm sorry," Giselle moaned.

"It's okay Giselle," he said. He whispered something in her ear.

"All clear guys," Vik said from the doorway.

They went inside and closed the door. Jim leaned against the closed door as Jeff started a fire in the fireplace. Connor carried Giselle upstairs behind Phil. Vik walked up to Jim.

"She's going to die, I think."

Jim nodded solemnly.

Jeff muttered something under his breath.

Phil came downstairs a couple of minutes later.

"Hey Jeff, see if there's any bottled water please," he said.

"Okay Phil," Jeff replied, walking into the darkened kitchen. A few seconds later, he ran upstairs carrying a few bottles of water.

"Jim, come look at the tower," Vik said.

Jim walked over to watch the fire. The whole complex was burning. Suddenly a huge cloud of embers shot upward from behind the tower.

"I guess the concourse collapsed," Vik said quietly.

"Yeah."

A few minutes later the tower began to lean to the right a little.

"The tower look like it's leaning?" Jim asked.

Vik tilted his head. "Yes. It won't be long before it collapses. Look! The zombies are swarming around the tower!"

"Like moths drawn to a flame," Jim muttered. He looked down at his watch. It was just before midnight. "Hey, help me move the entertainment center in front of the door."

"Okay," Vik said as he followed Jim over to the entertainment center.

They took the TV off and carried the wooden entertainment center over to the door. That finished, they went back over to the window to watch the fire.

Jim heard footsteps behind him. He turned and saw Phil and Jeff walking down the stairs. "How's she doing?"

Jeff shook his head.

"We got her burns cleaned as best as we could. The burns on her torso are bad enough that she didn't feel us cleaning them," Phil said grimly. "She's asleep now. Connor's up there with her. If she lives through the night, we'll go look for antibiotics and pain meds tomorrow. That's a big if though."

Jim nodded as they walked over to the window. "Why not go tonight?"

Phil made a noise. "Where are we going to go? The closest hospital is more than two miles away. It's cold and snowy, it's dark, and there are thousands of zombies out there. If we send someone to go get antibiotics, I don't think they're going to make it back."

"Hey, where's Sherry?" he asked.

"Upstairs with them," Phil said.

"Man, look at it burn!" Jeff said in amazement.

Suddenly the tower began to lean even further to the right.

"It's going to go soon," Vik said.

Jim grunted in agreement.

It started to shift.

"There it goes," Jeff said.

It collapsed to the right, on top of where the concourse had been, with a tremendous roar. It sent a large plume of embers and flame and snow and dust skyward. Everyone whistled in response as the plume of dust swept over the house.

They watched the rubble burn for a while. Finally, Phil spoke up.

"Who wants first watch?"

"I'll take it," Jim volunteered.

"Okay. The rest of us should try to get some sleep. We can sort out our plans tomorrow."

"Goodnight guys," Jim said, sitting down in a chair near the window. It was now 1:34 am.

Zombies continued to shuffle across the field, drawn to the burning rubble. Jim watched for a while and gradually felt his eyes grow heavy.

"I'll just rest my eyes for a moment," he mumbled quietly.

He woke up with a start. How long had he been asleep? He looked out the window and saw that dawn was near. The sky was glowing a dark blue. Across the field the ruins of the New York Central Terminal still burned. He looked around. The house was quiet except for the crackle of the fireplace and the sound of three men snoring.

Jim shook his head. He had fallen asleep during his watch! What if a zombie had gotten in? At the very least he probably would have been bitten. He sighed.

Jeff stirred. "Hey! What time is it?" he whispered.

"A bit before six thirty."

"Get some sleep man. I'll take watch," he said, walking up to the chair.

"You sure?" Jim asked. "I just woke up myself. I must have fallen asleep at some point."

He chuckled. "Yeah man, go lay down. You still kept watch longer than any of us."

"Okay," Jim said, standing up. He walked over to the fireplace and placed another log on the embers. Then he lay down on the floor and fell back asleep.

"They both slept through the night," Jim heard Sherry say as he woke up later.

He sat up rubbing his eyes.

"Good morning sunshine!" Phil said.

"Hey," he replied groggily.

"Well, we'll see how she's doing today," Phil said to Sherry.

Vik and Jeff were over at the window watching the smoldering rubble.

Footsteps echoed upstairs. Jim turned toward the stairs. Connor walked down quietly.

"She died sometime in the night," he said softly.

Sherry and Jeff walked over to him and hugged him.

"I mean, I guess I was prepared for the possibility," he said. "I don't know. It just sucks. She suffered a lot."

"Yeah," Jeff said, hugging him.

The group spent the morning quietly grieving for Giselle. Around midday they wrapped her body in a white sheet, carried her outside and dug a grave for her with shovels from the house's garage.

"Giselle Janae Jackson was my girlfriend," Connor said shakily as Jim and Jeff lowered her body into the ground. "We hadn't been dating long, but we enjoyed a lot of good times together. She taught me that even in the midst of death, joy could be experienced."

The others murmured in agreement.

"In the short time we had together, I got to see that Giselle was a sweet young lady," Sherry said. "She had a real interest in others and she'll be missed."

"Yeah, she was a caring person," Jim said. "When we saved those folks on Bailey Avenue from zombies, she was busy comforting the women and children while we were killing zombies. She played an important part in our group."

They shoveled dirt onto her body until the grave was filled in. Then they turned and walked back into the house. It was bitterly cold outside. When Jim walked back into the kitchen he saw where the smell of death had been coming from; a dead woman sat in the corner slumped over on a stool.

That evening the group sat around the fireplace.

"So where do we go from here?" Vik asked.

"Well, I guess me and Jim are going to head west to Detroit to see if our dad is still alive. I mean, most of our family is to the west," Phil said.

Jim nodded. "Yeah, I guess we are going to head west."

"Well, I'm going to head east to New York City," Jeff said. "All my family is out there. It's nothing personal. Jim, you're my best friend. But I need to see if *my* family is okay."

"I understand Jeff," Jim said.

"I'll go with Jeff," Connor said.

"I guess I'll go with Phil and Jim," Sherry said.

"Me too," Vik said. "I'll go with Jim and Phil."

"Alright, we'll set out in the morning," Phil said.

CHAPTER SEVENTEEN

Randy Eccleston
Day 6

"Hey Randy, wake up."

He sat up in the dark. "What is it?" he asked.

"Jamie and Juan are downstairs," Adam replied. "Eating breakfast. We're all going to set out in a little bit."

"Thanks," Randy said as he rubbed his eyes. "What time is it?" He looked down at his watch. It was 6:00am.

"How'd you sleep?" Adam asked.

"Like a rock. You?"

"The same. It was nice to sleep on soft carpet."

"Yeah, it was."

"I'll see you downstairs," he said as he walked out of the dark room.

Randy stood up and stretched and then put his shoes back on. Then he walked downstairs. The others were all sitting in the dark dining room eating dry cereal and granola bars.

"Good morning Sunshine," Casey said as he munched on what appeared to be Froot Loops.

"Good morning Cupcake," Randy replied. "What's for breakfast?"

"Cereal and granola," Jamie replied. "Juan has Cheerios, Froot Loops and Frosted Flakes. Bowls are in the cabinet above the sink."

Randy walked over to the sink and grabbed a bowl from the cabinet. Then he grabbed the box of Cheerios and poured himself a bowl. He walked over and sat down at the table.

"If you're thirsty, there's still tap water," Juan said. "They cut the power a few days ago, but there's still plenty of water pressure. I noticed that some areas still have power, so they might have kept the water treatment plant going so they could have clean water too."

Randy nodded as he took a bite of dry cereal. "That makes sense I suppose."

"Alright guys, let's go over our weapon inventory. I don't want any of us to get killed out there," Jamie said.

"Agreed," Randy replied.

"Juan and I have three M-Four rifles with approximately six hundred rounds between the two of us. We also have three M-Nineteen-Eleven pistols with about a thousand rounds. We also have four M-Eighty-Four flash bang grenades. What do you all have?"

"We have nothing. All of our guns got burned up in the truck when the soldiers stopped us," Randy replied.

"There are five of you," Juan said.

"Yes, I had a machine gun, I think it was an AR-Fifteen," Casey said. "It got destroyed when those soldiers torched our truck."

"Ah," Juan replied. "You can use our extra rifle, if you'd like?"

"Sure," Casey said. "That sounds great. Thank you."

"The rest of you can take the pistols, if that's okay? There's a couple of crowbars out in the garage too."

Randy nodded. "That'll be fine."

"Okay, now that we have that figured out, let's discuss today's goals," Jamie said as he unfolded a map of the area on the table. He turned on a flashlight and aimed it down at the map. "Juan and I have covered from East Empire Street," he pointed, "all the way down south to South Morris Avenue," he pointed again. "We'd like to maybe send one group out along East Empire Street and have them go north along the perimeter, and then we'll have the other group go to South Morris Avenue and work their way down to the southwest corner of the perimeter and then back north. We'll leave as soon as we get our gear ready and then return here before sundown. Remember, the goal is to not get noticed. Attention is bad."

"Why don't we take the north route?" Randy suggested.

"That's what I was thinking too. We'll send Juan, Casey and Missy down to South Morris Avenue and me, you, Adam and Jillian will work our way from Empire Street to the north."

"Okay, let's do this."

"One last thing," Juan said. "If you encounter a zombie, only severe head trauma will kill it."

"Like a gunshot?" Missy asked.

"Yes. But I think any type of severe trauma that punctures the skull and destroys the brain will do the trick," he said.

Everyone walked out onto the front porch a short time later. Randy hugged Casey and Missy.

"Be careful guys," he said. "Come back here alive, okay?"

"We will man, you guys be careful too," Casey said.

"Alright, we should be okay walking out in the open for now," Jamie said as they walked south on North Linden Street. "Patrols come through here at Five-Thirty and Eleven-Thirty, AM and PM. Just be alert. If you hear any vehicles approaching, get out of sight as quickly as possible."

Randy nodded. "Sounds good."

They passed the eastern perimeter of ISU and kept walking. It was chilly.

"So, where did you grow up originally Randy?" Jamie asked.

"Chicago. I've lived there my whole life."

"That's cool. Big city boy?"

He laughed. "Sort of. I live in the city now. When I still lived with my parents, we lived pretty far out from the city center. Now they live in a suburb north of Chicago, near the lake."

"I'm originally from Des Plaines myself," Jamie said.

"That's cool."

"Yeah. We moved to West Virginia when I was little so my stepdad could find work. It sucked."

"I can imagine."

"So you have a brother in Chicago?"

Randy nodded. "Yeah, I have an older brother named Todd."

"That's cool."

"Yeah, I hope he's okay. I'm anxious to get up there and see how he, his wife and their kids are doing."

"Yeah."

"What about you? You said last night you have a little sister and siblings. Anyone else?"

"I've got a younger brother named Shelby and a little sister named Krissy," Jamie said. "I'm about three years older than Shelby and six years older than Krissy. I haven't talked to them in a while. Shelby lives down in Louisville. He and I had a falling out this last summer after our mom died. I don't know about Krissy. I know she lives in Alabama somewhere, but I haven't talked to her since before I went to prison."

"Wow," Jillian said.

"What about you, Jillian?" Jamie asked.

"Yeah, I've got an older brother who's stationed over in South Korea in the Navy. He's a doctor."

"That's really cool. You, Adam?"

"I'm an only child," Adam replied.

"Lucky," Jamie said as he laughed.

"I guess."

They crossed East Emerson Street and continued on. Randy marveled at how quiet the city was. Aside from the occasional distant gunshot and distant explosion, the city was still.

Suddenly Jamie raised his gun and fired ahead. Randy looked up and saw an infected person fall over.

"Whoa," Adam said. "I didn't even see him."

"Yeah. You've got to be careful. They can come out of nowhere and their bite is always fatal."

Randy nodded. "So you're sure they're undead denizens and not just people who are horribly ill?"

"You tell me," Jamie said. "Here comes another."

Randy saw an infected man stumbling toward them.

"Watch," Jamie said. He shot the infected man in the chest and he fell over. A few seconds later, the man got back up and resumed his approach. Jamie shot him again in the chest. The man fell over and got back up again.

Randy watched with curiosity and horror.

"Here, check this out," Jamie said. He laid his gun down and pulled a knife out. Then he walked over and slashed the man's throat. There was surprisingly little blood. He stepped back and everyone watched as the man got back up and continued his advance toward them.

"Wow," Randy murmured.

"Yeah. If that guy was alive, he would be seconds away from death right now. Instead, he just keeps coming. Oh yeah, do you smell that?"

Randy nodded. The man smelled like decay.

"He's rotting," Jamie said as he picked his gun back up. He pointed the rifle and fired at the man's head. He fell over, dead.

"I guess zombies are real," Adam said.

"Let's keep going, we're making good time."

They continued on. Jamie led them east on East Empire Street when they reached it. The streets were surprisingly clear. They passed a school.

"You see that up ahead?" Jamie asked, pointing.

Randy squinted his eyes in the morning sunlight. He saw several buses blocking the road. He nodded.

"That's the roadblock. Come on, we'll cut through that parking lot behind the building."

They walked for hours through parking lots behind warehouses and office buildings and stores. They would peek at the perimeter occasionally. The soldiers had set up a double layer of chain link fences topped with spiral razor wire along the road. Randy noticed a Humvee with a guard every few hundred yards.

Around 10:00am, they approached a stopped train on some tracks.

"We should climb up there to get a good view of what's ahead," Adam suggested.

Randy climbed the box car first, then Adam, Jillian and Jamie followed. He surveyed the path ahead and saw a large empty field stretching from their position all the way to the northern perimeter perhaps two miles away.

"Whoa," Jamie said. "We'd better circle around the edge of the field. See all the Humvees along the perimeter?"

Randy nodded.

"Follow me," he said as he climbed down from the black tanker car.

They followed Jamie southwest along the railroad tracks to an overpass. They left the tracks and climbed up an embankment to the road. The followed him north. As they passed an intersection, Randy saw that they were on Towanda Avenue. They passed a neighborhood full of mansions.

"Good old suburbia," Jillian said as they walked.

"Look alive, there might be a lot of zombies in these houses," Jamie said. "See all the red sheets in the windows?"

Randy nodded.

Gunfire echoed in the distance behind them. Explosions followed.

The neighborhood to the left gave way to a large field that led up to lots in various stages of development. Soon Randy and the others crossed East Raab Road and continued north. Towanda Avenue narrowed to two lanes. They were nearing the northern perimeter. The road inclined ahead.

Jamie motioned for them to crouch a little and stay quiet as the road entered a narrow grove of trees. They crept forward perhaps another two hundred feet and came to a break in the pavement. There had once been an overpass running over the highway here. The soldiers had apparently demolished it, however, for fifteen feet below a hastily constructed chain-link fence ran from east to west across the shattered remains of the bridge. Randy saw a trio of Humvees a few hundred yards to the west. Another trio sat parked about a quarter mile to the east.

"Come on," Jamie whispered. "This segment of the perimeter is too heavily guarded."

They walked south on Towanda Road and then Jamie led them west on Beech Street. A hilly embankment covered with yellowing grass sat to the right, obscuring their view of the interstate. To the left lay a neighborhood in the early stages of development. Up ahead, the road curved to the south, away from the perimeter. They left the road and cut through several backyards. Every third house they passed had scratching noises emanating from within.

"Do you suppose there are zombies in there?" Jillian asked.

Jamie nodded grimly. "Yes."

Around 1:00pm they reached North Main Street. As they had continued west, the perimeter had grown even more heavily guarded. Jamie had become discouraged.

"That's probably the most secure I've seen it," he said.

Randy nodded. "Even so, there has to be a hole somewhere, a weakness. We just need to find it."

"Yeah, well, let's get going south. We should start back to the house so we can make it by dark. As we get closer to the center of the area, we'll encounter more patrols that will inevitably slow us down," he said.

They walked for a while and came upon a large park to the right. Hundreds of zombies were swarming around a playground within the park.

"Look out guys," Randy said. "There are a bunch of zombies in there."

Jamie gasped. "That is a lot of zombies! They all look preoccupied though."

Suddenly Randy heard a woman scream from within the park.

"That sounded like it came from the center of the horde!" Adam said.

Jamie nodded.

"Help! Please help! I'm trapped!" the woman screamed.

"Come on guys! We've got to help her!" Jillian exclaimed.

"We don't know if she's someone we should be rescuing," Jamie replied.

"What if she's with the Wolf Pack?" Randy asked. "Still, Jillian's right. Let's get a little closer and see if we can determine who she is."

They crept toward the edge of the horde and toward the playground. The zombies had completely encircled the playground equipment. The zombies paid them no attention as the survivors tried to peer over them.

Randy saw a sycamore nearby that looked easy to climb. He looked up and studied it for a moment. The leaves had almost all fallen off the towering tree. He could perhaps climb halfway up and get a good view of the screaming woman. He reached up, grabbed a branch and pulled himself up. He clambered from branch to branch until he was about twenty feet up.

"Please help!" the woman screamed again. Randy could see her clearly from up here. She was standing atop the monkey bars of a jungle gym that stood about eight feet above the shredded rubber padding on the ground; she was just inches out of the reach of the zombies below her. She had shoulder-length curly brown hair and was wearing a dark red jacket. She also had a crossbow strapped to her back. She looked familiar, like he had seen her somewhere before.

"Who are you?" he called to her.

"What? Who are you?" she yelled back.

"Not important. What is more important to us before we attempt to rescue you is your identity," he replied.

"My name is Penny Holloway!" she yelled.

"Penny Holloway?" Jamie asked from the ground. "Isn't she the host of that show?"

"You're the host of Survive This, aren't you?" Randy asked her.

"Yes! I am the host! Please, just find a way to get me down!"

Randy looked around and saw a parking lot nearby that had several cars parked in it.

"Hey Jamie! These things are drawn to loud noise, aren't they?" he asked.

Jamie nodded.

"Let's go see if any of those cars have car alarms on them!"

"That's a great idea Randy! Come on guys, let's go make a ruckus!" Jamie led Adam and Jillian over to the parking lot while Randy remained in the tree.

"What's your name?" Penny asked.

"Randy, Randy Eccleston!"

"Please don't leave me Randy!"

"I won't," he yelled.

He heard the sound of breaking glass and several car alarms began to go off. He looked down at the surging mass of infected humans and wondered if this would work. Slowly, the zombies began walking away from the playground, toward the parking lot one at a time. Soon more and more of them began moving toward the cacophony. Eventually, they had all left.

He climbed down from the tree and ran over to Penny. He saw where she had shot a few zombies with her crossbow. He helped her down as the others rejoined them.

"Thanks Randy," she said, hugging him. She smelled horrible, like she hadn't showered in days.

"You're welcome Penny," he said, trying not to wrinkle his nose.

"Save the introductions for the walk back guys, we've got to get out of here fast. First, that's a lot of zombies we just momentarily distracted. Second, we just created a lot of noise that is going to attract the attention of more zombies and soldiers. We've got to scoot!" Jamie said.

They ran back to North Main Street and followed Jamie north to West Summit Street. They followed him to the right into an older neighborhood.

Suddenly, the sound of diesel engines could be heard.

"Hide!" Jamie said urgently.

They all ran into a carport and ducked behind a parked car as three APCs rolled by.

Jamie sighed in relief. "That was close," he said quietly.

Randy nodded.

"Who are you guys?" Penny asked.

"Just some people trying to get out of town, Miss," Jamie replied.

"Okay."

"I'm Adam Doss," Adam introduced himself.

"I'm Jillian Wilson," Jillian said.

"I'm Jamie Daniels," Jamie said.

"Alright, I'm Penny Holloway," Penny said.

"Alright, that's great. Now, let's get going," Jamie said.

They continued on, walking east on West Summit Street.

"How did you end up like that, on the playground?" Randy asked Penny.

"Well, I was running from a bunch of soldiers in hazmat suits and I thought I had given them the slip. Suddenly, there were zombies chasing me and as I ran,

I realized I was slowly being encircled by the undead! I saw the jungle gym in the playground and I hurriedly climbed it. Then I realized I was trapped. I figured either the zombies were going to get me if I fell off or if an especially tall zombie happened along, or the soldiers would get me with their flamethrowers. I honestly thought you guys were soldiers at first."

"Yeah, we thought you might be a soldier too," Adam said.

She laughed darkly. "Those guys are terrible! I passed by some kind of battle going on between them and a motley assortment of uninfected people today south of downtown. I can't believe they are using so many flamethrowers! From a tactical perspective, those are dangerous tools to dispatch zombies with. They don't have a very long range, they're heavy, they're dangerous to the operator, the list of cons goes on and on and on and on."

"But the psychological impact is tremendous," Randy said.

"Yeah, but who are they trying to spook? It's not like any of the people who succumbed to Owasa Disease are influenced by fear once they become zombies."

"Think about all the people you saw today fighting with the soldiers. How much do you think it would impact you to see your best friend get torched with a flamethrower?" Randy asked.

She visibly shuddered. "I had to endure and witness a lot of things on my TV show, but I had never seen a human being die by immolation."

"It's pretty awful," Jamie said as they turned on to North Linden.

"Where are you all from?" she asked.

"Me, Adam and Jillian are all from Chicago," Randy said.

"I'm from Southern Illinois," Jamie said.

"How did you all meet?" she asked.

Randy laughed.

"No, really! You guys are headed in opposite directions right?"

"I saved their skin," Jamie said.

"Yeah, we were about to get torched when he and another guy named Juan saved us," Adam said.

"Yeah, we have two other friends who are with Juan," Randy said. "Now, where are you from?"

"Phoenix," she said.

"Wow, you've come a long way in a short time!" Jillian said.

"I commandeered a helicopter and that got me most of the way here," Penny said.

"Wow," Randy said.

She laughed. "Well, you know, hosting that show helped me acquire some useful skills."

That evening they all gathered in a circle in Juan's garage. The group had grown to eight.

"So where are you all headed?" Penny asked.

"Chicago," Randy said.

"But you told me earlier that you all were coming from Chicago," Penny said, a confused expression on her face.

"No, that's where we are from originally; me, Adam, Jillian and Casey. We're coming from Saint Louis, Missouri though. Me, Adam and Jillian were there visiting Casey and Missy when everything went down. Then we decided to head back to Chicago," he explained.

"And we decided to come with them," Missy said.

"Oh, okay. That makes sense now," she said, laughing.

"I don't know where I am heading once I escape from Bloomington-Normal," Juan said.

"I think I'm going to go with them to Chicago," Jamie said.

"Well, it's funny that five of you are headed to Chicago, because that's where I'm headed too!" Penny said.

"Really?" Adam asked.

"Yup! I have extended family I hope to find there."

"Penny, your optimism is welcome here," Juan said. "But I don't think you'll find them."

She shot him a cold look. "Why would you say something like that?"

"I'm sorry Penny, I guess it's just the insurance guy in me," he said as he looked down at the floor.

"I really hope they're still alive! I mean, come on! My parents are dead! My boyfriend is dead! All of my friends are dead! If my family in Chicago is dead, then I have nothing left, no one left in this world!" She started to cry.

Randy stood up and walked over to her. He put his arm around her.

"Thanks Randy," she said quietly.

"I'm sorry Penny," Juan said. "I shouldn't have said that."

"No, it's okay," she said, blowing her nose into Randy's sleeve. "I mean, I see where you're coming from."

"Even so, I'm sorry."

"I forgive you Juan."

They all sat there for a few minutes in silence.

Finally, Jamie cleared his throat. "Alright, so in addition to rescuing Penny, we also followed the perimeter from Empire Street all the way north to North Main Street. It was pretty secure. What about you guys?"

"We followed it from South Morris Avenue, where you and I had left off Jamie, to West Washington Street. We saw a secure perimeter and witnessed several battles between soldiers and uninfected residents. It looks like several neighborhoods in Southwest Bloomington banded together to begin battling the soldiers," Juan replied.

"Really?" Jamie asked.

"Yeah, it looked like they were pretty evenly matched," Casey said.

"Huh, maybe we can help them retake the area," Jamie said. "Maybe we just need to find the rebels and link up with them."

"If I could add something?" Penny interrupted. "I saw similar battles from a different angle. It looked like the 'rebels,'" she made quote marks with her hands, "were getting their butts handed to them. Besides, I came in from the west side along College Avenue. After I passed the skirmish between soldiers and rebels, I saw thousands of zombies. Even if the rebels manage to defeat the soldiers, what are they going to do about the zombies?"

"She has a good point," Randy said.

"Penny, Randy, the zombies could be dispatched with organized resistance probably," Juan said.

"No, I disagree," she said. "I saw every military post between Phoenix and Albuquerque get overrun by zombies."

"What about the ones past Albuquerque?" Jamie asked.

"They were all overrun. Zombified soldiers roamed the grounds. I notice that all of you have guns. Those are great at taking care of flamethrower-wielding soldiers, but terrible at taking out zombies."

"How so?" Jamie asked.

"They require a great deal of accuracy to deliver a fatal blow to a zombie, they produce a lot of noise that attracts more zombies, and they require a limited resource: bullets."

"Okay, I see your point. But what about you? Your crossbow might not make much noise but it still requires a lot of accuracy and requires arrows," he said.

"Bolts," she said, correcting him.

"Yeah, whatever."

"Maybe so, but I can easily reuse bolts. Plus, I have a lot of training using a crossbow. I'm guessing you all don't have much training with guns, do you? Let's see, our motley group has an insurance salesman, a sound engineer, a Wal-Mart cashier, a blood bank guy, an accountant and a music teacher. None of those jobs screams 'expert marksman' to me."

"Okay, so what, we should walk around with swords?" Jamie asked.

"Well, if you can find one, sure. I'd recommend just having a handy weapon to crush skulls with, like a baseball bat."

"Or tire iron," Adam said.

"Or crowbar," Casey said.

"Sure," Penny replied. "Something that doesn't require bullets or ammunition that can still get the job done."

Suddenly the garage shook as several helicopters flew overhead.

"Helicopters?" Casey asked aloud. "I didn't know these guys had helicopters."

"We told you they had seized the airport east of here," Juan said. "Still, they hadn't flown anything in or out of it since seizing it."

"Hmm," Jamie said. "We should probably set up a watch rotation, so that we have someone awake tonight. The soldiers may have just gotten reinforcements."

CHAPTER EIGHTEEN

Adam Doss
Day 7

"Adam, wake up buddy, it's your turn at watch."

Adam sat up and saw Casey silhouetted in the dark.

"Quiet night?" he asked.

"Here, yes. There's been a lot of gunfire in the distance. There have also been more helicopters flying nearby. I guess the soldiers are dropping the hammer on the rebels."

Adam nodded. "Thanks." He stood up. "Get some sleep Casey."

"Thanks man, good night."

Adam walked downstairs and sat down at the foot of the stairs, pistol in hand. He heard the distant gunfire Casey had mentioned. He closed his eyes for a moment and sighed. He hoped it would be a quiet night.

He sat there for a while and then stood up to stretch. He walked around the darkened house and returned to the stairs and sat back down.

He thought about his parents. He wondered if they were still alive. He had honestly been optimistic, but Penny's description of what things were like now sort of shot down his hopes. Still, he was determined to return to Valparaiso and see for himself if his parents were still alive.

He thought about the little ranch style house he had grown up in; 250 Michigan Avenue. He thought about his dad. He had been a tax lawyer who had encouraged him to be an accountant. Adam had looked up to him so much.

Adam shook his head and realized he was crying.

He thought back to the last time he had seen his parents, during Labor Day weekend.

"So Adam, when are you going to pop the question to Jill?" his dad had asked him as they stood in the kitchen. Jill and his mom were outside on the back patio.

"I don't know dad. Probably in the spring."

"Good. You know son, I'm proud of you. You keep doing everything like you have been and I can see you ascending to the top by the time you're forty."

"Thanks dad."

"Have you and Jill talked about kids yet?"

"Yeah, we're thinking after we get married."

"Good, good. How's Mass been?"

"Honestly dad, I haven't been in a few months."

"It's okay son," he said, patting Adam on the back. *"I just figured I'd ask. You know how your mother is, she's always asking about you and praying for you."*

"Yeah."

Adam awoke with a start. What had woken him up?

He heard something on the front porch get knocked over. He peered around the corner and saw a shadowy figure standing on the front porch scratching at the window. He realized it was a zombie. He felt around for his pistol and found it on the step above where he was sitting. He picked it up and watched the zombie shuffle around on the porch. It looked like it was sniffing the air.

After a few tense moments it turned and ambled off the porch. Adam walked into the living room and watched it stagger out to the street and continue walking away. He looked down at his watch. It was 5:20am. Everyone would be getting up soon.

He yawned and stretched his arms as an explosion rumbled in the distance. It sounded like the soldiers' campaign to eliminate the rebels had been running all night.

He shook his head. They needed to find a hole in the perimeter and escape soon.

"Quiet night?" he heard Juan on the steps above him.

"Yeah," he said.

"The morning patrol should be coming through any minute," Juan said.

Adam nodded. "It sounds like a battle has been going all night."

"Yes, I'm quite concerned. We need to make escape a priority."

"I thought it already was a priority?"

"We need to make it more of a priority now," Juan said as he walked down and sat down a few steps above Adam. "With Penny, we can possibly divide into three groups to probe the perimeter now."

"Yeah, we can I suppose."

Soon several Humvees rolled by outside. They continued on without stopping. Everyone woke up soon after that.

"Alright, today we're going to split into three groups," Juan said as everyone ate breakfast. "Escape is our top priority."

"Me, Adam and Penny," Randy said.

Adam looked at Jillian. She shrugged.

"I'll take Casey," Juan said.

"Fine, I'll take Jillian and Missy," Jamie said.

"Alright, Jamie, why don't you and the ladies go back to where you left off yesterday on North Main? Randy, why don't you guys head west to West College and I-Fifty-Five and head south and Casey and I will go to West Washington and head north to Randy and crew?" Juan suggested.

"Sounds good," Jamie said.

"Sounds alright to me," Randy said.

"Alright, let's set out after breakfast."

A few hours later a cold wind blew as Adam, Randy and Penny crossed Cottage Avenue. They had walked for a couple of hours and had each found some tools to supplement their armaments. Adam had grabbed a crowbar, Randy had grabbed a baseball bat and Penny had grabbed a three-foot long piece of rebar.

It had been a quiet walk so far when they reached Cottage Avenue. Suddenly, zombies emerged from a house a few dozen yards away.

"Uh guys," Adam said. "I think we're going to get to test our weapons."

"Remember," Penny said. "Swing for the head."

Adam ran toward the zombies and swung the hooked end of his crowbar into the skull of the first one he reached. It collapsed with a growl. He pulled the bar out and swung it into the eye of another zombie.

He stepped back as Randy and Penny each dispatched a trio of undead.

"Nice work guys," Randy said.

"Indeed. It's nice to have some help," Penny said.

"So Penny," Adam asked as they resumed their walk west. "I think you've figured out by now that we're all huge fans of your show!"

She laughed. "I figured as much. You all recognized me."

"My favorite episode is when you were in the Atacama Desert and had to eat scorpions to survive!" Randy gushed.

She laughed again. "Yeah, I hear that a lot. That was actually my least favorite episode to tape. I seriously got stung by scorpions at least four times!"

"That sounds painful," Adam said.

"It was."

"My favorite episode is probably the one where you had to escape the glacier in Greenland. The ice caves were beautiful."

"Yeah, the aurora borealis were pretty too," Randy said.

"Thanks guys. I'd like to think that show prepared me for this," she said.

Adam nodded. "I'm sure all the survival skills help."

Soon they neared the perimeter. Adam watched as Penny studied it through binoculars.

"I see two Humvees and some chain-link fence up ahead," she said. She lowered the binoculars. "You know, I came in just south of here. If I remember correctly, nobody was guarding the perimeter down there."

"Let's check it out," Randy said.

They wound their way south through a subdivision to West Hovey Avenue, killing a few zombies along the way. They turned onto the road and walked west. Suddenly Adam heard gunfire up ahead and screaming.

They ran forward to a warehouse on the right. Adam peered around the corner and saw dozens of soldiers shooting at hundreds of zombies surrounding them. It was clear the soldiers were significantly outnumbered.

"Let's watch this," Randy said. "I want to see what happens."

"You're going to see what organized resistance with firearms accomplishes," Penny said grimly.

They watched for forty-five minutes as the soldiers were gradually picked off by zombies. At around noon the last soldier screamed loudly and then quit firing his gun. The field grew eerily quiet except for the sound of flesh being ripped from corpses.

Adam shuddered.

"We should keep going," Randy said.

"We just found a breach in the perimeter," he countered. "We should head back and wait for the others."

"Adam, they'll refill this place with soldiers by the time we get back here."

"Maybe, but we have to at least try! I mean, surely their numbers are getting depleted."

"Unless those choppers overnight were resupplying them. We have no idea how many soldiers there are now."

"Guys, I think Randy is right. We need to keep moving south," Penny said. "Even if we head back now, you guys said last night that you typically go late into the afternoon. So, no one will be at the house."

"Yeah, I guess you're right Penny," Adam conceded. "Still, we have to tell the others about this as soon as possible!"

"Well, let's get going," Randy said. "I'd like to not get surrounded by those zombies."

They continued south and a short time after they crossed West Hovey, they were forced to turn back. They had come upon a horde of zombies that stretched for hundreds of yards. There must have been thousands of zombies in the crowd. Additionally, Adam saw the telltale plumes of flames shooting up at the far edge of the horde; soldiers were fighting their way through the horde toward their position, presumably to provide backup to the group of soldiers they had seen get slaughtered.

They all walked back to the house and waited.

At 2:00pm Adam saw Jillian, Missy and Jamie walking toward the house. He ran out to meet them.

"You guys are back early!" Jamie said as he saw Adam running.

"You guys are too!" he replied. He embraced Jillian when he reached her. "I'm glad you're okay Jill," he said.

She kissed him. "I'm glad you're okay."

"Why are you guys back so soon?" Jamie asked.

"We ran into a huge horde of zombies," he said. "We couldn't continue any further south."

"Did you run into Juan and Casey?"

Adam shook his head.

"Hmm."

"Why are you guys back so soon?"

"We reached College Avenue and assumed you had been there already."

"Fair enough."

They walked back inside.

"We saw dozens of soldiers get slaughtered by zombies this morning," Randy said.

Jamie raised his eyebrows. "Interesting. Things are getting crazy."

Adam nodded.

"We saw at least six helicopters fly over us," Jillian said.

"Yeah, and they had different markings than the Wolf Pack's vehicles," Jamie said.

Adam nodded. "So what does that mean?"

"I don't know. I guess the Wolf Pack got more friends."

Juan and Casey finally returned at sunset.

Missy ran out to meet them and embraced Casey as though he had returned from war.

Juan looked exhausted when they entered the house.

"What happened today?" Jamie asked.

"We saw a three-way battle," Juan replied.

"What?" Adam asked.

"We saw the rebels fighting against Wolf Pack soldiers. We also saw a third group of soldiers fighting with the Wolf Pack and the rebels. It would seem the helicopters we heard last night belonged to the new group of soldiers. They are definitely not allied with the Wolf Pack."

"We saw zombies today," Randy said. "Lots and lots of zombies."

"We should leave first thing in the morning," Juan said.

"How? How are we going to get through the perimeter?" Adam asked.

"Hopefully all of the fighting has reduced the number of soldiers guarding the perimeter. We'll just have to find a vehicle and drive through a roadblock," he replied.

"That sounds desperate," Randy said.

Juan threw his hands up. "I don't know what else to do. If we stay here much longer, we are going to get caught in the crossfire or get eaten."

"They're likely to have the area we saw on the west side reinforced by now," Randy said. "So if we are going to make a break for it that rules the west out. What did you guys see on the southeast side and the southwest side?"

"The southwest side is where the heaviest fighting is," Juan said.

"So the majority of conflict is concentrated on the west side is what I'm hearing," Penny said.

"The southeast side was heavily guarded too. So was the northwest side," Jamie said.

"That leaves the northeast side," Jillian said.

"We'll set out tomorrow before dawn," Jamie said. "I guess we'll look for a large van tomorrow."

"Where is everyone going once we're out?" Missy asked.

"Well, we are going to Chicago," Randy said.

"I am too, so I guess I'll go with you all," Penny replied.

"I have nowhere left to go," Jamie said. "If it's still okay with you all, I'll go with you?"

Randy nodded.

"I too will go with you all," Juan said.

"That settles it," Randy said. "We're all going to Chicago."

Adam took first watch. Everyone except Jill went to sleep around 9:00pm. She sat on the stairs talking to him.

"Adam, today was scary. There were so many zombies," she said.

"I know Jill. It was terrible. We watched dozens of those soldiers get devoured by zombies."

She shuddered.

"Hey, I know I meant for this to be more romantic than this, but I really like you."

She giggled. "I really like you too."

"Well, I mean, I think with everything the way it is, now's as good a time as any to say this."

"Say what?"

"Jillian Michelle Wilson, I want to marry you."

"I want to marry you too, Adam Ryan Doss!"

"Will you marry me as soon as we get some place safe?"

She nodded. "Yes, I will!"

They kissed.

"I love you Jill."

She rested her head on his shoulder. "I love you too Adam."

They sat there for a while.

Around 11:00pm she spoke up. "I think I'm going to try to get some sleep."

"Alright, good night Jill."

"Good night Adam." She kissed him and then walked upstairs.

Adam sat there in the dark for a while, smiling. In the midst of everything that was going on, he still had his girl.

He was still smiling when he heard the sound of approaching diesel vehicles. He peered around the stairwell and saw two Humvees drive slowly past. A third Humvee turned down Linden Street. An APC drove by.

He realized something was amiss. He picked his pistol up and watched as a second APC stopped in the intersection of Poplar and Linden. It turned a spotlight on and shone it on the house across the street. Adam watched as five soldiers disembarked and walked to the house across the street. They fired their flamethrowers at the house and he watched in horror as it burst into flames.

He ran upstairs into the bedroom Juan and Jamie were in.

"Guys!" he whispered urgently. "The soldiers are torching the house across the street! Wake up!"

Juan stirred.

"Juan! The soldiers are torching the house across the street!"

He sat up quickly. "What?"

"The soldiers are torching the house across the street!"

He ran to the window and looked out. "They're also torching the one across the corner! Go get everyone else up!"

Adam ran to the room Randy, Casey, Missy, Penny and Jill were sleeping in.

"Guys!" he said urgently. "They're torching the houses around us! Get up! We've got to go!"

Randy sat up. "What? We're being attacked?"

"Come on! We've got to go!"

Adam ran downstairs and saw soldiers walking up toward the house. Everyone filed down the stairs quickly into the kitchen.

"We will have to run through the backyard!" Juan said quietly.

"We'll have to split up!" Randy said. "Does everyone know where ISU is?"

"Yes!"

"Let's meet at the Quad at ISU!" Randy said.

"I'll be the last one out!" Adam said. "Go!"

The others disappeared out the back door. Juan, Penny, Jamie, Casey, Missy and Jill all ran out into the backyard. Someone knocked hard on the front door. Adam heard the wood splitting. He raised his gun and aimed. When the door burst open he began shooting. The first soldier dropped. Another soldier dropped. As soon as the third soldier fell down Adam turned and ran out the back door. The others were long gone he hoped. He hoped he had bought them enough time.

He sprinted through the backyard and leapt over a short chain-link fence into the next door neighbor's backyard. As he ran he heard houses all around him bursting into flames. He heard helicopters and gunfire nearby. He ran as fast as he could.

He stopped after he reached Fell Avenue and turned to look back. He saw flames leaping skyward behind him but couldn't tell if he was being pursued. He turned and ran into the night.

CHAPTER NINETEEN

Jillian Wilson
Day 8

"Go!" Adam yelled.

Jill felt Randy practically drag her out the back door and she turned to run with them. Just hours before she had told Adam she wanted to marry him and now she was running from him?

She followed Randy and Penny through yard after yard. They hurdled short fences and soon reached the Quad at ISU. Randy and Penny sat down in the grass under a tree, panting. Jill bent over with her hands on her knees, panting. She looked up and saw Casey and Missy approaching. They sat down under the tree next to Randy and Penny, too out of breath to talk.

Jamie ran up a few minutes later. He was panting. "Juan is dead," he said sadly.

"What?" Randy asked.

"He's dead. We were running through a backyard and he must have gotten hit with a sniper's bullet because he dropped. I ran back to him and his head looked like it had exploded."

Jill grimaced at the news. Juan had been a gracious host and now he was dead.

"What about Adam? Where's Adam?" Randy asked.

"How long do we wait here for him?" Penny asked.

Jill turned and glared at her. "We will wait for Adam as long as we have to!"

"We can't wait forever for your boy toy," Penny shot back.

Jill walked over to her and slapped her.

Penny leapt up and tackled Jill. "Why you...!" she screamed.

Randy grabbed her and pulled her off Jill. "Come on ladies! We'll wait here until Adam gets here."

She glared at Jill as he pulled her off. "Don't ever touch me again!"

"Don't ever suggest we abandon my boyfriend!" Jill shouted at her.

"Ladies, if you don't quit your yelling, you're going to attract a lot of unwanted attention," Jamie said. "Now just calm down, I know we're all wound up. Getting mad at each other isn't going to help anything. I want you both to stand up and shake hands and apologize to each other."

Jill looked at Jamie and realized he wasn't kidding. She stood up and walked to Penny. She sized the other woman up for a moment. Penny was a little shorter than she was and she smelled terrible. Still, Jill was glad she knew how to use a crossbow. Jill extended her hand.

"I'm sorry Penny. I'm just on edge. I'm worried about Adam."

Penny ignored her hand and came near and hugged her. "I'm sorry too Jill. I shouldn't have been so callous."

"Why is everyone hugging?" Adam's voice came from the edge of the Quad.

"Adam!" Jill yelled. She turned and ran to him. "You're alive!"

He hugged her and kissed her. "I am alive. You are too!"

"We all are!" Penny said.

"Except for Juan," Jamie said.

Adam frowned. "What happened to Juan?"

"He got shot. He died," Jamie said quietly.

"I'm sorry to hear that man. I'm really sorry to hear that."

"It's okay, I mean it will be."

At 5:00am , Randy and Jamie disappeared to find a vehicle while the others waited in the Quad. Penny, Casey and Missy all slept next to Jill and Adam. Penny was snoring softly.

"Adam, I thought I'd never see you again," Jill said as she leaned back on her elbows.

He chuckled softly. "I thought the same thing. I thought I was going to get barbequed."

"That's not funny."

"Sorry."

"It's okay." She leaned over and kissed his cheek. "I'm just glad you're okay."

She heard the sound of an approaching vehicle. She sat up and raised her pistol. Adam sat up too. Sure enough, a van was driving across the Quad toward them. It stopped twenty feet away and flashed its headlights.

"Guys! Look what we found!" Randy called out from the van.

Jill stood and walked over to the van. It was a white 15-passenger van with ISU lettering on the side.

"Nice!" she said.

"Yeah, I think it was the debate team's or something," Randy said. "Get the others up! Let's go!"

Jill walked over and woke Missy and Casey up. Adam woke Penny up. Soon they had all climbed into the van and were driving slowly through the streets of Normal, Illinois. They drove past abandoned storefronts and burned out ruins of houses. Zombies shuffled aimlessly down the street. They turned onto another road as they drove past an abandoned mall.

Adam was talking to Jamie and Randy about something. Jill started to nod off.

She startled suddenly and sat up. It was daylight out and the Illinois countryside was slowly rolling by.

"Where are we? How long have I been out?" she asked.

Adam laughed. "We're about ten miles north of the perimeter. We drove through it about an hour ago. It is now seven o'clock."

"How did we drive through the perimeter?"

"We drove up to a roadblock and saw that it was abandoned. This roadblock was like the others; it was just a pair of Humvees parked sideways across the road, blocking it. Adam and Jamie got into them and drove them out of the way and then got back in the van and we drove on," Randy said.

"Oh." Jill saw that Casey, Missy and Penny were still asleep. "You didn't wake any of us up?"

"Honestly, after all that last night, we felt it best to let you all sleep. We're going to drive for a little bit and then stop and find some place to recuperate."

Jill smiled. They had done it. They had escaped from Bloomington-Normal.

She yawned and closed her eyes. She felt Adam slide his arm around her. She leaned against him and fell asleep.

"Miss Wilson?" the little boy asked. "What's the difference between a flute and a clarinet?"

Jill smiled at him. "It's really simple Jimmy. The flute is silver, it is long and skinny and it can make a higher pitched noise than the clarinet can. The flute, however, has even more differences! You make sound with the flute by blowing into an opening at the top of it. The clarinet, on the other hand, you play by blowing into a mouthpiece that has a reed in it."

Several hands shot up.

"Yes Lexi?" Jill asked.

"Miss Wilson, what's a reed?"

"A reed is a thin piece of wood that lays across an opening on the bottom of the mouthpiece," She held up a clarinet mouthpiece to show them. "It works by vibrating really fast when you blow across it. Here, let me demonstrate." She assembled the clarinet, moistened the reed, and began to blow into it. She played a C-Major scale. Then she laid the clarinet down and picked up the flute and blew across the mouthpiece. She trilled her way up and down a G-Mixolydian scale.

The kids all smiled as she laid the flute down on the desk.

"Now, we have just a few minutes left before the end of class. Does anyone have any questions?"

She snapped awake suddenly. The van was stopping.

"Where are we?" she asked sleepily.

"We're in Odell, Illinois Jill," Adam replied. "You sleep well?"

She nodded. "What time is it?"

"Just before noon."

"Oh. What's in Odell?"

"Randy hopes we can find some place to rest and recuperate."

She sighed. "I'm sad Juan died."

"Me too," Jamie said quietly. "I saved his skin more than once, but I guess I failed one time too many."

"Don't blame yourself Jamie, you didn't know that would happen," Casey said.

"Yeah," Adam added. "How would you have stopped a sniper's bullet?"

"Still, it just kills me that I couldn't save him."

The van exited the highway and pulled into the parking lot of a feed store.

"Well guys, I guess this looks alright as a place to spend the night," Randy said.

"It does," Adam said.

Everyone got out of the van and Jill immediately noticed it was a lot colder than it had been when they had left ISU. She folded her arms.

"Cold?" Adam asked as he put his arm around her.

She nodded. "It got a lot colder."

"Yeah, it did."

"Guys, I'm going to go to sleep when we get in there," Randy said.

"Me too," Jamie said.

They walked into the darkened feed store after Jamie picked the lock on the front door. It was cool inside, but not cold. It was quiet too.

Jill followed Adam back to the back storeroom. He smiled in the dim light when they got back there.

"This is perfect! There's actually room to stretch out!"

"Yeah, it is," she replied. "I guess you're going to go to sleep?"

He nodded. "Yeah, I'm exhausted."

"Okay, I think I'm going to stay up for a while."

"Okay, be careful."

"I will be. I love you Adam."

"I love you too Jill," he kissed her as he said it.

She walked out to the showroom and saw the others talking.

"I think I'm going to stay up and keep watch," Missy said.

"You sure babe?" Casey asked as he put his hands on her hips. "I don't want you getting overwhelmed."

"Yeah, well you need sleep!" she replied, laughing as he kissed her neck.

"Fine," he turned to Jill. "You staying up too Jillian?"

"Yeah, I figure I slept all the way here, so I might as well stay up."

"Okay, get some rest." He walked back to the back room alongside Randy and Jamie.

Penny looked out the door. "I'm going to take a walk," she said.

"Be careful," Missy said.

Jill sat down on a bar stool behind the front counter next to Missy.

"How you holding up?" Missy asked.

Jill shrugged. "I don't know yet. I don't know if my family is still alive, I don't know if my co-workers are still alive, so I just don't know. You?"

"Well, we were going to be losing the house either today or tomorrow, so there's that."

She nodded. "So what happened? I mean, why did you guys enter foreclosure?"

She frowned. "Casey lost his job about six months ago. The recording studio went under."

"I'm sorry to hear that."

"It happens, I guess. It just sucks."

"Yeah."

"Where does your family live?" Missy asked.

"Cleveland, Ohio."

"Wow. How'd you end up in Chicago?"

"I did my undergrad at the University of Illinois in Champaign. Adam got a job in Chicago when he graduated, so I did too."

"What did you do?"

"I was a music teacher at an elementary school." Jill frowned. She began to wonder what had happened to all the kids at Dan Ryan Elementary School. She thought about all the first graders in Mrs. Kirkpatrick's class. They had been so fascinated by woodwind instruments.

"Do you know how to play any musical instruments?" Missy interrupted her sad thoughts.

"Yeah, I can play a bunch of woodwind instruments and piano."

"That's cool. I played clarinet in elementary school," she replied with a smile.

Jill grinned. "I liked playing clarinet. How long did you play for?"

"Until second grade. That was the year my dad died."

"I'm so sorry honey!" Jill hugged her.

She shrugged. "I was seven when it happened. I guess I've had time to get over it."

"Still, that's got to be tough."

"Yeah, I mean, after my dad died everything kind of fell apart. My mom couldn't find a good enough job so we lost the house and wound up living in a trailer. My mom dated several men throughout my childhood. Some were good men, most were trash."

"That's awful."

"Yeah, I mean, I guess I've tried to get over it, but haven't really succeeded."

"Do you have any siblings?" Jill asked.

"Yeah, I have an older brother and a younger brother. My older brother, Brian, wound up in prison about seven years ago after he murdered a rival meth dealer."

Jill felt her eyes widen involuntarily. "Wow."

"Yeah, he was a jerk anyway. My little brother Aaron joined the army after he graduated from high school last year and got killed in Somalia."

"I'm sorry. I'm so sorry."

"It's okay, I mean, you know, he was serving his country. My mom was actually able to buy a house with his death benefit."

"So you and Casey have been dating for two years now, right?" Jill asked, changing the subject because she was becoming uncomfortable.

She nodded. "Yeah."

"How'd you guys meet?"

"I went to a house show his band was playing at and I stayed for a while after they finished their set."

"What did he play?"

"Guitar. He used to play in a band with Randy, actually, back in high school."

"That's cool."

"Yeah, anyway, he asked me to go on a date and we went to Applebee's a few nights later and yeah...I think it was a combination of his long hair and guitar playing ability that attracted me to him initially."

Jill smiled.

"How did you and Adam meet?"

"We met at a social event U of I held at the beginning of my second year of college."

"That's cool. You guys have been dating for a long time, huh?"

She smiled again. "Yeah. Casey sounds like he's a great guy."

"Yeah, he's got his moments. He really helped me out when we started dating. I had this crazy ex-boyfriend who was stalking me and Casey took care of him."

"What did he do? Spook him?"

Missy frowned. "No, he waited outside of Matthew's work one night about a year and a half ago and beat him up after work."

"Knocked some sense into him?"

"I guess. I mean, Matthew left me alone after that, but Casey was lucky he didn't press charges. Casey put Matt in the hospital for a week!"

Jill gasped. "Wow."

"Yeah, I had mixed feelings about it at first, but I realized he just did what he thought was necessary to get Matthew to leave me alone."

She nodded. "Yeah."

"Hey look! There's a zombie out there!" Missy pointed out the front door.

Jill looked and saw a zombie staggering around in the parking lot.

"Should I kill it?" she asked quietly.

Jill shook her head. "No, let's wait. If you run out there and shoot it, the noise might attract more."

"Good thinking Jillian!"

"Just call me Jill," she said.

"Okay Jill," she said, smiling.

CHAPTER TWENTY

Andy Gibson
Day 18

When they had arrived at Becker's room, the man could still be heard clawing at the door. Robbie nodded at Sterling.

"*Who* is in the deceased OIM's quarters?" Sterling demanded.

"The OIM," Robbie said. "I think he's tripping on bath salts."

"What?"

"Sir, Mister Becker attacked Doctor Kulik and attempted to attack Robbie," Andy said.

Sterling shook his head. "Open the door. Let me see."

"Are you sure sir?" Robbie asked.

Sterling nodded.

"Can I at least stand in front of you sir? In case he tries to attack you?"

Sterling sighed. "Go ahead."

Tyrell inserted the key into the doorknob and turned it. Then he stepped back and Robbie turned the knob. He pushed the door open and Andy saw Becker standing by the opposite wall, facing it. An overwhelming stench wafted from the room.

"Carl? You're alive?" Sterling asked, confused.

Carl spun around and staggered forward, his entrails dangling from his abdomen.

"Carl! You're badly hurt!" Sterling gasped.

"Sir, now would be a good time to close the door," Robbie said nervously, readying his baton.

Carl growled and stumbled forward, arms outstretched.

"We have to help him!" Sterling yelled.

Robbie raised the baton in a defensive gesture. "Get back sir! I don't want to hit you again!"

Carl lunged forward, jaw snapping. Robbie bashed him in the forehead with the baton. Carl fell backwards as Sterling cried out.

"Sterling, sir! Carl isn't normal anymore! He's a ravenous monster!" Andy yelled.

Sterling looked at Andy as Robbie quickly pulled the door closed. "Did he really bite Dan?"

He nodded.

Sterling sighed. "Tyrell, write up your report. Andy, follow me."

Suddenly the loudspeaker crackled. "*Attention crew, I apologize for ringing you at this late hour but this is Carlos Rodriguez, acting OIM. All crew must report to the galley immediately. Any crew who do not attend will face disciplinary action.*"

Sterling looked at Andy. Andy looked at Sterling. They both ran to the galley.

"It has come to my attention that there has been a fatal encounter with security by a member of our crew," Carlos said as Andy sat down near the wall.

The acting OIM looked exhausted. "Sterling, do you have a report of what happened?"

Sterling stood. "Yes, I think I do."

"Let's have it then. I want to quell the panic that is rising," Carlos said.

"OIM Becker is not dead, first, but he is incapable of continuing leadership." Everyone gasped.

"What? How?" Carlos asked, confused.

"Becker attacked Doctor Dan Kulik and bit him this morning. Security confined him to his room while trying to sort out what happened. He seems to be under the influence of some sort of psychoactive substance. Then about an hour ago, Doctor Kulik attacked and killed Doctor Claire Maclin. Security was forced to use deadly force to subdue him," he finished with a sigh.

Carlos looked shocked. "Alright people, here's the deal. Whatever happened to Doctor Kulik and Master Becker, it has a logical, scientific explanation. There is no Voodoo being performed on this platform. However, do not go near the former OIM's cabin, or you will face discipline. Protocol indicates that we are to quarantine anyone displaying symptoms we cannot identify. That said, we are going to mourn the dead and we are going to continue attempting to make contact with someone on shore. Need I remind you it has been more than two weeks since we heard from the shore?"

"We are going to continue our attempts until December First. If no contact is made by then, we will abandon ship and make for shore in the lifeboats. If we see any kind of disruptive behavior, discipline will be enacted. We are not just co-workers. We are family! We will live as such. Do I make myself clear?"

The crew murmured their agreement.

"Alright. Now, get back to work or bed, whichever you are scheduled to do," he said.

Andy stood.

"Andy!" Royce called out.

"What?"

"Come with me."

Andy followed his friend away from the galley, down the hall to the infirmary.

"What is it?" he asked.

"It's Claire. She…she came back from the dead."

"What? Are you crazy?"

Royce turned and gave him a look. "After everything else that's happened today?"

They reached the infirmary and Andy noticed that a bed had been knocked over.

"What happened?"

"She tried to attack Doctor Shah and Scott about ten minutes after we left the infirmary earlier."

"But Dan ripped her face off."

"Yeah, Scott told me that it was the most terrifying sight he had ever seen. He could see her bare skull."

Andy felt nauseous. "What did they do with her?"

"Shah restrained her and they threw her overboard."

"What? Why? How?"

Royce put his arm on Andy's shoulder. "I'm just kidding man. What, do you think zombies are real?"

Andy punched him in the chest. "That's not funny!"

"I'm sorry, I couldn't resist. No, they did throw her overboard earlier. They just boxed up her body and Dan's body and did a little ceremony while Carlos addressed everybody. Then they threw the boxes overboard."

Andy nodded grimly. "Really though, that's not funny man."

Royce shrugged. "Scott did say he thought he heard a noise coming from the box Claire was in right before they cast it overboard. He just thought he was hearing things."

Andy shook his head. "You're a jerk."

The crew spent the next two weeks planning and preparing. A list of who would be on each lifeboat was published on the 18th.

Andy was assigned to Lifeboat D, along with the rest of the Fire Team, the Geologists, and Security; Sterling was D's designated coxswain and Andy was the backup. As he scanned the list he was glad to see he wouldn't be riding in Lifeboat A. Carl Becker was assigned to that boat. Andy assumed he would somehow be kept under lock and key, but still.

He was sad to see that Milo was assigned to Lifeboat A. Milo was a good friend and Andy had a bad feeling about his being in the same boat as Mr. Becker. Whatever was wrong with Becker, Andy had concluded he didn't want to be locked in the same tiny boat as the former OIM.

One night, a few days before Thanksgiving, Andy sat in his room playing poker with Royce and Milo. Milo laid down a Flush.

"Read 'em and weep!" he said with a chuckle.

"I would but I've got a Full House," Andy said as he laid his cards on the table.

"Sorry ladies," Royce said, "I think four Aces beats both of your hands." He laid four Aces on the table.

Milo sighed. "Man!"

"There's always the next hand, if you have chips left," Andy said.

Milo grumbled under his breath. "Alright, come on!" He placed more chips in the center of the table.

"So, what do you think is really wrong with Becker?" Royce asked.

"I don't know. There's no way it's drugs. He's been in his room for two weeks now, and he is still violent and moving around. I don't know, logic can't explain it," Andy said. "He's got a giant slit in his belly, his entrails are hanging out, and he has a broken jaw. There shouldn't be any way he's walking around. And when I wrestled him off Doctor Kulik, I thought he was so pale and so cold. It felt like I was wrestling a corpse off someone," he said as Milo placed the flop down.

"I'm just going to come out and say it," Milo said. "He's a zombie. I think the man's odor gives it away. He smells like rotting flesh."

"A zombie?" Royce asked. "I think a better term for whatever he is and whatever Kulik became after being bitten is a creeper. Becker just creeps around his room. I mean, look at what Kulik did when he killed Doctor Maclin! He just crept around the Infirmary with her face in his hands."

"That's disgusting!" Milo said as he placed the turn down; he laid down a Seven of Hearts.

Andy looked at his own hand and frowned. "I agree with Royce," he said. "I think creeper is a better name. Zombie is just too corny."

"Fine!" Milo said. "But you know, revenant might be a good term too."

Royce laughed. "Revenant? Someone's been playing too much Dungeons and Dragons!"

"Hey man! I was into role playing games when I was a kid, who cares?" Milo laughed.

"Well, whatever he is, he's going to be in your lifeboat when we abandon ship," Andy said as he folded.

"What?" Milo exclaimed. "No!"

"Yup, so I'd be careful," Andy said.

Milo shook his head. "That's crazy!"

"Yeah, the whole cook staff is assigned to that lifeboat."

"Can I ride in yours?"

Andy laughed. "I doubt Sterling will let you, but who knows?"

On November 26th, the crew celebrated Thanksgiving. Andy stood up on the helideck while everyone waited for dinner to be ready. He watched the sun slowly set behind puffy cumulus clouds, painting the western sky a brilliant blend of fiery colors.

"What are you thinking about?" Royce asked.

"Shelly and Isaiah," he replied.

"I guess you still can't get a hold of them?"

Andy shook his head. "We might as well not even have phones on this rig. I don't know, I'm worried man. Even if Teddy was a catastrophic hurricane, why haven't we been able to get a hold of anyone? Surely there are ships out here in the Gulf within range of our broadcasts? Why can't we reach the Coast Guard? I mean, it's surprising we can't reach HQ or Ops, but it's shocking that we can't even reach the Coast Guard!"

"I know man. I mean, that fire a few weeks ago, what would have happened if it had been worse? We would have had to abandon ship!"

"Yeah," Andy said as a warm breeze blew across the helideck. "I don't know man. I'm not sure what we're going to find when we get ashore. I'm wondering if I'll even find a plate from my house. And I'm worried sick about Shelly and Isaiah."

"I'm sure they're fine Andy," Royce said, patting his shoulder.

"*Attention crew, Thanksgiving Dinner is ready. Please report to the galley at your convenience,*" Milo announced over the intercom.

"Well? You up for some turkey?" Andy asked.

"Sounds good man," Royce replied.

They walked downstairs to the galley. A number of crew members were already there, sitting at tables. Andy saw that the food had been set up buffet style, with a line area for people to walk through. Cooks Pat McKinney and Newton Thomas stood behind the table, ready to assist.

He looked around and saw Milo sitting at a table with Oscar, Fyodor and Well Services Tech David M'Kumbe. He walked over and Royce followed.

"Andy! Royce! Have a seat guys!" Milo exclaimed, motioning to two seats. Andy and Royce both sat down.

"Hello Andrew," David said, extending his hand.

"Hey David, how's it going?" Andy asked, shaking his hand.

"As well as can be expected I suppose. We were all, all of us in Well Services anyway, just crushed to learn of Mike's death. But, as they say, we are still alive, I am still alive. So I should rejoice," he replied.

"It was pretty awful," Fyodor said. "I'm glad that Andy and Royce acted so quickly or we might all be dead."

Andy shrugged. "We were just doing our job."

"Yeah, but you saved us!" Milo said, laughing.

"Yes," Oscar said. Oscar was a tall Hispanic man from Atlanta. He had moved his wife and children there from Mexico and had been hired by CPG as a Production Technician. His job was to make sure oil and gas kept flowing smoothly during normal operation.

"How are you holding up Oscar?" Royce asked. "Your whole team got lost, didn't it?"

Oscar shrugged. "Well, Raul died in that fire and Dave, I'm not really sure what happened to Dave Sappins. We think he went outside during the storm and must have fallen overboard. My supervisor Josh is okay though. And they'll hire more technicians when we get back home I'd imagine."

"You really think there's anything left at home?" Fyodor asked.

"I hope so," Andy said. "What do you think?"

"Come on man, we haven't been able to contact anyone onshore since before the hurricane. I mean, I've checked the transmission equipment and our radio is in great condition! I can see the writing on the wall; something terrible and expansive happened onshore," he said. "Perhaps there was a nuclear war. Perhaps a meteor hit New York. I don't know."

David nodded. "I hate to be a pessimist, but I have to agree with Fyodor's assessment. Something awful has happened, or at least so it would seem."

"You think civilization has collapsed?" Andy asked.

Fyodor shrugged. "I saw some terrible things growing up in Russia. But nothing I saw compared to this. Our radio has a great enough range that we should be able to hit any receiver on the Gulf Coast. At the very least, we should be able to listen to any unencrypted traffic along the Gulf Coast. Andy, you know as well as I do that there's only been static since the evening we were supposed to be evac'd. I don't know what happened, but it must be bad."

Third Mate Dale Speith stood at the front of the room near the food and cleared his throat. "Hey, if I could, uh, have your attention! We are going to begin eating now. When the table next to you has come up, your table may come up. We want you to use this time at your tables to express what you're thankful for. Alright, let's eat!"

After dinner Andy returned to the helideck to gaze upon the stars. He silently prayed that somewhere, whether in Hattiesburg or Bay Saint Louis,

Shelly was looking up at the same stars slowly circling the sky. A warm breeze continued to blow across the Gulf.

He heard footsteps climbing the stairway. He turned and saw Tyrell emerge onto the deck.

"Hey Tyrell," Andy said.

"Andy, I hope your dinner was good?" he asked.

"It was. Not like what Shelly can cook, but not bad," Andy replied.

"Hey, I wanted to talk to you alone. So we've received reports that someone in the crew is planning to cause a fire or explosion or something that would cost CPG a large amount of money, kind of as payback for abandoning us out here. We haven't received any reports of who is planning this or when it will happen, but I just figured you should know so that you can keep the Fire Team on their toes."

"I see," Andy replied, stroking his chin. "A lot of us are mad at CPG, so I can't say I'm surprised someone's considering that."

"Yeah, I know. Even so, such behavior would clearly open them up to prosecution once we got ashore. If we really resent CPG for what they did, court would be a more appropriate outlet."

"I agree Tyrell. But, I mean, the platform isn't pumping right now and likely won't resume pumping until after we go ashore. So there isn't much they could do to cause catastrophic damage to the platform, at least not without risking everyone's lives."

"Fair enough. I just figured I'd let you know."

"Thanks Tyrell. How are things going with Becker?"

He sighed. "Man, I don't know what to call it anymore. Something horrific happened to Becker and Kulik," he shuddered. "I have nightmares most nights about that Infirmary. I mean Dan just didn't even look human anymore!"

"I know. It was a horrifying scene to stumble upon."

"Yeah! He was eating her face! Faisal said that she was probably alive the whole time he was tearing her face off. I watched the security tapes and it would seem she was. It was sickening to watch."

Andy shuddered. "That's awful."

"Yeah! And the way he just kept trying to attack me! I've never seen anyone not cry out in pain after being hit by a Taser!"

"Yeah. What do you think happened to him? To Becker? To make them so violent?"

He shrugged. "I don't know man. It just seems like something straight out of a horror movie."

Andy nodded. "Yeah, like Night of the Living Dead."

He sighed. "Well, I'd better go down and relieve Robbie. Have a good night Andy."

"You too Tyrell."

The last few days of November passed without incident. Andy had the Fire Team perform a final drill and everyone packed what they needed to take with them in their backpacks.

On the morning of the last day before they were to abandon ship, Andy awoke to find a note that had been slipped under his door in the night. He unfolded it and read it.

"Attention crew,

On Monday, November 30 we will be conducting some tests on the pumping and drilling equipment to make sure the equipment of Bald Point 3131 is still operational before we leave for shore. These tests will be conducted before the lifeboats are loaded and launched. The testing will begin at approximately 10:00 and end around 19:00. At the conclusion of testing, the platform will be mothballed.

Testing will be conducted by the Drilling and Production Teams. All members of Drilling Crew and Production Crew should report to the drilling shack at 9:00. Additionally, the Derrick hands, Floor hands, Lease hands, Mud Engineers and Well Services Team should be present no later than 9:00. Control Room personnel should report to the Control Room by 8:30. Fire Team B will be on call in the event of an incident. Finally, all crew should report to their designated lifeboat stations at 6:00 on Tuesday, December 1.

Signed,

Carlos Rodriguez

Andy glanced at his watch. It was 8:48am. He hurriedly dressed and ran downstairs to Sterling's office. He knocked on the door.

"Come in," Sterling said.

Andy opened the door and entered his office, waving the letter. "Who authorized this?"

"Carlos did," Sterling said as he leaned back in his chair. "You look like you disagree with the decision?"

"I do," Andy said, sitting down.

"Why?"

"Did Tyrell not tell you about the supposed conspiracy to destroy the platform?" he asked.

Sterling nodded. "He did, which is why we have a Fire Team on duty."

"Why not Team A?"

"B Team is just as capable."

"Why didn't I know about this?"

Sterling stared at him for a moment. "Andrew, you've been working a lot lately. I know about the extra shifts. I appreciate the work, I do, but you could use a break. Nick came and told me about how hard you work. I figured you could use the break. Besides, it's just routine testing. It makes sense."

"Why did they wait until now?" Andy asked suspiciously.

"Nathan and Josh wanted to perform the testing three weeks ago but Maintenance had to repair a lot of equipment on the production deck that was damaged in the storm. Maniczewski just signed off on the repairs yesterday."

Andy sighed. "I don't think this is a good idea."

He shrugged. "Take the day to pack and rest."

Andy exited Sterling's office and grumbled under his breath. So Nathan Howell, the head driller, and Josh Hammond, the director of Production had wanted to perform the testing for a while?

Andy shook his head as he walked back to his room. It made sense to test the equipment following a major storm to see if it still worked. The platform could have been knocked loose from the well during the storm, for instance. Still, something didn't feel right.

CHAPTER TWENTY-ONE

Randy Eccleston
Day 10

The group stayed in Odell for a day and a half and then set out again, heading toward Chicago. They saw a few zombies while they were resting at the feed store, but didn't see nearly as many as they had seen in Bloomington-Normal. Randy was also grateful they hadn't seen any more soldiers.

It was cloudy and cold when they left the little village. Randy was startled by how desolate the prairie looked as they drove through it. In less than two weeks it seemed, civilization had collapsed. They drove by abandoned cars on the side of the highway every mile or so.

"You know," he said as they drove past an exit for Dwight, Illinois, "I'm starting to think it's unlikely my brother and parents are still alive."

Adam patted his shoulder. "Hey man, I know it looks bad. You have to hold out hope though."

He shrugged. "I guess. I don't know, I think I was hoping to see more signs of normalcy as we drove north, but everything I've seen so far is indicative of continued collapse."

"We could try the radio," Casey suggested.

Randy turned the radio on and scanned through the available stations on FM first. Nothing but static. Then he tried AM.

"Static," he murmured as he swept the dial down the frequency range.

Suddenly he heard speech. He stopped and turned the radio up.

"Attention all who can hear this radio broadcast. My name is Sergeant Rory Niedemeyer with the United States Army. My group of soldiers has seized Bloomington-Normal and has defeated the Wolf Pack. We offer safety to every able bodied citizen. Come and find salvation," a man's voice droned.

Randy turned the radio off. "See?" he asked. "The only thing we've seen that hasn't been utterly indicative of societal collapse has been soldiers fighting over the establishment of a fiefdom in Bloomington-Normal, and that's still a troubling sign of collapse. Who knows how many houses the Wolf Pack torched before they were subdued? Besides, there were so many zombies." He shook his head.

"Still, we don't know who survived," Adam said. "There are surely a lot of people who didn't succumb."

"You all are the first group of survivors I've encountered who haven't been crazies or perverts," Penny spoke up from the back of the van. "And there have been lots of crazies and perverts."

"I haven't really heard your story," Randy said. "What exactly happened that brought you up here?"

"I woke up a week and a half ago and heard my parents growling from their bedroom. You see, I lived with them when my show wasn't taping. Anyway, I woke up and heard them growling. I thought they were just, you know, doing married people things," she said.

Randy suppressed a laugh and heard others in the van snicker.

"Anyway, my dad burst out of their room and he was covered with blood. He was missing half of his face. He tried to attack me but I held him off. I roundhouse kicked him into the wall repeatedly. Then I saw my mom. I guess my dad had disemboweled her at some point in the night, but she was still walking around with the same ravenous look in her eyes as my dad. I ran away. I ran to my boyfriend's house, but he was the same way. Everyone in Phoenix was the same way. So I got in a car, I drove to an airport outside Albuquerque, I stole a helicopter and I flew as far as Oklahoma. Then I stole another car and drove as far north as Bloomington and then I met you guys. But seriously, you are the only sane people I've encountered."

Randy nodded. "That's tough."

"Yeah, I guess that several years of hosting Survive This prepared me for the apocalypse, sort of."

"I wish they hadn't kept your show on the Hardcore Network," Jamie said. "Your show should have been on a major network. Primetime, you know?"

She laughed. "Well, my producer said we were in talks with NBC about a month ago. But, my guess would be that's going nowhere."

They drove over the Kankakee River. Randy knew they were getting close to Chicago. A few minutes later they crossed the Des Plaines River.

"So where does your family in Chicago stay Penny?" Missy asked.

"Real close to the Magnificent Mile," she replied. "My aunt and uncle live there."

"That's cool," Missy replied.

Randy looked in the rearview mirror at Jillian. She rolled her eyes as Penny spoke.

She and Penny had fought a few nights before, very briefly. Even though Randy and Jamie had broken up the fight, it was clear that neither Jillian nor Penny liked each other very much.

They suddenly approached a traffic jam on the highway as they passed through Joliet.

"Whoa," Adam said as Randy slowed the van to a stop.

Ahead, decaying arms reached through the windows of stopped cars.

"Zombie highway," Casey said.

"Can we go around?" Penny asked.

"Yeah, it looks like we can squeeze the van onto the right shoulder," Randy said as he drove to the shoulder. There was just enough room to drive by the jam.

Rotting hands beat angrily on the side of the van as they passed the stopped cars. It took several hours for Randy to thread the van through the fifteen-mile long jam, but they finally emerged onto open highway just south of Bolingbrook.

"Ah Chicagoland," he sighed as they passed a burned out Ikea just off the highway. Zombies roamed the parking lot.

The highway was clear until they passed I-355. Then it became more crowded with abandoned cars. Randy had to slow down significantly to steer around stopped cars. Finally, around 5:00pm they reached the Des Plaines River again. They crossed it and Randy was forced to swerve to a stop as they approached the Chicago Sanitary and Ship Canal; the bridge had been destroyed.

Randy got out and walked to the edge of the pavement and looked down. The bridge deck had collapsed into the canal. He saw several corpses tangled with the wreckage of the bridge far below. Rusty rebar stuck out from the edge of the pavement, arcing downward toward the river. Across the collapsed span, an old Mitsubishi sub-compact dangled over the edge.

"Well, now what?" Casey asked as he walked up alongside him.

"I don't know," he replied. "Look!" He pointed upriver. "Those bridges are out too."

Casey nodded. "How much gas does the van have?"

Randy frowned. "The needle's on E. We don't really have enough gas to drive around looking for a river crossing."

Casey murmured under his breath.

"It's getting late. We should find some place to spend the night. We can come up with a solution tomorrow," Randy said as he looked down at the canal.

"You know," Casey said, "if we could find some little boats, we could just float down the canal pretty much all the way to your brother's."

"Yeah, that's probably not a bad idea Casey."

They spent the night in an abandoned mechanic's shop near the highway. The next morning as they ate breakfast, Randy stood up.

"Okay guys, we are going to try to find some jon boats to go down the canal in. The canal eventually joins the Chicago River. We can bypass all of the traffic on the roads and we can avoid a bunch of zombies," he said.

"We're going to your brother's house, right?" Adam asked.

"Yeah, they live just north of Wrigley Field," he replied.

"I think me and Jill are going to go with you until we get there, then we're going to go look for our families," Adam said.

Randy nodded. "I understand that."

"Me and Missy are with you all the way Randy," Casey said.

"Me too," Jamie said.

Randy looked at Penny.

She shook her head. "I think this is where we need to part ways," she said.

"You know, you're welcome to come with us. I mean, if your family didn't make it, you could go with us," he offered.

She shook her head. "No, I need to go alone. If my family is alive, that's great! If not, I don't want to be a burden on anyone."

"You wouldn't be a burden," he replied.

"No Randy. Thank you, you've all been great, really. But I must go the rest of the way alone."

"Okay Penny. If you change your mind, come to Twenty-Fifty-Four West Dakin Avenue, just north of Wrigley Field. That's where we'll be, either way."

She nodded. "Okay. Thanks Randy. Twenty-Fifty-Four West Dakin Avenue, just north of Wrigley Field."

"Alright guys, let's get going. I don't know how far we'll have to hoof it," Randy said.

Everyone gathered their belongings and walked out into the chilly morning. Casey walked down to the riverfront ahead of the others. Randy heard him laugh.

"Guys! There are boats down here!" he yelled.

Everyone walked down to him and Randy saw two small metal jon boats tied to a dock.

"That's great!" he exclaimed. "Look! They even have motors! This might not take too long at all!"

"Okay, this is where we part ways," Penny said. She hugged each of them. "Be careful out there. I hope you all find what you're looking for."

"I hope you find what you're looking for too," Randy said.

"Goodbye guys," she said. Then she turned and walked back up the embankment.

"Goodbye Penny!" he called.

Casey, Missy and Jamie boarded one boat and Adam and Jillian boarded the second boat with Randy. They all untied the boats and fired the engines up. Then they began motoring down the canal.

They spent the morning steering around fallen bridges and floating by abandoned chemical plants and factories. Here and there they passed corpses floating in the foul water. Gradually the skyline of downtown Chicago came into view.

"I'm glad Penny didn't come with us," Jillian said.

Randy laughed. "You and her didn't see eye to eye, did you?"

She shook her head. "No, I think everything was fine until she suggested abandoning Adam the other night."

"What? She wanted to abandon me?" Adam asked. He seemed taken aback.

Jillian laughed. "Yeah, when we were waiting for you to catch up to us when we escaped to the Quad at ISU, she suggested we just leave without you."

"Wow," he said.

"Yeah, I slapped her and tackled her. I wasn't about to leave my man!"

He laughed. "Man Jill, you're tough, aren't you?"

"Well, she was pretty tough too. I'm glad Jamie broke things up."

Randy laughed.

"What's so funny Randy?" She sounded offended.

"I'm just laughing at the fight the other night," he replied.

She punched him mockingly. "Don't mess with me." She laughed.

"Aw Jill, you know he just thought Penny was cute," Adam said.

Randy laughed. "Even though she smelled terrible, yes, I must admit I thought she was pretty hot back in her TV days. I think with a good scrubbing she'd be hot again."

Jillian shook her head. "Either way, I'm glad she's out of our hair."

It took them all morning to float down the canal and up the Chicago River. As they floated past downtown Chicago, Randy saw thousands of zombies on Lower Wacker Drive. He and the others floated past Goose Island and finally landed just north of the Cortland Street Bridge. He and the others killed several dozen zombies when they disembarked from the boats and made their way to Ashland Avenue.

As they walked north they passed dozens of burned out shops. The streets were littered with trash. Orange body bags lay piled up on the sidewalks, presumably with corpses inside them. Some buildings were wrapped in huge sheets of orange and white plastic with large biohazard symbols printed on them.

"So this is what a pandemic looks like," Adam said somberly as they walked through the desolate streets.

"Yeah," Randy said quietly.

They passed a block of stores with boarded up windows. Missing person posters lined most of the sheets of plywood. Randy walked over to the sidewalk and surveyed the posters.

"Have you seen my sister? Have you seen my brother? Have you seen my son?" he murmured as he read the posters aloud. He saw photos of children, of smiling women, of older people, of happy families. He shook his head.

"Hey look!" Jamie said suddenly.

Randy turned and saw a group of about two dozen people approaching. They were wearing hockey goalie equipment and all had baseball bats.

"Who are you?" the one in front called out.

Randy put his hand on the grip of his pistol; it had been tucked into his waistband. "Why does it matter?" he yelled back.

"Because you're trespassing!"

"We're just passing through!" he called back.

"It doesn't matter! Kill them!" the leader yelled.

Several of them took off running toward Randy and his friends, bats raised.

Randy raised his pistol and aimed at the lead runner. He fired and the runner fell to the street with a cry. Casey, Adam and Jamie all began shooting too and soon they had dropped all but three of the group of thugs.

The leader raised his hands and stepped backwards. "Fine! You can have these streets!" He turned and ran, his two surviving companions beside him.

Randy and the others continued on.

They walked until they reached West Addison Street. Then they turned right and continued on past homes with boarded up windows and shops with broken windows. The desolation was shocking; this was normally a bustling tourist district. Randy noticed more and more body bags as he and his friends neared Wrigley Field. They turned left at Wrigley Field and cut through a parking lot to North Seminary Street. They passed abandoned military tents that were filled with more body bags.

"This is creepy," Jillian said.

Randy nodded.

They walked the final few blocks to West Dakin Street and turned onto the street. Randy's brother lived in the second house on the left. He looked up at the large stone house. He looked back at the street and saw his brother's car parked in front of the house.

"Wait here guys, I want to be the one to see if...if they didn't make it," he said. He opened the wrought iron gate and walked up the steps to their porch. He paused, hesitant to knock on the door. What if they weren't alive? What if they were dead? What if?

He slowly curled his fingers into a fist and raised his arm. He took a deep breath and knocked. Then he waited. Several seconds went by. He knocked again.

"Todd! Vicki! It's Randy! If you're in there, please let me in!" he called out.

He heard footsteps. His heart practically skipped a beat.

He heard several locks' tumblers turn. The door opened. And there, in the doorway stood his brother, Todd Eccleston.

CHAPTER TWENTY-TWO
Randy Eccleston
Day 11

"Randy! You're alive!" Todd practically screamed. He stepped forward and embraced Randy in a tight bear hug.

Randy hugged him back and realized he was crying. "I thought you were surely dead!" he exclaimed.

"I thought you were too!" Todd replied.

"Where are Vicki and the kids?"

"Inside, napping."

"Oh man, I'm so glad you're alive!"

"Who are these folks with you? I recognize Adam and Casey, but who is everyone else?"

Randy turned to the rest of his group. "That's Adam's girlfriend Jillian, that's Casey's girlfriend Missy and that is Jamie, a man we met in Bloomington who saved our lives."

"Hey guys! Come on in! All of you!" his brother stepped aside and they all entered. Once they were inside the house, he closed the door and locked the deadbolt and doorknob and then he moved a book case against the door.

Everyone walked to the living room while Randy looked around at the interior just inside the door, taking it in. His brother had bought a large, old house when his business had started turning a profit. The entrance room had a stairway to the left of the door that went upstairs. To the right was a large, spacious living room with a tiny office tucked into a corner. Down the hall was a half bathroom and the kitchen and dining room. The whole first floor had ten-foot high ceilings and dark chestnut hardwood floors.

He heard footsteps coming down the stairs.

"Uncle Randy!"

He looked up and saw his nieces, Hannah and Laci, running down the stairs.

"Hannah! Laci!" he exclaimed.

They both wrapped themselves around him in a tight hug when they reached the bottom of the stairs.

"Randy! It's good to see you!"

He looked up and saw his sister-in-law Vicki standing at the top of the stairs. She looked sleepy.

"It's good to see you too Vicki!"

"Okay girls, let Uncle Randy breathe!" Vicki admonished the girls.

They let go and Randy walked into the living room. He saw his friends sitting on two of the couches. He sat down in a recliner across from Todd as Adam recounted their journey.

When he had finished, Randy cleared his throat. "So Todd, have you talked to mom or dad?"

Todd looked at him and the expression on his face told Randy everything.

"What happened?"

"Randy, I don't know. I went to their house a few days ago; I rode my bike. They were both dead. I think," his voice cracked, "I think they must have taken a fatal dose of pills."

Randy's face fell. His parents were dead. He sat there quietly for a moment.

"I'm sorry Randy!" Todd stood up and walked over to him.

Randy stood up and hugged him.

"I talked to dad for the last time about two days before quarantine was enacted. He was talking about buying a sail boat and asked me if I thought it would be a sound investment."

Randy nodded quietly.

"I don't think they suffered. They were lying in bed embracing one another. I buried them in their backyard. I'm grateful they didn't turn into zombies."

Randy nodded. "What about Vicki's family?"

He stepped back and shrugged. "We don't know. She talked to her dad the same night the quarantine was enacted, she said he told her it would all blow over pretty quickly. She also talked to her brother in Buffalo, but that was weeks ago. I mean, her dad lives in Detroit, her mom lives in New York City, she has two brothers who live in Buffalo, New York and an older brother who lives in Bay Saint Louis, Mississippi."

Randy looked at Vicki. She was sitting down. She looked calm.

"Vicki, how are you holding up?" he asked.

She shrugged. "I'm just living one day at a time."

"She was actually working when it all went down!" Todd exclaimed. "In the ER!"

"Whoa, really?" Randy asked.

"Yeah, it was crazy," Vicki said. "I was there for my normal shift when a bunch of people came in vomiting blood. My boss had us all put on Tyvek suits and face masks and latex gloves. Once I saw how crazy it was, I quit. I had to come home to my family. I barely made it home."

"Wow."

"Yeah, I'm not sure what happened to all my co-workers. I hope some of them made it out okay."

"I'm sure some did," Randy said.

She shrugged. "Yeah, I hope so."

Later, as it was getting dark outside, Randy sat in the dining room with Todd, Adam, Casey and Jamie. The women were upstairs with his nieces.

"So Todd, you owned a brewery?" Jamie asked.

Todd nodded. "Yup. Parachutes Brewery. I opened it in Two-Thousand-Sixteen after I'd been home brewing for a few years."

"Hey, yeah, you guys made Shiver IPA, didn't you?" Casey asked.

Todd nodded. "Yup. We won some awards with that brew. I actually have a few cases out in the shed."

"That's great!" Randy said. "That's definitely my favorite beer!"

Todd laughed. "Thanks little brother."

"Man, when was the next brew fest scheduled for?" Adam asked.

Todd frowned. "The next A Rush of Brew to the Head Festival was scheduled to start yesterday. But, it seems like civilization has collapsed, so I'm not sure I should be that disappointed. You know? It's like when you compare the loss of your business to the apocalypse, it sort of puts everything in perspective."

"Yeah," Randy said. "Have you seen a lot of zombies around here?"

He shook his head. "No, we saw some rioters at first, but I think it helped that almost everyone in the neighborhood ignored the quarantine orders and tried to escape. Vicki talked me into staying. She had seen the virus and its effects first hand and she didn't want to risk any of us catching it. The rioters though, they looted some of the houses down at the other end of the block those first few nights, but even that has died down the last few days. No one goes out at night now, so that also makes it easier to watch for suspicious activity."

Randy nodded. "So how much food do we have here? Ammo? Water?"

He laughed. "You worry too much Randy. We've got a healthy supply of beer in the backyard, we have about a hundred gallons of potable water in the basement and we have enough dry goods to last a few months. We've also got a couple of compound bows and rifles. We'll stay here as long as we can. And your friends are all welcome to stay too."

"Thanks Todd," Jamie said. "I, for one, appreciate the hospitality."

"No problem Jamie," Todd replied.

Randy stood and walked out onto the back porch. An El-Train line curved over the back half of the backyard, the wrought-iron frame of the trestle had one pillar in the back corner of the yard. He looked up at an old maple tree that stood in the opposite corner from the iron column. The old tree probably stood close to eighty feet high, towering over even the El-Train line. It still had about half of its leaves, all of which had turned yellow or red.

"Enjoying the scenic view?" Todd asked as he stepped out onto the back porch.

Randy chuckled. "Yes. So elegant."

Todd laughed.

"How long do you think we'll be able to hold out here?" he asked.

Todd shrugged. "Well, I had initially made my projections assuming I only had myself, Vicki and the girls to account for. That said, I think we have enough food and drink to last a few weeks. We can always go forage if we need to."

"Adam told you about Bloomington, right?"

Todd nodded.

"So what happens if a hostile group comes along and tries to take our supplies?"

"We'll fight them off."

"Todd, I mean really. What happens if a well-armed group comes along?"

"We'll leave then."

"Do you have a backup plan?"

Todd laughed. "You worry too much Randy. We'll be fine. We've got the means to gather food, we're probably in the best place to go foraging, we have some ammo, and we're in an obscure location. You can't even tell anyone lives in this house from the street."

Randy nodded. He wasn't sure he was fully convinced. "If you say so Todd."

"Trust me little brother. We'll be fine."

CHAPTER TWENTY-THREE
Andy Gibson
Day 33

At 10:00 am on November 30th,the familiar whir and hum of machinery that had been silenced in advance of the approaching hurricane more than a month before, began again. Andy watched movies in his room, trusting that the platform was in good hands with Kenny leading Fire Team B.

At some point he fell asleep.

He was suddenly standing near Lifeboat D.

"You ready to go?" Sterling asked.

"I am. You? You know this is a one-way trip?" Andy replied.

"Yeah. I can't wait to punch someone at Corporate in the face."

"Same here."

"Could be worse though. At least we didn't have a blowout. I'd hate for this to be the next Piper Alpha."

Andy was awakened by the phone in his room ringing. He looked at his watch. It was 6:42pm, eighteen minutes before the test was to conclude. He answered the phone.

"Hello?"

"Andy, it's Kenny. We have a situation," he said.

"What, what is it?"

"The well is blowing out," he said gravely.

Andy sat upright quickly. "Blowing out?" he asked in disbelief.

"Yes. It's spraying mud out of the top of the derrick. Nothing's on fire yet," Kenny replied. "The gas alarms have been going off for a few seconds."

"Has someone activated the blowout preventer?"

"Nathan's supposed to be doing it."

"Well get it done!" Andy exclaimed. "The last thing we want is for an-"

The whole platform shook violently as he was thrown forward out of bed. He landed on his chest on the floor at the foot of the bed. The deafening roar left his ears ringing.

He pushed himself to his feet, dazed. "Oh no," he cried, "Please no, please no!"

Andy ran out of his room and saw others in the hallway, dazed.

"What just happened?" someone yelled.

"Get to the lifeboats!" Andy yelled back. "There's been an explosion!"

He went back into his room and hurriedly threw on his overalls and a hard hat and then he ran down the hallway to the stairwell. From there he ran down to the main deck. When he opened the door, he gasped. Flames enveloped the derrick and adjacent crane as liquid mud rained down. Bodies littered the deck. Where was the Fire Team?

"Help me!" someone screamed. Andy ran to where the screaming had come from and found Royce lying under a fallen beam.

"Are you okay?" he yelled as he lifted the beam.

"Yeah!" Royce nodded. "Just got knocked down by the beam!"

"What happened?"

"A blowout!" he yelled.

"Get to the lifeboats man, we're going to have to abandon ship!" Andy yelled.

"Not without you!"

"Where's the Fire Team?"

"I don't know! Nick had them all out over by the drilling shack!"

Andy turned and saw the drilling shack engulfed in flames. "I hope not," he said.

"What can I do?" Royce asked, interrupting his dark train of thought.

"Well, if you're going to be out here, help me get the fire-fighting measures activated! Go down to the Control Room and have those numbskulls activate them!" he yelled.

Royce nodded. "Got it boss!" He ran to the accommodation structure.

Andy turned and looked up at the geyser of flame jetting upward toward the darkening sky. Thick black smoke rose upward from the flaming column. He turned and ran to the Fire Room and was dismayed to see no one in it.

"What if they all got killed?" he asked himself. He ran back outside and to the Control Room.

"Get everyone to the lifeboats!" he yelled. "Why isn't the alarm sounding?"

Andreas, one of the Control Room technicians looked up at him. "I'm sorry! I didn't know what to do!"

"Hit the alarm! Activate the blowout preventer! And get to a lifeboat!" Andy yelled, infuriated.

The alarm klaxons began blaring, echoing through the facility.

Where was the Production Crew? The Drilling Crew?

He descended the stairs to the production deck past pipe work that snaked through the floor. The sound of oil rushing through the pipes droned near his head as he descended. When he reached the bottom of the stairs, he saw the Production Manager kneeling and weeping among the pipes.

Andy coughed. The air was filled with gaseous vapors.

"Josh! Are you alright?" he yelled, running up to the kneeling man. "What happened?"

"We tried to get them!" he yelled mournfully.

"What are you talking about? We've got to get out of here!" Andy said urgently.

"No, no. We tried to get back at Cypress for abandoning us! It was just supposed to ruin some of the drilling equipment!"

"Are you saying *you* caused the blowout?" Andy yelled.

"Yes! We caused it!" he howled.

Andy balled up his fist and punched the man in the eye. He fell backwards.

"You killed good men!" Andy screamed. He bent down and grabbed the Production Manager by the shirt collar.

He was weeping. "I'm so sorry! I am so sorry!"

Andy yanked him to his feet. "Come on! We've got to get out of here!" he yelled as he released the shirt.

Andy ran toward the stairs expecting Josh to be behind him. Suddenly he was knocked off his feet by another explosion. Dazed, he sat up and looked back. Josh was lying face down on the deck enveloped by flames shooting from a nearby pipe.

"Josh!" he yelled. He realized that if Josh was somehow still alive, he was too grievously wounded to survive the trip to shore. Andy ran back up the stairs to the main deck where the whole platform was in disarray.

He saw someone who was in flames leap over the safety railing and off the platform.

"We're all going to die!" someone screamed.

"Get to the lifeboats!" Andy yelled again.

Suddenly, another blast knocked him off his feet. Dazed, he sat up. His ears were ringing. No one else was moving on the deck. He saw flames all around. He slowly stood and stumbled to the North Lifeboat Deck. He stepped over dead bodies and broken machinery. Small explosions went off all around him as cylinders of gas detonated and rocketed skyward.

When he reached the deck, Andy saw from the stairs that it was ablaze. He ran back toward the South Lifeboat Deck as his sense of balance returned. The whole platform was bobbing up and down in the sea. He realized that soon the whole spar would be on fire as the millions of gallons of crude oil stored within the floating structure ignited.

He descended to the South Lifeboat Deck and saw that both lifeboats there were gone. He looked out and saw three lifeboats a few hundred yards from the platform. He looked down over the railing at the sea. If he jumped, he'd fall about eighty feet; the fall might kill him. He looked back and saw a wall of fire behind him. He turned again to the precipice.

He took a deep breath and leapt from the platform. As he fell through the cool evening air, he felt an intense sense of calm sweep over him. He pointed his toes downward, squeezed his legs together and reached upward.

Andy felt a shock as he plunged into the cool Gulf water. He descended downward. He looked up and opened his eyes. He could see the burning platform above, its image distorted by the rippling water. He waved his arms and kicked and managed to surface. The roar of the inferno overhead was nearly deafening. He could see the rainbow sheen of oil on the water nearby.

He kicked again and looked for the lifeboats. Where had they gone?

He swept his arms forward and began to swim in the direction he thought the lifeboats were in. Behind him, more explosions took place as the platform burned. Flaming debris splashed in the water nearby. Andy swam all the more furiously.

"Andy! Is that you?" a familiar voice yelled. He looked up and saw a lifeboat ten feet away; Milo was standing in the hatchway.

"Yes!" Andy yelled, swimming to the boat. He reached up and felt hands around his forearm. He was pulled into the boat. He looked up and saw only four other men in the vessel: Milo, Royce, Bob Taylor from Maintenance and Oscar from Production.

"Where's everybody else?" he yelled.

He noticed Royce was weeping. So was Bob. Oscar sat in a seat silently, his face in his hands.

Milo spoke up. "They're either dead or in the other two lifeboats man."

"What? Why did this boat launch with only you guys in it?"

The cook looked down. "We didn't have a choice. It was either launch or be cooked!"

"What?"

"That second explosion almost killed us!" Oscar yelled.

More explosions rocked the platform behind them.

"We have to go back!" Andy said. "What if people are left on the platform?"

Royce shook his head. "No. You were the only one. We thought you were dead. Bodies have been dropping off that rig by the dozens; most of them in flames."

The radio crackled. *"Lifeboats, this is Carlos Rodriguez. Please state your presence and number aboard. This is Lifeboat A. We have fifteen aboard. Over."*

"This is Merle Hoskins, coxswain of Lifeboat B. We have ten aboard."

Andy walked to the radio console and picked up the microphone. "This is Richard Andrew Gibson, acting coxswain of Lifeboat D. We have five aboard."

"Alright, where's C?" Carlos asked.

Milo looked at him. "It was destroyed in the third explosion. Everyone aboard was killed."

"One of the gentlemen on my boat said he saw Lifeboat C get destroyed in the third explosion," Andy said.

He heard gasps from one of the boats.

"That's distressing news. Crew leads, we will now go through the various crews and list how many are present. If someone on your boat got on the wrong boat, have him speak up please. We need to determine who is missing," Carlos said. *"Alright. Culinary. We have three on A according to Chef Keel."*

"We've got Milo on D," Andy said.

"Alright, Culinary is fully accounted for. Medical staff has one plus Carl Becker. They are fully accounted for. Second and Third Mates?"

"They were scheduled to be on C if I recall correctly," Merle said sadly.

"Alright. Let's see, Tool Pusher, Drilling, Derrick, and Floor hands and Lease hands were scheduled to be on C. So were the Mud Engineers."

Oscar shook his head and began to cry.

"Scaffolding is fully accounted for," Carlos said. *"Control Room is fully accounted for. Production? Is anyone still alive out there?"*

"Yeah," Andy said. "Oscar Mendez is on D."

"Fire Team?" Carlos asked.

"We only have two on D," Andy said. He felt tears welling up in his eyes as he realized how severe their loss was.

"Anyone else? Okay," Carlos sighed. *"Geologists? Security? We've got Tyrell Cook with us. What about Robbie?"*

"He's not on D," Andy said.

"Engineering?" Carlos asked.

"Five of us," Merle responded. *"All accounted for."*

"Maintenance?" Carlos asked.

"All accounted for except for Bob Taylor," came the response.

"Bob's on D," Andy said.

"Alright. Well Services? Welding?"

"We've got one welder on B," Merle said.

"Crane Operators?"

No one replied.

"Alright. We are going to steer to a safe distance while we send out distress calls. Is anyone on any boat injured?" Carlos asked.

"Kyle has some burns on his right side, but he's okay. Otherwise we're okay on B," Merle said.

"No one's injured on D," Andy said.

"Well, that's good. If no response comes to our distress call then we will make for Port Fourchon."

Andy sat down in the coxswain seat and started the motor. He followed the other two boats away from the burning platform. Once they were about a half a mile out, they all stopped.

Andy stood and walked to the hatchway and watched the installation burn while the others wept behind him. He and Royce were the only survivors from the Fire Team. They were the only survivors besides Tyrell from the entire Safety Department.

He sighed and turned to the others. "Alright, what happened up there? We need to piece this together."

Royce sighed. "After I went to the Control Room, I heard a huge explosion. I ran down to the lifeboat platform and saw that it was in danger of being consumed by flames. We launched, even though we knew we had room for more because we knew more folks weren't coming. Man, the whole drilling crew was up there when that first explosion went off! The whole Fire Team was too."

"So what caused the first explosion?" Andy asked.

"I don't know," Royce replied. "I guess that gas was gushing up with the mud that was blowing out. It probably spread out and hit an ignition source. The gas alarms were all going off. The first explosion was huge. I'm lucky I was standing behind some machinery talking to Mikhail." He sighed again. "I just got knocked out and stuck under a beam. Mikhail wasn't so lucky."

"Man, this is bad," Andy said.

"Yeah, I was in the galley washing dishes when the first explosion hit. I woke up lying in front of the fridge. I couldn't make it to Lifeboat A because the hallway was filled with rubble and gas. So I hightailed it to the other lifeboat deck. When I got there Oscar was already seated. I thought about launching when the second explosion went off. Seriously, the fireball missed our boat by no more than twenty feet. It must have come from the drilling deck," Milo said.

"Mitch and Dale showed up for C and then Greg showed up. We tried to convince them to launch when the second explosion happened, but they wouldn't listen," Bob said. "I came here for the same reason Oscar did. It was the closest lifeboat to where I was when the first explosion happened."

"Yeah, we launched because it got too hot in there," Milo said.

"We knew no one would be able to make it here through the flames. And about ten seconds after we launched, the third explosion happened and we watched C get destroyed," Royce said. "Man, why did this happen?"

"Because Josh Hammond sabotaged the shutdown process," Oscar said.

"What?" Milo asked angrily. Andy saw Bob's face turn red.

"Josh told me about five minutes before the first explosion," Oscar said. "He said he had the Mud Engineers pump too much mud out of the well. He wanted to cause a minor blowout to damage the derrick. He assured me it would be safe when I objected. He said it would just be mud coming out. I told him that if gas came up, we wouldn't be able to smell it," Oscar said tearfully. "He said that the alarms would catch it! The Fire Team was nearby, ready in case something bad happened. Then I went to go find Greg and tell him since he was Josh's supervisor. I was about thirty feet away when drilling mud started pouring onto the drilling floor. I had just descended to the drilling deck because someone said Greg was down there when the first explosion happened." He sighed. "A lot of good men died today."

Andy nodded. "I found Josh on the production deck. He confessed to me. He was killed by the second explosion."

"Alright crew, let's set a course for Port Fourchon. Set these coordinates in your navigation systems: Twenty-Nine-Point-One-One degrees North by Ninety-Point-Two degrees West. We should make it there around Five A.M. Stay close," the radio crackled.

Andy looked back at Bald Point. The geyser of flame shooting skyward had stopped.

"I guess someone did activate the blowout preventer," he said softly. He walked to the coxswain seat and fired up the engine again. They set a course for Port Fourchon using the coordinates Carlos had radioed over.

A lot of good men had died because of the vengeful decisions of a few. Andy felt the tears coming again. And unlike a disaster during normal times, there wouldn't be a rescue ship coming. There would probably not be any attempt to stop the leakage of oil from the wrecked spar, at least not until they got to shore and someone could be mobilized.

He wondered how much dispersant would be sprayed on the water to reduce the oil slicks to sinking molecules. He wondered how much oil would be spread across the sea floor like a blanket of foul, dark death no creature could easily escape.

The ride north was quiet except for the whoosh of the lifeboat cutting through the water and the dull buzz of the engine. At one point, Andy looked back and saw everyone except Bob asleep. His face was still red.

He looked up at Andy. "Those imbeciles that caused this got what they deserved. I hope they rot in hell."

Andy nodded. "The justice they'll face is more intense than any they will have ever witnessed in life. The blood of dozens of men is on their hands."

He nodded. "I've never felt so angry. What would possess someone to do something so idiotic?"

Andy shrugged. "The thirst for blood is a powerful and destructive motivation. When Sterling told me they were planning to do some drilling tests the day before we were scheduled to leave, I had a strong suspicion some kind of sabotage would take place. Tyrell told me a couple of weeks ago of rumors that something like this would happen. But, if it happened like Royce suggested, there was no way to do anything except try to vent the gas."

"Awful, just awful!" Bob shook his head.

They sped toward the Louisiana coast for a while longer and finally Andy saw pinpoints of light on the horizon. His relief quickly turned to horror as they drew closer; the lights turned out to be oil platforms that were ablaze, their wells burning out of control.

The radio crackled as they passed a point thirty miles from shore. Andy could hear commotion in the background noise of the transmission.

"This is Tyrell Cook on board Lifeboat A. We have a serious problem. Carl Becker has gotten loose and has bitten people. I fatally wounded him but people are now gravely ill. Carlos is severely wounded. Can anyone assist?"

Andy shuddered in horror. Why had they brought Carl Becker?

Suddenly the radio crackled again.

"Uh D, did you see that?" Merle asked.

Andy looked to the right and saw a small boat that was on fire, a small mushroom cloud of flame rising above it. "What was that?" he asked.

"I think that was Lifeboat A."

"Tyrell? Tyrell? Can you hear me? This is Andrew Gibson from Lifeboat D. Do you read me?" Andy said urgently into the microphone.

"Uh we are going to circle around and see if we can find any survivors," Merle said.

Andy turned the boat and cut the throttle. "Us too."

Royce and Milo stirred as they neared the flaming wreckage.

"What happened? Why are we going slower?" Milo asked.

"I think Lifeboat A just exploded," Andy said tentatively. "Open the hatch."

Royce stood and opened the hatch. A cool breeze carried the fumes of burning rubber into the boat. They pulled alongside the burning wreckage as it started to sink. Andy killed the engine and walked to the hatch.

"Hello out there!" he yelled, cupping his hand to his mouth. "Can anyone hear me? Hello! Can anyone hear me?"

No response came. The only sound was the surf.

"Hello out there!" Merle yelled from about twenty yards away. "Can anyone hear me?"

Silence.

"I think they're all dead!" Merle yelled.

"I think so too!" Andy yelled back as the remains of Lifeboat A sank beneath the waves.

"Let's continue on!" Merle yelled. "When I find those fools at CPG I'm going to strangle them!"

Andy started the engine again and they continued on. Everyone sat in stunned silence. They passed more burning and ruined oil platforms as they neared the coast. Andy saw flames dancing on the shore as they passed a buoy indicating a remaining distance of two miles to the jetty.

"Uh Merle, I don't know about this. Fourchon looks like it's in pretty bad shape," Andy said nervously into the radio.

"Well, wait at the jetty and we'll go ashore first. We'll let you know if it's safe," he replied as the radio crackled.

Andy killed the engine as they entered the jetty and waited. Everyone behind him woke up.

"Where are we?" Oscar asked.

"In the jetty at Port Fourchon," he replied. "The whole port looks like it's on fire. Merle is taking Lifeboat B ashore first. He'll radio back to let us know if it's safe."

The radio crackled. *"Pulling up to a dock now. There are a lot of folks on shore but they're walking kinda funny,"* Merle said. *"Hey! What's wrong with you? Hey! Stop right now!"* Andy heard growls in the background and screams. It sounded like a terrible struggle.

"D! Run! Run for your lives! Do not come ashore here!" Andy recognized Scott Maniczewski's voice. He was screaming. More screaming in the background and then the radio went silent.

"What just happened?" Royce asked.

"I think we're the only survivors from Bald Point," Andy said quietly. Oil tanks burned in the night in front of them, sending pillars of smoke toward the sky.

CHAPTER TWENTY-FOUR

Katie Barnes
Day 17

They came around a bend in the highway as the clouds above thickened. They had been driving all day and were now just north of Pittsburgh.

"We'll be exiting the highway soon!" Joel yelled over the din of wind and motor. He motioned to Rachel who was on the other moped with the bags.

They had left the cabin in the Allegheny National Forest that morning just before dawn, when the forest glade was illuminated by civil twilight. They had loaded their gear onto the moped Rachel would drive while Katie rode on the back of Joel's. Each bike had a spare tank of gas. Everything had been tinted gray in dawn's early light.

Rachel had tearfully bid the cabin goodbye and they had sped off into the forest. It had been chilly. Really chilly. So Katie had hugged Joel tightly.

They sped through rural Pennsylvania, following US Route 62. The Allegheny River was to their right most of the time. They drove through mostly deserted towns. Sometimes Katie saw Infected shuffling through towns on the opposite bank of the Allegheny; sometimes she saw them just a block away in empty towns.

The hilly arboreal landscape reminded her of Canada. She thought back to when she had arrived in Toronto.

When she had disembarked from the airplane at Toronto Pearson International Airport, Katie expected her aunt and uncle to either fail to show up or to be unhappy to see her; she had been projecting her father's failures on them. She was stunned when she saw a brightly colored sign saying,

WELCOME HOME KATIE!

A tall slightly chubby man with graying black hair stood next to a slender blonde who looked strikingly like Katie's mother. They were both holding the welcome sign. Katie walked to them and they hugged her tightly. They were so excited to have her in Toronto. Their accents and attitudes contrasted sharply with Katie's father's. When they got outside the terminal, she saw that a light snow was falling.

Uncle Martin drove them back to a house near Casa Loma in his old Toyota Camry. They drove to 288 Spadina Road. It was an old Victorian style house with a gabled roof that was rather imposing from the street. Katie would have been more reluctant to enter if Martin and Catherine hadn't been so welcoming.

"I'll be right back ladies," Martin said after carrying Katie's luggage in. He walked back outside.

Catherine smiled. "Katie, I know you must really be hurt by what your dad did. I'm sorry you had to face that. We love you and we intend to treat you like you're the daughter we never had."

"Thanks," Katie had murmured uncomfortably.

Any awkwardness dissipated when Martin returned with Chinese food. They shared the first of many meals together and Katie concluded living in Toronto might work out as she ate a crab wonton.

After she had been there for a few days, her aunt took Katie to work with her, after Katie expressed an interest in art. Catherine worked at the Art Gallery of Ontario as a photographer and did a lot of photography on the side.

As Catherine took her on a tour of the Gallery, she saw a lot of beautiful paintings by artists such as Picasso and Cézanne and Dalí. When they walked up to the second floor they entered the Canadian Art section.

Something caught Katie's eye as she and her aunt entered a room. There on the opposite wall was an oil canvas depicting a lonely pine tree on the shore of a lake in vermillion and green. Katie felt drawn to it by some unseen magnetism and, so compelled, walked to it.

She studied the detail, the way the mountains in the background weren't obscured by the lonely pine in the foreground. The clever use of vermillion as an undercoat drew her attention too, as it contrasted with the other colors on the canvas.

"Ah, I see you found The West Wind," Catherine said, as she walked up behind Katie.

"I did," Katie replied, as she looked at the plate on the wall next to the painting. "Who was Tom Thomson?"

"Tom Thomson was a Canadian painter who died in Nineteen-Seventeen. His paintings heavily influenced a group of painters known as the Group of Seven. Together, they are among the most influential and significant artists in Canada's history. The Gallery here has some of his work and some of his work is in the National Gallery in Ottawa. Do you like what you see?"

"I do, I really do."

"I'll tell Martin; he's been wanting to go visit Ottawa for a while," she chuckled and hugged Katie.

Katie was snapped out of her thoughts of Canada as the moped decelerated, exiting the highway. They drove around onto East Street and crossed a bridge over the highway. Katie saw mountainous forests surrounding them. Joel veered left onto a road that wound up the side of a mountain. They passed a few burned out houses. A few turns later, they drove into a desolate neighborhood. Red sheets hung in many windows and some of the houses were boarded up with signs spray-painted on them,

INFECTION WITHIN. BIOHAZARD. KEEP OUT.

They came around a bend and suddenly houses became sparser. Katie saw a house on the left up ahead that had a brick wall around the property. Light shone from the windows within.

"That's Austin's parents' house!" Joel yelled, pointing at the fortified home.

They drove up to the gate.

"I guess we'll see who's home," Joel said nervously as he stepped off the bike. He tried the intercom. It beeped.

"What do you want? If you're here to loot, be advised the brick has an electrified layer at the top. You will be electrocuted if you attempt to climb the wall. If you make it in, we will shoot!" a modulated voice replied back.

"Uh, is this where Austin Collins lives?" Joel asked.

"Who wants to know?" the voice queried.

"An old friend."

"Joel, is that you?"

"It is. Joel Ryan in the flesh!"

Katie heard a clanking sound. The gate opened automatically.

"Come on up to the house!" the intercom squawked.

When they reached the house, Austin ran out and greeted them jubilantly. "You guys are still alive!" he yelled.

"*You're* still alive!" Joel yelled back, hugging him.

"Well come on in! We have to catch up!" Austin said eagerly, waving toward his house. "We have hot water, so if you need a shower please help yourself."

Katie noticed that Austin's hair had been combed back in to cornrows.

"What happened to the 'fro Austin?" she asked.

He laughed. "Man, when the zombies rose up, I felt like I needed to have my hair under control. You know, an afro is an easy thing for a zombie to grab."

She nodded. "That's true."

"Plus, I figure this makes me look a bit more intimidating, in case some miscreants try to get in."

Katie and the others followed him into the house. The house was a large brick structure. The entry room had a staircase leading up to the second floor and several rooms to the right, left and back. The floors appeared to be made of cherry wood.

"Do you smell that?" Rachel asked.

Katie did indeed smell the aroma of pumpkin pie. This could work.

They walked back to the kitchen and Austin prepared some plates for them. Then he sat down at the table. The other three all sat down across from him and they began to relate what had happened in the last two weeks.

"So after we returned from D.C., I had to come back here because my grandma was sick with Owasa Disease. I had no idea how much the media censored what Owasa Disease does to a person! It was the most horrifying thing I'd ever seen when I visited her," Austin said. "Of course she died after a few days and the CDC recommended a quick burial. I thought I heard scratching at the inside of the casket at the funeral, but I just dismissed what I heard as the product of not having slept much.

"Then October Twenty-Eighth happened. The government declared quarantine and people who had been infected with Owasa Disease started coming back to life and attacking people. It was almost like the virus was controlling their bodies!

"My dad got stuck downtown at the beginning of the quarantine at the Allegheny County Courthouse and we couldn't get a hold of him because all the cell towers were down, so we were freaking out! When the County Administration realized what was happening, they let their employees leave.

"So on October Thirtieth I was awakened by the sound of my dad's motorcycle roaring up our driveway. We were so relieved! He told us about what he had seen, with the dead rising and stuff. Since then we electrified part of the wall around the property, reinforced the gate and have just been biding our time hiding out here," he paused. "So, what's new with you guys?"

"Where to start?" Katie asked. "I was chased by Infected all over UB's North Campus, we were arrested for violating the quarantine orders then mercifully dropped off at my house; we hid out in our house for about a week. We watched things spiral out of control. It was me, Joel, Rachel, Michelle, Megan Costanza, you knew her right? And Amber and Anthony were there too. We saw horrible things, people being torn apart by the Infected and coming back, that kind of stuff. One even broke into our house. I killed it with my baseball bat." She saw Austin's jaw drop. "After about a week of watching society collapse, we opted to leave. Anthony, Amber, and Megan went back to Amber's house and we left to go to Rachel's dad's cabin up in northern Pennsylvania.

"When we got there, Rachel's dad had been infected. And he bit Michelle," she paused, feeling tears welling up in her eyes. "I'm sorry, it's just..." Katie looked at Rachel. She was starting to cry too.

"Michelle got infected and died. I killed her when she came back to life," Joel said. "We determined it would be a bad idea to try to overwinter at the cabin, so we decided to make our way here, to see if you were still alive. And here we are."

"Wow," Austin said. "I don't know what to say. Michelle died?"

Katie nodded.

"I'm so sorry guys," he said, standing up and hugging Rachel and Katie.

Katie heard footsteps coming down the stairs. She turned and saw an older man with a salt and pepper beard approaching.

"Austin, who are your friends?" he asked.

"Dad, these are my friends from college. That's Joel, my roommate, his fiancée Katie and her roommate Rachel," Austin replied.

"Ah, pleased to meet you all! Did you all come here from Buffalo?" Austin's dad asked.

Katie nodded. "We came on mopeds."

"Wow! What's it like out there?"

"Bad. Really bad," Rachel said grimly. "Society has basically collapsed."

"Wow. That's terrible. I guess we've been a little insulated in here. The brick wall out there helps," he replied. "Oh goodness! Where are my manners? I'm Gary Collins, Austin's father!" He extended his hand and shook all of their hands. "My wife Valerie is around here somewhere. Welcome to Collins House!"

After that, Katie, Joel and Rachel settled in pretty quickly. Katie was amazed by how well the Collins retained a sense of normalcy! They generated their electricity from solar panels on the roof and used electric heaters to keep the house warm. All of their drinking water came from a well and they recycled gray water from the washing machine for the garden growing in a greenhouse behind the house. Valerie had a green thumb and had been growing fruits and vegetables year round in the greenhouse for a while. Austin and Gary went hunting once a week in the woods behind the house and primarily caught small game with traps and these weapons they called gigs.

The gig resembled a spear, but was made of a long wooden rod. One end was split into four equal tines that had been sharpened. There were pencils stuck into the grooves between the tines to hold them apart. Honestly Katie thought the gig was an intimidating tool.

Katie even went outside a few times and played Frisbee golf with Joel, Austin and Rachel. It was like being in a bubble of normal in a sea of tumult! It was incredible! They filled in the rest of the time working on chores around the household.

Gary helped Katie modify her bat to make a more effective weapon. He attached small steel pegs around the circumference of the bat at its tip. That made the bat a little heavier, but also more effective.

On Thursday, November 26th, the group even celebrated Thanksgiving! Somehow, Gary had caught a turkey in the woods behind the house. Katie enjoyed it thoroughly.

When they moved in with the Collins, Katie learned they lived in a 4-bedroom house. Valerie and Gary had the master bedroom, which was downstairs connected to the office. Austin had a smaller bedroom upstairs. Rachel got a room and Joel and Katie shared the last room.

At last they had found a safe place to stay.

CHAPTER TWENTY-FIVE

Jim Gibson
Day 37

"So that's it then?" Jim asked as dawn broke over the snowy field and the smoldering ruins of the New York Central Terminal. "We're going our separate ways?"

"I'm afraid so man," Jeff replied. "You've got your family, you and Phil, and I have my own. They might still be alive, they might be dead, I just don't know. That said man, you inspired me. You walked across the city to find your brother, and you're getting ready to drive across the country to find your family. I respect that and I honestly wish we were heading in the same direction, but we can't. Your way is west, mine is to go to the Big Apple, or whatever's left of it."

"I understand man, it's been good. Good luck," Jim said as he hugged Jeff. "May we meet again."

"Indeed," Jeff replied, lifting his bag into the bed of the 1983 Ford F-150 he had found in a neighbor's garage. "May we meet again. Goodbye Jim, goodbye Phil. I hope you find what you're looking for. Bye Vikram, bye Sherry!" He turned and opened the door of the truck. Then he climbed in and started the ancient vehicle. Gray exhaust erupted from the tailpipe as the engine roared to life. He shifted the truck into gear and he and Connor drove off.

"Alright, let's get going," Phil said. "We might be able to reach dad's house by nightfall."

Jim walked back to the driveway and climbed in the front seat of the gold 1997 Jeep Wrangler which had been the other car in the neighbor's garage. Sherry and Vik were already seated in the back. Phil got in the driver's seat and shifted the already running Jeep into first. Mercifully the heat worked in the old Jeep, as the thermometer on the front porch of the house they had been sheltering in indicated the temperature was 21°.

Jim still couldn't believe Antoine and Giselle were dead and that the place they had been hiding in had suddenly burned to the ground. He wondered how Phil was coping with his best friend's unexpected death as they pulled south on Memorial Drive. The Jeep turned left on to Williams Street and continued east.

As they drove through a darkened underpass that snaked beneath railroad tracks, Phil carefully steered around abandoned police vehicles and zombies. They continued east past zombies shuffling along sidewalks and turned right on Bailey Avenue.

Jim looked back as they drove south on Bailey under another rail overpass. Sherry flashed a little smile as he stared past her. A few miles north lay the University at Buffalo. He wondered about the blonde girl he had asked out a few weeks earlier.

She had been in his Statistics and Probability class and usually sat across the room from him. Her long wavy blonde hair and blue eyes were eye catching. She was the prettiest woman he had ever seen! Katie Barnes was her name, and she had actually lived down the street from him and his family when they lived in Baltimore.

Back in October, a few weeks before the epidemic, Jim had gone down to a bar near Saint Canisius College one night and run into her. He asked her out on a date but she reluctantly declined. It turned out she already had a boyfriend and had plans with him.

Jim had been shaken but not defeated. He could wait and see if she became available. And, of course, if she didn't, there were always other girls. Nevertheless, with all of the recent events, he couldn't help but wonder if she had survived or been turned into a zombie. He supposed he'd never know.

He heard Phil cuss and he looked up. The Jeep was approaching I-190 and it was obvious the freeway was clogged with abandoned cars. Phil punched the steering wheel and slowed the Jeep to a stop. Jim pulled out a road atlas and handed it to his brother.

Phil studied it with furrowed brows flipping between the map of Buffalo and the map of New York.

"Okay," he said. "We will get out of Buffalo on the side streets and try getting on the interstate once we are in a rural area."

"Hey Phil," Vik said nervously. "We should get moving, now!"

Jim turned and saw zombies within two yards of the Jeep. "Phil, yeah, we've got zombies!" he said.

"Geez guys, quit twisting my arm!" Phil sighed, shifting into gear. The Jeep moved forward away from the undead denizens. "We'll take the scenic route!"

He reached up and turned the radio on. Surprisingly the old Jeep had a CD player!

A song with an electronic feel started. A man sang with a woman providing backing vocals.

They listened to the album for a few songs before Phil ejected it and studied the CD.

"The Postal Service? This band sucks!" he said as he cracked his window and threw the disc from the Jeep.

"Hey!" Sherry protested. "I like that band!"

"Too bad," he replied looking through the CDs on the visor. "Do you like The Black Keys?"

"They're okay," she replied.

"I like them," Jim said.

"Me too," Vik said.

"Alright, the tribe has spoken," Phil said inserting the CD.

The track started with a gritty blues riff.

Phil steered carefully as they drove south, as the snow obscured parts of the road. They drove through an empty toll plaza and merged on to I-90. Thankfully the few cars they passed were almost all parked on the shoulder or in the median.

The entire landscape in every direction was covered in white. The sun had been out earlier in the day but it was now cloudy.

"Man, I can't believe Antoine was so stupid," Phil said, shaking his head.

Jim grunted in reply.

"I mean the guy was an electrical engineering student! He knew he was in a room full of highly energized equipment! Why not lure the zombie out of the room before trying to slice and dice? Zombies are dumb. They're easily led into a situation bad for them. It's such a waste."

"I'm sure Antoine was doing what he thought was best," Sherry said quietly.

"Even so it resulted in him dying, him getting Giselle killed, almost getting Connor and the rest of us killed and our home burning to the ground. It was stupid!" He let out an anguished laugh. "I mean he was my best friend!"

"I know man, it hurts," Jim said.

He shook his head. "Such a waste, such a waste."

They stopped for the night in Willoughby, Ohio just outside Cleveland. Phil parked outside the loading dock for a small hardware store located about a mile from the interstate. Together, Phil, Vik and Jim forced the garage door up and carried their gear in, closing the door once everyone was in.

It was chilly in the store but not unbearably so. Sherry and Phil went one direction in the store while Vik and Jim went in the other direction to make sure it was zombie free. Sure enough, there were only a few of the creatures roaming the aisles of the former hardware store. They were easily dealt with.

When that was finished everyone gathered in the back and Phil spoke up. "Alright, we need to take advantage of our temporary shelter. First, we need to make sure it's secure and defendable. Then, we need to see if we can find some battery powered heaters or something, you know, the kind contractors would use. Then, we might as well use the opportunity afforded us here to find better weapons. Jim, your little pry bar looks like it could use an upgrade. Vik, your puny claw hammer could be upsized. My knife could probably be upgraded and Sherry, your knife could be upgraded too."

Vik pointed out the windows were already covered with plywood. Then he found a battery powered garage heater that he carried to the back room where they would be sleeping. He rigged it up and turned it on.

Phil found a machete he liked. Jim found an axe he liked. Vik found a long-handled sledgehammer he liked and Sherry found a crowbar she liked. Their tasks finished, the group sat down in the back room and warmed up while eating trail mix.

"So Vikram, you're from Mumbai originally?" Phil asked.

Vik nodded. "Yes. We came to America when I was little. My father was a doctor in India but he and my mother wanted better opportunities for me and my brother Raj so we moved to Houston, Texas when I was two."

"That's cool man."

"Thanks. Unfortunately, my parents died in a plane crash two years ago when they were flying back to India to visit family. Their airplane crashed in the Pacific Ocean."

"I'm sorry to hear that."

"Yeah, it sucked. But I think I have recovered a lot from it. I still occasionally feel sad about it, but it is in the past."

"What about your brother?" Sherry asked.

"He is a mechanical engineer in Nairobi, or he was. I don't know if he's still alive and I suppose there's no way I'll ever know."

"Where did you hope to end up working after you graduated?" Phil asked.

Vik laughed. "Well, I've always hated hot weather. You know, I don't remember much from living in Mumbai, but I remember it was hot. Of course Houston was hot and humid too! So I was hoping to eventually get a job somewhere cold, like Canada or Alaska, maybe Russia. Vikram Patel, the Indian man with a Southern accent who grew up in Houston and who wound up building dams in Russia. Wouldn't that be a hoot?"

Everyone laughed.

"So your dad worked with the Detroit Tigers?" he asked.

"Yeah, kind of," Phil replied.

"He was a radio announcer for them. He got to travel around with them all over the place. He was actually an employee of a radio station in Detroit, I can't remember which one," Jim piped in.

"W-X-T-M," Phil said.

"That's cool," Vik said. "You guys get to go to any games?"

"Yeah, he took us to Game Two of the Two-Thousand-Twelve World Series," Jim replied. "We got to meet Prince Fielder and Justin Verlander. It was pretty cool."

"It was, even though the Tigers got swept," Phil added.

"Yeah," Jim said.

"That's really cool man," Vik said.

Jim heard snoring behind Vik and realized Sherry had fallen asleep.

"She makes a good point," Phil said, chuckling. "It's late. Who wants first watch?"

"I'll take it," said Vik. "How long should our shifts last?"

"Let's say four hours," Phil said.

"Okay, I'll go keep watch near the front of the store. Jim, I'll come wake you in four hours?"

"No, let him sleep until the last shift. I'll wake him when my shift is done," Phil said.

"Okay," Vik replied, standing up. "I'll come get you all if I need help. Goodnight guys."

Jim fell asleep quickly.

"Hey, wake up!" he heard Phil whispering.

Jim opened his eyes. He felt like he had just fallen asleep.

"It's your turn for watch buddy," Phil said.

"Okay," he replied, sitting up and rubbing his eyes. "Didn't I just fall asleep?"

Phil chuckled. "No man, you laid down and you were out."

"Oh."

"Wear your coat, it's chilly up front. Vik set up a chair at the cash register. It's a good place to sit."

"Okay," Jim said as he stood up and grabbed his axe. "Goodnight Phil."

Phil chuckled. "Goodnight Jim. I guess it will be daylight soon."

"Okay," Jim said, buttoning his coat and grabbing his flashlight. He walked to the front of the store away from the dim orange glow of the heater. The temperature fell sharply as he neared the front of the store.

He sat down in the chair at the cash register and listened to the wind howl outside. He wondered how many zombies were shuffling across the wastes outside. He also wondered if his dad was still alive. The snow made Jim think of him.

Jim and his siblings had to visit him several times each winter per the terms of his visitation rights. He had bought a house in Saint Clair Shores, a wealthy suburb north of Detroit. His house sat in a cul-de-sac at the end of a street that jutted out on a peninsula into Lake Saint Clair. In the summer they would go swimming in the lake, but in the winter it usually froze over enough to go ice fishing.

His girlfriends always seemed to be terrible cooks. Jim could never understand as a child why they were unable to do something as simple as read the directions on a box of brownie mix.

Jim saw light begin to shine in through the gaps in the plywood. He realized the sun was coming up. He walked back and woke the others and they set out again.

They merged onto westbound I-90 as the sun peeked above the horizon behind them. They drove toward Cleveland. As they approached downtown, with Lake Erie on the right, the freeway suddenly became choked with abandoned cars.

Phil turned the Jeep around and drove back to an exit they had passed earlier: Eddy Road. They exited the highway and drove to Saint Clair Avenue. They continued west on it, passing abandoned homes and businesses. Some buildings were burned out ruins. Others were boarded up. Some had red sheets hanging in broken windows, blowing in the wind. Others were boarded up and spray-painted with warning signs indicating contagion was present within.

They passed dilapidated Victorian houses and crumbling brick structures. Zombies shuffled through the snow all around, so Phil was forced to drive carefully.

"We're about one-hundred-seventy-five miles from Detroit," Jim said, studying the Dist-o-Map.

"Good, we should make it there today," Phil replied.

"Hey, why'd you guys let me sleep all night?" Sherry asked. "I could have kept watch."

"I figured you needed rest," Phil said.

"Okay, thanks!"

As they continued west toward downtown Cleveland, the snow became slushy. The morning sun was causing it to melt. Soon they reached areas where the road was free of snow.

They passed over an interstate that was crowded with abandoned cars. Zombies swarmed around below. Jim wondered if they would encounter a similarly sized horde before they left Cleveland.

The tall office buildings of downtown Cleveland loomed ahead. Soon the Jeep was driving among them. Some showed evidence of fire damage. Some were leaning precariously. Most were missing some or all of their windows. Throughout the downtown area, broken glass glimmered on the pavement and sidewalks.

They approached a plaza to the left. As the Jeep came around the adjacent building, Jim saw two large regal buildings standing one street over. He also saw thousands of zombies swarming around a fountain in the center of the plaza.

"Oh man!" Phil exclaimed, accelerating past the mall. They passed more towers as the road sloped downward toward a river. They passed West 10th Street and Phil slowed to a stop. They were at the riverfront. To the right stood a fallen bridge over the river. To the left stood an intact bridge.

Phil turned left down West 10th Street and they approached the bridge. West 10th Street passed under the bridge's approach.

"Aha!" he exclaimed, seeing a side street they could use to find access to the bridge. As the Jeep came around the corner the road ahead was blocked by hundreds of zombies. Phil slowed to a stop and backed the Jeep up. The zombies saw the survivors and began to stagger toward the Jeep.

Phil turned around and drove down West 10th Street back to Saint Clair Avenue. At that intersection there was a street that ran diagonally toward the bridge. It too was clogged with zombies.

"Go right!" Vik yelled.

The Jeep continued up the hill on Saint Clair and when the group reached West 9th Street, Phil hurriedly turned right as a large crowd of zombies was approaching from the east. He sped down the street and as he turned right on Huron Street, apparently where the bridge's approach was located, the Jeep slid through the slushy intersection and flattened several zombies.

Phil floored it and the Jeep motored across the bridge, downtown Cleveland and the horde of zombies receded into the distance behind them, the Cuyahoga River below. Everyone let out sighs of relief when the Jeep reached the western terminus of the bridge and they saw the area was devoid of zombies. Phil slowed to a stop and pulled the atlas back out. He flipped through the pages, studying it.

"Okay," he said. "If we go left here, we'll get back to Interstate Ninety."

The Jeep turned left and continued on. Phil ran down several zombies in the street as they sped south. Soon they merged back on to westbound I-90.

"You know that river we drove over used to catch on fire all the time," Sherry said.

"Oh yeah?" Jim asked.

"Yeah. My uncle lived in Cleveland for a while and said that the Cuyahoga used to be one of the most polluted rivers on Earth."

"Wow," Jim said disinterestedly, watching the wintery landscape speed by.

He soon fell asleep.

It was mid-afternoon when he woke up. He saw downtown Detroit in the distance. As he rubbed his eyes he became aware it was snowing again.

"Have a good nap?" Vik asked.

"Yeah," he replied. "How long was I asleep?" He looked to the left and saw the idled smokestacks of the River Rouge complex nearby. Zug Island was to the right with its towering blast furnaces.

"Like four hours," Phil said. "I just figured we'd let you sleep."

They followed I-75 as it snaked through the city of Detroit. The skyscrapers of downtown passed by on the right.

"Jim, do you remember when dad had us over for Christmas eight years ago?" Phil asked.

"Yeah, vaguely. Was that when he was dating Deanna?"

"No, he was with Charlene at that point I think."

"Yeah, I remember."

"Man, I remember Charlene just couldn't cook! Remember how she tried to cook a Christmas goose and burned the bird?"

"Yeah," Jim laughed. "Dad had a thing for women who couldn't cook."

Sherry and Vik laughed from the backseat.

They passed Ford Field on the right and continued along I-75. Soon they merged onto northbound I-94. Jim knew they were getting close. The snow had stopped by the time they exited at East 11 Mile Road.

"I wonder how far Jeff and Connor have made it," Jim said.

"If their car held out, they could be in New York City by now," Sherry said.

"Yeah," he said as Phil turned on to Shorewood Street. The Jeep crossed a small bridge and drove past houses that were all, surprisingly, intact. Most had boarded up windows, a few had graffiti spray-painted on them that indicated the presence of Owasa Disease. Phil slowed as they reached the end of the block and pulled into a driveway. The old man's car was nowhere to be seen. The windows of his house were all boarded up. There wasn't a zombie in sight.

"Alright," Phil said as they pulled into the driveway. He turned toward Sherry and Vik. "Me and Jim are going to go inside to make sure there aren't any zombies. You two stay out here."

"Okay Phil," Vik said.

Jim and Phil got out. A frigid gust of wind swept off the lake blowing snow around them. They walked up the unplowed driveway to the covered porch of the humble one-story L-shaped brick house on the shore.

"Alright," Phil said, inserting his key into the lock. "We don't know what we are going to find in there, so be ready for anything. Dad could be gone. Dad could be alive, holed up in there with a machine gun and an itchy trigger finger. He might be a zombie. If he is, a zombie that is," he paused, "let me do it."

"Okay," Jim said.

"Alright, let's do this. Get my back."

Jim turned his flashlight on as Phil opened the door. The darkened house was quiet. They walked in and Phil shut the door quickly.

Jim looked around at the interior. The furniture was coated with a thin layer of dust. He looked at the photos on the wall. Baby pictures were prominently displayed alongside Tigers memorabilia.

Phil walked into the kitchen and Jim followed. Bananas sat moldering in a fruit basket on the counter. Jim looked out the small window over the sink and saw the blue waters of Lake Saint Clair rippling in the wind.

They searched the house. All of the bedrooms were empty. So was the bathroom.

"I guess that leaves the basement," Jim said grimly.

"Yeah, I'll go first," Phil said, walking to the basement door in the kitchen. The floor creaked underfoot as they walked across it.

Phil opened the door and the faint scent of death wafted up from the darkened basement. He looked at Jim and shrugged. They started down the stairs, Phil in front.

When they reached the bottom of the stairs Jim swept the beam of his flashlight around the dark basement. He illuminated concrete walls and a washer and dryer with shelving in the corner. And there alongside the shelving, in the corner, their dad hung from a joist in the ceiling, a noose around his neck.

CHAPTER TWENTY-SIX

Andy Gibson
Day 34

Andy set a course to the east following the coastline after the horrifying events at Port Fourchon. The others had all been horrified by the radio broadcast and what seemed to be Scott Maniczewski's last words. By now the sun was coming up, making visual navigation considerably easier.

Royce offered to navigate and steer the boat to give him a chance to sleep. Andy laid down in the back of the lifeboat and tried to fall asleep. Despite the bumpy ride, he sank into slumber very quickly.

He had nightmares about the oil platform. He could hear others around him crying out for help, but he couldn't move. He was frozen in place.

He bolted upright suddenly, wide-awake. He was back on the lifeboat. Bob lay a few feet away, snoring softly. Oscar and Milo were praying together. Royce was still steering the boat. The radio beeped softly.

"What's on the radio?" he asked sleepily.

"Another warning message, warning us to stay away from New Orleans. You can listen to it if you want? I turned the volume down so you and Bob could sleep," Royce replied.

Andy sat up and looked out the porthole in the side of the boat. He saw the coast in the distance. It was cloudy out and the water was a deep stormy blue color. He walked to the front and sat down next to Royce.

The radio was beeping Morse code in what sounded like an S.O.S. The beeping paused for a moment.

"This is Rear Admiral Charles McCann of the United States Coast Guard. By the time you hear this message, I will likely be dead or worse. I am broadcasting from New Orleans, Louisiana. If you receive this message do not come here. I repeat, do not come here. Infection containment protocols have failed and Owasa Disease is rampant. Do not come here. If you come here, you will die or worse."

The beeping continued and then the message repeated.

Royce looked at Andy. "What do you make of that?"

He shrugged. "I guess it's a good thing we aren't going to the Big Easy."

"What do you make of him talking about containment and infection?"

He shrugged. "Who knows?"

"Sounds bad. Did some sort of epidemic happen while we were out at sea?"

"*That* sounds apocalyptic. *But,* it also sounds plausible. I mean, why haven't we been able to make contact with anyone on shore? What if civilization was wiped out by some lousy flu virus and then the hurricane just damaged infrastructure even further?"

"Maybe it was Ebola," Royce said.

Andy shook his head. "Fyodor did suggest nuclear war, back on Thanksgiving."

"Man that sounds bad. We'd better stop talking like that," Milo said, interrupting them. "That sounds like some kind of disaster movie!"

"Relax," Andy said reassuringly. "I'm sure it's not as bad as it sounds."

"I'm going to go back to praying I think. We'll see how bad it really is once we get to shore," he said. "It looks like it's much worse than it sounds."

The next morning Andy awoke after having slept poorly all night. He couldn't stop thinking about Shelly and Isaiah. He had been delightfully surprised when Shelly had learned she was pregnant. The pregnancy had gone smoothly and Andy had been looking forward to taking a month off work from the platform in Brazil.

When Shelly woke him at 3:00 in the morning telling him she was having contractions, at first Andy told her she was just having Braxton-Hicks contractions; Isaiah's due date was still a few weeks away. There was simply no way he would be coming so soon Andy thought. Andy could remember telling her to take a hot shower to see if the contractions went away.

When she began crying out in agony in the shower, he leapt out of bed and realized she was having real contractions. He drove her to the hospital in Bay Saint Louis and at 6:32am, his tiny little boy Isaiah Alexander Gibson was born.

Andy remembered the first time he held Isaiah; he was so tiny and Andy knew in that instant that he would do anything to keep Isaiah safe. All of the late nights after Isaiah came home, all of the sniffly noses, all of the dirty diapers, all of it just made Andy love him more. He was so happy to be a daddy.

Somehow, having Isaiah helped Andy fall even more deeply in love with Shelly. She had been the love of his life since before they had been married. But now he worked to put the phone away when he was home and really be present with her and Isaiah.

So of course Andy was worried when he couldn't reach them via phone after the hurricane. Of course his worry grew as time passed and he still couldn't reach them. And of course it grew further still when he saw the destruction at Port Fourchon and heard the broadcast from New Orleans.

He put on a brave front to the other guys in the lifeboat, but inside he was filled with turmoil. He relieved Bob from steering at 8:00am and took over.

At 9:00am, he cried out. "I see the bridges! We're approaching Bay Saint Louis!"

Royce stood and looked out the front window. "We sure are!"

As they drew near, Andy saw that the rail bridge at the mouth of the bay had large sections missing. The US-90 Bridge also looked badly damaged. Gradually the shore came into better view. Trees had been stripped of their vegetation and uprooted. Houses were missing their roofs and some buildings appeared to have even been washed out into the bay.

Andy grimaced. "This doesn't look good."

"Where are all the people? Where's FEMA?" Royce asked. He patted Andy's shoulder. "Hey, I'm sure Shelly and Isaiah are alright."

Andy nodded. "Thanks."

As they passed under an intact section of the rail bridge, Andy noticed that the rails had been twisted. The level of destruction astonished him. Even more astonishing was how deserted the city appeared from the bay.

As they approached the US-90 Bridge, Andy saw that it would be impossible to continue north in the inlet; the only portions of the bridge that hadn't collapsed into the water were the concrete columns the spans should have rested atop. The rest of the bridge, every segment, lay in mangled piles between the supports.

"Looks like we'll have to beach the lifeboat," he said, steering the boat toward the sandy expanse. The boat shook a little as it scraped the sand just offshore and then shook violently as they ran aground. Once they had stopped, Milo opened the hatch and all five men exited the lifeboat.

Andy looked around at the desolation. Palm trees had been snapped like twigs. Houses had been knocked off their foundations or had their roofs peeled back like a can of sardines or had been crushed by falling oaks or had burned down. In some places, he could see concrete slabs that had been swept clean of any structure.

They walked up the beach, climbed up the seawall and walked to North Beach Boulevard. Andy listened carefully; all he could hear was the sound of the surf punctuated occasionally by one bird calling to another. The air smelled strongly of saltwater.

"I've heard about what this place looked like after Hurricane Katrina, but this has to be just as bad," Bob said. "I had an uncle who lived here in Oh-Five. He said it was the worst storm he had ever seen."

"Man," Milo whistled. "I hope it isn't this bad in Bayou La Batre!"

Andy nodded, his worry growing. They crossed US-90 and saw cars that had been turned upside down; rotting corpses hung from the seats, bound in place by seatbelts.

Once they were north of the highway, the damage became less catastrophic. Here houses only appeared to have water damage. Nevertheless, Andy had a strong feeling he would only find a single stilt remaining of his house.

As they passed a marina on the right, Andy was overcome with anxiety. He started to trot.

"Hey! Wait up!" Royce yelled.

"I'm sorry! I can't wait! One-Oh-Eight Engman! The street's up ahead on the left!" he yelled as he quickened his pace. "One-Oh-Eight Engman! Just catch up!"

He broke into a dash and ran the final mile and a half. As he came around the corner, sweaty and out of breath, he saw his worries about the house had been unfounded! It was still standing! His garage was still standing too! He saw a water line on both buildings about seven feet high. Of course that's why the house was up on stilts.

He noticed the side door of the garage was open. And he caught a glint of dark blue in the darkness behind it. Shelly's Passat was dark blue! Andy sprinted the final three hundred yards to the garage and ran through the door.

He couldn't see anything in the dim light except the vague outline of the Passat. The garage smelled foul, like mold and something else. He walked to the garage door and pulled it open and flooded the water-damaged garage with light. It was then that he saw the car in detail. The car wasn't water-damaged, so he knew it had arrived after the storm. He saw something in the car and as he approached the driver's side, his vision grew blurry with tears. He pulled the driver's door open and cried out.

His wife and son lay dead in the car.

The Passat's windows were cracked and the key had been turned. Andy guessed that Shelly had started the car with the garage door closed and the windows down and had asphyxiated herself and Isaiah with carbon monoxide. The moldy smell in the garage had masked the lingering scent of car exhaust and the terrible odor of decay. When he opened the car door, though, Andy could smell it more strongly. A note was taped to the steering wheel. He grabbed it and read it as he wept.

He was still in the garage, weeping and vomiting when the others caught up to him. Later, he recalled being led into the house by Royce and Milo.

He sat on the couch in his living room for a while staring ahead. Finally, his senses returned. He stood up quickly. His dramatic change in demeanor must have scared the others. "I need to bury them," he said resolutely. "I have two shovels in the garage. Will someone help me?"

"We all will man," Royce said. Milo, Oscar and Bob all voiced their affirmation.

The men all exited the house, walked down the stairs and went back to the garage. The sun had finally emerged from the clouds and was hanging low in the sky as the sandy earth received his wife's and son's linen-shrouded bodies.

"I met Shelly during my first semester of college," he said sadly as he and his friends stood over the fresh graves. "She and I started dating after we realized we were going to the same church. We got married a few weeks before we graduated from college and we had Isaiah a little more than a year ago.

"You all know this about me. I am a committed Christian. Shelly was too. She was the anchor that God provided me in stormy waters. She was my best friend. She was my lover. She-" he began to choke up. "She and I loved each other so deeply! And Isaiah, he was my little boy!" he cried out and fell to his knees.

"May they rest in peace," Royce said softly, patting his shoulder.

They finished filling the graves as the sun dipped below the horizon, bathing the clouds in brilliant splashes of color. The others went back inside and left Andy at the graves. He stood there for what seemed like a long time reading the note from Shelly over and over.

"Andrew, I am so very sorry. I am so sorry," he murmured as he read it.

The sky faded from pink to orange to red to purple to black and soon it was too dark to read the note. The stars emerged and eventually Andy could even see the milky white outline of the galaxy, stretching across the night sky.

"Goodbye Shelly, goodbye Isaiah," he said calmly, as the moon rose in the east, over the bay. "Rest in peace beloved wife and beloved son." He stood there for a little while longer.

"We travel through a barren land with dangers thick on every hand but Jesus guides us through the vale, oh the Christian's hope can never fail," he sang. "Sometimes we're tempted to despair, but Jesus makes us then His care. Though numerous foes our souls assail, oh the Christian's hope can never fail." He walked back to the stairs and climbed them to the house. He walked in and sat down at the kitchen table with the others.

"So I suppose Oscar and I will set for Atlanta in a couple of days," Bob said a little later.

"I'm going to follow them as far as Bayou La Batre," Milo said.

Andy nodded. "There's nothing for me here. I have family scattered all over the northeast quadrant of the country. I have a sister in Chicago, my father's in Detroit, two brothers live in Buffalo and my mother lives in Manhattan. If it's alright, I too will follow you all as far as Milo's before I head north."

"That's cool with me," Milo said.

"I'll stick with Andy," Royce said.

"Alright," Milo said. "I guess we all leave here two days thence?"

CHAPTER TWENTY-SEVEN

Jim Gibson
Day 38

Phil and Jim both gasped. They ran over to the body. His skin was gray, firm and cold. There was a note pinned to his orange plaid flannel shirt. Phil grabbed it and read it aloud.

"If anyone finds me like this, please know I didn't want to do it. I believe myself to have no other options though. The house is surrounded by monsters who crave flesh. It is growing cold as winter approaches as well. I have no means of escape and I do not wish to become one of those monsters should I lose my mind and leave the house. The date is now November 24. If you can, if civilization is ever restored, please find my children and tell them their father loved them very much. Their names are Richard Andrew Gibson of Bay Saint Louis, Mississippi; Victoria Anne Eccleston of Chicago, Illinois; and Philip Joshua Gibson Junior and James Daniel Gibson both of Buffalo, New York. May Detroit rise from the ashes and be great once more!

Signed Philip John Gibson Senior"

Phil dropped the note and looked up at their dad. "Help me cut him down," he said tearfully.

Jim cut the rope holding his father up and laid the body on the cool concrete floor with Phil. Jim sat on the floor beside him silently. Phil kept walking in circles, crying.

"Guys?" Vik yelled from upstairs. "Is everything okay? You've been down there for a while."

"No," Phil yelled. "Our father is dead!"

Jim heard footsteps as Vik ran downstairs. His roommate gasped when he reached the bottom.

"What happened?" he asked.

"He hung himself," Jim said quietly. "A couple of weeks ago. I guess the cold preserved his body."

"Oh my, I'm so sorry!"

Phil stopped walking in circles and looked at Vik. "Thanks."

Jim stood and they all went upstairs. By now it was dark outside. Sherry sat in the living room, building a fire in the fireplace.

"Their dad is dead," Vik said.

Sherry stood and ran over to Phil, embracing him. "I'm so sorry!"

Phil buried his face in her shoulder weeping.

Jim noticed all of their bags had been brought in and set on the floor. He supposed Vik or Sherry had brought them in. He sat down in front of the fireplace and watched the flames slowly consume the log that had been placed in the hearth.

Vik sat down beside Jim and watched the fire with him.

"I'm sorry to hear about your father," Vik said finally. "I know what it is like to suddenly and unexpectedly lose one's parents."

"Thank you Vikram," Jim said.

"If you wish to talk, I will listen. If you simply desire silence, I will be silent."

Jim nodded. It had always greatly bothered him that his dad had screwed up his marriage with his mom. He was a good father, or at least he tried to be. Jim just never understood why he was continually unfaithful. Didn't he realize what had been at stake?

Phil and Sherry sat down beside Jim and Vik, around the fire.

"Sometimes," Jim said, "I wonder why mom married Steve."

"Me too," Phil said quietly.

"I mean, Dad had a thing for the ladies, but at least he was a nice guy and tried to be involved in our lives. Steve was a jerk who spent so much time in the office and who spent most of his free time with his own snotty nosed kid. Phil, after you went off to college, I don't know if I ever told you about how Steve decided to take Mom and Tyler to Hawaii with him and made me stay home to watch the house?"

"They went to Hawaii together?" Phil asked indignantly. "Huh, I guess at least you weren't the only one who missed out. I didn't even know they had gone to Hawaii. I'll bet Andy and Vicki didn't either."

Jim nodded. "But dad, on the other hand, was a good guy! I remember he took us to Tigers baseball games every summer and usually let us travel with him on road trips. Do you remember when he let us go with him to Tampa when the Tigers played the Devil Rays? We had box seats for every game!"

"Yeah, that was awesome," Phil said, grinning. "Remember when he took us to the All Star Game in Minneapolis?"

"Yeah, I remember we got lost in a shady neighborhood. Dad was so flustered!" Jim laughed.

"Yeah," Phil replied, wiping his eyes, "Dad was pretty fun to be around."

"Yeah. I'll miss him," Jim said.

"Me too."

Everyone sat there quietly for a while. Then Phil jumped up and ran to the back of the house. Jim heard him digging around in a closet. A few minutes later he returned with a couple of cloth items bundled up. He laid them out on the floor behind everyone.

Jim turned and saw a giant Detroit Tigers flag stretched across the living room. In the middle of it, Phil laid an autographed gray and orange Cecil Fielder jersey with the number 45 emblazoned on the back.

"We have to bury Dad," Jim said.

"Yeah. Tomorrow we're going to procure the neighbor's bass boat, we're going to dress dad in Cecil Fielder's jersey and we are going to wrap him in the Tigers flag. We will have a short ceremony for him on the lake and bury him in the lake," Phil said.

"Sounds good," Jim said.

"Do you guys want help?" Sherry asked.

"No," Phil replied. "This is a task for me and Jim and just us. You guys can stay here and hang out while we pay our last respects to our dad."

"Okay," she said.

"Now, my dad used to keep a solid supply of beer and wine here. It's not water, but it's probably the only safe thing to drink in here," he said walking into the kitchen. "Bingo!" he said triumphantly. Jim heard the clanking of cans and Phil returned to the living room holding two six packs of Red Stripe.

"Rehydrate my friends!" he said, laughing.

Jim grabbed a can and opened it. The distinctive pop sounded delightful. The cold brew quenched his thirst as he took a drink.

"Of course, in the event of the apocalypse dad wouldn't have bottled water!" Phil exclaimed, laughing. "Instead he had Jamaican lager!"

Everyone laughed.

The next morning Jim awoke to the feeling of sunlight on his face. He sat up. Beams of light were filtering through gaps in the plywood sheeting over the windows. Everyone else was still asleep.

He stood up and walked out into the backyard. It was chilly out, but warmer than it had been for the last few weeks. The lake stretched toward the horizon, the blue surface broken here and there by small chunks of ice. Jim turned and looked at the wooden privacy fence surrounding the backyard. It was still intact.

He sat down at the picnic table in the backyard and sighed. He had been pretty optimistic about finding his dad alive. It had been crushing to find him dead. Jim's father was dead.

He dwelt on that for a moment. His father was dead.

He felt a tear fall.

He shook his head.

Of course, because of this finding, he was no longer optimistic about finding his brother or his sister or his mom or even Steve. Jim dreaded going to Chicago now.

He shook his head again. He had to be strong. For Phil and for the others he had to be strong. He wiped the tears from his eyes. He took in a deep breath and sighed.

"Aren't you cold?" Vik asked, interrupting his thoughts. Jim heard the frozen grass crunching under his friend's feet.

"I'm fine," he said. "You sure you want to live somewhere cold? You seem to dislike this."

"No, no. I just figured you'd be cold, that's all," Vik said, as he sat down on the bench beside Jim.

"I'm fine."

"How are you doing man? I mean, with your dad and stuff?"

Jim shrugged. "I'm managing I guess."

Vik patted his shoulder. "I know it hurts."

"Yeah."

"I ever tell you how I found out that my parents died?"

Jim shook his head. "I guess it happened before we met, huh?"

"Yeah."

"Huh."

"I had just finished my last final before Winter Break. It was a few weeks before Christmas. My parents flew back to India to visit family for Diwali. They were going to fly home a few days before classes started for the spring semester.

"They called me every day while they were in India. I was back in Houston housesitting for them. I remember they called me before they got on the plane to fly back. They said they would be back around noon the next day.

"My dad's co-worker Dave was supposed to pick them up from the airport. Well, noon came and went and I received no call from them. I assumed their flight had been delayed. At three that afternoon, Dave called me and asked if I had heard from them. I hadn't.

"Then I got the call from the airline. Their plane had disappeared from radar a thousand miles southwest of Midway Island. They were searching for the plane but couldn't make any promises. I knew then that my parents were dead."

"Wow man."

"Yeah. They found some fragments of the airplane and a few suitcases floating in the ocean about two weeks later, but they never found any large parts of the airplane or bodies. They think it experienced some sort of mechanical failure that caused the plane to break up in the sky. Investigators told me it was extremely likely my parents didn't feel anything.

"So needless to say, I missed the first couple of weeks of class that semester. It was awful. But friend, I can tell you now that you will survive. Eventually the pain will fade enough to no longer be so piercing." Vik patted his shoulder again.

"Thanks Vikram," Jim said.

"You're welcome friend."

Jim heard the sliding patio door open. He turned and saw Phil and Sherry walk outside.

"Chilly, huh?" Phil asked.

"Yeah. At least all the snow melted," Jim replied.

"We going to do this?"

"With dad?"

"Yes."

"Yeah. Let's do it."

"Okay, go next door and take old man Warren's bass boat."

Jim walked around to the front yard and climbed over the neighbor's chain link fence. As he walked through the backyard he saw a zombie pressing against the glass patio door of the house, its flesh hanging from its bones in places.

Jim walked to the little dock on the shore and climbed into the bass boat. Then he untied it from its mooring and started the motor. He steered it over to his dad's yard and tied it off at the dock.

"See anything over there?" Phil asked as Jim walked up toward the house.

"Yeah, Warren is a zombie now."

"Ha, that guy was always a grouch."

They walked inside. Phil grabbed the flag and the jersey and he and Jim went downstairs to their dad's body. He lay on the concrete floor looking peaceful.

"Help me lift him into an upright position," Phil said.

The brothers wrestled him into an upright position; his body was stiff. Then they put the jersey on him and buttoned it. When they were finished they carefully laid him on the spread out flag and wrapped it around him tightly. When they were finished, they both looked at each other.

"I'll get the shoulders if you get the feet," Phil said.

"Okay."

The brothers lifted their dad's body up and carried him up the stairs out of the basement. They then carried him out the backdoor and to the bass boat. They lowered him into the boat and then Phil walked over to the shed. He came back with rope and several dumbbells.

"We're going to weigh him down so that he sinks and doesn't float back to shore," Phil said as he climbed into the boat and began wrapping rope around the flag near their father's shoulders and knotting it together.

Jim climbed in and grabbed a length of rope and began tying it around their father's legs and knotting it. He grabbed two of the dumbbells and tied them to the ends of the rope.

"Alright guys," he said. "We will be back soon."

"Be careful," Sherry said.

"You know you have our condolences," Vik said.

"Thanks," Jim said as Phil untied the boat. Jim started the motor and steered them out away from the shore.

It was a clear day and the wind was calm. The brothers motored out to a spot a couple of miles offshore.

"I guess this is a good spot," Phil said.

Jim killed the motor and they coasted to a stop.

"Philip John Gibson was my father," Phil said solemnly. "I am his namesake. He was my father, he was my mentor and he was my friend. He died before his time, but he is honored in death. May he find rest at the bottom of Lake Saint Clair."

"Indeed. Philip John Gibson was my father," Jim said solemnly. "He taught me right from wrong, he gave me a love of baseball and film. He was not a perfect father, he made mistakes. But he accepted responsibility for his mistakes and he taught me to do likewise. He is honored in death and may he rest in peace."

Jim and Phil stood up carefully, trying not to tip the boat over. They slowly lifted the body and lowered it into the lake. It sank quickly, bubbles coming up as it descended.

The brothers sat back down in the small boat and sat there at that spot in the lake for a while.

"I guess you listened in on that phone call too, huh?" Phil said finally.

"Which phone call?" Jim asked.

"The one where he called mom and confessed everything to her and took responsibility."

"Yeah. I remember he called and you answered and then ran to your room after mom took the phone and quietly listened in. I did too."

"Man, how old were we when that happened?"

"I was eight. It was right before we moved to New York."

"Wow, so I was ten. It's funny Jim, I remember that call like it was yesterday."

"Me too. He said, 'Now Judith, I know you divorced me because I was unfaithful to you. I confess I committed adultery at least ten times with ten other women.' I remember there was silence and then mom said-"

"Well Philip, it's about time you came clean!'" Phil said.

"Yeah, and then dad apologized and took responsibility! It was crazy!"

"Yeah. He tried Jim, he tried so hard."

"He really did. I mean, I guess many a man has been led astray by his desires."

"Yeah. Let's head back to shore."

They arrived back at shore around noon. Vik ran up to greet them. "Hey! I think when we leave we should take your dad's Lincoln!" he yelled as Phil tied the boat off.

"Ha! He hasn't been buried for a day even and you're wanting us to divide up his assets!" Phil yelled, laughing.

He and Jim climbed out of the boat and followed Vik to the garage. Their dad's orange Lincoln Navigator sat in the middle of the room. Phil examined it.

"Well Vik, I guess you're right. The Lincoln has a full tank of gas, compared to the Jeep's quarter of a tank, and it is more spacious inside," he said.

"How much longer are we staying?" Sherry asked.

"Another day, we'll leave tomorrow," Phil said. "Me and Jim are going to go through our dad's stuff today to see if there's anything we want to take."

"Okay, and then where are we heading?"

"Chicago," Jim said. "We're going to look for our sister, see if she's still alive."

"Okay," she replied. "And then to Omaha?"

"Sure, it's on the way west," Phil said.

That afternoon Sherry went for a walk around the neighborhood. Phil advised her to stay close and to carry her crowbar with her, just in case. Jim and Phil stayed inside to sort through their father's possessions.

"How do these look?" Phil asked.

Jim looked up from the box he had been sorting through and saw Phil was wearing an old pair of aviator glasses. He chuckled. "They look good on you. Where'd you find those?"

"In his nightstand."

"Cool."

The brothers dug some more. Phil searched his dad's closet while Jim looked under the bed.

"Score!" Phil shouted.

Jim turned and saw him holding a shotgun. "Whoa!" he exclaimed.

"Yeah! Now just to find the shells!"

Jim found a box of 12-gauge shells under the bed. He handed them to Phil.

"Now we can be just like the zombie killers in the movies!" he said laughing.

"Yeah," Jim laughed.

Phil chambered one of the shells. Suddenly a blood-curdling scream came from outside.

"Sherry!" Phil said urgently. He and Jim both ran out of the bedroom. Jim grabbed his axe as he ran out the front door. Vik was right behind them.

CHAPTER TWENTY-EIGHT

Jamie Daniels
Day 14

A chilly breeze blew down the street as Jamie Daniels walked toward the lakeshore. The morning sun hung about 45° above the cold blue water of Lake Michigan. He sighed and a small cloud of steam blew forth from his mouth.

"Winter is coming," he muttered as he shivered. He lit a cigarette and took a drag as clouds moved east over the water. He glanced south toward the ruined buildings of downtown Chicago. He had been to the Windy City once before; it was a bitter memory. He had come to purchase a package of heroin for a partner of his in Kentucky.

In retrospect, he wasn't sure if the drugs he had been high on were making him more anxious than usual or if it was just cold, but the dealer had called him 'Shakes.'

A few months later Jamie had been arrested after robbing a convenience store and then he had spent a long time in prison.

He shook his head. He had been a junkie off and on since he had been a teenager. So much wasted time, so much wasted money, so many burned bridges and ruined relationships.

He inhaled another puff of tobacco and chuckled bitterly. He had been clean for four months. The collapse of society had made it significantly more difficult to relapse. Still, he felt the draw of the sweet needle from time to time.

He shook his head again, remembering what his brother had told him the last time they had spoken.

"Once a junkie always a junkie," Shelby had said so bitterly.

"Yeah, you don't know nothing about recovery!" Jamie had screamed.

"And you don't know a thing about integrity!" Shelby had screamed back, tapping Jamie's chest with his finger. "Once a junkie always a junkie."

He chuckled again. Shelby's words had been the catalyst he had needed to finally get clean. Shelby would probably never know what kind of influence he had been.

A rustling in some nearby bushes snapped Jamie out of his thoughts. He turned and saw an infected man emerge. The ghoul staggered toward him. Its clothes were slashed and hung from decaying shoulders.

He stood there, watching the infected man stumble toward him. He waited until the zombie was perhaps four feet away. He reached out and grabbed its arm just below the shoulder. The rotting thing growled as it jerked forward and Jamie threw it into the lake.

He sighed and walked back to Todd's house.

"Remember when the Jeep got a flat tire in the Mojave Desert?" Randy asked at dinner. It was late, the kids were in bed.

Todd laughed. "Yeah."

Randy nodded. "Yeah, I remember you tried jacking the Jeep up but the jack was broken! We had to walk three miles back to a gas station and wait for a tow truck."

"Yeah, we waited for what, like four hours?" Todd replied.

"Yeah! And it was so hot! And the gas station attendant was so rude!"

Todd laughed as he sipped some beer.

"Hey Todd! This beer is good! What's it called again?" Casey asked.

"Paradise Lager."

"It's smooth!" Adam said.

"Thanks guys."

"It is pretty good," Jamie said as he drank some.

"So Jamie, where are you from?" Todd asked.

"Des Plaines originally," he replied. "But I grew up in West Virginia. My mom married a guy named Dwayne when I was eight and we moved to a little town in West Virginia when I was ten, after Dwayne got a job as a shift supervisor at a coal mine."

"What part of West Virginia?" Todd asked.

"About an hour east of Charleston, up in the Appalachians."

"What a beautiful part of the country!" Todd exclaimed.

"Maybe, but between my stepdad beating me, my mom and my brother and molesting my sister, I wanted to escape as soon as I could."

"That's terrible!" Vicki exclaimed. "I'm so sorry that you had to go through that!"

He shrugged. "I moved out as soon as I could. I married my high school sweetheart and we moved to Ashland, Kentucky. About the only good thing that came out of that relationship was my daughter Madeleine," Jamie replied. "Tamara, my wife, was crazy. We were both heroin junkies. She and I divorced about seven years ago when she got clean and I haven't seen either her or my daughter in a long time."

"Wow Jamie, that sucks," Todd said.

Jamie looked down at his plate. Canned corn and spam lay mingling in one another's juices. He sighed. "I don't know. I made a lot of bad choices when I was younger, you know, sometimes we have to bear the fruit of what we've done."

"How long have you been clean?" Todd asked.

"Four months."

"Wow. That's good man!"

He nodded. "It's been tough, but here I am today, clean and sober."

"Indeed!" Todd raised his beer. "A toast! A toast to Jamie and his continued abstinence from heroin."

Everyone murmured agreement and took drinks from their beverages.

A few days passed. On the Fifteenth Jamie went scavenging with Todd, Randy and Adam. They walked north along the shore of Lake Michigan. It was cloudy and cold and a bitterly cold breeze blew in off the lake.

"So dad was thinking about buying a sailboat?" Randy asked as they passed several burned out cars.

Todd nodded. "Yeah. I think he had some grand notions of being able to sail anywhere in the world."

Randy laughed. "Yeah, he always wanted to show mom the Seven Seas!"

Adam patted Jamie's shoulder. "Hey, I'm sorry you had such a rough upbringing."

Jamie shrugged, uncomfortable at the hint of pity in Adam's voice. "Not your fault."

"Still."

Jamie frowned. "You're kind of awkward, you know that?"

"I'm sorry, I just, I guess I've never known anyone who..." he trailed off.

"Has spent time in prison? Has been divorced? Has been a junkie? Has robbed someone else?" Jamie asked, trying to finish his awkward sentence.

He looked down. "I'm sorry, I am awkward."

Jamie laughed and patted him on the back. "It's okay Adam. I've heard it all."

The awkward boy smiled. "Thanks."

"What do you think happened to Penny? Think she found her family?"

He shrugged. "I don't know. I hope so. She was pretty."

Jamie laughed. "She was indeed. Although she smelled like a zoo."

"What do you think?"

"I think she was sweet but sort of a bimbo. I'd be very surprised if she even makes it to her family alive."

"What? She was a crazy survivalist!"

"She was also lacking in people skills."

"She made it this far!"

"Luck man, it was all luck."

"We'll have to agree to disagree."

"Hey, for her sake I hope you're right," Jamie said.

"Hey, I don't mean to break up the pow wow back there," Randy said suddenly, "but we have zombies approaching!"

Jamie looked up and saw a crowd of about fourteen zombies approaching slowly. They all possessed a hungry, dead look in their eyes. Most were disfigured and maimed.

He raised his hammer and ran at a zombie on the left flank. He hacked at its head with the claw end of his tool and it dropped. He moved on to the next zombie as the others worked. They quickly dispatched the crowd and continued on.

"We're getting close to Loyola University," Todd said. "We're going to look through their medical offices for antibiotics."

"Why?" Jamie asked.

"In case any of us gets sick. They could prove useful."

"Good point."

Jamie looked around. "There are fewer zombies than I expected."

Randy shrugged. "Yeah, it is a little strange."

"I noticed they seem to move in waves across the city," Todd said. "It's like they wander until they find a larger group to join up with and so on and so forth. I saw a crowd that probably had several thousand zombies in it a few days before you guys showed up just wandering around on Lower Wacker Drive in downtown. When I came back a few hours later, they were all gone."

"So we need to be careful," Randy said. "We could turn back and come face to face with a massive herd of zombies."

"I'd worry more about the thugs than the zombies," Adam said. "We can outrun zombies."

"True, they're not very fast," Jamie said.

"Yeah, but I would still avoid getting cornered. I'd be worried about getting boxed in pretty quickly," Randy said.

"Here we are," Todd said.

Jamie looked up and saw a tall Art Deco style building to the left next to a four-story concrete building. The road curved around the complex.

"Is that the university?" he asked.

"Yeah," Todd replied.

"Do you know where to go?" Adam asked.

"I've been here dozens of times over the years," Todd said. "I know exactly where to go."

Jamie looked to the left as they left the road and saw an abandoned transit bus turned sideways on the street. It was covered with missing person fliers.

They followed Todd down a trail that wrapped around the four-story building and followed the rocky shore of the Lake. They passed a blocky concrete chapel and approached a three-story structure with a red roof.

"Here," Todd said.

"Why don't I stay outside?" Jamie suggested.

"And keep watch?"

"Yeah. I need to smoke a cigarette."

"Sure, just holler if you need anything. We're going to the second floor. There's a medical lab up there."

"Sure thing Todd."

They entered the building as Jamie pulled a cigarette out of his jacket pocket. He pulled his lighter out, a cheap transparent orange Bic and lit the cigarette. He took a drag of it as the water bobbed up and down along the rocky shore. He looked out over the deep blue water and exhaled.

Jamie noticed some debris bobbing up and down on the waves about a hundred feet out. It looked like several wooden boards. He squinted his eyes to get a better look and realized he was staring at several dozen corpses floating in the lake. He grimaced and took another drag from the cigarette.

A few minutes later the others emerged from the building, each carrying a plastic bag.

"Did you find what you were looking for?" he asked.

"Yeah," Todd said. "This should restock our medicine cabinet nicely. Any trouble out here?"

Jamie shook his head. "No, it's been quiet."

"Good, let's get going."

On the Eighteenth, Jamie was awakened by the sound of the girls playing in the room next to the room that Adam, Randy, Casey and he were sleeping in. He sat up and rubbed his eyes. Casey was snoring. Adam and Randy were gone.

"What time is it?" Jamie mumbled. He looked at the alarm clock and saw that it was just before 10:00am. He stood up and walked downstairs. Randy and Adam were in the kitchen with Todd.

Todd smiled. "Good morning sunshine!"

"Hey," Jamie said. "Is there coffee?"

"Yeah, over there in the pot. It's cold brewed," he replied.

"That's fine," Jamie said as he walked over to the coffee pot. He grabbed a mug from the cabinet and poured a cup.

"Hey, I was going to take the guys to Wrigley Field," Todd said.

"Why?" Jamie asked. "Aren't there just corpses there?"

"Well, it was where the military attempted to evac everyone. It was a dismal failure," Todd replied.

"We wanted to see it," Randy said.

Jamie shook his head.

"Besides, there's probably some ammo there," Adam said.

"You make a good point Adam," Jamie conceded.

"Yeah. We're going to head over in a little bit, if you want to come?" Todd said.

"Sure, let me drink some coffee first."

They set out around 11:00am. It was unseasonably warm out as they walked south on Seminary Avenue. The trees in the park on the right side of the road had shed most of their leaves by now. Jamie turned his head and saw a trio of deer grazing in the center of the park.

"This is where I've caught two deer," Todd whispered in his ear.

Jamie nodded. "Plenty of land to graze on. Do the zombies go after them?"

Todd made a noise that sounded like a soft laugh. "Sometimes. It's kind of funny to watch. Usually the deer get away. Those zombies are so slow. I guess it's a consequence of being dead."

Jamie nodded.

"So you have a daughter huh?" Todd asked.

"Yeah."

He squeezed Jamie's shoulder. "I'm sure she's okay."

Jamie nodded.

"How old is she?"

"Sixteen."

"A teenager. Wow."

Jamie shrugged. "Yeah. I haven't seen her in years."

Todd put his hand on Jamie's shoulder again. "I'm sure she misses you."

Jamie nodded. He was growing tired of the others' sympathy. He was mainly annoyed by Adam and Todd, but even Randy seemed to give him piteous looks from time to time. Would he ever get beyond being someone's object of pity? He had seen the same look in Shelby's eyes, before he had stolen from him. He had seen the same look in Tamara's eyes the last time she had visited him in that roach-infested rat hole of a prison. He hated that look.

"Hey, look!" Adam called out.

The outer shell of Wrigley Field loomed ahead. Dozens of olive green military tents stood in the lots around the stadium. Body bags were stacked all over; some stacks stood four or five bags high. As the survivors approached the scene, Jamie saw that some corpses were dressed in fatigues, some in scrubs, and others in denim. A few were naked. Nevertheless all were swollen and blackened.

The stench of decay was nearly overwhelming. Adam yelled as the black blanket on one nearby corpse turned out to be a swarm of millions of flies.

"I warned you all," Jamie said. "I didn't think this was a good idea."

The group turned down Waveland Avenue and walked toward a breach in the wall around the stadium. As the field came into view, so too did the mangled wreckage of several military helicopters. Hundreds of zombies stumbled about the outfield aimlessly.

"We should get back," Todd said quietly.

Jamie nodded. "Don't make any loud noises guys," he said quietly to the others. "Let's head back the way we came."

They quietly retraced their steps back to Seminary Avenue and walked back toward Todd's house.

"There were a lot of zombies in there," Adam said as they passed a burned out video game store.

Todd nodded quietly. "We might need to get out of the city soon."

"We drove up from Bloomington in a fifteen-passenger van," Randy replied.

"Oh yeah? Where's this van now?" Todd asked.

"Stopped near a fallen bridge on the Stevenson Expressway over by Midway. We couldn't drive it the rest of the way because it was out of gas and the bridge was collapsed."

Todd nodded. "I suppose we could go try to recover it."

"Sounds good. What do you think? Me, you, Casey and Jamie?" Randy asked.

Jamie felt Todd sizing him up and weighing his value.

"You any good with that gun Jamie?" Todd asked.

Jamie nodded. "I fought off dozens of deranged soldiers in Bloomington with it, so I'd like to think I am."

"Good."

"Hey, if you guys are heading that way, I think me and Jill are going to head east to see if our family survived," Adam said.

Todd looked at him and Jamie could see the doubt in his eyes. "You're going to walk to Valpo?"

"If there isn't any other way, yes," Adam replied. "And then we are going to head to Cleveland."

Todd glanced back at Jamie. "No. We will find a car in the neighborhood we can hotwire for you. We'll look when we get back."

"Thanks Todd."

"Maybe I should go with them?" Randy said.

"No Randy, you don't have to do that. Stay with your brother," Adam protested. "Besides, if we don't find any," he paused. "If we don't find any family who survived, we are going to come back."

Randy nodded uncertainly. "Still, I'd feel better if I could go with you." He glanced at Todd.

"It will probably take a few days to get to Cleveland and back," Todd said. "Go with them Randy."

"You sure Todd?"

"Yes. Take my car."

"The Land Rover?" Randy asked.

"Yes." He turned toward Jamie. "It'll be me, you and Casey going to get the van. You okay with that?"

Jamie nodded. He hoped it would be a quick journey to retrieve the van. He also hoped Randy, Adam and Jillian would be okay.

But the next day it was sharply colder and rainy. So too was the day after and the day after that. Finally, a good day arrived for one trio to go west and the other trio to go east. They began loading up the Land Rover before dawn.

Later Jamie was packing some supplies in a backpack as Todd handed Randy a rifle. The gun appeared to be several decades old.

"Where did this gun come from Todd?" Randy asked.

"Vicki's grandpa, if you believe it. That was a wedding present from her Grandpa Elmer," Todd replied as he handed Randy a box of bullets.

Jamie followed Todd, Randy, Casey, Adam and Jillian outside to the Land Rover. The majority of the supplies needed to travel east were already loaded up in the silver vehicle. Jamie realized he had never seen a Land Rover up close.

"Randy, be careful," Todd said as he embraced his brother tightly.

"I will be Todd."

"I hope you guys find surviving family," Todd told Adam and Jillian.

"Thank you Todd. If we don't, we'll be back," Adam said.

Jamie wondered how Randy would return if either Adam's or Jillian's families were still alive. Would they send him back on his own? What if the Land Rover couldn't make it to Cleveland?

"How much extra gas do they have?" Jamie asked.

"About fifteen gallons. Should be enough to get them to Cleveland and most of the way back. They should be able to scavenge the rest. I gave them the tools to siphon gas from cars," Todd replied as the three got into the Rover and started it. Everyone waved as the Rover pulled forward and then suddenly Randy, Adam and Jillian were gone as the Rover disappeared around a corner.

"We'll set out in a few minutes," Todd said. "We'll make our way to the river and try to find a motorized boat we can take upriver to the van. Maybe we can be back before sundown. You have a bag packed with supplies Casey?"

Casey nodded. He was wearing a black hoodie and had a canvas backpack. Jamie's own bag felt surprisingly light in spite of the load of ammunition, water and food.

"We'll head east toward Lake Michigan," Todd said. "There's a harbor southeast of here. We'll look for a boat there."

It was eerily quiet as they walked. The only sound besides their footsteps was the rustling of leaves as a gentle breeze blew. They passed boarded up storefronts and burned out cars as they moved toward the Lake. Every now and then Jamie would spy a few crows fluttering away from a rotting corpse as they approached. As they turned right on North Broadway, Jamie noticed a faint noise that sounded like the noise a stick makes when it hits a metal barrel. He suddenly felt disquieted. They walked through the parking lot of an abandoned gas station as they headed east on Sheridan Road.

"It's so quiet," Casey said.

Jamie nodded. "Do you hear that thumping noise up ahead?"

"What do you think it is?" Casey asked.

"I don't know," Jamie replied.

"Look alive guys," Todd said. "Could be trouble."

As they neared the lake, Jamie saw what was causing the commotion; hundreds of cars were stopped on a highway up ahead. Each car had a zombie trapped in it and the creatures were hitting the inside of the car windows trying to break free.

"Alright, let's squeeze between the cars. See there? There's a pretty good gap between that semi and the little brown Volvo in front of it," Todd said.

As they neared the stopped cars, an overwhelming stench hit them. Jamie gagged.

"They stink," Casey said.

"You wouldn't smell too good either if your corpse had been trapped in a car for a few weeks," Todd replied.

As they crossed in front of stopped cars, Jamie saw the putrid zombies reaching for them, clawing at them.

HONK!

The sudden noise made Jamie jump as the semi's horn began to blare. That caused the car alarm on a nearby car to start going off. The air was quickly filled with the cacophony of car alarms and truck horns. The sound was deafening.

"We'll go that way!" Todd yelled, pointing south. "The harbor is-" His lips were moving but Jamie couldn't hear anything else he said over the noise.

Jamie covered his ears with both hands as he, Casey and Todd began to run south through a parking lot that sat adjacent to some tennis courts. He looked back and saw dozens of zombies staggering toward them.

"Guys!" he yelled as they put some distance between themselves and the blaring alarms. "Behind us!"

Todd and Casey stopped and turned around. Todd's jaw dropped when he saw the zombies. "Run!" he yelled. "This way!"

Jamie and Casey followed Todd down a running path as a mostly empty harbor came into view.

"There!" Jamie yelled as he pointed toward a gray jon boat tied off at a dock about three hundred feet away. He looked back and saw they were now being followed by hundreds of zombies.

The trio all climbed in the little boat and Todd fired up the engine as a dozen zombies emerged from a nearby bar and grill. Todd eased the boat out away from the dock and soon they were speeding out into Lake Michigan, away from the horde. The abandoned towers of downtown Chicago towered over the water south of them. The boat veered toward downtown.

"We got away!" Casey yelled triumphantly.

"Be that as it may, those car alarms are going to be going off for a while," Jamie replied. "And sound seems to attract zombies."

"Let's just hope we can get back to the house," Todd said. "Vicki has a few guns, and she knows how to use them. Let's hope she doesn't have to use them. Besides, the front door is nice and sturdy and the windows are more than six feet off the ground."

As they floated into the mouth of the Chicago River, Jamie was struck by how quiet the city was. They floated past a horde of several hundred zombies on Lower Wacker Drive as Todd turned the boat to follow the South Fork of the river. A chilly breeze blew in from behind as the river curved to the west. They passed abandoned factories and burned out warehouses. Here and there Jamie noticed submerged cars near the river's banks. He was surprised by how desolate the once bustling city was. Even the birds were quiet, although he supposed that was because most had already flown south for the winter.

They crossed beneath Western Avenue. A trio of men hung from nooses on the bridge's west side. Jamie realized one had been disemboweled; he couldn't tell if that had occurred before or after the man had been hung. He felt sick but he couldn't take his eyes off the macabre scene. He wondered who had hung the men and wondered if they were waiting for more victims. He turned and looked back at the city. That was when he saw it. The sun reflected off something in the water. He squinted his eyes to figure out what it was.

"We're being followed," he said calmly.

"By what?" Todd asked.

"Don't know. Looks like it might be a small fishing boat."

"Hmm," Todd huffed. "Probably one of those cars we passed."

Jamie wasn't sure about that.

"Besides, if it's someone who wants trouble, he'll have to deal with us and our guns," Casey said, patting his rifle.

"You sound awfully confident Casey," Jamie said.

"He's just young," Todd said laughing. "How old are you anyway Casey?"

"Twenty-six," he replied, as the wind blew his hair out.

Jamie chuckled. "You were a Goth in high school, weren't you?"

Casey smiled. "I was."

"I can tell."

"I remember when Randy met Casey, my parents were freaked out!" Todd exclaimed. "Here this Goth kid with white makeup was befriending their youngest son."

"They thought I was a vampire," Casey said matter-of-factly.

"No they didn't," Todd said. "They were just freaked out."

"No, your dad asked me if I preferred B Positive or O Negative."

At that they all laughed.

"Well? What was your preference?" Jamie asked.

"I told him I liked pessimists, so O Negative."

Jamie smiled. "Witty."

"Hey Jamie, I think you were right," Todd said abruptly. "Look. Whatever that is, it's got to be powered. It's following us upstream. We don't know whether it's carrying someone who is friendly or hostile, but either way we need to be prepared. Have your guns ready." He turned up the throttle and as the engine grew louder the little jon boat accelerated.

Jamie breathed a sigh of relief as the little vessel pursuing them seemed to shrink. They were outpacing it.

"Hey, we're getting close to where Randy said you guys abandoned the van," Todd said a few moments later. "Right?"

"Yeah," Casey said. "This all looks familiar."

Distant gunfire broke out to the north. Jamie looked at Todd. "We'd best be getting out of here quickly once we reach the van."

Suddenly it grew quiet around them. Jamie raised his eyebrows. "I don't like this."

Todd reached back and killed the throttle for a moment. All around them it was quiet. Not a sound came from the urban landscape to their north and not a sound came from the woods to the south.

Jamie looked back and saw their pursuers getting closer. He saw that it was a small fishing boat pursuing them. "Come on," he said, "let's get goi-"

His voice was suddenly drowned out as two single-prop stunt airplanes flew over them at high speed. The airplanes were only about ten feet above Jamie, Todd and Casey as they flew over the river heading north. They were flying so fast that their livery blended into a colorful blur. Jamie looked upriver at a bridge they were approaching and suddenly the bridge exploded in a massive fireball; he felt the heat on his face as the shockwave almost knocked him backwards out of the jon boat.

"What the-" Todd yelled.

Suddenly mortars began arcing overhead from the north and from the south, whistling as they flew over the river. Explosions began to ring out all around them as the bridge up ahead collapsed in a fiery cloud.

"Get to the south bank!" Casey yelled. "Those people are still chasing us!"

Jamie spun around as something whistled by his head. He saw the fishing boat was less than five hundred feet away. He saw another muzzle flash and realized they were being shot at. "They're shooting at us!" Jamie yelled as he raised his rifle. He aimed and fired and saw someone fall off the fishing boat into the river.

The jon boat scraped gravel as it ran ashore on the south bank. Jamie, Todd and Casey leapt out and ran up into the brush. Bullets ricocheted all around them. A slender birch tree splintered less than five feet from Jamie.

"We'll have to jump that fence!" Casey yelled.

Jamie clambered over the seven-foot tall chain link fence and realized they were in a large scrap yard. "Over there!" he yelled, pointing at some shipping containers. They ran and entered one. Jamie's heart was pounding. He heard the fence jingling and realized they were still being followed. He readied his rifle as footsteps neared the shipping container. His finger moved to the trigger.

Suddenly four gunshots rang out. Jamie waited for what seemed like a long time.

"Come out of the container!" a young man called from outside. "You were being chased by four Stickneyans. I shot them and they are dead. You are safe now! Come out, all three of you!"

Jamie looked at Todd and Casey and shrugged. Todd nodded. Jamie walked out and heard Todd and Casey follow. He looked around. The sun was directly overhead. Four dead men lay only a few feet away. About twenty feet away stood a wiry young man holding an assault rifle. He was tanned and looked nervous. He was wearing a camouflaged jacket and had a red bandana tied around his head.

"My name is Mahmoud Razza," he said. "You are safe with me."

"Where are we?" Todd asked.

"Near Garfield Ridge, over by Midway. We aren't in safe territory. I'm sure you heard the skirmish up north of the river."

"Skirmish? It looked more like all-out war!" Jamie exclaimed.

Mahmoud nodded. "Those mortars were flying directly over where we are standing. We need to get somewhere safe. We're standing in contested territory. I have a safe house over in Summit, about a mile west of here."

"How do we know you're leading us to safety?" Jamie asked suspiciously.

"Why would I be leading you into danger?" Mahmoud asked. "I just saved your lives."

"We don't know you. But, I know that you shot four armed men in less time than it takes me to sneeze," Jamie replied. "If we are in contested territory, as you said, how do we know you aren't taking us to be prisoners or something?"

Mahmoud shrugged. "I guess you don't. If you want to be standing here when more Stickneyans cross the river in a few minutes, go ahead. They sure seemed like they liked you guys."

Todd sighed. "We'll follow you."

Jamie looked at Todd and raised his eyebrows. Todd shrugged.

"Great! Let's get going. Zombies will surely be approaching this area soon."

One by one they followed Mahmoud to the entrance of the scrapyard and then west toward Summit. Jamie hung back behind the others. He didn't like this. The young man had saved their lives, which was true. Still, Jamie wasn't so sure he had saved them for purely altruistic reasons. Could it be he was going to deliver them to a fate far worse than they had been saved from? Jamie fingered the trigger of his M4.

"Where are you all from?" Mahmoud asked.

"The city," Todd replied.

"Me too," Casey said.

"Ah, you know, I forgot to ask your names," Mahmoud sighed.

"I'm Todd, that is Casey and our quiet friend is Jamie," Todd said.

"Where are you from Jamie?" Mahmoud asked.

"All over," Jamie replied. "You?"

"The same. My family immigrated here about a year before I was born."

"Where did they immigrate from?" Casey asked.

"Yemen. Where are you guys headed?"

"West, to see if a friend is still alive," Todd said.

"I hope they are still alive."

Jamie noticed that the gunfire was fading behind them. He looked back and saw a few zombies stumbling toward the clamor. He saw smoke rising in the distance. He turned and saw the landscape around them becoming more suburban.

"There, that house over there," Mahmoud pointed at a light yellow one-story house with boarded up windows. "That's my place. Stay with me for a bit and then I'll show you how to get out of here."

Jamie followed them through the yard upto the porch. Mahmoud fumbled through his pocket and pulled a key out. He slid it into the lock on the doorknob and turned it. Jamie noticed the door had scratch marks all over it.

As Mahmoud opened the door, the smell of incense wafted out from the darkened house. They entered. Jamie noticed that pinholes had been drilled in the plywood over the windows allowing a small amount of light in. Jamie saw a beat up leather couch in the living room. He also noticed the faint scent of marijuana.

Todd sat down on the couch and Casey sat on the floor. "Do you have anything to drink?" Casey asked as Jamie sat down in a recliner.

"Is wine okay?" Mahmoud asked.

"Sure," Todd replied. "What do you have? Merlot?"

"Shiraz. Sorry, but it's cheap stuff from the corner liquor store. At least you won't get sick from drinking it. I'll be right back." He disappeared into the darkened hallway.

"I don't trust him," Jamie whispered to Todd.

"I don't either," Casey said quietly.

"I don't either guys. We'll drink some wine and then be on our way. If he can get us around all the fighting, it's worth sharing a glass of wine with him. I don't know about you guys, but I don't feel like we are equipped to go against someone who has airplanes and mortars," Todd replied.

A few minutes later Mahmoud returned with a bottle of wine and three glasses. He set the glasses on the coffee table and then poured wine into each. "Drink up gentlemen."

Jamie grabbed a glass and swirled the wine around in it, eyeing it suspiciously.

"You guys have any family out there?" Mahmoud asked.

"Yeah, we all do. You?" Todd asked as he took a swig of the red liquid.

"Yes. I have a younger sister named Zia. She is fifteen. She disappeared a few days ago."

"Where did she go?" Casey asked.

"I don't know," Mahmoud replied pensively. "She disappeared while I was out looking for food. That was a few days ago."

"Any ideas what happened?" Jamie asked.

"I think one of the warring groups kidnapped her."

Jamie nodded as he took a sip of wine. It was delicious. He took a larger sip and then quickly downed the rest of the glass. "This wine is good Mahmoud!"

Todd nodded. "It's delicious."

"Yeah, it is!" Casey piped in.

"Thank you, you all honor me," Mahmoud smiled. "More?"

"Yes please," Jamie said, holding out his glass. Mahmoud topped it off and it seemed to Jamie like he inhaled the second glass. His eyes began to feel heavy. He looked over and noticed that Casey had fallen asleep. Todd was leaning forward. What was going on?

Mahmoud was saying something about his sister. Jamie saw Todd fall forward into the coffee table with a crash.

"What is in this wine?" he slurred at Mahmoud. "You drugged us?" He tried to stand up and suddenly his legs felt like jelly. The room began to spin.

"I am sorry Jamie. I have to get Zia back," Mahmoud said as he helped Jamie lay down on the floor. "Sleep now."

And that's what Jamie did.

CHAPTER TWENTY-NINE

Andy Gibson
Day 34

Andy sat in his bed reading the note Shelly had left over and over again.

Andy, I am so very sorry. I'm so sorry.

I pray this letter never finds you. It would be better for you to have died at sea than to come ashore and discover the horrible fate that has befallen mankind...

He couldn't help but weep softly and think about how he would never hold her again. He would never kiss her again. That conversation where he had told her helicopters weren't coming was the last conversation he ever had with her and he hadn't even gotten to say goodbye.

He wondered what her last thoughts had been. Had she concluded he had died at sea, on the platform, in the hurricane?

He shook his head. He knew she was in a better place, but that did little to mollify his pain. And Isaiah, little Isaiah was gone too.

Andy had been so delighted to learn they were going to have a son. He had been ecstatic with joy when Isaiah had been born. He would just count the boy's tiny fingers and toes all the time, marveling at how little they were. He and Shelly threw a huge birthday party for him on his first birthday. And now he too was gone. Andy would never get to tickle his belly and hear his hearty laugh ever again. He'd never get to read him a bedtime story ever again. He'd never get to hear Isaiah call for him ever again.

Andy finally fell asleep around midnight.

The next morning, he heard a scratching at the front door. He sat up and realized he had been crying in his sleep.

"So much for being tough," he muttered. He climbed out of bed and quietly tiptoed past the guest bedroom where Bob was still sleeping. He crept past Isaiah's room where Royce lay sleeping on the floor. As Andy entered the living room, he saw Milo on the couch and Oscar curled up on the floor. He looked at the window; it was still boarded up. He snuck to the front door to see what was causing the soft racket. Was it a stray dog?

He gasped quietly when he looked through the peephole; a ghastly creeper stood at the door, scratching at it mindlessly.

He slowly stepped back from the door and walked back to his bedroom. He opened the closet and pulled his shotgun bag down from the top shelf. He unzipped it and assembled the shotgun. He heard footsteps approaching the room. He looked up and saw Milo.

"What's up man?" the cook asked. "Why do you have a shotgun?"

Andy motioned in the direction of the front door. "There is a creeper on the front porch," he said as he chambered a shell. He stood and walked back into the living room as Milo followed.

Milo looked out a gap in the plywood and gasped loudly. "Guys!" he exclaimed. "We've got a problem!"

The scratching at the door became fiendish.

Andy glared at Milo. "Thanks!"

"Sorry man!" he exclaimed. "That guy brought his buddies!"

Andy walked over to where Milo stood in the kitchen as Oscar stirred behind them. He looked through the gap and saw hundreds of creepers in the yard. He gasped.

"We do have a problem," he said, looking at Milo.

"What's all the commotion about?" Royce asked as he walked into the kitchen, yawning.

"Creepers," Andy said. "A lot of them."

"What?" Royce asked.

"See for yourself," Andy said, stepping away from the window.

Royce walked over and whistled as he peered out the gap in the wood. "Geez! They've got us surrounded!"

"What should we do about them?" Oscar asked.

"First we should wake Bob up," Andy said.

Milo walked out of the kitchen. "Hey Bob! Get up!" he yelled. "We've got creepers! Creepers by the dozens!"

"What?" Bob yelled back from the guest bedroom. "What are creepers?"

"Zombies!" Royce yelled.

Andy heard a growl from the front porch.

"Hey guys," he whispered. "Maybe we should keep it down in here."

"What's the plan?" Bob asked quietly as he walked into the room to join them. He was dressed only in his underwear.

"We don't have one yet," Oscar said.

"What kind of weapons do we have in addition to your shotgun Andy?" Bob asked.

"I've got a pistol too. It's in my bedroom closet on the top shelf. I also have a tire iron and fireman axe out in the garage, but obviously those won't do us any good right now."

"How much ammo you got?" Milo asked.

"Uh something like twenty shotgun shells and eighty bullets for the pistol. It's a semiautomatic pistol," Andy replied.

"Hmm," Royce said, peering out the window. "That's probably not enough to kill all those creepers."

"So what?" Oscar said. "Should we just go out there, guns blazing, and make a break for it?"

Andy shook his head. "I guess if we're reduced to that as our only option, but let's try to devise some other way."

"Andy's right," Milo said. "Running out there would be like running straight into a death trap. I'd like to not die."

"How sturdy is your front door?" Bob asked.

"Solid oak. I think it will stand the mad scrabbling of a creeper," Andy replied.

"Okay. I've got experience with pistols. What kind is it?" Bob asked.

"A nine millimeter Sig Sauer," Andy replied.

"Okay good. Would it be alright if I used it?" he asked.

"Sure."

"We should try to conserve our ammo," Milo said. "It's a long walk to Bayou La Batre from here!"

Andy laughed. "Yeah, good point."

"And Bob, could you put some pants on man? You're making me kind of uncomfortable in your, uh, tighty whiteys," Royce said.

Bob laughed. "Sure, sorry."

Thunder rumbled in the distance.

"What was that?" Royce asked.

"Sounds like it's going to storm," Andy said. "Why don't I slip out on the back balcony?"

He walked down the hallway to the backdoor and slid it open. He walked out on the balcony and saw dozens of creepers twelve feet below. The balcony provided a good view of the east and south. He saw dark clouds moving in overhead. It looked like it would rain.

He looked out toward the bay. Waves were tipped with white out in the middle. He wondered how strong the storm would be.

He looked at his house. It had withstood a major hurricane. It would probably survive whatever this turned out to be.

It began raining shortly after he walked out on the balcony. The rain intensified as the day wore on. The wind did too.

At 3:00pm that afternoon Oscar spoke up. "This is another tropical cyclone, isn't it?"

"They're pretty unusual this late in the year," Royce replied.

"True, but they do happen," Milo said. "Think about it; it's been raining harder and harder all day now. It's also been getting windier and windier all day. I suppose the only thing left to see is a storm surge of some sort."

"He's right," Andy said. "This is probably a tropical depression or tropical storm. Don't worry. This house stood up to a Category Five hurricane about a month ago. It'll handle this."

"I hope so man, I don't swim that well," Oscar said nervously.

"We won't float away, don't worry," Bob said.

"Yeah, this house is securely bolted to the concrete pilings," Andy said. "We have enough water to last five days, but food's a little sparse so we'll have to ration."

The storm shook and rattled the house for the next two days as the street and yard were slowly submerged beneath the storm surge. Gradually the creepers disappeared from view beneath the rising tide.

The others passed the time playing poker and resting. Andy spent a lot of time in his bedroom, reflecting on the last few weeks' horrible events.

Nearly everybody on Bald Point had died. His lovely bride and beautiful son now laid in the soil beneath the stormy tide of an offseason tropical storm. He wondered if anyone in his family was still alive.

He planned to go first to Detroit to see if his dad was still alive. From there, he reasoned, he could determine whether it would be wiser to go east to Buffalo and Manhattan where his brothers and mother were or west to Chicago where his sister Vicki lived.

On the December 7th, the rain died down and the storm water began to recede. Andy looked out the window and cried out in shock.

"They're gone!" he yelled.

He ran to the living room, opened the door and looked around. The yard was deserted. Large puddles of water filled depressions on the lawn. Two-year old saplings the neighbor had planted had either drowned or been uprooted. The only audible sounds were the tide and seagulls.

"Well, I guess this is as good a time as any to leave," Royce said.

"Yeah, let's head out," Andy said.

They set out walking south on North Beach Boulevard after Andy recovered the axe and tire iron from the garage. He gave the iron to Milo and Oscar took the axe. As they neared the marina Andy saw two creepers stumbling up the road toward them.

"Hold on!" Milo exclaimed. He brandished a tire iron and ran up to one of the creepers and began striking it in the head repeatedly. After a few such strikes, the creeper lay still on the ground.

Bang!

The remaining creeper stumbled as it took a shot to the chest from Bob's pistol. It stood back up though, and continued advancing toward them.

"Head shots guys!" Milo exclaimed. "You've all seen zombie movies, right?"

Bang!

The creeper dropped as Milo leapt backwards.

"You trying to kill me Bob?" he yelled angrily.

"Thought you trusted me!" Bob yelled back, laughing. "I told you I was a good shot!"

Everyone except Milo laughed.

"Alright wise guy, just remember, your pistol has a limited number of bullets; my tire iron doesn't," Milo said. "So when you run out of bullets and I save your life, we'll see who's laughing then."

"Yeah yeah," Bob said. "When your arm gets tired of swinging that thing, my trigger finger will still be fine."

They continued on.

"I've noticed a few things guys," Oscar said as they passed ruined mansions. "Doctor Kulik became a creeper after Becker bit him, right?"

"Yeah," Andy said. "I guess he did."

"Okay, so it seems that whatever it is that causes someone to become a creeper is spread by biting. So don't get bitten. I've also noticed that only wounds to the head seem to wound them fatally. Remember that."

"I'm telling you, those things are just like zombies!" Milo exclaimed.

When they passed the fallen US-90 Bridge, Bob shook his head. "I came down here with my church after Katrina and helped with the rebuilding efforts. I'll never forget the devastation. I'll also never forget the resilience of most of the people here. They were determined to rise from the watery mess and rebuild."

"How far do you think the devastation extends from here?" Oscar asked.

"I don't know," Andy said. "Sterling tried reaching HQ, Ops, and the Coast Guard. No response came from any of those places. So it would seem that the entire Gulf Coast has been affected. I have a hard time believing it would still be this desolate more than a month later if there weren't bigger issues away from the coast. I don't know, we were all thinking the hurricane was the cause of the silence, but it looks like the creepers really were. It's not looking good."

They approached a ruined church on the right. Its windows had been broken out and one of its towers lay on the ground in the parking lot, shattered by the fall.

Suddenly noise came from within the darkened entrance. Everyone froze and crouched down, preparing for whatever would come staggering out of the desolate church. Andy raised his shotgun as Bob raised his pistol.

A large buck came leaping out of the entrance running toward them. It leapt over the driveway and through the lawn.

Bang! Bang!

Bob fired two shots at it and it collapsed immediately, sliding across the grass.

"Man! You're a dead eye!" Royce exclaimed.

Bob shrugged. "I've gone deer hunting for years. Who wants venison?"

They carved some meat from the dead buck and carried it down to the beach. They laid the large cuts of meat on the concrete steps that led down to the beach and set about building a fire to roast the meat over. They cut the meat into more manageable sizes and speared it on some skewers Oscar found in a destroyed house across the street.

The deer turned out delicious and refreshing. After they had eaten, they continued south along the shore.

Suddenly Royce yelled something and took off running as they came around a bend in the road. As Andy came around the bend he saw why Royce had taken off running; a sailboat lay on its side up the beach.

They found that the boat was miraculously undamaged. It must have been pushed ashore during one of the storms. Bob found a functioning tractor inland and drove it to the beach. They managed to drag the boat toward the water during low tide. They boarded it and waited for the tide to come in.

At high tide, the boat began to float in the water and Bob steered it out into the bay. As it was late in the day at this point, they dropped anchor a few hundred feet out and spent the night there.

When Andy woke up the next day, they were sailing past the ruined casinos of Gulfport, Mississippi. He stretched and saw that Royce and Bob were the only other ones awake. He joined them.

"Hey Andy, I'm really sorry about your wife and baby boy," Bob said, hugging him. "I'm sorry I didn't say anything until now too."

"Thanks Bob," he replied.

"Hey Bob," Royce said. "You have family in Georgia?"

"Yes," Bob replied. "I've got an older daughter who lives in Sandy Springs, up north of Atlanta. I wonder if she's okay. She's a mechanical engineer."

"I'm sure she is," Royce said. "Sounds like she probably has a level head."

As they passed Biloxi, Oscar and Milo woke up.

"Where we at?" Milo asked.

"We're passing Biloxi," Royce said.

"Awesome!" Milo exclaimed. "I hope my Momma's still alive! I ever tell you guys about my family?"

"Just that your mom can cook like no one's business," Andy said.

"Let me tell you a little about them. My Momma is married to a guy named Ray. Ray is my step dad and in many ways, he's a better dad than my own father was. He's a doctor in Mobile. I've also got a younger sister named Monica. She lives in Boston."

"Boston?" Andy asked. "What's she doing up there?"

"She's about halfway done with her undergrad work at Boston University."

"That's cool," Royce said.

"Yeah, I hope everyone's okay."

"I too hope my family is alright," Oscar said.

"Where do they stay?" Royce asked.

"Just east of Atlanta, in Decatur. I have a wife and two little boys." He sighed. "I hope they're okay."

"I'm sure they are man," Milo said, patting his back.

They continued sailing east until 3:00pm. The navigational chart indicated they were nearing Bayou La Batre, so Bob steered the boat north toward the shore. At 3:30pm, he pulled it up to a dock and Royce tied it off.

They walked up the dock to Shell Belt Road. The level of devastation there was shocking. Trees had been stripped of their leaves and snapped off near the ground. Ruined houses lined the street, having been pushed off their stilts. The smell of the surf mingled with the stench of decay.

They started up the street toward town and Milo started murmuring under his breath.

"Where's your house Milo?" Andy asked.

"North of town, inland, a little way from the bayou," he replied nervously.

"Hey," Andy said, putting his hand on Milo's shoulder, "I know you are anxious. You're worried about your family. Just remember, no matter what, we are here with you."

He nodded. "Yeah, I know that."

The ground was littered with dead fish that had been washed ashore. The men passed a dead dog and other skeletal remains.

The road cut through a saltwater marsh ahead. Heavy construction vehicles were half sunk in the mud; their deceased operators still strapped into their seats.

A gurgling sound came from a stand of tall reeds to the left of the road. A creeper staggered out of the vegetation and up the embankment toward them. It growled when it saw them.

Andy whacked it in the face with the butt of his shotgun and it staggered backwards. He followed it down into the weeds and bashed its head three more times with his shotgun. Its skull made a cracking sound the second time he struck it and caved in with the third hit.

Andy climbed back up to the street and saw four more creepers approaching. Oscar yelled and swung his axe down on one's head. He hacked at it repeatedly as Milo engaged two creepers with his tire iron.

It was almost comical hearing the others cry out ninja-like noises as they bludgeoned the creepers. Royce simply knocked the final creeper down and stomped on its head.

The men continued on.

"I don't see how these things could have destroyed civilization," Milo said. "They're slow and weak."

They passed a ruined shipyard, where broken shrimp boats and toppled cranes lay twisted together. They continued on past ruined quays and collapsed seafood plants; the smell of rotting meat became stronger.

As they neared another mangled shipyard, Andy heard the growls of creepers. When they crossed Rabby Street, he saw the source; dozens of maimed creepers lay trapped beneath inverted cars.

"Man, this doesn't look good," Milo said quietly as they passed the mangled wreckage. The frame of a lift bridge stood behind the ruined buildings on the left side of the street.

They turned on to South Wintzell Avenue and Royce spoke up as Andy noticed the deck of the bridge was partially raised.

"Guys, we've got a problem!"

Andy turned and saw hundreds of creepers behind them. They were moving toward the survivors, arms outstretched.

"Run!" he yelled.

They ran toward the bridge. The deck appeared to be raised about eight feet. Several cars were stopped at the precipice, leaning precariously over the side.

"How do we get up there?" Royce yelled.

"We'll have to hop on a car and jump!" Andy yelled.

He scrambled onto the trunk of a maroon Oldsmobile and climbed up o the bridge deck. He turned and helped Oscar and Milo up. Beside him, Royce had climbed up from the trunk of a blue Lincoln Towncar. He helped Bob climb up on the deck. Behind them the creepers surged forward. As the ghouls climbed atop the precariously balanced vehicles, Andy heard loud groaning noises as the cars began to tilt forward. With an awful noise, the cars splashed into the bayou below, taking dozens of creepers with them.

He turned and saw the bridge deck was choked with cars that had decaying arms reaching through windows toward them.

"Alright guys," Andy said. "Be careful. I doubt good would come from being grabbed by one of those greedy claws."

"Yeah, look! We could just climb up and over the cars," Milo said.

They walked forward and Andy hopped up on the trunk of a Mercedes. As he walked on the roof of the car, he heard angry scratching at the underside of the metal roof. He jumped to the next car, a newer Ford.

Carefully, the men picked their way across the jam and paused at the northern end of the deck. The road ahead was creeper free. Andy saw the others looking down at the street below. It appeared to be roughly an eight-foot drop.

"Alright guys," Royce said. "Be careful. We don't want any broken ankles."

They climbed down one at a time. First Royce lowered himself down, then Milo, then Bob, then Oscar. Finally, it was Andy's turn.

He turned and started to lower himself off the deck when he suddenly lost his balance and fell. He landed on his feet and felt a searing pain shoot up his right leg.

"Andy!" Royce yelled as he ran over to Andy. "You okay?"

"I think so," Andy said. He stepped forward and felt intense pain in his ankle. He tried to take another step and the pain worsened. "No, I'm not."

"You're hobbling like you broke something," Milo said. "Hey, you don't look so good."

Andy's vision became blurry and it felt as though everything was spinning around.

"Andy? Andy? You okay?" he heard Royce ask, but his friend's voice sounded distant.

"I think I am," he mumbled. Then everything went dark.

CHAPTER THIRTY

Jamie Daniels
Day 25

Jamie awoke as he was being jerked to his feet. He tried to move his arms, to demand his freedom but he must have still been drugged. He heard Todd yell something as he blacked out again.

The next time he woke up he was being lifted into the back of a police van. He realized he was bound with zip ties. Had he been arrested again? He was confused. It was as though he was seeing everything through a haze.

The haze cleared when he heard Mahmoud's voice. He looked up and saw the treacherous snake standing next to a teenage girl. Mahmoud was arguing with a very large man. Suddenly the man grabbed Mahmoud's right hand and squeezed. Mahmoud screamed in agony as the bones in his hand were crushed. The man then raised his gun and shot the girl in the face. Mahmoud's anguished scream was the last thing Jamie heard before he blacked out. He thought he tasted bile as he lost consciousness.

"Wake up Jamie!" Todd was yelling.

Jamie opened his eyes and realized he was blind. He was laying on a cold tile floor. "What? What happened?" he asked. He had a pounding headache. "I'm blind."

"No you're not. We are in a completely dark room. That snake Mahmoud betrayed us. He traded us with some gang for his sister."

"They shot his sister."

"Yes they did. He was demanding money and ammo in exchange for us. He felt like he was being short-changed by only getting his sister back in exchange for three healthy hostages."

"He was being greedy."

"That thug agreed with you. Mahmoud argued his sister's life away."

"Where are we?"

"Midway Airport. I regained consciousness in the van."

"Where's Casey?"

"Asleep somewhere over there."

"How long was I out?"

"They let me keep my watch at least, so I think we've been here for a day and a half."

"I was out that long?"

"Yeah."

"Wow. Whatever Mahmoud drugged us with must have been strong."

"That it was. But, I barely finished one glass of tainted wine before I passed out. How many did you have? Two?"

"Almost three."

Todd chuckled. "Ah, you just got way more of the drug than me or Casey did. Makes sense now that I think about it."

Jamie noticed the scent of urine. "I guess we don't have a toilet?"

"No. No we don't. There is a trashcan though. It's pretty big. It's over in the corner, about ten paces to your right."

"How do you know?"

Todd chuckled again. "I tripped over you a few times."

Jamie shook his head. "Has anyone come by to tell us why we're being held?"

"No. They threw us in here and seem to have just thrown away the key."

Jamie didn't like the sound of that. He had been detained many times before and had always received his civil rights. Of course, that was before society collapsed. He growled. "This is stupid."

"Yes, it is," Casey replied from the darkness. "I'm glad to hear you're awake Jamie. I thought you might be dying."

"Thanks Casey."

"What time is it Todd?" Casey asked.

Jamie turned and saw two glowing watch hands about ten feet away. He realized he was staring at Todd.

"Just after noon," Todd said.

Suddenly there was a clanking sound coming from one of the walls and then Jamie was blinded by intense white light. He threw his arms up to shield his eyes as Casey cried out.

"What the…what is this?" a man with a husky voice demanded. "Is this the way to treat our guests?" There was a loud gunshot that echoed in the small room. It made Jamie jump. "Carry this sad piece of trash away," Husky Man said. "I don't care what you do with him. Feed him to the zombies for all I care."

Jamie lowered his arm as his eyes adjusted to the light. He saw a tall, thin, older man with long gray hair that was pulled back in a ponytail. The man wore a green track jacket and tight jeans and had a cigar tucked behind his left ear.

"Forgive my men," he said apologetically. "They have become too accustomed to the sacks of rotting meat that prowl the streets. My name is Sergei Popov. I am one of the bosses in our little gang. Who are you three?"

"Just a trio of travelers," Todd said.

"That's what everyone says," Sergei replied. "Who are you really?"

"We live over on the lake shore," Casey said.

"Why are you in our neighborhood then? You're quite a few blocks from Lake Michigan," Sergei replied with a smirk.

"My brother and his friends came this way and we are looking for them," Todd replied.

"Ah, yes. Well, you know it's funny. I don't know if you saw what we did to Mahmoud, the slippery young man who sold you to us?"

"Your men broke his hand and shot his sister," Jamie replied warily.

"Yes. Well, he lied to us. He told us that he had three senior members of Stickney's leadership. Imagine my man's surprise when he reviewed Todd's driver's license and saw an address that's over by Wrigley Field!"

"So let us go," Jamie said.

"It's not that simple I'm afraid," Sergei sat down at the interrogation table in the center of the room. "Stickney thinks we have three high value hostages. It just so happens they have some very important members of our gang held captive. They are willing to trade for you."

"So you're just going to traffic us around?" Casey asked.

"Well, we will see. The Stickneyans might let you go."

Jamie saw that Sergei had a pistol holstered on his hip. Two men stood outside the room wielding automatic rifles. It seemed unlikely Jamie and his friends would be able to strong arm their way out.

"Why are you doing this?" Casey asked. "What are you and the Stickneyans fighting over? Haven't you seen what it's like out there? Civilization has collapsed! There's zombies everywhere."

"Yes, yes young man, I know this. We are fighting to define what the future will look like, to control it. You see, most of humanity seems to have succumbed to what the media briefly dubbed Owasa Disease, but not everyone did. Have you ever heard the phrase, 'nature abhors a vacuum?'"

Todd nodded. "I have."

"Good. So you know then, that in the absence of authority, for instance, people will coalesce around whatever figure of authority they can find. My goal here is to make sure the Stickneyans don't become that authority; rather, that I do."

"You're just pursuing a kingdom of sand," Casey said.

Sergei laughed. "Just a few weeks of apocalypse have made you rather jaded!"

"So what's the plan then?" Todd asked.

"Well, we're going to hold you three until Stickney agrees to a prisoner exchange. Until then, we are going to provide you with meals and we'll leave the lights on for you." Sergei smiled as he leaned back. "You boys like beef stroganoff?"

Jamie realized he was extremely hungry. He felt his stomach rumble. "That sounds delicious," he confessed.

"Great! We'll bring you some. Now don't think about doing anything squirrelly. You all heard me shoot a man because he left you in the dark. I won't think twice about crippling each of you and feeding you to my dogs. Now, excuse me," he said as he stood up. "Jayden, get them a new trashcan," he barked at one of the guards as he walked out.

Jamie looked at Todd and Casey as a clean trashcan was dragged into the room by a pimple-faced teenager. As the boy walked out, he closed the door. Jamie heard a lock turning.

He turned toward Todd.

"We have to figure out how to escape," Todd said quietly.

Jamie nodded. "We seem to be at a disadvantage. They have guns. We seem to have left our guns at Mahmoud's house."

Todd nodded. "We could try to escape when they take us to be exchanged."

Jamie nodded. "That could work."

"But how? How do we do it?" Todd asked.

"We need a diversion," Casey said. "You know, zombies are drawn to noise."

"These guys seem to have military power," Todd said.

"Maybe. But all it would take is enough zombies being drawn in and our captors will be overwhelmed," Casey pointed out.

"And how do we avoid being eaten and escape?" Todd asked.

Jamie shushed the other two with a motion as footsteps approached the door.

"Alright gentlemen, I have three plates of beef stroganoff!" Sergei said cheerfully as he entered the room. He laid a large platter with three plates on it down on the table. Jamie noticed steam rising from mounds of creamy noodles. He also stole a furtive glance out the door and saw a shuttered McDonald's across the hall.

Sergei smiled. "Enjoy gentlemen." Then he turned and walked out, closing the door behind him.

Jamie noticed a carafe of water on the table with four Solo cups. He realized he was quite thirsty too. He walked over to the table and poured himself a glass. The water felt cool and refreshing as it went down his throat.

"So when will be the best time to escape?" Casey asked quietly as he took a bite of stroganoff.

"Not here," Todd replied.

"No, we're in the wolf's den," Casey said. "So when they take us to be exchanged?"

"Perhaps," Jamie said. "Although they'll probably be expecting us to attempt escape. Maybe we'll get lucky and things will go sideways when they try to exchange us. Maybe the folks from Stickney will decide to start shooting at our captors when they realize we aren't high value targets."

"Perhaps," mused Todd. "Perhaps they'll shoot us too."

"I'd rather not think about that," Jamie said. Suddenly he heard nearby gunfire.

"What's that?" Casey asked.

"Sounds like automatic weapons," Jamie replied. He walked to the door and pressed his ear against it. He could hear distant yelling.

"What is it?" Todd asked. "What do you hear?"

"Sounds like some kind of fighting. I can't tell much else. There's yelling down the hall, it sounds like..."

The room shook.

"Sounds intense," Casey said tentatively.

Jamie stepped back from the door. "I don't know. Hopefully it doesn't make things worse for us."

"Maybe we'll be liberated."

Todd shook his head. "No, I don't think so. In the Gospel of Matthew, Jesus told a parable. He said there was a man possessed by a demon. The demon was cast out and then traveled around and found seven more demons to come back with it. They all returned and possessed the man, so his final state was even worse than the original state."

"So you think if Sergei's gang is displaced we'll be even worse off?"

Todd nodded. "Yes. Let's hope the captor who gave us water and stroganoff doesn't get killed."

The gunfire echoed for a while longer while the three men sat in the room. Suddenly gunshots rang out just outside the door. Jamie turned the table in the room over and he, Todd and Casey ducked behind it.

Someone laughed manically from out in the hallway and there were more gunshots.

Jamie looked at Casey and noticed the young man had his eyes closed. His lips were moving silently.

After a while, the commotion in the hallway died down and gradually the gunfire faded into the distance. Then there was just silence outside the room.

"Who do you think won?" Jamie asked Todd.

He shrugged. "Hopefully the man who gave us stroganoff."

There was a knock on the door. Jamie heard the lock turning and the door opened. He peered over the table and saw Sergei standing in the doorway.

"Hello gentlemen, I see you heard all the hullaballoo out in the hallway, huh?"

Todd stood up. "What happened?"

Sergei waved his hand dismissively. "Some gang from the south thought they'd try to steal our home from us. They were dealt with."

"Who are you Sergei?" Jamie asked.

"I was a TSA agent, back before all this epidemic nonsense. Now I'm one of the bosses of our little army. Don't worry gentlemen, I think we will have an envoy from Stickney this evening. We might be able to arrange an exchange."

Jamie nodded.

"Now then, I don't think we'll have any more incursions this evening. Sleep well gentlemen." Sergei nodded at them and walked out, closing the door as he left.

"Did you guys see the body behind Sergei on the floor?" Casey asked.

Jamie shook his head.

"There was a dude who must have been shot five times!"

Jamie shrugged. "There was some kind of a battle out there."

Todd sighed. "We need to get out of here."

Jamie nodded. "Yes we do."

"No, I mean, when we get back to the house we need to get out of Chicago. That is, if we get back to the house."

"You don't think we'll be safe at the house?" Casey asked.

"Do you?" Todd asked. "Look, you all told me about Bloomington. This sounds like that. And it sounds like there are at least three groups fighting over this little square of land. It won't be long before the violence spreads east."

"Where are we going to go?" Casey asked.

Todd shrugged. "We'll have to think about it and talk about it with the others. But I think if we head north, you know, there are thousands of lakes in Ontario. Much of Ontario is remote. We could probably find an abandoned cabin on the shore of one and hide out up there."

"That's certainly an option," Jamie said.

A distant explosion made the room shake.

"We have to get out of here first," Todd said.

That night the three men all had a difficult time falling asleep, but eventually they did. The next morning, Jamie awoke before the others did. He noticed that the lights had been turned off sometime overnight.

As he laid there in the darkness, he thought back to the last time he had seen his brother. Shelby had been such a good man. While Jamie had used their terrible upbringing to justify diving into a life of crime, his little brother had turned out to be an honest, hardworking man.

Shelby had taken him in following his release from prison. Then, Jamie had gone to Joliet to live with their mother as she lay dying from cancer. Her death at the end of the previous January had been his excuse to lapse back into an addiction to heroin.

As Jamie laid there, he felt a darkly familiar desire come over him. It wasn't like thirst or hunger and it was stronger than lust. He had craved the sweet release of heroin before, in life's stressful moments. Now, however, he felt himself wanting it more and more. Life had been nothing but stressful for the last few weeks. Now all he wanted was a release.

He shook his head. Maybe Shelby had been right. Jamie had shown up on his doorstep in March. Shelby and his wife Lana had taken him in and driven him to job interviews all over the Louisville area. Jamie remembered how he would play Cowboys and Indians with his nephew Jared. The little boy idolized his uncle. Then Jamie had inadvertently found an account statement for an IRA. The three letters had been just another meaningless acronym to him, but the account balance hadn't been.

"Eighty-Thousand dollars," he mumbled to himself in the dark. He had traded his family for the money his mother had left her grandson Jared when she had died. He had called the Edward Jones adviser, had requested a disbursement, had successfully impersonated Shelby and had then walked three miles to get the check. He had then cashed it and spent it so quickly. He had gotten so high that even now, he was surprised he hadn't overdosed.

He remembered when Shelby realized what had happened. It was a testament to his brother's character, Jamie felt, that he hadn't killed Jamie. He hadn't hit him. He hadn't even pressed charges. He had simply told Jamie to leave and to never come back.

"Once a junkie, always a junkie," Jamie whispered bitterly. He wondered if Shelby and Lana and Jared had survived. He thought about his daughter and his ex-wife. Had any of them survived?

Suddenly he heard tumblers in the door turning. He sat up as Sergei opened the door.

"Wake up gentlemen. We're going to go for a drive," their captor said cheerfully.

He led them through the terminal and the concourse across a sky bridge to a parking garage. A white cargo van was waiting for them. They all got in and the van took off.

"Has Midway always been so dumpy?" Jamie asked.

Sergei laughed. "For a long time, yes."

Jamie noticed that the five other men in the van were all heavily armed.

"Where are we going?" Todd asked.

"Shut up," one of the gangsters said.

Jamie looked out the back window of the van and saw Midway passing by on the left. Once they were past the airport, all he could see were the abandoned buildings they passed. After about fifteen minutes the van came to a stop on a bridge.

Sergei got out and a few seconds later he opened the back door of the van.

"Gentlemen, please step out of the van," he instructed Jamie, Casey and Todd.

They climbed out as the gangsters exited behind them.

"What now?" Todd asked.

"We wait," Sergei replied.

Jamie looked around and realized they were standing over a river. He looked north and saw trees all along the shore of the river. It was cloudy and cold outside.

They waited for what seemed like hours. Finally, a single car came rolling across the bridge from the north. It stopped 300 feet away. It appeared to be empty.

"Go check it out Casper," Sergei told one of the soldiers.

Casper walked out to the car. When he reached it he peered in the windows. He turned and yelled back, "There's nothing in it!"

"There must be something!" Sergei yelled. "Pop the trunk!"

Casper walked around to the driver's side. When he touched the door handle, the car suddenly exploded. Gunfire erupted from the north bank of the river at the same moment.

"Get back in the van!" Sergei screamed.

The four remaining gangsters herded Jamie, Todd and Casey back into the van. As they did so, two of them were shot.

The driver spun the van around and they sped away from the bridge.

Sergei was furious. "Those treacherous snakes!" he screamed in rage.

Jamie became a little carsick as the van raced back to Midway. Once they arrived back at the airport, the two remaining gangsters led Jamie, Casey and Todd back to the room they had been locked in.

Once they were left alone, Casey spoke up. "That was crazy."

Todd nodded. "We're lucky we didn't get killed."

Explosions rang out nearby.

"We may get killed yet," Jamie said.

Gunfire echoed outside for what seemed like hours. Suddenly gunshots rang out in the hallway outside the room. A bullet ricocheted off the outside of the door and suddenly the door came unlatched. The three men ducked behind the table as the door cracked open. The lights went out as a loud explosion boomed down the hall. Ceiling tiles fell on Jamie and Todd. The three men sat there silently as screaming gunmen ran up and down the hall outside the door.

"Did you hear that?" Jamie asked suddenly.

"Hear what?" Todd asked.

"Zombies," Casey whispered.

A telltale growl came from the hallway. More gunshots rang out just outside the door.

"If the gunfire moves away from here, we should make a break for it," Todd said quietly.

Jamie nodded. "Yes."

Gradually the fighting moved down the hall away from the room.

Jamie stood and walked to the door. He opened it a little more and saw Sergei lying on the floor, face down in a pool of blood, just a few feet from the doorway. He appeared to have been shot at least a dozen times. He turned and motioned to the other two as he looked up and down the hallway. They were alone in this part of the terminal.

Jamie walked out into the hallway as Todd and Casey followed him. He reached down and took Sergei's pistol. He glanced out the window and noticed it was dark and rainy. He ran down to the end of the terminal to the last jetway and kicked the door open. The three men descended an emergency staircase from the jetway and emerged on the tarmac. Wrecked airliners lay all around them.

"This way!" Todd yelled.

Jamie and Casey followed him southwest across the tarmac to the service entrance on the south side of the airport. They finally emerged onto the road as the sounds of battle continued back by the terminal.

"Do you remember where Mahmoud lived?" Todd asked.

"I do," Casey said. "This way."

He led them through the night past block after block of abandoned buildings. The three men easily stepped around most of the zombies they encountered. Finally, as the sky was beginning to lighten, they stopped in front of a building Jamie recognized. Mahmoud's sister's body still lay on the sidewalk.

Jamie walked up to the door and kicked it open. It stank of decay inside the dark house.

"Mahmoud!" Jamie yelled. "Where are you?"

He heard a moan come from another room. He walked into the room as Casey and Todd searched the front room for their guns.

Two candles burned in the bedroom providing a dim source of light. Mahmoud lay in a bed in the center of the room. He shivered beneath several blankets.

"We've come for our weapons Mahmoud," Jamie said.

"Take them," the weak man replied. He coughed. "I'm sorry I betrayed you."

"You threw away your sister's life," Jamie replied.

Mahmoud coughed again. "Yes, yes I did. I think I'm dying."

"What happened?"

"Those goons beat me after they shot my Zia and broke my hand. One of my wounds is infected. I've got a fever."

"Your apartment stinks."

"I'm dying."

"Good," Jamie said.

Casey walked up behind him. "I found our guns Jamie," he said.

Jamie nodded as he stared at the dying man. "You know Mahmoud, I spent ten years in prison. You know what they do to traitors there?"

He nodded and coughed again. "Please do it. Please kill me. Put me out of my misery."

"No," Jamie said.

"Please!" he whined.

"No. Come on Casey, let's go."

He heard Casey follow him out of the bedroom as Mahmoud yelled for them.

"Come back! Come back Jamie! Please! Please put me out of my misery!"

"Where's Todd?" Jamie asked.

"He's outside waiting. The rain stopped."

"Come on, let's go."

As they walked out to the wet street, the dying man's cries faded behind them.

CHAPTER THIRTY-ONE
Randy Eccleston
Day 23

Randy turned the key in the ignition and the Land Rover's engine roared to life. He looked out the window at Todd, Casey and Jamie. He waved at them and shifted the SUV into gear. Then he pushed down on the accelerator and drove east on West Dakin Street. He turned right onto North Sheffield Avenue and drove south on it.

"You guys want to listen to music?" he asked.

"Sure. What's in the CD player?" Adam asked.

"I don't know, let's see," Randy said as he steered around several burned out cars. He turned the radio on and the sound of a rhythmically strumming guitar came through the speakers.

"Bones sinking like stones, all that we've fought for. Homes, places we've grown, all of us are done for," a British voice crooned. *"We live in a beautiful world, yeah we do, yeah we do. We live in a beautiful world."*

"I like Coldplay," Jillian said from the backseat.

"Me too," Adam said.

"I guess we'll listen to them," Randy replied as they drove by a mound of hundreds of body bags stacked ten feet high on the sidewalk. Zombies shuffled around everywhere. He carefully steered the Land Rover around greedy claws.

"I can't believe how much things have changed," Adam said.

"Me neither," Randy said. "It's crazy. Just a few weeks ago, this was all bustling and busy. Heck, just about a month ago, the Cubs were in the playoffs!"

Jillian chuckled. "The Curse lives on."

"Whatever," Randy said. "There was no curse. Just bad management. Terrible management for many years."

Adam laughed. "Yeah."

Randy turned right onto West North Avenue. They drove past old warehouses converted into retail stores and eventually crossed the Chicago River. The towers of downtown Chicago stood to the south. They drove a little further and eventually came to the onramp for Interstate 90. Randy turned onto it and steered around stopped cars.

"Hey look, the express lanes are empty!" Jillian pointed out.

Randy saw a section where the dividing wall between the normal traffic lanes and the express lanes had been knocked aside. He steered over to the express lane and soon they were speeding south. They weren't able to go fast for very long, however. After a few minutes, he had to steer onto the left side of the interstate to remain on I-90. Of course this side of the highway was choked with cars too, so he had to steer slowly around stopped and burned out cars.

After several hours of slow going, they reached a section of I-90 that was a toll road. Here, the road was much clearer. They made good time from there, passing into Indiana. Randy exited the highway at IN-49 and drove south. The road here was completely choked with cars, so Randy drove on to the median.

Several more hours passed but eventually they drove past the sign welcoming them to Valparaiso, Indiana.

"Huh, I thought we'd see buildings by now," Randy said.

"We should have," Adam replied. "Wait, look!"

Randy looked around and realized the road snaked through a section of town that had been burned completely to the ground.

"Turn right up here," Adam said.

Randy turned onto the road and drove past burned out ruins for several miles.

"Stop up ahead."

Randy slowed to a stop and Adam leapt out of the Land Rover.

"Adam! Wait!" he yelled, but it was no use. Adam was already a hundred feet away running into the charred ruins of a house.

Randy and Jillian climbed out of the Land Rover and Randy noticed several dozen zombies just a few hundred feet away.

Adam cried out and Jillian ran to where he had gone. Randy slowly walked to the ruins. He knew what his friend had found. As he came around a blackened column, he saw Adam kneeling in the ashes next to two charred corpses. Jillian was holding him as he wept.

"Adam, I-I-I'm so sorry," Randy said quietly.

Adam nodded.

Jillian looked back and then whispered something to Adam. Randy looked back and saw that the zombies were approaching.

Adam stood and walked back to the Land Rover without saying a word. Randy watched as he pulled his crowbar out and started walking toward the zombies.

"Adam! What are you doing?" Randy yelled.

Without a word Adam swung the crowbar into the skull of the first zombie he encountered. He let out a primal scream as he hacked at zombies with the curved end of the metal bar.

"Adam!" Randy watched in horror as his best friend was surrounded by zombies. He ran to the Land Rover and grabbed his bat. He then ran to the throng of undead and began swinging the bat. He slowly whacked his way through the horde to Adam. His best friend dropped the crowbar as the last zombie was dispatched. He was covered from head to toe in gore. He was panting.

"Are you okay Adam?" Jillian asked.

He nodded. "I will be."

"Did you get bitten or scratched?" Randy asked.

He shook his head. "No." He stepped through the circle of corpses and walked past Randy and Jillian back to the burned out shell of his parents' house.

Randy and Jillian followed him.

By the time Randy caught up to him, he saw that Adam was sitting in the ashes again staring at his parents' bodies. Jillian walked back over to him and held him. Randy turned and walked back out to the Land Rover. He looked across the street at the dead zombies. By his estimate there were at least thirty zombies lying in the grass. He stared at the blackened desolate landscape for a few minutes.

"Let's go," Adam said behind him.

Randy turned and saw that he and Jillian had walked up quietly.

"You okay?" he asked Adam.

His friend nodded. "I will be. Let's go."

They all got into the Land Rover. Randy noticed that Adam smelled terrible.

"You want to try to find some clean clothes?" he asked.

Adam nodded. "I guess I got pretty filthy killing those zombies, huh?"

Randy steered the SUV out of the burned out subdivision and drove back toward I-90.

"You know, I think I hoped they'd be okay," Adam said quietly. "But I guess I was also thinking it was likely they weren't. It just, I don't know, it just hurts."

Randy nodded.

"I mean, I guess I should be grateful that at least they didn't turn into zombies. But still. They were burned to death!"

"Yeah man. That's tough."

"Yeah," Adam replied.

Randy saw a hunting supply store up ahead on the right. He steered into the parking lot and saw that the front door had been busted down. "You want to look in here?" he asked.

"This looks as good as any other place," Adam admitted. "I mean, there probably isn't any more ammo in there, but maybe they left some clothes."

The trio exited the Land Rover and walked into the store. Broken glass crunched under Randy's feet as he walked past several shelves that had been completely looted. He walked back to the ammunition counter and saw that all of the glass display cases had been ransacked. It indeed appeared as though the weapons had been thoroughly looted. He frowned. He turned and saw Adam sizing up a shelf of blue jeans. Jillian was holding a pack of undershirts and a red flannel button up shirt.

Randy walked over to the camping supplies. He saw a few hand warmers had been left on the shelves. He quickly pocketed them. He wondered how cold winter would be. He also wondered how Todd, Casey and Jamie were doing. His thoughts were interrupted as Adam walked up behind him.

"How do I look?"

Randy turned and saw his friend was now wearing a camouflage jacket over a black and red flannel shirt. He was also wearing a new pair of jeans and a pair of work boots.

"Looks better than gore-encrusted clothes," Randy replied.

"Good."

"I guess, let's get back on the road, see how far we can make it before it gets dark."

They walked out to the Land Rover and Randy steered the SUV back on to the road. A little while later they reached I-90 and Randy merged onto it going east.

"You're being awfully quiet Jillian," he said.

"Yeah. I think I'm worried about my parents," she replied.

Randy nodded. "Yeah."

The sun was nearing the horizon when he steered the Land Rover off the highway just outside Rolling Prairie, Indiana. He parked at a mechanic's shop and the three friends spent the night in the shop's office.

The next morning, they got back on the road. A light snow began to fall as they passed through South Bend and when they entered Ohio, the snowfall began to intensify. They drove slowly through the day and into the night, taking turns driving, and eventually reached Lakewood, Ohio the following morning. The snowfall had abated a few hours earlier.

"Jillian, be prepared," Adam said to her.

Randy looked in the rearview mirror and saw her nod. "I turn here, right?"

"Yes. It's at Twenty-One-Ten Wyandotte. Third house on the left."

Randy eased the Land Rover to a stop in front of a white two-story house with a covered porch. Two red Adirondack chairs sat on the porch. The windows were intact and the door hadn't been knocked down. He also noticed there were no red sheets hanging in the windows. There was a thin dusting of snow on the lawn.

He and the others got out of the SUV. He looked down the road in both directions and noticed there were no zombies in sight. He turned and followed Jillian and Adam up the walk to the front porch. Jillian knocked on the door.

No answer came from within the house.

She knocked again.

No answer.

She reached down and pulled a key from under the doormat and unlocked the door. She opened the door and the trio walked in.

"Mom? Dad?" she called.

Randy heard a growl come from the kitchen. "Jillian, I think there are zombies in here."

"Mom? Dad?" she yelled.

Suddenly a zombie staggered out of the kitchen. The skin on its face was stretched tight, but Randy couldn't help but notice its resemblance to Jillian.

"Mom?" she asked, confused.

Randy shoved the zombie backwards into the arms of another zombie that had staggered out of the kitchen.

"Mom! Dad!" Jillian screamed. She began to cry hysterically as Adam grabbed her. "Let go!" she screamed as Randy shoved the zombies back a second time.

He used his bat to push the zombies back into the kitchen. He ran around and opened the back door and led the two zombies out into the backyard. Once they had stepped on to the grass he swung his bat into their heads and killed them.

Jillian ran out into the backyard and collapsed beside her parents. She was crying. Adam followed her out and tried to hug her. She shoved him away.

"Mom! Dad!" she yelled.

"Jill do you want to remember them this way?" Adam asked plaintively.

"I want to remember them!" she screamed back at him.

Randy walked back into the house to make sure there were no other zombies within. It only took a few moments but he was relieved to find the house was empty. He walked back outside and saw Adam holding Jillian. She was leaning on his shoulder weeping bitterly.

"Hey guys, let's go inside. It's cold out here," Randy suggested.

Adam led her inside and Randy followed. They all sat down in the living room as her cries turned into soft sobbing. Randy handed her a box of tissues.

"Thanks," she said, as she blew her nose.

"You're welcome," he said.

"I'm going to go take a nap," she said.

"Okay."

She stood and walked upstairs leaving Randy and Adam alone in the living room.

Adam shook his head. "This is terrible."

Randy nodded. "It is."

"I guess we should bury them."

"Yeah, we should."

Both men walked out to the backyard. Adam walked over to the shed and pulled out two shovels. He tossed one to Randy and they both began to dig graves for Jillian's parents. It took the rest of the morning and part of the afternoon, but eventually they had both dug graves four feet deep. They laid her parents' corpses in the graves and buried them. Randy was covered with sweat by the time they finished.

"You guys buried my parents?" Jillian asked suddenly from the back porch.

"Yes," Adam replied.

"Thank you."

They all went back inside and sat in the living room quietly for a while. At length Jillian spoke up. "Let's spend the night here and head back to Chicago tomorrow," she said quietly.

Randy nodded. "That sounds like a good plan."

Adam and Jillian went to bed shortly after the sun went down while Randy kept the first watch. At 2:00am he woke Adam up and went to bed himself.

The next morning, he awoke shortly after dawn and walked downstairs. He saw Adam asleep at the bottom of the stairs and chuckled softly. He walked into the kitchen and poured himself a bowl of Cheerios. He then walked back into the living room and sat down. As he munched on some dry cereal, he noticed movement in the front yard. He stood and walked to the front door and opened it.

Two overweight young men stood on the front porch wielding shotguns. The younger one stared at Randy for a moment before aiming the gun at him. "Good morning sir. My name is Donald Chambliss. This here is my brother Doug Chambliss. We both live across the street and I must ask, is Jillian Wilson with you?"

CHAPTER THIRTY-TWO

Jillian Wilson
Day 25

"Good morning Miss Jillian," a familiar voice said.

She opened her eyes and saw an overweight young man with thin brown hair standing over her. He was holding a shotgun and had it trained on her face.

"Doug? Doug Chambliss?" she asked, confused.

"The one and only."

"Why are you aiming a shotgun at me?"

"To make sure you come with us."

She slowly sat up and sized up the younger Chambliss brother. She had known both Doug and Donald since her childhood. They had both been a little slow and very strange. "Where are you taking me?" she asked.

"Across the street to our house. Mama wants to see you. She thinks you can help Papa."

"What's wrong with your father?"

"He's sick. He's grouchy. He needs some cheering up. Mama thinks you could do it. Papa always thought you were cute."

Jillian shuddered. She remembered the salacious old man from her teenage years. He would often sit on the front porch in the evening during the summertime, staring at neighborhood girls as they rode their bicycles by. She remembered that her parents never trusted the man. Her dad especially had warned her to never talk to him.

"Come on now, get up," Doug said softly. "I know Donald doesn't want to hurt your friends, but you remember right? He's got that nasty temper."

She got out of bed, wondering what they were going to do to Adam and Randy.

"Now, put on your coat and let's go downstairs. Donald's waiting for us."

She complied and walked down the stairs in front of Doug as she zipped up her coat. She was relieved to see that Randy and Adam were both okay.

"Hey Jill," Adam said quietly.

"Hey."

She also noticed the older Chambliss brother standing by the door.

"Come on," he said. "Papa's waiting."

She followed Donald outside. It was much colder now than it had been the day before. She shivered as she walked across her parents' front yard. She looked back and saw Adam and Randy behind her, following. Adam raised his eyebrows and shrugged.

She turned back around and looked up at the Chambliss brothers' house. It stood directly across the street from her parents' house and, like the other houses in the neighborhood, had an identical floor plan. She noticed that the tan siding was peeling off in many places and several windows were boarded up. Weeds poked up through the snow in the front yard.

"Right this way Miss Jillian," Donald said. He led her and the others around the side of the house to the backyard. He paused to open a gate and then led them to the back door.

She noticed three unburied zombies stacked in the corner of the yard. She felt herself growing nauseous as Donald reached down and grabbed her wrist. He pulled her close to himself. He smelled of onions and stale pipe tobacco and something else, some sickly sweet odor. She did her best not to gag as he leaned down toward her face.

"Don't try anything stupid Miss Jillian. My mother doesn't want us to hurt you, but she didn't say nothing about your two friends," he whispered ominously.

She nodded.

"Right this way then," he said as he stood back up and opened the back door. He pulled her into the kitchen and she noticed right away that the whole house had the same sickly sweet odor. She looked down at the cracked yellow linoleum on the floor. The wallpaper depicted a floral scene drawn in abstract shapes. She saw dirty dishes piled up in the sink. A woman coughed from the living room.

"Hey Mama!" Doug yelled as he closed the backdoor. "We got Miss Jillian! We also brought her friends!"

"Friends?" the woman called from the living room. "Friends?" Her voice sounded husky, as though it had been distorted by decades of chain smoking.

Jillian noticed the floor shaking. She looked up and saw an absurdly obese woman walk through the hallway into the kitchen. The woman wore black horn-rimmed glasses and her curly gray hair was in rollers.

"Hello Jillian," the obese woman said. "I'm Mama Chambliss. I'm sure you remember me?"

Jillian nodded.

"Can you help my sweet husband?" she asked.

"What's wrong with him?"

"He's sick. I think he needs a cute redhead to snap him out of it. Boys, please put Miss Wilson's friends in the basement. If they resist, break their hands."

Jillian turned and watched as the two Chambliss Brothers herded her fiancé and friend into the basement.

"Don't you dare hurt Jill!" Adam yelled as he disappeared into a stairwell.

Mama Chambliss laughed. "We won't son. Now listen to my boys or they'll break your hands!"

Jillian turned and looked at her. "Look ma'am, I'm not sure what you have in mind here, but you can't just abduct people at gunpoint."

"Miss Wilson, one day if you get married you'll understand my desperation."

The two brothers returned to the kitchen and closed the basement door. There was pounding on the door. She could hear Adam and Randy yelling.

"Miss Jillian," Donald said. "Please tell your two friends to shut up."

Jillian walked to the basement door. She cleared her throat. "Adam! Randy! Relax! I'm okay. They're not going to hurt me. I think this is all just a big misunderstanding. We'll get out of here soon."

"Jillian, be careful!" Adam said.

"I will Adam."

"Take Miss Wilson up to Papa's room," Mama Chambliss said.

Donald picked Jillian up and threw her over his shoulder. She cried out in surprise.

"Be quiet Miss Jillian, I don't want you to agitate Papa," the oaf said. Then he walked into the living room and climbed a staircase. Jillian wondered where she was being carried. He paused and unlocked a door. Then he led her up a narrower staircase. It was dark up here. She heard a familiar growl come from the top of the stairwell. Donald paused again and unlocked another door and carried her into the room. Then he set her down in a corner of the chilly and dimly lit attic.

She looked around. As her eyes adjusted to the darkness, she saw multiple storage chests and cobwebs. She also saw the elder Chambliss man chained to the opposite wall. It took her a moment to realize he was a zombie. She gasped. Suddenly she felt a cold and heavy manacle close around her ankle.

"I'll come back up here this evening for you Miss Jillian," Donald said. "Please talk to my father, try to snap him out of this." He turned and walked out of the room. She heard the door's lock turn after it had closed and she heard footsteps going down the stairs.

It took her a moment to realize she had been locked in the attic with a zombie.

"Wait!" she yelled. She stood and tried to walk to the door and only made it about two feet before her chain went taut. She tripped and fell over. She looked back at the wall and saw the chain was anchored on a steel plate bolted on to a stud. She tugged at the chain. There was no give.

She turned and saw the zombified Mr. Chambliss gazing at her. Part of his face had sloughed off, exposing the fascia and bone. She suddenly felt nauseous. She turned and threw up. Her stomach heaved as her vomit splashed on the hardwood floor. Papa growled.

She sat up. "What's wrong with these people?" she wondered aloud.

Papa began to crawl toward her. She cowered against the wall. Papa's chain grew taut finally, stopping him about four feet away from her. Mercifully, she was out of reach. She took a deep breath and leaned against the wall. He reached for her with his left hand and gazed at her. His eyes had faded white and lacked any sign of warmth. He growled and strained against the chain.

"Please let me out!" Jillian screamed as loud as she could. She stomped on the floor. "Please let me out! Come on! Come on!"

She screamed for what felt like hours before she finally gave up. They had locked her up in their attic with a zombie. She glared at Papa.

"You got what you deserved, you pervert," she muttered.

Finally, after several more hours, the door unlocked and Doug walked in. "Hi Miss Jillian. Are you hungry?"

She glared at him. "You locked me in a cold, dark room all day with a zombie and you ask if I'm hungry?"

He knelt down in front of her. "Miss Jillian, please don't say such things when we get downstairs. You know, Donald's got a temper and Mama won't suffer no one to talk ill of Papa. He's sick, we know that."

"He's dead!" Jillian said.

Doug shook his head. "I've tried telling Mama and Donald that, but they won't believe me."

She stared at him. "Let me go. Let me and my friends go now and we'll pretend this didn't happen."

"I'm sorry Miss Jillian, Mama made it clear you all can't leave until you've healed Papa."

He unlocked her manacle and led her downstairs. It was at least much warmer on the first floor. She was led into the kitchen where Mama, Donald, Adam and Randy all sat around the table.

"Did you make any progress with my sweet husband?" Mama asked.

"No ma'am," Jillian replied. *Careful, don't say anything stupid*, she thought. "I am still trying to determine how to help."

The fat woman smiled. "Good. I'm sorry that our dinner will be so meager, but the boys foraged some bacon and some crackers. Eat up!"

Jillian looked down at her paper plate. It had two strips of bacon and a pile of wheat crackers. She munched on the food and realized she hadn't eaten a proper meal in a couple of days. She quickly devoured what was on the plate.

She looked up at Mama and wondered if the brothers would carve bacon from their sow of a mother if they couldn't find food.

"Now Miss Wilson, once you heal Papa, you and your friends are free to go," Mama said.

"Thank you. I will work hard on it tomorrow," Jillian said. She realized she had no idea how she was going to get her or Adam and Randy out of this. She hoped they had a more productive day in the basement.

"Now, Miss Wilson, we are going to allow you to spend the night with your friends down in the basement," Donald said as he stood and walked over to her.

"Oh, you are?" she asked.

"Yes. I think most of the spiders have died by now."

She shuddered. "That's nice." She noticed the shotgun resting on the kitchen counter.

After everyone had finished dinner, Jillian, Adam and Randy were led down into the basement. It was dark and cool, but at least it wasn't as cold as the attic had been.

"Sleep well folks," Doug said as he walked up the stairs and closed the door behind him.

"So you're okay Jill?" Adam asked.

"Yes," she replied quietly.

"What was in the attic?"

"A zombie."

"A zombie?" The surprise was evident in his voice.

"What kind of zombie?" Randy asked.

"The brothers' father," she replied.

Randy sighed. "Wow. That sucks."

"Yeah."

"We need to figure out how to get out of here," Adam said quietly. "If he's a zombie, there's nothing Jill can do for him besides kill him."

"Wait, I have an idea," Randy said.

"What's that?" Jillian asked.

"What if we released the zombie into the house and sicced him on the hick family?"

Adam huffed. "We're not doing anything that puts Jill in danger."

"I wouldn't be able to do that anyway," she said. "He's chained up on one side of the attic and I'll be chained up on the opposite side. Besides, the door is locked too."

"I found a few keys in a jar over on a shelf down here earlier today. Maybe one of them would work," Randy said.

"You know, if one of those works, I could unchain myself, unchain the zombie, hide in one of the chests up there and maybe even unlock the door and let Papa go feed on his family," she said.

"That sounds like a good idea," Adam said. "We'll be safe down here too."

"Then once the carnage settles down, Jillian can come down, finish off the zombies and let us out," Randy said.

"Sounds like a plan," she said. "Where's these keys you found?"

"Hold on," Adam said. She heard him fumble around in the dark and then she heard jingling. "Where are you?" he asked.

"Over here."

She heard nearby footsteps and she reached out and touched his knee. He knelt down and handed her five keys.

"Hopefully one of these works," he said.

"Yeah."

She felt his arm slide around her shoulders.

"I'm glad you're okay," he said.

"Me too," she replied.

Eventually she heard Randy snoring. She realized Adam was asleep too. She laid down on the cold, hard floor and gradually fell asleep.

When she awoke, she saw sunlight shining in through a window near the ceiling. Adam and Randy were both still asleep. She heard footsteps up above and then heard the basement door open.

"Miss Jillian? It's time to go help Papa!" Doug yelled from the top of the stairs.

Adam stirred.

"I'll be up in a moment!" Jillian called. She stood and stretched. She checked her pockets to make sure she still had the five keys. She bent down and kissed Adam on the forehead as he opened his eyes.

"Be careful," he whispered.

"I will be. I love you Adam."

"I love you too."

She walked up the stairs and saw Doug and Donald both waiting for her. This time they permitted her to walk up the stairs to the second floor and then up to the attic. Donald fixed the manacle around her ankle and then the brothers left. The zombified Mr. Chambliss growled from the corner.

When she had been in the attic for a while, she pulled the keys out of her pockets and tried them on the manacle's lock. The first three didn't work. The fourth key, a small gold key did, however and soon she was free of the chains. She stood and stretched and then tiptoed to the door. Surprisingly, the first key worked. She left it in the lock. She carefully opened the door and listened. She heard conversation echoing up from far below. She couldn't understand what was being said, so she quietly crept about halfway down the stairs.

She heard Mama talking.

"Now look boys, tonight when they're asleep, I want you to go downstairs and kill those two men. We are going to grill them up and we'll have meat for the winter!" the obese woman yelled.

Jillian suddenly felt sick. She wondered if the bacon from the night before had actually been bacon. She quickly crept back up the stairs.

Before, she had wondered if she would be doing the right thing unleashing a zombie on her captors. Now she was convinced it would be the right thing to do. Now to release Mr. Chambliss without getting bitten.

She walked over toward the zombie and sized him up. His chain appeared to be about six feet long. She realized if she knocked him over, she could have enough time to try a key and then scoot back out of reach if it didn't work. She looked down at the four keys in her hand. She wondered if the lock on his manacle was keyed the same as the other lock. She'd have to try it to find out.

She reached out with her foot and pushed the zombie over. She ducked down and tried the first key on the lock. It didn't fit. She quickly rolled out of the way as Chambliss reached for her. She knocked him back again and tried the second key. It didn't fit either. She rolled away again. She kicked him over a third time and tried the next key. It worked. The manacle fell off Chambliss' emaciated ankle. She stood and ran over to an armoire leaning against the wall as the zombie stood and hissed. She opened the door, shoved some old clothes aside and climbed in. She closed the door as Chambliss clawed at it. She heard him growling.

After a few tense moments she heard him shuffle away. She heard the door creak open and then heard him tumble down the stairs. A few more moments passed and she heard Mama Chambliss scream. She heard the brothers screaming. A few seconds passed and she heard the boom of a shotgun. Then all she heard was Mama crying. She wondered what had happened.

She slowly crept out of the armoire and made her way downstairs. She paused at the top of the stairs to the first floor; Doug lay at the bottom, limbs splayed. There was a pool of blood beneath him; he wasn't moving. She slowly crept down the stairs and saw Donald lying next to his brother. His throat had been ripped out. She peered around the corner and saw Mr. Chambliss' corpse lying next to Mama with the shotgun on the floor between them. The obese woman was on her back in the living room, atop the shattered ruins of the coffee table. She was bleeding profusely from her left arm. She saw Jillian and glared.

"You! You! Because of you my boys are dead!" she roared. She flailed for the shotgun.

Jillian carefully stepped around the brothers' corpses and walked into the living room. "What did you feed us last night?" she asked pointedly.

The obese woman glared. "Bacon! You ingrate! We fed you store-bought bacon!"

"Oh? Then why were you telling your sons to kill my fiancé and friend tonight so you'd have meat for the winter?"

Mama's expression changed to one of fear. "We... we...we..." she stammered.

"You what?"

"We weren't going to hurt you!"

"You're not going to now," Jillian said. "Now, did you feed us real bacon last night?" She knelt and picked up the shotgun. She pulled the slide and discharged a spent shell.

The obese woman nodded. "Yes! Yes! I was just thinking ahead! You know, winter is coming and what would we do for food?"

"Where's the box for the bacon?"

"In the kitchen, next to the sink! Please, you have to help me!"

Jillian ignored her plea and walked into the kitchen. Sure enough, there was a box for microwave ready bacon resting on the counter. She sighed in relief and walked to the basement door. She unlocked it and opened it to see Adam and Randy waiting at the foot of the stairs. They walked up.

"Everything okay?" Adam asked as he hugged Jillian.

"Yes, it is now," she replied.

Suddenly Mama shrieked something incomprehensible from the living room. Jillian, Adam and Randy ran into the room to see the now reanimated brothers feasting on their mother. Randy gasped.

"Come on, let's get out of here," Jillian said quietly.

"You and Randy go outside," Adam said. "I'll be out in a moment."

They walked outside. It was cold and cloudy outside. A moment later Adam joined them.

"What did you do?" she asked as they walked back to her parents' house.

"You'll see. I didn't want anyone mistaking that house as safe."

"I guess we'll head back to Chicago," Randy said.

"Yeah. There's nothing for me here. Not now anyway," she said.

The trio grabbed their bags from Jillian's parents' house and as they walked back out to the Land Rover she saw flames erupt from the front windows of the Chambliss' house.

"Oh," she murmured.

"Yeah," Adam said as he climbed into the back seat of the SUV. Jillian climbed in next to him.

"Are you guys okay?" she asked as Randy got in and started the engine.

"Yeah," Randy replied. "You sure that you are?"

"I will be," she said. "I will be."

Flames shot skyward from the Chambliss' house as the trio drove away.

CHAPTER THIRTY-THREE

Casey Newburgh
Day 29

Once they had escaped the gangs, it was easy enough to find the van. Mahmoud only lived about a mile from the van. The white ISU van was actually still sitting in the same spot it had been in, about twenty feet from the edge of the pavement. Finding gas for the van was a bit harder, but Jamie had located a commuter parking lot about a quarter of a mile back and had siphoned gas from a few cars. With that, the van roared to life.

Casey had been relieved to get in the van and be on the road again. It had been quite a harrowing experience being held prisoner at Midway. He watched the ruins of suburban Chicago coast by as Todd drove north on North 1st Avenue. Soon they passed over the Des Plaines River and through the ruins of Maywood. Every other cross street they passed had zombies staggering down them. Casey was surprised by how many zombies there were.

"You guys seeing this?" he asked as they passed over I-290. It looked like hundreds of thousands of zombies were staggering around on the interstate.

"What did you expect Casey?" Jamie asked. "This is Chicago we're in. The city had what, ten million people living in it before the epidemic?"

Casey laughed. It was true. He supposed he shouldn't have been surprised. He wondered how Missy was, if she was worried, as the van drove past a dense forest. At some point he nodded off.

When he woke up Todd was parking the van in front of his house. Casey looked around and saw the Land Rover was still gone.

"Where do you think your brother is?" Jamie asked Todd.

Todd shrugged as he turned the van off. "I don't know. Maybe Adam or Jillian's family was still alive."

They all walked upto the house and when they entered, Casey watched Todd get tackled by his daughters. Vicki ran up and hugged him when he stood back up.

"I'm glad you guys are all still alive!" she exclaimed. "Did you get the van?"

Todd nodded.

"What took so long?"

"Gangsters. Has Randy been back yet?"

She shook her head.

"Where's Missy?" Casey asked.

"Upstairs sleeping."

Casey ran up the stairs as he heard Todd and Jamie talking with Vicki about the gangs. He found Missy asleep in the guest bedroom. He walked in and sat down on the bed next to her.

"Missy?" he asked.

She turned over and opened her eyes a crack. "Casey?" She sat up and kissed him. "You're okay!"

"I am!" he said as he hugged her.

"What took so long? You guys were gone for four days!"

He laughed. "We got kidnapped by a gang and held prisoner down at Midway."

She gasped. "Are you okay?"

He nodded. "It was pretty crazy. We escaped when another gang attacked."

She hugged him tightly. "I'm glad you're back."

He nodded.

That evening at dinner, Todd spoke up.

"Look, I don't know if Randy, Adam and Jillian are coming back or not. We need to make plans to get out of here soon," he said. "There were several gangs fighting over the west suburbs. It won't be long before they are fighting over the city proper."

"But Todd, you said we'd be safe here," Vicki protested.

"I did; that was before I saw gangs with airplanes and mortars!"

"Todd, your brother made it back here. What about my family?"

He raised his eyebrows. "Vicki, it's been almost a month. Surely we would have heard from someone by now?"

She nodded quietly. "Do you think they survived?"

A grim expression crossed his face for a moment. "Maybe. It's definitely possible. But still, we don't know that they'd come here. Your mom lives in New York."

She pursed her lips. "So where are we going to go?"

"I'll look over the maps, but I think we should try to make it to one of the lakes in Southern Ontario. We could hide out in a cabin over the winter. We can take the van."

"What about Randy, Adam and Jillian?" Casey asked.

Todd looked down at his plate. "I don't know. We have to leave soon. I say we give them a few more days. If they make it back, we'll go together. If they don't, we have to leave."

Casey shook his head. "We can't just leave."

"What would you do Casey?" Todd asked. "We can't just go look for them. There's a lot of territory between here and Cleveland. All we can do is wait for a few days and then head out with or without them. Today is November Twenty-Sixth. We'll give them until December First. If they aren't back by then, we will leave without them."

"But Randy is family, your family."

"I know that Casey. Vicki and the girls are too, though, and my first responsibility is to them. If you want to wait here for Randy when we leave, you can, but if they're not back by the First, me and my household will have to leave without them."

"Todd, they've only been gone for four days. It could have taken that long just to get to Cleveland," Jamie said.

Todd stared at him. "Even so. December First is as long as I'm going to wait."

The next morning Missy woke up with a terrible cough. She had a fever too. Vicki suspected she had the flu. Casey brought her water and broth throughout the day but she was still sick the next day and the next and the next and the next.

In addition, Randy, Adam and Jillian were still missing.

December 1st came and went and they still weren't back yet. But now, Missy and Vicki both had the flu. Casey was glad they would have to at least wait until Vicki was feeling better.

Missy's fever broke the next day and on the 3rd she was up and walking around.

Vicki's fever broke on the 5th. Todd announced they were going to leave the next day, with or without Randy, Adam and Jillian.

Casey was sitting on the front porch that evening when the Land Rover came driving down West Dakin Street. He leapt up in joy when Randy climbed out.

"What took you guys so long?" he exclaimed as Adam and Jillian got out.

Randy laughed and shook his head. "We got a flat tire on the way back and then a ball joint broke. We had to find a mechanic's shop and fix it ourselves. That took a while because, you know, I'm not a mechanic. Neither is Adam or Jillian. Then we got caught in a crazy snowstorm. Seriously, we must have gotten more than three feet of snow dumped on us."

Casey laughed. "I'm glad you guys are okay!"

The front door opened. "What's all the commotion about?" Todd called out.

"Todd!" Randy shouted.

"Randy?" Todd ran out the door and leapt off the porch. He embraced Randy in a big bear hug.

"I guess you guys didn't…" Casey started, but then he trailed off.

Adam shook his head. "No. My parents were dead. So were Jill's."

"I'm sorry to hear that man," Casey said as he walked over and hugged Adam.

"It's okay. I think we'll be okay. Thank you."

"I see you guys got the van back!" Randy exclaimed.

Todd laughed. "Yeah. We'll need to catch up inside. A lot has happened since you left."

"Tell me about it!"

They all walked inside.

Over dinner they regaled one another with tales of abduction and escape.

As they ate dessert Todd cleared his throat. "We have to head north. We'll leave first thing in the morning. Randy, I'm really glad you guys made it back. We are going to head north for the lakes in Southern Ontario."

Randy nodded. "Let's do it."

The next morning, they loaded their gear into the van and the Land Rover. Casey walked with Randy and Todd through the house as they checked to make sure they had everything. The house was spotless, the beds were made, and the floors were clean.

"Man, this is tough," Todd said when they reached the foot of the stairs. "I hope we make it back here someday. This house was falling apart when we bought it. We fixed it up and man, this is tough."

Randy hugged him. "We'll be back man."

Todd nodded. "Yeah. I hope so." He turned to Randy. "You okay driving the Land Rover?"

Randy nodded. "Yeah. Hey Casey, do you and Missy want to ride with me, Adam and Jillian?"

Casey nodded. "Sure."

They walked out of the house as Jamie, Vicki and the girls climbed into the van.

"If we get separated, we'll meet at Solon Springs, Wisconsin," Todd said. "There's a high school close to the highway there."

Randy nodded. "Sounds good Todd. We'll follow you the best we can."

"Excellent! Be careful Randy."

Todd got into the van as Randy, Casey, Missy, Adam and Jillian clambered into the Land Rover.

"This ought to be fun," Randy said as he followed the van down the street.

"Should be. How about we listen to some music?" Casey suggested.

"Sure. There's a CD by a band called Yeasayer in the CD player now."

Casey turned the radio on and turned it up.

"Live in the moment, never count on longevity, please," the singer sang over and over.

"I don't like this," Casey said. "It's too depressing." He turned the radio off.

Randy laughed as they pulled onto Interstate 90.

The going was slow that day and the sun was going down by the time the van and Land Rover reached Rockford, Illinois. The survivors hid out in a derelict truck stop. The next day they made slightly better progress and made it as far as Madison, Wisconsin. Casey held Missy that night as they slept in a Walgreens. On the 8th they passed through Eau Claire, Wisconsin and then had to stop for the night in Bloomer as snow began to fall. On the 9th they were snowbound in Bloomer. The next day, they managed to get back on the road and they made it to Spooner. The next day, however, the van and the Land Rover got separated just north of town.

Randy growled when he realized the van had somehow wound up way ahead. He sighed and looked at Casey. "I guess we'll meet them in Solon Springs."

They drove all day through heavy rain and finally came to Solon Springs in the evening. The van was parked in the parking lot of the school there. Randy parked the Land Rover and he and Casey got out. The rain had finally let up right before they drove into town. Todd was standing outside the van. Casey noticed its hood was raised.

"What happened?" Randy asked.

"The transmission is busted," Todd said. "It started slipping gears just a few miles back and now I can't even get it in motion."

"What do you want to do?" Randy asked.

"I don't know. Any of your friends have experience changing a transmission?"

Randy grimaced. "No."

"I guess we can try to find another car. I'm glad she held out long enough to get us here at least."

"Where's everyone else?"

"In the school," Todd pointed. "They're holed up in the gym."

Casey, Missy, Randy, Adam and Jillian all followed Todd into the school. It was dark inside. Casey and the others followed Todd through the labyrinthine halls to the dimly lit gym where Vicki and the girls were asleep in the corner. Jamie was reading something by the light of a flashlight.

"Hey, I'm going to take a walk," Missy told Casey. She kissed him.

"Okay, be careful," he said.

"I will be, I love you."

"I love you too."

He turned to Randy as she walked away. "Quite a drive, huh?"

Randy nodded. "Yeah."

"So those people who had you held captive were going to eat you guys?"

"Me and Adam anyway, I think they liked Jillian." Randy seemed to shudder.

"I'm glad you guys are okay," Casey said.

Suddenly, he heard Missy scream from down the hall. He grabbed his rifle and a flashlight and took off running. "Missy!" he screamed.

"Help!" he heard her scream.

He cursed the layout of the school. He turned one corner and then another and realized the screams were coming from the opposite direction. He slid to a stop and turned around. He ran back the way he had come, his feet pounding on the tile floor, sending echoes up and down the dark halls.

"I'm coming Missy!" he screamed.

He came running around a corner and collided with a zombie. The impact knocked the zombie over and sent Casey flying over the creature. His gun and flashlight rolled away. He jumped to his knees and ran forward to the flashlight. He spun around as the zombie fell toward him. He rolled out of the way and shone his light around. He saw his rifle a few feet away. He quickly crawled to it and grabbed it. He fired at the zombie. It collapsed as the deafening gunshot echoed through the halls.

He heard Missy scream again from down the hall. By now he heard screams from the gym. He knew there were zombies everywhere now. His ears were ringing and his muscles were burning. He ran toward where Missy was. He didn't hear her screaming any more. He came around another corner and saw a zombie leaning over Missy. She was laying on the floor motionless. Blood was pooling around her.

"Missy!" he screamed.

The zombie sat up and turned to look at him. Its face was covered with bright red blood.

"Missy!" he screamed again. He shot the zombie in the face and ran to her.

She stared up at the ceiling blankly. Her throat had been torn open. Her skin was pale and a terrified expression was frozen on her face.

"Missy! No!" he screamed again. "No!" He shook her shoulders. This couldn't be. He had shared his life with this woman for the last two years, he had bought a house with her; he had loved her! He realized she was dead. "No!" he screamed. He turned and began to punch a locker door. He punched it as hard as he could again and again and again. He felt something crack in his hand but he kept punching.

"Casey! Missy!" he heard Randy yell. He felt arms around him pulling him away from the wall.

"No!" he screamed. "No!"

"Casey! Casey! There's nothing we can do! I'm sorry!" Randy was yelling. Everything faded red for Casey as he heard distant gunfire.

CHAPTER THIRTY-FOUR

Jim Gibson
Day 39

Sherry was in the yard of the house next to the Warren's home. It had tall weeds. She was lying in the driveway crying. Her ankle bled profusely.

Phil, Jim and Vik ran up to her. Jim heard a growl from the grass. He turned and saw a legless zombie lying in the grass trying to pull itself toward Sherry.

Boom!

Jim jumped as Phil shot it in the head. He and Phil turned to Sherry.

"What happened?" Phil asked, kneeling by her side.

"I was cutting through the yard and it bit me in the ankle!" she screamed. "It hurts so much!"

Phil examined her ankle and grimaced. She had been bitten by a zombie.

"Phil, I know what we saw in the movies but you have to try to save me!" she yelled.

"Phil, we have to kill her," Jim said.

Phil looked at him. "Are you crazy? We can save her! Here, help me tie my belt around her calf as a tourniquet! Come on! Help me!" he yelled.

"What do I do?" Jim asked frantically.

"Lift her into a sitting position!"

Jim put his hands under her arms and lifted her to a sitting position. She screamed in pain as Phil wrapped the belt around her leg just below her knee. Then he inserted a thick stick into the loop and began twisting it to tighten the belt.

"This is going to hurt Sherry. I'm sorry!" he said. "Jim, give me your axe."

"What? What are you doing?" Jim asked.

"Give me your axe. Trust me, we have to do this or she'll die," he said calmly.

"Wait! Phil, what are you doing?" she screamed as he raised the axe over his head.

"Hold her legs down Vik! Jim, cover her eyes! Sher this will be over quickly. I'm sorry!" he yelled.

Jim covered her eyes as Vik held her legs down. She relaxed, sobbing.

Jim looked away as Phil swung the axe down. Sherry jumped as Jim heard the sickening sound of metal cleaving muscle and bone. Then she let out an earsplitting scream. She kept screaming.

"Come on! We've got to get her inside!" Phil yelled. "Vik! Go get the fireplace going! We're going to have to cauterize her leg!"

As the brothers lifted her up, she cried out again. "Phil, just kill me!" she squealed.

"No! We can save you Sherry!" he yelled as they ran back to the house.

They carried Sherry inside and set her down in front of the fireplace. Vik held a skillet over the fire with an oven mitt.

"Really?" Jim asked incredulously.

"What else do we have that is metal, clean and flat?" he asked.

"It will work," Phil said. "It has to."

By now, despite the presence of the tourniquet, Sherry had lost a lot of blood. Vik turned and pressed the flat end of the skillet to Sherry's stump. She screamed in agony as it made a sizzling noise and then passed out from the pain.

"Come on, help me carry her to the guest room," Phil said then.

Jim helped his brother pick her up and carried her to the guest room and laid her on the bed. As they did so, Jim noticed the bleeding had been stanched.

Phil grabbed a blanket and covered her up. "Alright guys. I guess we'll see how she does. She's probably in shock. She lost a lot of blood out there and in here before we cauterized her wound. When she wakes up we will have to give her water. Some of these houses nearby must have water. Jim, will you and Vik go search?"

Jim nodded. "Yeah, we'll go look."

"Thanks," he replied.

He and Vik walked out of the room and walked outside. Jim realized he had left his axe in the driveway. He ran over to it and paused. The blade was still red with Sherry's blood and the amputated part of her leg lay in the driveway still, a small pool of blood beneath it. He picked up his axe slowly and stepped back.

"Whoa," Vik said.

They walked to the Warren's house.

"Be ready Vik, there's at least one zombie in there," Jim said as they reached the front door.

Vik raised his hammer and swung it at the door near the deadbolt. The door swung open as the bolt was broken. Jim walked in, axe raised. Vik followed. Warren appeared to be the only zombie in the house. He stumbled toward them.

He had been a mean old man for as long as Jim could remember. Whenever he and Phil came to visit their dad, Jim remembered how if a ball was thrown over the fence into his yard he would come out and scream at them.

Jim stared at him for a moment and then swung the axe down into the old man's head. He fell to the ground motionless.

"Alright, let's see if he's got bottled water," Jim said, walking into the kitchen. Sure enough, he had a whole case of it!

Jim and Vik carried it back to the house and cleaned the blood off the floor in the living room. Then they waited.

Phil spent the night in the guest room with Sherry while Jim and Vik slept in the living room again.

The next morning Jim awoke at dawn. He stood and walked to the back of the house. Sherry was awake. Phil was still asleep on the floor beside the bed.

"Hey," Jim said.

"Hey," she said weakly.

"How are you feeling?"

"Alright, I suppose, for someone who's missing half of their leg." She forced a smile.

"Good."

"Thank you for bringing me water."

"No problem. I'm glad I could help."

Phil stirred. He sat up and looked around. "You're awake!"

"I am," she said.

"Good!" He stood and stretched.

"Hey, is there any ibuprofen here?" she asked. "My leg really hurts. I also have a killer headache."

"I'll go look," Jim said. He turned and walked to the bathroom. He opened the medicine cabinet and saw a bottle of ibuprofen. He grabbed it and walked back to the bedroom. As soon as he reached the room, Sherry made a strange noise.

"Are you okay?" Phil asked.

She shook her head. "I don't feel so good."

"What's wrong?"

"I-" suddenly she screamed in agony and arched her back. She sat up and began throwing up. In the dark room her vomit looked black. She was vomiting blood.

Phil jumped back. "No, no, no!" he yelled.

"Phil, what's happening to me?" she asked, wiping her mouth. "Do I have Owasa Disease? Am I going to become a zombie?" She started crying. Her tears left black streaks on her face.

Vik ran back to the bedroom. "Guys we have a problem! Uh, what?" He stopped in his tracks.

"Yeah we do have a problem! Sherry has Owasa Disease!" Phil yelled.

"Phil, you might want to look out front."

Jim ran into the living room and peeked out the window through a crack in the plywood. He gasped. There must have been hundreds of zombies in front of the house, stretching into the street.

He heard Phil cuss. He ran back to the bedroom and saw Sherry had fallen back asleep.

"Phil, we have to kill her!" Jim said.

"No! We can't!" Phil said, starting to cry. He shoved Jim aside and walked into the living room. Jim followed him out of the guest bedroom, leaving the stench of blood and vomit behind. Vik sat down in the hallway outside the bedroom.

Jim sat down in the recliner. Phil sat on the couch across from him, his face in his hands. He was bawling.

"What are we going to do?" he asked. "Sherry is going to die and we are surrounded by zombies. We are all going to die."

"No, we aren't. We'll get out of this. For now, though, our most pressing problem is that Sherry is sick. I'm sorry I said we should kill her," Jim said.

"It's okay. I know that I said we would have to kill someone who was bitten. But that was then, I mean I didn't really realize this is what that would be like."

"Yeah."

"So what now?"

"I guess we wait."

A few hours later, Phil walked out into the backyard. Vik walked into the living room.

"So what are we going to do?" he asked.

"I don't know. I guess we'll wait and see what happens," Jim said quietly.

"Yeah."

At dusk they heard vomiting and choking noises come from the bedroom. Jim and Phil ran back and saw Sherry convulsing. Then she was still. Phil walked over to her and put his finger on her neck.

"She's dead," he said. He started to cry again.

"Here's what we're going to do," Jim said. "We are going to take her outside and build a funeral pyre in the backyard. Then we will cremate her. Then we will figure out how we are going to escape."

"Okay," Phil sniffled.

"Vik, help me carry her out. Grab her ankle."

"Okay," Vik grabbed her ankle.

"Be careful not to get any blood or vomit in your eyes or mouth," Jim said.

"Okay," Vik replied as he and Jim lifted her up and carried her out. They carried her out the backdoor and laid her bloody body in the grass as the sky faded from red to black.

Jim and Vik quickly gathered firewood and built a pyre. Phil walked out as they were finishing up. Jim then used some rope to bind her wrists.

"Alright, help me lift her on to the pyre," he said.

He and Vik started to lift her when she growled. They dropped her immediately.

"Sherry?" Phil asked as she opened her eyes and growled again.

"No, not Sherry," Jim said. "Not anymore."

She struggled against the rope and began to sit up. Jim put his foot on her chest and pushed her back down. She growled angrily.

Phil walked up with a rod of rebar. He looked down at her. "I'm sorry Sherry," he said as he jabbed the rod down into her forehead. She became still. He pulled the bar from her head, threw it aside and stepped back.

"Vik, help me lift her up on the pyre," Jim said, grabbing her leg. They lifted her up and laid her on top of the firewood. Phil approached with a gas can. He poured gasoline over her and the pyre.

"Get back," he said as he pulled out a matchbox. Jim and Vik both stepped back as he struck a match and dropped the burning stick near Sherry's corpse. The pyre ignited with an intense fireball. Flames leapt upward into the dark night sky. The fire roared as wood and Sherry were both consumed.

"Sherry Walker," Phil said. "We had a rocky relationship, it's true. At times you loved me, at times you hated me. I think at different stages I felt the same. But these last couple of months saw our relationship stabilize and you were actually an excellent companion to have. I will miss you," Phil said.

They all stood there for a while watching the pyre burn. The growls of zombies from the front yard grew louder.

Jim put his hand on his brother's shoulder.

Phil turned to face him.

"We need to go," Jim said quietly.

"How?"

"Well," he stood there thinking. "We could take the bass boat to a safe spot and steal a car or walk out or, wait! I've got it!"

"Yeah? What's your idea?" Vik asked.

"I'll sneak through the backyards of neighboring houses and flank the horde. I'll lead them away from this street and when it's clear, you guys bring the Lincoln and pick me up."

"Wait, wait," Phil said. "I don't like that idea. I'm fine just taking the boat."

"No, if we do that, we lose a perfectly functioning car! I can do this!"

"Jim, if I lose you, I don't know if I can keep going!"

"Phil, trust me!"

He growled. "Fine, but you'd better come back alive!"

"I will! Trust me! I'll lead them north on Jefferson."

Jim ran back into the house and grabbed his axe and flashlight. He also grabbed his knife, strapping it to his ankle. Then he ran to the garage, grabbed a small box and a lighter and ran back outside.

"Wish me luck!" he said as he ran past Phil and Vik to the privacy fence. He swung his axe and hacked a hole in the fence. He climbed through to the next yard and was relieved to find it was zombie free. He circled around the house as it sat on the corner of the peninsula jutting into the lake. He glanced across the canal and saw dozens of zombies pressing against chain-link fences, their eyes glowing menacingly in the moonlight. Some of the zombies seemed to be glowing faintly.

Jim then hopped the neighbor's chain-link fence and ran through the next yard. He hopped the fence on the other side of the yard and encountered a zombie standing in a gazebo. As he ran through the gazebo, Jim swung his axe and swiftly scalped the zombie. It fell to the wooden deck with a thud. Jim continued on and ran through a yard without a fence. He paused when he reached the driveway and saw zombies in the front yard. He needed to go further still.

In the next yard Jim encountered a zombie standing near a ceramic birdbath. He swung the axe into its head. It fell and knocked the birdbath over. Jim continued on and ran through three yards without fences.

He hopped a yellow chain-link fence into a yard with three zombies. They were quickly dispatched. Finally, he reached a yard with a wall of hedges bordering the driveway. He looked down the driveway and saw the coast was clear.

Jim ran out to the street and saw that he was about fifty feet past the horde. He pulled a firecracker out of his pocket and lit the fuse. He dropped it and stepped back a few feet. It went off with a loud bang.

Several zombies turned around and saw him. He started jumping up and down, waving his arms.

"Hey! Zombies! Come and get me!" he yelled.

The horde turned and started moving toward Jim. He walked backwards, catching his breath. "That's right, keep coming," he mumbled.

He climbed up on a Hummer parked on the side of the road and looked down the street toward his dad's house. He saw the flames from the funeral pyre leaping skyward and saw the horde retreating from the house. He climbed down and continued walking away from the zombies, leading them away from Phil and Vikram.

Jim reached Jefferson and turned north on it.

"Come on! You're going to have to work for your meal!" he yelled. The zombies continued to follow him.

He passed Worthington Street. The horde stretched out in front of him as they spilled off of Shorewood Street. He heard a car honking and saw the Lincoln turn onto Jefferson heading south, away from him. It stopped and started honking. The horde stopped and turned away from Jim. They changed directions and started walking toward the Lincoln. The SUV drove off slowly, turning right on the next side street.

"Yes!" Jim whispered. He looked up at the night sky. The stars shone brightly, the moon even brighter.

He heard a car approaching from the north. He looked up and saw the Lincoln's headlights approaching. The SUV slowed to a stop and the driver's side window rolled down.

"You look cold, get in!" Phil said.

Jim laughed.

"Actually, I have a better idea. Feel like driving?"

"Sure," Jim said.

"Great!" Phil shifted the car into park, unbuckled his seat belt, got out and climbed in the back seat.

Jim climbed into the driver's seat, rolled the window up, buckled the seatbelt and shifted into gear. The Lincoln pulled away. Jim drove to Interstate 94 and merged onto it going south.

"Do you remember how to get to Vicki's?" Phil asked.

"Yeah, I think," Jim replied.

"Okay, just let me know if you get lost. I'm going to get some shut eye."

"Good night Phil."

"So, good work back there Jim!" Vik said as they drove up to an elevated section of I-94.

"Thanks," Jim said, looking around. Small fires burned all over Detroit.

"Wow, there's a lot of fires out there," Vik said.

"Yeah. I guess we aren't the only ones who avoided becoming zombies."

"Huh. How are you doing with your father's death?" he asked.

"I'm doing better, I think. How are you doing with Sherry's death? I know you guys grew kind of close."

"I'll be okay."

"Okay. I'm worried about Phil. They were really close."

"I think he'll be fine."

Jim drove through the night and they arrived at 2054 West Dakin Street in Chicago at dawn the next day. Jim parked the Lincoln in front of his sister's house. Everyone climbed out to stretch.

"Huh," Phil said.

"What?" Jim asked.

"Their cars are gone."

Jim shrugged. "Maybe they got stolen. Look, there aren't any red sheets in the windows. And, for that matter, none of the windows are broken."

"Yeah, true. Let's see," Phil said. They walked up to the porch together. Phil looked under a ceramic frog on the stoop and found the spare key. He unlocked the door and the brothers walked in.

The old two-story house smelled of air freshener and faintly of greasy food. It was chilly inside.

"Hello?" Phil yelled. "Vicki? Todd? Laci? Hannah?"

No answer.

"You guys search down here and in the basement. I'll look upstairs," he said, climbing the stairs.

Vik and Jim walked around downstairs. The living room looked nearly undisturbed. So did the kitchen and the office. Jim reluctantly opened the door to the basement and he and Vik walked down the stairs.

Jim was relieved to find there were no bodies hanging from nooses. He and Vik walked back up to the first floor as Phil walked downstairs.

"Anything?" he asked.

Jim shook his head. "You?"

"No. The beds are made, but there's no sign anything bad happened here."

"Huh. Maybe they tried to escape?"

"Maybe. I wish we knew where they had gone off to!"

Jim sat down on the couch. "I guess we may never know," he said glumly.

"Maybe," Phil said, sitting down beside him. "But this might mean they survived."

"Yeah, I guess."

"Well," he looked at Jim and Vik. "You guys must be tired. I know I am."

"Yeah, I'm exhausted," Vik said.

"Me too," Jim admitted.

"Well, there are four bedrooms in this house, I guess let's go upstairs and get some rest," Phil said, standing up.

Jim locked the door and walked upstairs with them.

Vik went into Jim's niece Laci's room and lay down on a bed that was too small, comically too small. Jim walked into the guest bedroom and laid down on the bed while Phil walked back to the master bedroom.

Jim covered up and fell asleep quickly.

CHAPTER THIRTY-FIVE

Jim Gibson
Day 41

"Well, I knew somebody ate my porridge and was sleeping in my bed! Who do you think you are, anyway? Goldilocks?" a strange woman asked.

Jim opened his eyes and saw a crossbow pointed right at him. A curly-headed brunette was holding it.

"Have a nice nap did you?" she asked suspiciously.

"Who are you?" Jim asked reaching for his axe.

"I already moved your axe. How about you tell me who *you* are!" she replied angrily.

"Um, I think there's been a misunderstanding. Is it okay if I sit up?"

"Slowly. Don't try anything fishy!"

Jim slowly sat up. "Who are you?"

"Penny Holloway. Who are you?"

"My name is James Daniel Gibson. Now, what are you doing in my sister's house?"

"Your sister's house?" she asked.

"Yes! My sister's house! What are you doing here?"

"Um, how do I know you're not just telling me this is your sister's house? Huh?" She jabbed the crossbow at him threateningly.

"What's going on?" Vikram walked into the doorway.

She spun and pointed the crossbow at him. "Who are you?"

He threw his hands up.

"He's with me! Look, if you don't believe this is my sister's house, just go look at the photos on the wall! Me *and* the other guy here you haven't seen yet are in them!" Jim said angrily.

She lowered her crossbow. "Okay, James, if that's your real name. You wait right here," she said, pushing past Vikram.

Vik raised his eyebrows, confused.

Jim shrugged. "A vagrant I guess."

"What did you call me?" she angrily demanded when she returned a few moments later.

"I called you a vagrant. Is that not what you are?" Jim asked defensively.

"No, I am not. But I guess you are the brother of the people who lived here." She lowered her crossbow.

"Now, where are you from?"

She sat down on the bed. "Well, I'm from Phoenix originally. But I had cousins who lived here in Chicago, so I came here to find them. I guess they're dead."

"I see."

"So how does that bring our sister's house into this?" Phil asked from the hallway.

"Who? Oh, hello tall, dark and handsome! You must be the big brother?" she responded coyly.

"Answer my question," he said, leveling his shotgun.

"Oh, you're not smiling," she said. "Well, my cousins lived nearby and when I reached their house, it had, shall we say, burned down. I was being chased by zombies when I saw this house and managed to duck in here and hide. I realized this was where Randy's brother lived."

"Randy's brother?" Phil asked. "You mean Todd?"

"I guess. They were going to try to make it here when I left them over on the west side of Chicago. I don't know if they made it here or not. By the time I made it here, the house was empty."

"How long have you been here?" Phil asked.

"Three days."

Phil turned to Jim. "You think Vicki is still alive?"

"Maybe. But who knows where they are now? If this vagrant has been here for three days, then they've been gone for at least three days."

"Hey!" Penny protested. "I'm not a vagrant!"

Phil tilted his head. "You've been here for three days you said?"

"Yes."

"Okay, there's still a good four hours of daylight. Better get walking," he said and walked away.

She looked at Jim. "You guys want me to leave?"

"Really?" Vik asked. "Are you that dense? Really? We don't know you, you don't know us. You're trespassing! These men are the next of kin of the former owners, thus this house is theirs to do what they want! And, you held both myself and Jim at gun point!"

"Crossbow point," Jim corrected him.

"Alright, alright," she replied, a hurt expression on her face. "I can take a hint." She stood. "I guess you'll put a little lady out in the cold, huh? Good thing there's still a few hours of daylight, maybe I can find an overpass to sleep under and a metal barrel to start a fire in. At least I was able to take a shower here before you all showed up."

"What do you want?" Jim asked.

"Well, let me stay here a few more days. Where are you guys headed?"

"Well I guess the plan is to keep heading west."

"Really? I'm heading that way too!" she said enthusiastically.

"Oh?"

"Yeah! We could travel together!"

"Uh, we probably need to talk about that," Jim said.

"We *are* talking about it!" she laughed.

"No, I mean me, Vik, and my brother will have to talk it over."

"Talk what over?" Phil asked as he walked back into the room. "Hey, I thought I told you to scoot?!"

"Well, you did, but James here said I could travel with you guys as far as Sioux Falls, right?" She grinned.

"Uh what? I said no such thing!" Jim said angrily. "I said we would have to talk it over!"

She winked at Phil.

Phil glared at Jim.

"Phil! I didn't invite her to stay here!" Jim said defensively.

"I know that! Come here, let's discuss this privately."

Jim stood and followed his brother downstairs to the kitchen.

"What on earth? What happened?" Phil asked.

"I told her to get out. Vik told her to get out, then she suggested that she travel with us!" Jim replied.

"Really? It happened like that?"

"Well, she made a good point. She asked how we could send her out on the streets. It is getting to be winter."

Phil threw up his arms. "She's got you entranced I guess!"

"No she hasn't! She's annoying!" Jim protested.

"Well, I guess we could let her stay here a few nights while we prepare for the next step of our journey," Phil said.

"What?"

He shrugged. "We still have consciences, right?"

Jim sighed. "Yeah, I guess."

"Okay. What's her name?"

"Penny," he replied.

Phil laughed. "Okay, let's go tell Penny she can stay here for a few nights while we sort everything out."

"Okay," Jim said.

They walked back upstairs. She was talking to Vik. Phil cleared his throat.

"Okay, Penny, we decided you can stay here for a couple of nights while we figure out our next move. You have to respect our space though. And please, no pointing crossbows at any of us."

"Really? I can stay here?" She seemed surprised.

He sighed. "For a few nights."

She jumped up and hugged him. His eyes widened.

"Where can I sleep?" she asked.

"The little kids' bedroom," Vik said testily.

"Okay, I can do that," she said. "I like girly stuff." She grabbed her crossbow and walked to the other bedroom.

Jim, Phil and Vik looked at each other, wondering at the strange events that had just transpired.

This will be interesting, Jim thought.

That evening Penny left for a little while and returned to the house holding several dead squirrels by their tails.

"Where did you get those?" Vik asked, alarmed.

"I shot them with my crossbow in the cemetery just down the street!" she said happily. "Wait, you're Indian, does that mean you don't eat meat?"

"Uh, well my parents were Hindu but I'm not, so I have no problem eating meat. Are those on the menu tonight?" he asked nervously.

"Well yeah, assuming we have the means to roast them!" she said.

"There's a gas grill out back. Get the meat prepared and we can grill them," Jim said.

"Ever had squirrel?" she asked.

He shook his head.

"You're in for a treat! I survived on these things on the way here from Arizona! Well, come on! You can get the grill lit while I field dress the squirrels!" She walked out the backdoor. Jim followed her with a lighter in hand.

The silver grill sat on a wooden deck elevated about two feet above the tiny backyard. Dead ivy covered the privacy fence at the rear of the property and a large oak tree towered over the house. The wrought iron frame of elevated railroad tracks curved over the back quarter of the yard.

Jim walked over to the grill and opened the hood. It was nearly spotless inside. He reached underneath the grill and twisted the knob on the propane tank. He heard the hiss of flowing gas and pressed the ignite button. The gas lit in the grill burner and produced a satisfying blue flame. He closed the hood and turned to see Penny standing on a squirrel's tail.

She grabbed the hind legs of the dead rodent and pulled upwards. As she did so, the squirrel's hide separated from its body, exposing its red and pink flesh. Jim watched with a mixture of awe and horror at seeing the creature get flayed.

She laughed. "So, after you get it skinned, you have to remove its head. Then you crack it open and remove its entrails," she paused. "I can tell I'm making you a bit uncomfortable."

"Well, it's funny," he said. "I've killed dozens of zombies upto this point. I watched my brother amputate one of our friend's legs with my axe and I've seen more gore than years of watching slasher movies prepared me for. So, I guess I'd expect to be a little desensitized to this. And I am, to be clear. I guess I've just never seen an animal get field dressed."

She laughed. "My dad took me hunting all the time. He was a big game hunter, but he always told me that if I found myself in a survival situation, I should catch small game."

"Why is that?" Jim asked. "Wouldn't it be better to catch big game? More meat!"

She shook her head. "How many buffaloes have you seen on your journey here?"

He was silent.

"Exactly. Squirrels and rabbits are everywhere. I'd even consider a coyote to be small game. These little critters are all muscle too, so there's a lot of good protein in them," she said as she eviscerated the small creature. "Here, now one thing you want to look at when you're eating squirrel is its liver. Is the liver a deep healthy solid red? Or is it off-color or spotted? You always want a rich, deep red liver. Any other color or pattern indicates the squirrel might be diseased or otherwise unhealthy."

"I see."

"So, I'll bet your sister and her husband hated living practically underneath an El-Train line, huh?" she asked.

Jim turned and looked up at the hulking iron trestle. "I guess. She never really complained about it. She was a trauma nurse at one of the local hospitals, so I guess she was busy worrying about other stuff."

"What did Todd do?"

"He was the owner of some microbrewery."

"That's neat."

"Sure."

"How close were you to them?"

"I guess we were close when we were younger. She hated our stepdad though, so she skipped out of the Big Apple as soon as she finished high school. She moved out here for school and never came back. The distance kind of caused us all to grow apart."

"I see. You guys grew up in New York City?" Penny asked.

"Yeah, kind of. Baltimore really but we moved to New York when I was eight."

"That's cool. Is that where you guys were when the zombies arrived?"

Jim shook his head as she snapped the feet off a squirrel. "No, we were in Buffalo when it all started. We were all students at the University at Buffalo."

She laughed. "No way! My cousin was going there! His family were actually the people I came here searching for! I mean, his parents lived in D.C., but his dad's brother lived here. Oh, it's complicated."

"Really? What was his name?"

"Joel, Joel Ryan."

Jim scratched his head. The name sounded familiar.

"You know him?" she asked.

Jim shook his head. "He may have been a friend of a friend. I'm sorry."

She shrugged. "It's okay. I mean, my family is probably dead anyway. I think I just concluded that everyone I knew and loved is either dead or a zombie now."

"How did you reach that conclusion?" he asked.

She shrugged as she skinned the final squirrel. "Well, my boyfriend became a zombie and ate his whole family. My parents became zombies. I found them one morning after I woke up. Of course, when everyone in your town becomes a zombie and when pretty much the only uninfected people you encounter on your trek north across the Great Plains are either dead or scum, you lose faith in humanity pretty quickly."

"Huh," Jim said. "You're the first living, uninfected person we've run into since leaving Buffalo."

"Really?" she asked, a surprised look on her face. "What way did you guys come? Did you just canoe across the Great Lakes?"

He laughed. "No, we drove to Detroit first then we came here."

"What was in Detroit?"

"Mine and Phil's dad."

"Oh," she said.

"At least he wasn't a zombie," Jim said.

Penny walked over and hugged him. He grimaced as her hands were covered with squirrel blood. She stepped back and saw his expression and looked down at her hands.

"Oh my! I'm sorry!" she exclaimed.

"It's okay, I've gotten zombie blood on other clothes. I'll manage," Jim said. "Those squirrels ready to grill?"

She nodded. She placed them on the grill and waited to turn them.

"So you ran into Randy?" he asked.

"I did. He and some of his friends saved me from a horde of zombies down in central Illinois."

"That's good. That sounds like something he'd do."

"Were you guys close?"

"Not really. I mean, I saw him occasionally, but I wasn't close to him."

She nodded. "Good people. I hope they made it."

"Where were they headed?"

"Here."

Jim furrowed his brow. "I guess they didn't make it."

"Or they did, and you just missed them."

Jim frowned. He didn't like the sound of that.

"You said you had to chop someone's leg off on your way here; what happened?" she asked.

"Well," Jim took a deep breath. "One of our group, Phil's girlfriend actually, was out walking around when we were in Detroit and she got bitten on her ankle by a zombie."

"Oh no!" she gasped.

"Yeah. We heard her screaming so we ran outside and saw her. Phil took my axe from me and cut her leg off below the knee hoping we could save her," he said, trailing off.

"She didn't make it, did she?"

He shook his head.

"I'm sorry James! It sounds like you guys had a rough journey here!"

He shrugged. "That's life I guess. I guess the current situation of the world has just accelerated what has happened naturally for millennia. You either die before your friends and family do, or you are the last one standing at the end, left alone."

She grimaced. "Yeah, I suppose that's one way to look at it. It's probably time to turn the meat."

Jim opened the hood and turned the squirrels with some metal tongs. Then he closed the hood. "I'm going to go grab a tray to put these on when they're done."

"Okay!" she said.

He ran inside and grabbed a large metal tray from one of the cabinets. He saw Vik and Phil sitting in the living room playing chess. He laughed quietly and went back outside.

"So what's your Indian friend's story?" she asked as Jim sat the tray on the patio table.

"My Indian friend has a name you know," he said.

"Sorry! What's his name again?"

"Vikram. He goes by Vik though."

"Okay, so what's Vik's story?"

"He's my roommate from college. He's also my friend. He's one of our group."

"Why does he have a Southern accent?"

"Because he grew up in Houston."

"Oh. Was he one of those babies you see advertised on TV who got adopted by an American couple?"

"Really?" Jim asked incredulously.

"What?"

"Do you hear yourself talking?"

"What did I say?"

He sighed. "Vik's parents immigrated to the United States when he was two. They settled in Houston."

"Oh, did they own motels?"

Jim glared at her. "You sure are familiar with stereotypes, aren't you? His dad was a neurosurgeon!"

"Sorry!" she said. "I just went to high school with some Indian kid whose parents owned a chain of Best Westerns. I just assumed I guess."

"You know what happens when you assume, right?"

She laughed. "Sorry."

"It's cool."

"Smell that?" she asked, sniffing the air.

"Yeah, it smells good."

"It's probably done."

Jim opened the hood and saw the meat's pinkness had faded to white. He lifted a squirrel off the grill and cut into the meat on its leg. It was all white. He placed the squirrel on the tray and then removed the other cooked rodents. He turned the propane off and closed the grill hood and they walked inside.

"Gentlemen, dinner is served!" Penny announced, laughing.

Jim noticed it felt much warmer than it had inside. He peered into the living room and saw that the fireplace had a fire burning in it. They all sat down at the dinner table to eat. The squirrel was actually pretty good. Jim could tell Vik and Phil were as surprised by it as he was.

The survivors all went to bed after dinner. Jim laid down in the guest bedroom and stared up at the ceiling. He tried remembering what his brother-in-law looked like. He had only seen Todd a few times. He hadn't seen his nieces in a few years. He wondered if his sister's family was still alive. He wondered where they were if they were still alive. He fell asleep pondering such things.

"Hey, I'm sorry about yesterday, with the whole sticking a crossbow in your face thing," Penny said the next morning.

"It's okay," Jim said.

"I'm going to go hunting. Anyone want to come with?" she asked, looking around the room.

"I guess I'll go with you," Phil said. "I've been feeling a bit stir crazy."

"Alright, I'll meet you outside," she said, walking out to the porch.

"Phil, you sure you trust her to not put an arrow in your back?" Vik asked quietly as Phil put his coat on.

"Yeah," he said. "She seems harmless." He grabbed his shotgun and walked outside, closing the door behind him.

"Hey, Jim," Vik said, walking over. "Let me show you something I found in the basement yesterday."

"Okay, show me."

He walked into the kitchen and to the basement door. Jim followed him. They descended into the darkened basement. Daylight shone in from a window near the ceiling, dimly illuminating the concrete-walled room.

"Over here," Vik said, walking into a dark corner.

"This isn't where you're going to secretly kill me, is it?" Jim asked, laughing.

Vik turned and looked at him, partially illuminated by reflected light. "Why yes, I am. James, it is time to meet your maker." He stared at Jim for a moment and then started laughing.

Jim punched him in the arm. "Funny man, real funny! Now what is it you found?"

"Look at this!" he said, shining his light on an old wooden chest.

"So what's in there?

Vik opened the flat lid and shone his light in. Jim gasped. There, in the bottom of the chest, resting on red cloth, lay a stainless steel semiautomatic pistol with a black grip and an old rifle with a bayonet attached. There was a small notebook between the guns with boxes of bullets on each side. He picked the notebook up and read it aloud.

"One M-Nineteen-Oh-Three Springfield thirty caliber rifle, circa Nineteen-Oh-Six. One box of thirty caliber Ball Cartridge. One M-Nineteen-Oh-Five Bayonet Blade, circa Nineteen-Oh-Six, sixteen inches long. One Beretta Nine-Two-FS Inox, nine millimeter, date unknown. One box of nine-millimeter rounds. Purchased from a neighbor in exchange for cash and fair consideration on July Third, Twenty-Fourteen." He lowered the notebook. "These could be useful."

"They could indeed! Which gun do you want?" Vik asked.

"I guess the pistol. But I like the bayonet. Hmm," Jim said, thinking.

"Well, what if I take the rifle and you take the pistol and bayonet?"

"That works." Jim picked up the rifle and removed the bayonet. He then handed the rifle to Vik and grabbed the pistol. "We can put the ammo in our bags before we leave. Go ahead and load the rifle though."

"Good thinking," Vik said, picking up the box of bullets. "It looks like this box has a hundred rounds."

"Have you ever fired a gun before Vik?" Jim asked.

Vik stared at him. "What do you think? I grew up in Texas. Of course I have!" He laughed.

"Okay, good."

Jim sat the bayonet back in the chest and grabbed the box of 9mm bullets. He pulled the lever on the side of the pistol and ejected the clip; it was empty. He slid bullets into the metal clip one at a time. Then he slid the clip into the pistol and engaged the safety. He put the box of bullets back in the chest with the notebook, the other box of rifle rounds and the bayonet.

"Why are you leaving the bayonet down here?" Vik asked.

Jim shrugged. "I don't know; I just have a feeling it should be left down here until we leave."

"Okay," he said. "What do you think Phil will say of our find?"

As they walked back to the stairs, Jim replied. "I think he'll be happy and a bit jealous. Hey though, we all have guns now and decent close quarters weapons."

Phil walked in a few hours later.

"What did you guys get?" Vik asked as he walked in.

"We killed a deer and got some of its meat," he said. "Penny is dragging it back in a red wagon we found. If you guys want, go help her carry the meat in. It's wrapped in butcher paper we found and just needs to be cooked. Whoa, where'd you guys find those?" he asked, surprised by the guns.

"In the basement," Jim said quietly. "They were the only ones."

"Wow!"

"Pretty cool, huh?"

"Yeah! So Vik gets the World War One era rifle and you get a pistol?"

Jim nodded.

"That's good! Now go help Penny."

Jim stood and walked outside. Penny stood there with a little red wagon full of packets wrapped in brown butcher paper.

"So you shot Bambi?" he asked, walking down the stairs in front of the house to the wagon.

She nodded, smiling.

"Where'd you guys find this deer?"

"We found the deer and wagon down in Lincoln Park."

"I'm excited to eat it!" Jim said. He grabbed some packets and carried them inside. Then he walked out to the backyard and laid them on the patio table. He fired up the grill and walked back to the front to carry more deer meat up.

They spent the afternoon cooking the venison. Then they ate it for dinner along with some beer Penny had found in the backyard.

And that's all Jim could remember from the night before when he woke up the next morning. He had a slight headache. He sat up and rubbed his eyes. How much beer had he drunk the night before?

He felt stiff as he climbed out of bed. He looked around. Where were his pistol and axe? Had he left them downstairs?

He walked out of the bedroom and walked past Penny's room. She was gone.

"Probably out hunting," he mumbled as he walked by. He walked downstairs and found Vik asleep on the couch. Neither the axe nor the pistol was downstairs.

Jim tried to remember where he had left them. He shook his head. He really couldn't remember anything from after dinner. He walked over to Vik and shook his sleeping roommate.

"Wake up Vik!" he said.

"What do you want?" Vik asked sleepily.

"Have you seen my pistol or axe?"

"No! Let me go back to sleep!"

Jim sat down on the adjacent couch. Where had he left them?

He heard Phil yell from upstairs suddenly.

He ran to the stairs. "What is it?" he yelled.

"My shotgun is gone! So is my machete!" Phil yelled back. "Have you seen it? We must have gotten really drunk last night! I can't remember anything from after dinner!"

"Me neither!" Jim yelled back. "I can't find my axe or my pistol!"

Phil walked downstairs. "What the heck did we do last night?" He looked at Vik. "Wake him up, we need to figure out what happened."

"Vik! Wake up!" Jim yelled.

"Shut up!" he yelled back, pulling a pillow over his head.

"Where's Penny?" Phil asked.

Jim shrugged. "I figured she had gone out hunting."

"Hey! Vik! Come on man, get up!" Phil said. He tossed a throw pillow at the sleeping man.

Vik sat up rubbing his head. "Man, I've got a killer headache. Did we get hammered last night?"

"That seems to be the case," Phil said. "Let's try to piece this together. What's the last thing you remember Jim?"

"Um, I remember finishing my deer steak and quickly drinking the rest of my bottle of beer. I think that was around nine," he said.

"Okay, Vik?" Phil asked.

"I remember you said something about Sherry, right before Penny asked something about the Lincoln."

"Okay, I remember her asking me how much gas the Lincoln had. I was feeling pretty woozy at that point. And Jim, you were acting really goofy."

Vik walked into the kitchen and walked over to the case of beer. As he picked it up, he seemed to notice something on the counter. He sat the six pack down and picked up a blister pack of pills.

"What's that Vik?" Phil asked.

"I don't know. It says Roche on it. They're little white pills," he said. He dropped the pack when he realized what he had said. "Oh."

"She slipped us roofies!" Jim exclaimed. It made sense. "Vik, where's your rifle?"

"Over by the..." he started to point toward the front door but lowered his hand when he saw it was missing. "...Door."

"She robbed us!" Jim said.

"She sure did. Well, she couldn't have gotten too far. Let's see if we can catch upto her!" Phil said. "Get your stuff."

Jim ran downstairs and was grateful to find the bayonet and bullets were still in the chest. He ran back upstairs and gave the box of rifle bullets to Vik. Jim put the 9mm bullets in his backpack and took a quick inventory of his remaining gear: he had his knife, his compass, his watch, the bayonet, several shirts, a hoodie, a coat, and shoes.

He walked downstairs to meet with the guys. They walked to the door and Phil opened it. They walked out on the porch.

Phil cussed.

"You've got to be kidding me!" Jim exclaimed.

"She is a devil!" Vik yelled.

The Lincoln was long gone.

CHAPTER THIRTY-SIX

Adam Doss
Day 45

Adam grimaced. They had killed ten zombies in the gym, including some zombified teenagers, plus the two Casey had killed in the hallway. The creatures in the gym had almost gotten Vicki and her kids. The thought made him shudder. The zombies in the hallway had gotten Missy. He looked down at the man on the cot.

Casey was sound asleep on a cot in the nurse's office. Randy and Adam had found him kneeling over Missy's bloody corpse punching a locker over and over. Randy had tackled him. Randy and Adam had then carried the grief-stricken man into the gym. When they brought Casey into the large room, Jamie had forced him to take a pill that quickly sedated him.

"What did you give him?" Adam had asked Jamie.

"I gave him some Tramadol," the older man had replied.

"Will he be okay?" Randy had asked.

"Well, Vicki set the bones in his hand. But he'll be okay."

"He broke his hand?" Adam asked.

"You tell me? You saw him punching the locker like a mad man."

Adam stared down at Casey. He was peaceful now. Adam decided he wouldn't tell Casey about having to kill Missy when she had come back as a zombie. Not now anyway. That would come later.

"Man, Casey," he said as he looked at the bandages wrapped around Casey's right hand. "I hope that heals right." He shook his head. Casey had nearly punched a hole into the locker door.

Adam stood and walked out into the hallway. The sun was coming up outside. He walked down the hall to the gym and saw Jill sleeping on the floor next to Todd and Vicki and the girls. He walked to the main entrance and saw Randy standing outside talking to Jamie. Jamie was smoking a cigarette.

Adam walked outside and joined them.

"Hey Adam," Randy greeted him.

"Hey."

"Anyway," Jamie said. "It's going to be a long walk to Canada if we can't find another vehicle. Let's see, we have capacity in the Land Rover for five people and some luggage. We have nine people plus luggage, so if we can find a functional car nearby, we could just get back on the road. Otherwise, we're going to have to walk."

"We'll find something," Adam said.

"I don't know about that," Jamie replied. "This is a little town out in the middle of nowhere. This is a bad place to have broken down. Especially with it getting to be winter."

"We'll find something," Adam insisted. He walked back inside and ran into Todd.

"Hey Adam," Todd said sleepily. "Are you and Randy up to going out in the Land Rover to look for a car we can use?"

"Uh sure," he replied. "When?"

"How about now?"

"Sure." He turned and walked back outside. "Hey Randy, Todd wants us to go look for a car with the Land Rover."

Randy looked at him. "Okay. Now?"

"Yeah."

"Okay, let's go."

The two walked to the Land Rover. It was chilly outside. When they got in, Randy started the SUV and steered it out of the parking lot. He drove east into town. The two combed the streets all morning but didn't see a single functional car. They barely saw any cars at all.

"I guess most of the folks here fled," Adam said.

Randy nodded. "Yeah, I guess they did. I guess we'll head back. Maybe we can drive to the next town over this afternoon and look."

He turned the SUV around and they drove back toward the school. As they turned onto East Baldwin Avenue, the Land Rover hit a patch of ice and began to spin.

"Hold on!" Randy yelled as it slid off the road and hit a ditch.

Adam felt the world spinning around him and was momentarily grateful he had thought to put his seatbelt on. Shattered glass flew around him as the Land Rover rolled over and over. Finally, it came to rest upside down next to a tree.

"You okay?" he asked a moment later.

"Yes. You?" Randy replied.

"Yeah." Adam slowly undid his seatbelt and crawled out of the wrecked SUV. "What happened?"

"I don't know," Randy replied as he climbed out. "I guess I hit some ice. Todd's not going to be happy."

They limped back down the road to the school. When they arrived, Todd ran out to them.

"What happened?" he asked.

"I flipped the Land Rover," Randy confessed.

"What?"

"We hit ice coming around a corner and went off the road and the Land Rover flipped several times," Adam said.

"I'm glad you're okay!" Todd exclaimed as he hugged Randy. "This is unfortunate though. Did you guys see any other cars?"

Adam shook his head. "No. Just a few burned out wrecks. Nothing we could use."

Todd tilted his head and looked upward for a moment. "I guess we'll have to walk. I mean, if nothing else, maybe we can find somewhere better to hole up than this school."

Randy nodded. "Yeah. I guess so. When do you want to leave?"

"Let's give Casey a day to recover. Then we'll set out."

They spent the rest of the day preparing to walk, redistributing supplies between bags. Casey woke up around noon and walked around the school silently all day.

Adam saw Randy walk out and talk to him. Adam walked over to Jill. "How are you holding up?" he asked.

She shrugged. "I'm hanging in there. You know, it's tough."

"Yeah." He hugged her.

"I'm glad I have you Adam," she said.

"I'm glad I have you."

They all slept poorly that night. The next morning, they set out on foot from the school. Todd and Vicki walked in front, followed by the girls, and Casey, Randy, Adam, Jillian and Jamie brought up the rear. Adam was happy at least that it was warm, compared to how it had been.

They made good time at first, walking past mile after mile of silent forest. They all stopped at an abandoned gas station on the side of the road to eat lunch around noon and then they continued on. Todd, Randy, Adam and Jamie all took turns giving Hannah and Laci piggyback rides. Around 2:00pm, Adam noticed that dark black clouds were moving in from the north. He wondered if it was going to rain.

A cold wind suddenly hit them and it began to snow. Soon the snow was falling so heavily that Adam could only see a few hundred feet in any direction. He and the others quickly bundled up and continued on. Soon visibility dropped to a few feet in any direction.

"Hold hands!" Todd yelled from somewhere up ahead.

They formed a human chain and continued on very slowly. Hours seemed to pass. The snow rapidly piled up around them. Adam guessed they were walking through snow at least a foot deep. Eventually he realized they weren't walking on pavement anymore. He wondered where they were walking to and he began to wonder if they were going to freeze to death in this blizzard.

"Todd!" he yelled as loud as he could.

"What?"

"We need to find shelter!"

"Where? We passed the last building more than an hour ago! We have to keep walking! If we stop we'll die!"

Suddenly the chain stopped.

"Guys! Come up here!" Todd yelled.

Adam walked forward and almost tripped over a wooden step. He slowly crawled up it and realized they had run into a large covered porch in front of a large farmhouse.

"Maybe we can take shelter inside!" Todd yelled over the roaring wind.

He stepped toward the door as Adam and Randy walked toward it too. Adam reached for the doorknob and suddenly the door swung open.

He looked up and saw an old man standing in the doorway holding a double-barreled shotgun. The old man stood about six feet tall, had thick black-rimmed glasses, wore a blue flannel shirt and had a black beanie covering his head. He had a bushy white mustache. He looked at the survivors warily. His eyes narrowed.

"What are you doing on my farm?" he demanded as he cocked the shotgun.

CHECK OUT OTHER GREAT ZOMBIE NOVELS

DEAD ASCENT
by Jason McPhearson

The dead have risen and they are hungry...

Grizzled war veteran turned game warden, Brayden James and a small group of survivors, fight their way through the rugged wilderness of southern Appalachia to an isolated cabin in the hope of finding sanctuary. Every terrifying step they make they are stalked by a growing mass of staggering corpses, and a raging forest fire, set by the government in hopes of containing the virus.

As all logical routes off the mountain are cut off from them, they seek the higher ground, but they soon realize there is little hope of escape when the dead walk and the world burns.

CHAOS THEORY
by Rich Restucci

The world has fallen to a relentless enemy beyond reason or mercy. With no remorse they rend the planet with tooth and nail.

One man stands against the scourge of death that consumes all.

Teamed with a genius survivalist and a teenage girl, he must flee the teeming dead, the evils of humans left unchecked, and those that would seek to use him. His best weapon to stave off the horrors of this new world? His wit.

CHECK OUT OTHER GREAT ZOMBIE NOVELS

RUN
by Rich Restucci

The dead have risen, and they are hungry.

Slow and plodding, they are Legion. The undead hunt the living. Stop and they will catch you. Hide and they will find you. If you have a heartbeat you do the only thing you can: You run.

Survivors escape to an island stronghold: A cop and his daughter, a computer nerd, a garbage man with a piece of rebar, and an escapee from a mental hospital with a life-saving secret. After reaching Alcatraz, the ever expanding group of survivors realize that the infected are not the only threat.

Caught between the viciousness of the undead, and the heartlessness of the living, what choice is there? Run.

THE DEAD WALK THE EARTH
by Luke Duffy

As the flames of war threaten to engulf the globe, a new threat emerges.

A 'deadly flu', the like of which no one has ever seen or imagined, relentlessly spreads, gripping the world by the throat and slowly squeezing the life from humanity.

Eight soldiers, accustomed to operating below the radar, carrying out the dirty work of a modern democracy, become trapped within the carnage of a new and terrifying world.

Deniable and completely expendable. That is how their government considers them, and as the dead begin to walk, Stan and his men must fight to survive.

CHECK OUT OTHER GREAT ZOMBIE NOVELS

DEAD PULSE RISING
by K. Michael Gibson

Slavering hordes of the walking dead rule the streets of Baltimore, their decaying forms shambling across the ruined city, voracious and unstoppable. The remaining survivors hide desperately, for all hope seems lost... until an armored fortress on wheels plows through the ghouls, crushing bones and decayed flesh. The vehicle stops and two men emerge from its doors, armed to the teeth and ready to cancel the apocalypse.

TOWER OF THE DEAD
by J.V. Roberts

Markus is a hardworking man that just wants a better life for his family. But when a virus sweeps through the halls of his high-rise apartment complex, those plans are put on hold. Trapped on the sixteenth floor with no hope of rescue, Markus must fight his way down to safety with his wife and young daughter in tow.

Floor by bloody floor they must battle through hordes of the hungry dead on a terrifying mission to survive the TOWER OF THE DEAD.